Variations on
the Beast

Variations on the Beast

Henry Grinberg

The Dragon Press

Variations on the Beast
Copyright © 2006 Henry Grinberg
The Dragon Press

Author's note: This is a work of fiction. Some of the events described in this book happened as related; others were expanded and changed. Some of the individuals portrayed are composites of more than one person, and some names and identifying characteristics have been changed as well.

For more information about this title, please contact:

The Dragon Press
270 Lafayette Street - Suite 401
New York, NY 10012
www.thedragonpress.com

Book design by:

Arbor Books
19 Spear Road, Suite 301
Ramsey, NJ 07446
www.arborbooks.com

Printed in Canada

Library of Congress Control Number: 2005910595
ISBN:0-9768181-1-6

To my wife, Suzanne Noguere, for her unfailing love
Like to the lark...

Acknowledgments

The following friends aided me immeasurably with their insights and knowledge of languages and classical music: Sylvia Adams, Arnold Freed, James V. Hatch, Henry R. Huttenbach, Kate Light, Seymour Lipkin, Arthur Mortensen, Marian Olah, and Fred S. Worms, OBE.

In addition, each of the following friends read the manuscript and generously provided helpful comments that sustained me during the writing: Doris Barkin, Elise Braun, Robert Braun, Saul Brody, David P. Celani, Howard M. Epstein, Frances Gellerman, my son, Gordon J. Grinberg, David Handel, Pamela Laskin, Janice Levit, Neil McKelvie, and G. L. "Willie" Watkins.

Special thanks to Martin Mitchell for all of the above reasons and for his immense and expert care in vetting the manuscript.

This novel is purely a work of fiction. However, it is based on the horrors of the Nazi regime during the Third Reich. For an understanding of that dreadful episode in human history, I am indebted to the scholarly work of, among others, Antony Beevor, Max Hastings, Sir Martin Gilbert, Michael H. Kater, Ian Kershaw, Claudia Koonz, Pamela M. Potter, and Richard Overy.

I am particularly grateful to Roger E. Kohn, my friend of many years standing, who served as my legal adviser.

To David Salvage, all gratitude for his enthusiasm and support.

Contents

Variations on
the Beast

Theme

Vienna 1960

The great chandeliers dimmed. Washed in light before me, the players ranged, almost a hundred of them. Violins, violas, cellos, basses—bows poised to strike. Woodwinds and brass raised to lips. Timpani ready to pound. Abruptly, I raised my baton. All chatter and coughing hushed. Breaths were held. Starched shirtfronts ceased their crackle, sumptuous ball gowns their rustle. The moment I relished most: the whole world waited for me.

The baton slashed. The first chords hammered out: the overture *Consecration of the House*. Thus, the immortal Beethoven proclaims, "Watch out, it's a new day!"

Here, at this inaugural concert, I am hymning a paean to the indestructible spirit of mankind. Most of the war ruins are gone. Vienna has been reconstructed. Also gone, unhappily, is any sense of proportion. The ultimate civic effort was to repose in this hall, which turned out to be ugly in the extreme. But here we are, alive, well, and prospering.

This Wiener Festspielhaus—Vienna's new festival hall—is hideous but striking, a building in tune with the latest architectural horrors of the midcentury. Glass, steel, terrazzo, travertine, jagged concrete loops and pillars swooping up and down at irregular intervals on the outside. Pale blue velvet plush on the inside. Pale blue! Is there no more red and gold? The orchestra sprawls in some outlandish spot halfway up the south wall. And the audience intrudes on all sides—even behind the players! So that there is never a refuge from their silly faces nodding to the music, attempting to aid me by beating time—disastrously out of time, their looking so dedicated.

One was obliged to approve of Krummhorn's design, what with the whole city behind him. The Festspielhaus represents the new Europe, they told me. It is a break from the past of feudal principalities, minor kingdoms, Hapsburg pomposities, and, most of all, from the so-called evils of the Anschluss—the union of Austria with the Third Reich—redeeming it from its status as a backwater after the loss of Imperial Austria-Hungary.

Good, good. So be it. I was never one to stand in the way of history. But the sound of these new concert halls! So bright, so naked, so lacking in mystery! Is this really Europe? Hardly. America, the efficient stepchild from across the Atlantic, is lashing out at its progenitors with a vengeance. Let me tell you what I think. It's all typical American hyperexposure. Who but they could have seized with such indecent haste upon Freud and his Jewish friends to make a public pastime of licking each other's psychic sores?

Gessler, my manager—I manage him, not the other way around—had fussed dreadfully about it. But he needn't have bothered. Rotten taste usually triumphs. The main thing is that it is I who triumphed. My personal struggle was over and done with when I had been appointed Generalmusikdirektor of the Österreichische Symphonie and its opera. And, unhappily, of this place.

As I say, I will not stand in the way of history. I give them Mozart, Haydn, Beethoven, and Brahms in the new transatlantic style, piercing and bright. I do it in the same way at the Royal Festival Hall in London, Philharmonic Hall in New York, the annual festival in Edinburgh, of which I am co-director, the Teatro de la Revolución in Buenos Aires, where I conduct a half-season each winter, the Salzburg Festival every other year, Wagner at Bayreuth, also every other year, and now here at this new Vienna concert hall, of which I am now—forgive my satisfied repetition—permanent, residing, reigning Generalmusikdirektor. And don't think I haven't got my eye on my old rival, von Karajan, in Berlin!

But this is dreadful. I have not introduced myself. It is so easy to be swept up in this postwar informality. The name, as everyone must know, is Kapp-Dortmunder. Hermann Kapp-Dortmunder. I started life as plain Hermann Kapp. I added the Dortmunder after accepting leadership of a provincial opera house in the Ruhr. I concluded that it was good for a conductor to have such a name. You have to have lots of syllables for the tongue and jaws to work on. It inspires respect. I am certain that other maestri thanked heaven for their multisyllabic names: Toscanini, Stokowski, Furtwängler, Klemperer, Schmitt-Isserstedt, Mengelberg, von Karajan, and so on. You will have noticed that those with short names are invariably known at large by both the first and last. I refer of course to such as Charles Münch, Fritz Stiedry, Malcolm Sargent, Henry Wood, Thomas Beecham—as well as the Jew Schlesinger, who understandably chose to conceal himself behind the name *Bruno Walter*. We, the single-named Barbirollis, Stokowskis, Koussevitskys, and Kapp-Dortmunders, bear a tangible advantage. To be known simply as Kapp-Dortmunder is eminently satisfying.

My wife does not care for the name—she is my second wife, I should point out. Many wonderful women have wished to share my life. One young woman, Krisztina, I loved and lost. We never married, but I have never ceased to think of her. I think she would have desired to be simply Frau Kapp. More about her later. Margot, my present wife, owns an international chain of design consultants. Very chic. She has great beauty, enormous flair, and business sense. So you can understand why she elected the euphonious sobriquet of Margot St. Monarque. That is not her real name, however, even though she is Swiss. We travel a great deal; I on my tours, she on hers.

The next part should really come from others, but you see I am perfectly candid. I am fifty years old, but look at least fifteen years younger. I have all my hair, somewhat en bouffant, interestingly streaked with gray. Even though I limp noticeably, because of frightful injuries suffered in the recent war, I hike, climb mountains, sail, drive racing cars, ski on land and water—and visit the masseur. In addition, I am agreeably tall and have a lean build, an aquiline nose, and high cheekbones. I'm told that I am handsome. Then of course, besides the inner repose and meditation that I bring to my profession, the conductor's trade itself is physically stimulating. One works hard and perspires generously. There is much swinging of the arms, twisting of the body, crouching low, and on occasion, flinging oneself in the air. This is excellent for the circulation, the liver, the digestion, and the lungs. Thus I am quite fit, and barring unfortunate accidents, there is no reason why I should not join the ranks of other noted maestri in living to a ripe and healthy old age.

Back to the concert. I had to resist with all my might the forceful representations of a faction within the Society for Austrian Culture that had dredged up from God-knows-where a certain spindly, hook-nosed gentleman, Nussbaum by name, introduced to me with hushed reverence as a *survivor*. You know, one of those professional survivors who seem to manage well while many a brave soldier who has bled for the Fatherland must do things that would make his mother blush in order to live. This Nussbaum, of course a Jewish drifter, was a musician, had become a naturalized Frenchman, and won the Prix de Rome, if you can believe it. He had produced a new canta-ta, *Grüss an alle Menschen,* his fatuous "Greetings to All Mankind," set to a poem of Lustig's. It purported to hail the brotherhood of man under the fatherhood of God, or some such sentiment that Beethoven and Schiller had already achieved a thousand times bet-ter in the Ninth Symphony.

Don't misunderstand me. I was perfectly cordial to both the Gesellschaft and Nussbaum. It is the thing to be these days. I handled the score reverently as though it were the Host itself. I ran through pas-sages on the piano in my study. It was horrid! One of those horribly jagged, astringent—no, *acid*—ugly things that we have to endure after the Second Viennese School, as you know, heavily Jewish and (leaving aside *Verklärte Nacht*) ugly. The Uglies, I call them. Berg and Schönberg, Webern, and that repulsive Krenek—full of ugliness. This thing by Nussbaum was of that ilk. It came laden with the requisite howls and discords—nasty, ear-stabbing trumpets in dissonant sec-onds. That section was labeled *Buchenwald.* In thoroughly bad taste. It ended—would you believe it—with a boy soprano intoning the nine-ty-eighth psalm.

> The Lord hath made known his salvation:
> His righteousness hath he openly
> shewed in the sight of the nations.
> He hath remembered his mercy and his
> faithfulness toward the house of Israel:
> All the ends of the earth have seen the
> salvation of our God.

I leave it for others to judge how appropriate that is to the feelings of Germans within the supposed spirit of reconciliation.

I had to play my cards with care. My future hinged on working well with the Gesellschaft. In another sense, it was grotesque that a Kapp-Dortmunder's career had to depend on a Nussbaum. *Nussbaum!* Oh, I was properly troubled, serious, diplomatic, full of concern for Nussbaum and the sufferings of all his tribe. The Gesellschaft wished me to understand—and they did so with irritating frequency—how fitting it would be for the opening concert at the Festspielhaus to reflect magnanimity and the coming together of mankind after the horrors of the European continent during the past quarter-century. As if I were a stranger to those horrors! And how better to utter this new feeling than through Nussbaum's wretched cantata.

But gentlemen, I said, how much better, with all respect and admiration for fellow-artist Nussbaum, than to express our thankful feelings through the great musical and humanistic tradition of Vienna. A concert of Viennese music: the composers of the great past, untouched and unclouded by the smirch of this tragic century. The officers of the Gesellschaft murmured together. Whom did you have in mind? they asked. Why, I said, Mozart, Beethoven, and Schubert. Let us transcend our differences and extend the hand of brotherhood by way of these true Viennese immortals, whose roots flourish in their true Viennese native soil. And I smiled gently at Nussbaum.

And that's how we did it. As you well know, what I had told the Gesellschaft may not have been entirely true, but its effect was as satisfactory. We got Nussbaum a fairly decent seat somewhere in the middle of the hall, completely drowned in an ocean of ministers, ambassadors, consuls-general, and their ladies in brocades, silks, and flowers. Quite an impressive sight, even in that hideous place.

There was a charming ceremony at the beginning: one delightful short speech after another. The East German ambassador presented me with a framed holograph page of the *St. Matthew Passion* that had been the envied possession of the Leipzig people for generations—I was deeply moved.

After the mighty *Consecration of the House*, I gave them Mozart's polished and witty Symphony No. 35 (*The Haffner*). There was a charming reception at the intermission, after which I did an impressive Schubert's Ninth. There was some derisive comment from one or two irresponsible critics who wrote something stupid about this having been a "tame" or "conventional" program. It meant little and was barely noted. They said that, if I insisted on trotting out warhorses, I should have performed the *Beethoven* Ninth, not the *Schubert* Ninth. Idiots! I had already given them a Beethoven, if they hadn't noticed. That concert was exactly what I intended. Nothing flashy or vulgar. I defy anyone to devise a program of greater worth or majesty for the inauguration. Far better than the screeching and howling of Nussbaum's choirs.

I'll tell you a secret about my Schubert's Ninth. I have always been extravagantly praised for it, and this has puzzled me. Maestro, they breathe, how do you achieve such presence, such spaciousness, such depth? What mysteries have you gazed upon? How does any mortal have the power and grace to reveal such beauty to his fellows? We Germans! Everything has to have a source in mythology, in the depths of vast, gloomy forests.

What answer could one give? They would be wounded by the obvious: *You don't know how to do it, and I do!* If you studied night and day at the conservatory a hundred years, it would still be a mystery. Knowing how is the key. Once you have that, you do what you want. The orchestra is mine. I take this piece of music—the Schubert Ninth—and ravish it, devour it. It becomes part of me as much as my own arms and legs, my brain, my feelings. It belongs to me, as precious as my own eyes. It is mine to fashion. I spend hours on balance and intonation and insist on absolute, ravishing beauty of sound. This should be no news. The pauses are eloquent in themselves. The crescendi have all the room in the world to grow. Ritardi before new themes are not overdone—and that is about all. I have profound faith in the design I carry in my head. I insist that my players fulfill my plan. And they go wild over it. As I say, *I can do it!*

I am no philosopher, but I write thoughtfully for the *Zeitschrift der Musikalischen Kunst* and participate in televised symposia at which people drone on, discussing the never-ending search for truth and new ways to express the oneness of human experience. And they go wild over it. I was nervous at the beginning. They clustered about me, so many professors, deep thinkers, musicologists, all yammering away about the meaning and destiny of art. It is a particularly distasteful German habit. I long ago gave up trying to tell them—and it was a mistake to attempt. The simple truth is this. I have a gift, a knack for conducting. And it's no disadvantage to have the power to engage and dismiss players at will. In that position, you too might acquire that "all-important mystical control" over your men, as the *Frankfurter Zeitung* expressed it. You too would gain that "strange, almost uncanny ability to communicate the finest visions," in the words of the *New York Herald-Tribune*.

The Schubert ended gloriously with the accelerated final section. A wonderful blaze of sound. And then the cheering, the shouting, the tears! Bürgermeister Löwicz trundled up to the stage and caught hold of me as I came out for my sixth bow. It is strange to be clasped by a short weeping man. He kept whimpering, "Maestro, Vienna lives again! You make Vienna live again."

I said nothing but clung to him with my left arm and blew kisses to the screaming audience with the other. Margot was sitting in the fourth row, along the center aisle, looking utterly ravishing as usual. As usual, she did not applaud. She never does after my first bow. She sat, quite collected amid all the noise, hands resting quietly in her lap, smiling her peculiar smile. That smile has the capacity to depress me for days. I don't know why that should be. There is nothing for which I should reproach myself. But it is a knowing smile, and it disturbs me because of that. Margot doesn't permit me to share the joke.

I take great pride in knowing myself extremely well, but I do not care to have others know me. Not even Margot. *Particularly* not Margot, I should say. Margot appears to understand me, part of her world of illusion and fashion. She also never says much, which adds to her air of mystery. I have no objection to these affectations, but it is irritating to think that she may be manipulated by her own public relations techniques. There she sat, practicing this nasty sort of psychological assault—I mean her smiling at me in that odd way—while being clasped by Löwicz. At me, the idol of Vienna, the hope of postwar cultural recovery, at the peak of his reputation, his star of success and reward in the ascendant.

The evening was not over. A champagne supper at the Grand Marschallin Hotel. I was toasted, and I toasted back. I was made a Hochritter of the Austrian Republic, I was made a Grand Chevalier of the Légion d'Honneur and kissed on both cheeks by Monsieur l'Ambassadeur Charentan, I was knighted by the Government of Sweden, I was created an honorary knight commander of the British Empire by a representative of Her Majesty, and I had the pleasure of learning from Mr. Ten Drouton that a Presidential Medal of the Arts awaited me upon my next visit to Washington. And all the time Margot stood there, smiling that smile of hers. What could she mean by it?

I asked her later as Josef drove us out to the lodge in the Daimler. She opened her eyes and looked at me from far away. *She must be tired,* I thought. She has beautiful black eyes, but they glittered rather coldly in the lights of the Esslingenstrasse. What kind of smile? Never mind, I thought wearily. With one's wife, there are matters of propriety better not to pursue. The sweets of the flesh are everywhere, but not the sweets of understanding. It took two marriages and many, many other—*arrangements?*—to learn that much. If I wished really to upset myself, I would ask Margot why she married me. A ridiculous question, really. I am famous, I am rich, I am the repository of a world-class cultural heritage. I can recite all these reasons and still not understand. I shall not insult your intelligence by suggesting that she loves me. We are fond of one another. We look magnificent together. I don't think I really know what love is. I wonder if Margot does. I shall not burn myself up trying to find out. But she is surely the cleverest of my women. She has read, she is witty, she is sharp as a whip in the management of her enterprises. I believe she is unfaithful to me. I shall not burn myself up trying to find out. But when she smiles in that way, it disturbs me. The sweets of understanding, does she withhold them from me, or has she none to give?

"What did you think of the concert, Margot?"

Again that dreamy opening of the eyes.

"Do you really need me to tell you?"

I laughed and leaned over to kiss her. "Margot," I said, "do you really like music?"

She caught her breath. "Do I really—?" She roared with laughter, and I joined in. I took her hand in mine, and we drove out into the forest, both of us cackling like a pair of monkeys. I ask you, where are the sweets of understanding? I think, you know, that I was far cleverer when younger.

* * *

First Variation

Szombathely 1917

I began life as a bastard. My father, Wilhelm Kapp, was a minor official in the tax office at Szombathely, which lies in the Hungarian regions of what used to be the vast Austro-Hungarian Empire. He did not, as far as I gather, marry my mother until I was four years old. I am less inclined now to blame him for that. He struggled fruitlessly against a dreary existence that punished, even if it did not extinguish.

For a man of bourgeois aspirations, this was surely maddening enough. While sharing his modest portion with an aged mother, he had at the same time to expend great energy to conceal the fruits of his sexual indiscretion. That might have spelled instant dismissal from the Civil Service. Luckily, Szombathely, while now assuming some provincial importance, was in the early years of this century a quiet small town, where a man of my father's sort could accept small bribes to overlook irregularities in the doings of local merchants—and pay to have his own ignored. He was an occasional but devoted communicant of the church, and was nothing if not respectable.

As a civil servant, my father enjoyed a certain immunity from the exigencies of the war. He had, after all, served his conscription in the infantry at nineteen. But even his slight influence among friends in Vienna could not prevent his reserve status from reactivation in 1915. He was sent, oddly enough, as a noncommissioned officer to a Czech regiment stationed near Jihlava, which disgusted him. After years at Szombathely, which also disgusted him—he detested Hungarians too—he was never to get his chance to cleave to Greater Germanism. Hence his clandestine liaison with my mother; hence his reluctance to acknowledge me, the unwelcome offspring of a union that might tie him forever to the provinces of the empire.

My mother used to tell me in later years that associates had constantly reminded Father that our beloved emperor, Ferenc József Császár—the Kaiser Franz Josef—was king of the Hungarians, the Moravians, and all the others, as well as of the Austrians, that the empire embraced in perfect fellowship many races and peoples. But Father is said to have become enraged at this and to have shouted that our beloved kaiser had been misled by evil counselors to acquiesce, first, to the renunciation of the Concordat with Rome and, second, to tolerate as equal to Austrians the rebellious Czechs, Moravians, Bohemians, Slovenes, Slovaks, Serbs, Italians, Carpathians, Croats, Bosnians, Ruthenians, Poles, Rumanians, and other scum, who did nothing but plot sedition.

As for the Hungarians, they were the worst! Sly, lazy, and degenerate—hourly working to subvert stern Catholic Austrians into becoming vile parodies of themselves, to while away their hours and years at cafés and operettas. If only our dear Kaiser could tear himself loose from freethinkers, Socialists, and, particularly, the Jews, who surrounded him, he might soon discern that to the north lay the land of Prussian virtues—salvation for all true Germans. As for Vienna, its courageous Bürgermeister, Dr. Karl Lueger, had the right idea: if he couldn't kick the Jews out, at least keep them in their place!

You may remember that our beloved Ferenc József Császár had tried to coordinate the disposition of the imperial armies with those of his brother-emperor, Kaiser Wilhelm II. Now this was sometimes more of a problem to the Central Powers than an advantage. Father, for instance, said he wished to fight for his country on the Western Front against the French and the English. Unhappily, this privilege was not vouchsafed to many eastern regiments. Logistics and provincial loyalties demanded that they serve in their own regions. Whenever the High Command wished to order such-and-such regiment of the empire into action against the Serbs or Rumanians or Italians, someone had to remind it that the troops of such-and-such regiment were themselves Serbs or Rumanians or Italians—or whatever else—and how could they be asked to fight their own brothers?

In any case, denied the plumes of victory before Verdun or Flanders, Father drilled and polished, oddly enough, with that seditious regiment at Jihlava, poised comically for action month after month until, finally, it was discovered in 1917 that Czechs would not object to fighting Italians. Thus to the Isonzo Front, just in time for the great victory at Caporetto. Father, however, fell at Vittoria Veneto, and with him collapsed his dream of Greater Austria. The republic was proclaimed at the armistice. It made no difference, for after our Császár died in '16, his great-nephew, Károly, was merely the shadow of an emperor, a pitiful substitute for the rightful heir, Ferenc Nándor Föherceg—Archduke Franz-Ferdinand—cruelly assassinated at Sarajevo. What could Father have returned to?

My mother, Lukács Maria Terézia, was seventeen when I was born, twenty-one when she became Kapp*né*—or Frau Kapp, as my father would have preferred it. Orphaned at an early age, she did housework for a Szombathely shopkeeper until she retired to the Konvent of St. Gregorine to await her confinement. After my birth, she continued to maintain both herself and me at St. Gregorine by dint of her expert domestic and culinary skills. I believe that she was happy there. Mother Superior must have been kind, and I can still remember glimpses of laughing nuns who played with me at odd moments of the day. They took me into the kitchen gardens to gather eggs from the hen coops in gray smoky dawns, or to pick and eat big fleshy gooseberries in the heat of summer afternoons. St. Gregorine must not have been one of those ascetic houses but an easy and human sort of religion in which the good, kind nuns lived.

There was a lot of singing, I recall, and not always at devotions. A *pianínó,* a small cottage piano, was stored in an attic near our room. And in that hushed cool place, Mother would love to sit when the day's work was finished, fingering the yellow keys, singing melancholy songs of love in a tiny, pretty voice. I don't remember the first time it happened, but a practice grew among the nuns. They would gather there and hum simple melodies. I would pick them out on the piano. I remember their delight and amazement.

"You must teach him, you simply must, Maria Terézia. He has a gift, that one!"

I reveled in it. And Mother, overjoyed that her infant could create such a stir, produced from somewhere a creased and grimy beginner's book and began to teach me. Well, it was true. I had a gift. I galloped through quite a few of those beginner's books. By the time Father married Mother, and we had moved to the modest house on the Györ útca in Szombathely, the old *pianínó* went with us, and I was charming everybody with my performances of Clementi and little pieces by Mozart. Only five years old, mind you. Father stayed with us less than a year before he was sent to join his regiment; but during that time, I cannot remember his once ever playing with me or smiling at me. I do know that he tried to stop Mother from calling me by the name she had given me, Ferenc.

"That's no name for a German child," he shouted. "I want no Hungarian brats in this house. *Ferenc!*" This in a disgusted growl.

From then on, he called me Hermann. Not even *Franz*, as you might imagine.

I never learned Father's real opinion of my piano playing. He can hardly have liked it. Now that I think of it, it was further evidence of his barely repaired indiscretions, his being forever tied to the provincial life he despised, his ruined chances for advancement and a desired transfer to Vienna. And yet he was always confounded by the admiration my accomplishments aroused among his Civil Service cronies. One of them was Superintendent Mellnicz, the chief of his department. A fat gentleman with huge muttonchop sidewhiskers, he loved to visit on Sunday afternoons, sip Tokaji, pat Mother's hand, and listen to me play. What could Father do? He soon learned that Superintendent Mellnicz' interest in him was perfunctory.

"He has no children of his own. He has no grandchildren," Father hissed into my uncomprehending ear. "Be nice to him. He likes children." He gripped my face hard in his huge hand, staring fiercely at me. "Tell him he looks like the Kaiser Franz-Josef."

And so, week after week, I played my pieces for Superintendent Mellnicz, Father smiling with his lips only, but narrow-eyed, motioning violently behind his chief's back to the sepia portrait of our Császár that hung on the wall, in uniform with medals, his kind, sad, intelligent eyes that understood everything.

So before my new piece, I bowed low and piped: "A sonata by Haydn Ferenc József in honor of Mellnicz *úr,* who reminds us so much of our dear Ferenc Jószef Császár." Mellnicz *úr* glowed with pleasure, gravely raised his glass to the portrait, and gave me a couple of coins.

"But you are spoiling him," Father would protest.

"Nonsense, nonsense," Mellnicz *úr* boomed, jovially shaking paunch and meerschaum at him. "He is a rare little fellow, full of genius and charm. We must nurture him. Szombathely will come to be proud of him."

After Father's chief departed, Mother would stare at him, smiling faintly, but with indisputable triumph.

"But you always remind the boy to tell Mellnicz *úr* that he looks like our Császár," she said. "And Mellnicz *úr* is happy, and he shows that he is happy by rewarding the boy." She put emphasis on the word *boy*—why, I cannot tell. Perhaps it was because she refused to call me Hermann. Perhaps not.

Anyway, there was an exchange of looks, the import of which I could not gauge. Father would curse under his breath, then reach for his hat and spend the rest of the evening at a beer hall.

Some money would come in from Father's army allotment, which Mother stretched out by doing housework for hire. By 1917, effects of the Allied blockade were severe. We usually ate bread made of potatoes and sawdust spread with dripping. Sometimes there was an egg, more rarely meat or cheese. But there were always turnips—boiled, steamed, mashed in soup, and finely chopped with raisins for dessert. Turnip greens made a fine vegetable, Mother said. Somehow my plate was kept full, but Mother grew pale and thin, her nose became long and sharp. Whenever I screamed my revulsion at the never-ending diet of turnip, she would sigh and try to divert me by reading from an old thick book of fairy tales. I loved their magic and color, but I was quickly sobered by the thought of another dreary dish of turnips.

"The farmers send their food to our brave soldiers at the Front," Mother said as she wiped my tears. "We eat turnips so that Papa can be strong to fight for our dear fatherland."

Papa? We had not seen him for a year. We had a sepia snapshot of him, which, in a moment of homesickness, he sent us. I have not looked at that photo for at least forty years, but I can still see the stern face under a soldier's cap. No sad, gentle muttonchop whiskers like our Császár's, but the fierce, spiky upturned mustache, in tribute to that other emperor, Father's namesake to the north, the great Kaiser Wilhelm.

One Sunday, Mellnicz *úr* brought a visitor with him. It was a cousin of his from Vienna, Madame Polkovska, who had made a career as a concert pianist when younger. Now she had retired and given up her pupils. She was very old, with white hair and trembling hands, wearing a black gown that reached the floor. She entered the room slowly on the arm of Mellnicz *úr*, feeling her way with a cane. I had never seen anything so frightening in my life. She was the witch of all the fairy tales rolled into one. I fled at once under the table. Mother was all afluster. Mellnicz *úr* laughed.

The witch banged her cane on the floor.

"Quiet, Max!" she commanded in a surprisingly deep voice. "The boy is frightened."

For a moment or two, I heard nothing but strange whispers and scratchings. Then, slowly before my eyes, the tablecloth lifted, and the witch's cane intruded into my sanctuary. Swinging from the end of it was a tiny packet wrapped in gold paper.

"Take it, take it," said the deep voice.

Gingerly, I lifted off the small object and unwrapped it. It was…it was chocolate! The smell of it flooded my mouth with water. But in an instant, I thrust it back out into the room.

"It's poisoned," I wailed. "If I eat it, I shall go to sleep for a hundred years."

I heard Mother cry out in helplessness, while Mellnicz *úr* roared with enjoyment.

The deep voice again. "If you come out, we shall all have a piece, and then you'll see who goes to sleep for a hundred years."

I don't know how or why I did it, but I crawled out at last. Madame Polkovska, Mother, and Mellnicz *úr* stood in a row, staring at me, their hands poised dramatically in front of their mouths. They waited until I was on my feet and then, as though at a signal, all three placed pieces of chocolate on their tongues. Eyes bulging, they chewed. Mother looked tragic, tears in her dark-circled eyes. Mellnicz *úr* shook his head in admiration. Madame Polkovska, awesome in her long black skirts, white hair piled majestically atop her trembling head, was yet regal. At about the same time, all three swallowed their chocolates and watched me. I stared back. We must have stood there motionless for fully five minutes, the silence broken only by the slow ticking of the mantelpiece clock.

At last, I made up my mind. If anyone were to swoon into the sleep that was death-in-life until redemption by a lover's kiss, it would have happened by now. I decided to place my piece in my mouth. By all that is holy, that chocolate was good! Never before and never again would anything so delicious pass my lips. I struggled to express my rapture. The spell was broken. Mother laughed and clapped her hands. Mellnicz *úr* picked me up and danced a jig. But Madame Polkovska swept to a chair by the piano and rapped her cane.

"Come!" she ordered. "We are wasting time. Ask the boy to play."

Mellnicz *úr* ceased his dance and placed me on the piano stool.

"Yes, yes," he stammered, breathing hard after his exertion. "That is why we are here." He turned to Mother. "Madame Polkovska is a *müvésznö*—a great artist, a student of Ferenc Liszt's at the Budapest Conservatoire, a close friend of Clara Schumann's, a trusted intimate of Gustav Mahler's at the Vienna Opera, a *zongoramüvész*, a most distinguished pianist. Why, she and Cosima Wagner—"

Madame Polkovska spoke. "Be quiet, Max!" She fixed Mother with her eyes. "I am retired these days, Frau Kapp. I have decided for the duration of the war to move here, to Szombathely. Vienna is so grim now. The streets are full of soldiers and guns. The newspapers bear nothing but ugly tidings. It is best to be away."

"It is too great an honor"—Mother began, but Madame Polkovska waved impatiently for silence.

"My cousin, Superintendent Mellnicz, tells me that your boy has a great talent. Of course, who knows what discernment he has to render such judgments. But I like the boy. He has charm and honesty—these are to be greatly prized these days."

I was coaxed to the piano. "You will hear, Marthe," Mellnicz *úr* breathed. "He's another Mozart."

I was now six years old and much advanced over my simple Clementi days. I played for them the D major prelude and fugue from the *Well-Tempered Clavier*, which Mother had recently taught me. Quite challenging for one my size. Instead of struggling to stretch the octaves in the left hand, I cheated and played only the bass notes. My fingers—though toughened by two years of constant practice—had hardly the power or agility to do it justice. But it wasn't bad. I tumbled through the final stretto and wheeled around breathless on my stool. But instead of the customary salvoes of praise and applause, there was a long silence. Neither Mother nor Mellnicz *úr* dared speak. At last, Madame Polkovska stirred.

"Well, he is certainly no Mozart," she growled. "But still, he is remarkable. He plays with sense. He seems to know how music should sound." She turned to Mother. "And you have been his only teacher, Frau Kapp?" Mother nodded silently. I had never seen her look so frightened. Madame turned back to me.

"Now, my little one," she began, "play us something less ambitious, something more attuned to your diminutive size. Do you know any Mozart, perhaps, since it is apparently your fate to have your names forever linked?"

Yes, I did, I assured her, while Mellnicz *úr* coughed deprecatingly. I turned once more to the keyboard and played the variations on *Ah Vous Dirai-je, Maman*. They require fleet fingers. Thankfully, things worked better for me than they had with the Bach. At the conclusion, Madame grunted with satisfaction.

"Yes, good, good," she grumbled. "That is how a child can play children's music." Then a strange request. "Child, stand next to me with your back to the piano." I obeyed. Next, she asked Mama to strike one of the keys. It didn't matter which.

"Do you know what that note was?" she asked, one eyebrow raised.

The room became still. No one had asked me that before. I screwed my face in concentration. "It's a C-sharp."

From Mama, a cry. "How did you know that?"

I didn't know how I knew. They tried a few more notes. I named them all. Mama and Mellnicz *úr* looked terribly impressed.

"He has quite a useful attribute," pronounced Madame. "He possesses *absolutes Gehör*, perfect pitch."

Mama seemed to be in shock. "Why did I never realize before that he had perfect pitch?" she asked. No one answered.

Only Madame continued to look severe. She abruptly rose to her feet. "Frau Kapp," she announced, "I shall be pleased to teach your boy. You have done passably well with him, but you will agree that the effects of an inexpert teacher are painfully apparent. He must come to me right away to unlearn many bad habits. Next, he may no longer play upon this piano. It is ruining both his ear and his touch. For a precocious child like this, the damage might be beyond repair within a few months. Next, I am getting on in years, so I shall instruct him for one half hour at nine o'clock every morning except Sunday. And he will practice at my house for the rest of the morning, should he wish, but not for less than two hours. He shall receive suitable breaks, refreshment, and rest, and will return to you each day by one o'clock. He will be at liberty to use the contents of my library, transported from Vienna at great cost and hardship to me. Is that acceptable, Frau Kapp?"

Mother threw up her hands in struggle. "But, Madame," she stammered, "I had no idea this was in your thoughts. He is such a small boy. Where could I get the money for these lessons? It is impossible even to think about—"

Madame Polkovska banged her cane on the floor again, a sound with which I was to become familiar. *"Ach!"* she exploded. "Who spoke of money? My cousin has told you that I am retired. I am not interested in money. When the sainted Abbé Liszt took me as his pupil in Budapest, he had no interest in money." She permitted herself a momentary smile. "Of course," she added, "they tell me that I was beautiful when I was younger." She resumed her stern tone. "This, the greatest pianist I ever knew, desired to teach those who deserved to learn. I can do no less." She pointed her cane at me.

"Tomorrow, young man. And you shall be punctual!"

Both Mother and I nodded, speechless. Mellnicz *úr* guided Madame Polkovska out of our house. His eyes twinkled with happiness.

* * *

I would agree with you that the scene you have just witnessed could be described as far-fetched. But something like it happened. Madame Polkovska, who had guided to fame some of the most important musical artists of her time, who had smoothed the way to greatness for many soloists, divas, designers, and directors, had taken a fancy to me.

And so, the next morning, as the first movement in a pattern that was to coil out over the years, I turned up at the modest though to me incredibly imposing house on the Király út. An aged female servant, who seemed as old as Madame, opened up when I pulled the bell. Mother had washed and dressed me with particular care. I had been hugged and kissed and sent on my way with fervent wishes that I prove both diligent and worthy of the great good fortune that had befallen me. The servant showed me into a large parlor on the ground floor.

The entire space in the sunny bay window was filled by a massive grand piano, one that I never could have imagined. Beneath the festooned layers of inlaid gold and ivory-shaped leaves, I could make out on its swollen legs and sides carved grapes, apples, bananas, eagles, and fish carelessly entangled. The opened lid revealed bright-hued paintings of young men in satin breeches and wigs playing violins to, and gazing soulfully at, demure young ladies white of wig and pink of shoulder. There was much bright blue sky and many cherubs, radiant with golden wings, flooding all available edges and corners, puffing with bulging cheeks on long post horns, strumming lyres, or clashing cymbals. A rich blue ribbon snaked through the entire scene, visiting each cherub in turn, artfully concealing his sex. I had advanced to the piano and was studying all this with deep interest when a clock on the mantelpiece struck the hour with tiny, silvery chimes. At the same moment, Madame Polkovska entered the room. I immediately lost whatever composure I had mustered.

"Come." She beckoned me to the magnificent instrument. "I am glad to see you are prompt." There was no other greeting.

I seated myself on a red plush bench and read, inside the keyboard lid, the words *Bösendorfer, Wien* inscribed in a flowing golden script. Madame pointed to the music rack, and to my astonishment, there were the books of Mozart and Bach that Mama had been using with me. Only these were shiny and new. Those at home were yellowed and crumbling, creased and rippled with a thousand-and-one turnings. At Madame's prompting, I reached out and opened the Bach—a stiff page that she had to press back at the center; otherwise it would close again. Such a marvelous fresh smell arose from the leaves. Fresh ink. Pages that nobody had ever turned before.

Madame's voice intruded. "Let us begin with the C major prelude," she said.

I smiled, for that was easy. She did not return the smile. I sighed and placed my hands over the smooth snow white keys. My left struck middle C and E. My right, the G, C, and E. But I could not continue.

"What's the matter?" Madame asked. But at the age of six, I found no way of letting her know: I was thrilled by the sound and the way that the piano responded. It was not to be believed. First of all, the action. The piano was enormous, and I half-expected that I'd have to strain to press the keys. But it was completely the opposite. All I had to do was *touch*, and the hammers rose and fell without effort. Here I could *play*, whereas on Mama's old upright I did hard labor. To press a key at home was to lean and grunt with effort. My fingers felt that they were propelling blocks, were kin to creaking joints of cracked wood and worn felt, finally connecting to the rusted tin cans of the wires. But *this*? How wonderful! *These* keys I had timidly pressed instantly shot the message through to the hammers. My own nerves could not have been as swift. And the tone: strong and secure—I felt I stood on something solid. Every note was separate and alone—not mingled with the ghosts of a dozen others. I gave myself the pleasure of a thumping good E-flat major chord. Wonderful! I did it again, louder. Then, as hard as it was for me—but somehow much easier on this piano—an F major scale in octaves, both hands. It was like the organ on Sunday. The bass notes boomed out with a good, firm punch, and the trebles were clean and sweet. How could I explain all this to Madame? But without my having to say a word, she, who had been watching me with great attention, abruptly rose from her chair.

"Enjoy yourself, young Master Kapp," she said. "Find out all about it. We shall begin tomorrow instead."

No farewell, but I could not care less. She vanished and left me alone with that beautiful instrument.

* * *

Mother asked me all kinds of questions when I returned home. What had Madame asked me to do first? What second? What pieces had she started me on? What exercises and drills? Had she mentioned Czerny, or did she think him too difficult? Mama kept talking about this Czerny. I stumbled and sputtered because Mama's excitement gave me no chance to reply. When at last she did, and I said that I had been left alone to acquaint myself with Madame's piano, she gave me a confused look and said it wasn't nice to tease her. Mama asked if Madame had given me lunch. I replied, quite truthfully, that her servant had taken me into the kitchen and given me delicious soup, ham, custard, and fruit jelly. She became sad and told me again I should not tease her. No one had seen ham, custard, or jelly for years in Szombathely. But that's exactly what I had eaten. I went further, becoming excited, because I wanted to tell

Mama all about Madame's fantastic grand piano, what it looked like with all its paintings and carvings. And, most important, how it had sounded, the way it had stirred my spirit.

But Mother refused to listen. She accused me again of teasing her, of not telling the truth. She dabbed at her eyes with her handkerchief. She said she was glad that Father had not been there to witness my behavior. True or not, any such tale I might tell would only have made him angry. She left the room without looking at me.

For the life of me, I had no idea what had just happened. I tease Mama? Only later could I come up with something that made sense. We lived a humble life at our house on the Györ útca. Our means were humble. Our food was humble. Mother slaved that we might keep body and soul together. I suppose my description of what Madame had given me to eat brought her a profound sense of failure. Despite the hard work in store for me every morning, I could not help enjoying my growing sense of power at the piano keys—and absolutely looking forward to jams, jellies, custard, and fragrant soups at Madame's table. Of course, my mother would never have dreamed of saying it, but I could tell she felt betrayed. For my part, I felt offended that she might feel that, and I think I relished it. That's the first betrayal that I remember. You might say that I sold my mother's trust for a bowl of soup. Later, I thought it a slight thing—and certainly an understandable lapse (if indeed lapse it was), but I think Mother never forgot it.

I settled into the new regime in Madame's ornate front parlor. Right from the beginning, Madame spoke to me in German. I could not say that I was expert in that language, but because Papa used it in the house—except when his chief, Mellnicz *úr,* came to call—I was quite comfortable with it. I soon discovered rule number one for Magyars: learn another language. Nobody in the world wants to speak Hungarian!

At Madame's, I would have to be ready for a rigorous, sweaty stretch of exercises—scales in any key that she might call for, arpeggios with both hands together and in opposite directions, scales in broken chords, chromatic runs with both hands in unison, in thirds and fourths, slower exercises with both hands together—not for the sake of velocity, but slowly, to develop regularity and measured pace—all to develop *technique,* as Madame called it. *Technique!* I loved saying the word. Once, when Madame's old servant opened the front door for me, I jumped up at her and shouted, "Technique!" She just looked at me sourly.

Of course, all this technique took time to build, according to Madame's exacting demands. She would sit silently to one side of the keyboard, her head trembling, but listening intently. Every so often, she thumped with her cane on the floor, indicating that I should repeat what I had just played, or used it to beat time to show me how dreadful was my sense of rhythm. After these exercises, I was permitted to play music. Madame did not think much of my Bach or Mozart.

"I've heard you try to play those masters at your mama's house," she said with raised brow. "Despite your impressive acquaintance with both composers, you will forgive me when I say you are not ready for either. Oh, yes," she continued, "you can play the notes. But Bach requires utmost passion and intelligence, while Mozart demands utmost maturity and depth, which, once achieved, must be dropped so that you may truly play artlessly."

I stared at her, not comprehending a word. Her features softened for a brief moment, and I thought she was about to smile at me. But no. She merely gestured with her head toward a Beethoven sonata on the music rack. It didn't have any sort of nice name, like "Springtime" or "Evening Whispers," just that it was in the key of G minor with the label Opus 49, No. 1.

"It's time to try some Beethoven," she said, and this time actually smiled. "I think I have mentioned that my own teacher was Franz Liszt." She motioned to a profile portrait on the wall of an old man with long white hair and a big nose.

I nodded. "Yes, you have, Madame," I said. "Did he like Beethoven too? You have told me he was a great musician."

"That is correct, young Master Kapp." She sounded almost kind. "Would you like to know who was the teacher of Franz Liszt, *my* teacher?"

I stared at her.

For answer, Madame pointed to a book stamped in gold with the legend *Carl Czerny* and then, in English, *School of Velocity, 1846.* "He, that man on the cover, with whom you are already acquainted. Czerny was Liszt's teacher."

I studied Madame's aged face, and then the face of the aged Franz

Liszt, and felt dizzy. Too many years for me to hold in my head.

"Now," she continued, "this is the best of all." Her eyes actually shone, something I would not often see. "Now, who do you suppose was *Czerny's* teacher? I'm speaking of the teacher of my *teacher's* teacher."

I became really anxious. I began to shake. I had to get out of there. The room had become suddenly hot and stuffy; my head began to swim. These feelings became familiar over time, later explained as a kind of epilepsy. They occurred whenever I was made to think of too many things at the same time. I didn't know enough to say anything about it. Madame seemed not to notice. She continued.

"I know it's hard," she said. "It must be as hard as imagining who your grandfather's grandfather was." She was correct.

After minutes of excruciating concentration, I still couldn't think of an answer. I couldn't stand it anymore. "So please tell me, Madame, I truly want to know who was"—I looked up to the ceiling and spoke carefully so as to get it right—"who was your teacher's *teacher's* teacher?"

Again, a tiny smile on that severe face. "Why, it was Beethoven himself," she said, "the man whose music you are about to play. Beethoven taught Czerny, Czerny taught Liszt, Liszt taught me. And now I'm teaching you. What do you think of that?"

Again, my head began to swim. I could play the piano well, but I couldn't answer Madame's question. "Please, what should I think of it?"

I think I startled her. I thought I would receive a good talking-to. Instead, her smile persisted and even grew somewhat sad. "I don't know either," she said at last. "But when I think of it, I feel a great warmth about my heart."

Within a moment, Madame recovered her stern aspect. She cleared her throat with a series of rasps, and we returned to the Beethoven. Madame said it was an easy piece and not too long—and so it seemed when she ran through it to give me an idea of what it sounded like. Her playing gave my head a chance to clear. But when I took my place on the piano bench, the piece proved anything but simple. To start with, the opening phrase, although not rapid, was accompanied in the left hand by a falling and rising passage in thirds that I was not able to play smoothly enough for Madame.

"*Legato, legato,*" she demanded. "My god, you play like a butcher. Some refinement, please." She leaned over to show me what she meant. "You have got to shape with smoothness, with an ear for the soft. And the softer!"

I tried again, but was immediately baffled when, in the second bar, I had to strike a C and the D under it at the same time—wasn't that a discord? That couldn't be correct!

Madame gave me a look. "In this key, it is perfectly correct. Beethoven's full of surprises. You'll get used to them. Again, please."

She was right. The sonata wasn't difficult. I soon got the hang of the notes. What turned out interesting, however, was the restless way Beethoven used the left hand. I had been accustomed to Mozart in his simple pieces: for the most part comfortably predictable *Alberti* bass lines. But you had to be on your toes with Beethoven. It wasn't simply accompaniment. Even in this "easy" piece, the left and right hands together created feelings in me hard to describe: unnamable longings, for one thing, and a sort of pain in my heart—not real pain, but a sensation I didn't have words for. This was particularly true in the second movement, which began with an innocent tune. But not for long. It was followed by a moody, haunting, almost wild section. After I had played it, I felt that I was going to cry. I turned away and blinked. Madame took my chin in her hand and turned my face up to hers.

"Good heavens, child," she said in wonder, "are those really tears?" It was the first time she seemed bemused. She touched my cheek.

"Welcome to Romantic music—but this is still the early Beethoven. My god, what's going to happen when you listen to Wagner?" She pointed to the music book. "Continue," she commanded.

After that, I could not be pried from the piano. As usual, according to our arrangement, Madame left me alone to practice precisely when her mantel clock struck nine thirty. I ignored the requirement that I practice scales and other exercises. I *needed* to work on that Beethoven sonata, so simple but yet so difficult. I needed to discover the secret behind that mingled pleasure and pain, why I felt that I had to cry. Hours flashed by. Madame's servant appeared as usual at 12:30 to summon me to the kitchen. I looked up at her with impatience and dislike.

"Go away!" I sounded just like Madame at her most imperious. I felt in no mood for soups or bowls of jelly.

"You are not hungry?" the old servant asked. "It makes no difference to me. As a matter of fact," she continued, "if you leave the house now, I can begin my afternoon off. I'm looking forward to sitting in the park."

"I want to go on practicing this piece. Is that all right?" I spoke rudely.

"No, it is not all right, young Master Kapp," she said. "Madame has gone out, and she has given me no instructions about leaving you in the house by yourself."

I must have looked aghast, but it had no effect. "So if you want to eat lunch as usual, I am ready to serve it, young master. If not, I am ready to lock up the house behind the two of us."

I glared at her a moment and ran from the building, pausing only to slam the great front door with a thunderous crash behind me.

I ran home feeling a murderous fury because I hadn't been able to have my way. When I arrived, Mother was astonished at my being earlier than usual. I made my way over to our brittle piano, threw it open, and—without mercy—pounded the keys for minutes on end. Finally, she sat beside me and grasped my hands, holding them in hers as echoes of the tuneless jangle died away.

"Ferenc, szegény fiam, my unhappy child," she whispered, "what has happened to you?"

I could only stare at her like a wild thing.

"Have you been naughty? Have you made Madame Polkovska angry with you?"

I burst into tears. I felt so unhappy. It had nothing to do with Madame, nothing to do with her servant. Surely, the cause of my misery was Beethoven. But it wasn't really his fault either. I seemed to have embarked on a struggle, but who was my foe? Beethoven made the rules. I was like an outsider begging for permission to enter, but he was a stern gatekeeper. I sensed all this from that rondo, the second movement of the G minor sonata. The only trouble was that, once again, I could not explain.

Mama had a different solution. "You want to know what I think, my little genius?" she smiled. "There has been a bit too much hard work," she said. "For two years, you have spent every morning with Madame, studying, practicing at her house. After you come home, lessons with me. You're only nine years old. It would be good for you to have friends." She gave me an encouraging look. "Yes, you have to have a friend."

"Why don't I go to school like other boys?" I asked.

Her eyes reddened. "It's the money," she said. "I can't pay the school fees. Papa's pension just isn't enough." Her voice became hard. "I refuse to send you to the workhouse school. The good sisters at the convent taught me, and I can teach you. Besides"—she squeezed me to her—"you've got a wonderful gift for the piano—Madame is sure of it. And who knows where it may take you!"

Hugging me to her again, she wept and I joined in.

* * *

Second Variation

Szombathely 1923

I had reached the exalted age of thirteen. Mama was proud of me for having survived hard times. Oh, yes, also because I had become quite good at the piano. I had given four solo recitals in the past two years at the Szombathely Municipal Auditorium, courtesy of Madame Polkovska. She had also arranged for the review of the most recent performance by newspapers, not only from Szombathely but also from nearby Graz and Wiener Neustadt. Mellnicz *úr* had wondered why not also the Budapest papers. Madame Polkovska had responded that Budapest was certainly to be reckoned with, but that she knew Vienna much better. And it was on Vienna that she had set her sights. It meant something that an influential friend of hers in Vienna, a music critic, had responded to an invitation to attend that most recent recital. His review read in part:

> Master Kapp, a serious-looking young fellow, who, I learned on good authority, is at least three or four years from his first shave, began his performance with a Mozart sonata, the No. 14 in A Minor (K. 310). It was surprisingly good, thankfully free of the affections we sometimes see in young performers. But it does require authority in the first movement, mature expression in the second, and utmost security in the presto. He handled the two outer movements well enough, but the andante had, in my opinion, more of an *ersatz* melancholy than true expression. Master Kapp should remember that Mozart's notes may not be difficult, but he is often difficult to play.

His Beethoven was better. The Opus 28 in D Major was a delight. Compared to the Mozart, our young recitalist seemed to apprehend the meditative, lyrical lines of the first, second, and fourth movements. One held one's breath as he approached the final allegro, but one need not have worried; the conclusion was as dashing as one could wish. His thirteen-year-old fingers were up to the challenge. Unhappily, your correspondent found it necessary to leave at the interval in order to fulfill other obligations.

I was angry that he didn't hear the second part. I had played the second of the two Opus 79 Brahms Rhapsodies, the one in G minor—not easy, with its left-hand octaves. I ended the program with Bach's First Partita in B Flat, closing with its rollicking gigue.

Madame had tried to be severe while we were preparing for the evening. "*Ach*," she exploded in exasperation. "You are stubborn and perverse. Everybody in the whole world begins with Bach and works forward in chronology." She pounded the floor with her cane. "I should have insisted. You begin with Bach, then you play Mozart, and then you play Beethoven, and *then* Schumann. And only then—if you like—people like Debussy and Ravel." She snorted sarcastically and smiled in spite of herself. That smile told me Madame would be lenient about my violating traditional order.

On the strength of that review, Madame arranged an audition for me with another influential friend, Dr. Bruno von Hornberger, an extremely important gentleman. He would mount a Haydn festival in Eisenstadt at the Schloss Eszterházy, the palace of Haydn's noble patrons. Dr. von Hornberger was to drop in at Madame's on his way back to Vienna.

On the appointed morning, I appeared in good time. Dr. von Hornberger turned out to be a large man, quite fat, who made a whistling noise when he breathed. Upon entering the house, he bowed and kissed Madame's hand, but barely nodded to me, before seating himself on one of the huge brocaded chairs in the parlor. I had the impression that he was annoyed, that he didn't want to be there. Nevertheless, at Madame's signal, I played my Mozart sonata for him while he stared up at the ceiling. Out of the corner of my eye, I could see his foot languidly beating time. When I finished the first movement, I eagerly swung around on my stool to face him. He was still looking up at the ceiling. All I could see of him were whiskers, a round chin, a fat neck, and two enormous hairy nostrils. Minutes passed before he stirred.

At last, he spoke. A strangely gentle voice, considering his great size.

"Good, good," he murmured, "a talented lad indeed." He accepted a cup of chocolate from my bane, Madame's aged servant. "But how can I help you at Eisenstadt?"

"I'd like you to give this pupil of mine a place on this summer's program."

Dr. von Hornberger's response was a gust of laughter and a rapid wave of his index finger from right to left. "An impossibility," he chuckled.

"Are your plans for the Haydntage so firmly established?" asked Madame.

He laughed again. "You may be absolutely sure of it. You may remember, we have to make these arrangements *very* early, by a whole year—or more. Our artists travel throughout Europe, North America and South, to Buenos Aires and Lima." He gently chided her. "You remember what it's like, *Gnädige Frau*—I don't have to tell you. Their managers simply have to know where they're going to be. Steamships, sleeper cars, hotels, the luggage—you know what that's like, Madame. Everything has to be precisely arranged. Otherwise, life would be chaos."

"Nevertheless," said Madame, gazing at him intently, "I have heard that the number of world-class artists you have engaged is not large at all and that other young and promising people will appear as well."

Dr. von Hornberger looked annoyed. "But hardly this young," he objected.

"Young Master Kapp," continued Madame, "is ready for a debut, in which he must play for an audience that includes a range of listeners wider than I, his mother, my cousin Herr Mellnicz, and our neighbors in Szombathely. I would consider it a personal kindness if you could make room for him this September." Despite her trembling head, she stared him steadily in the eye. "A personal kindness," she repeated.

Dr. von Hornberger turned red and swallowed. I looked on in wonder. Madame, whose wishes I had lightly defied about the order of the pieces I might play, was actually causing discomfort to this grand gentleman from Vienna.

"By the way, something puzzles me," said Madame in a confiding voice. "I am curious. Why have you chosen Eisenstadt as the site of the festival?"

Dr. von Hornberger cocked his head. "Rather than—"

"Rather than Eszterháza, of course. I know that Prince Nikolaus moved the court to the new palace there in 1760-something, and took dear Papa Haydn and all the musicians with him. And I also know that what Haydn wrote there was meant to be performed there, at Eszterháza."

Dr. von Hornberger sighed. "I know, I know, Madame. But I also don't have to tell you that everything is politics, and everything is difficult. Look, the Kaiser Franz-Josef is dead. There is no more dual empire. Today I'm strictly an Austrian with no privileges in Hungary. There are two Eszterháza palaces connected to Haydn, one at Eisenstadt in Austria and one at Eszterháza across the lake in Hungary. The Hungarians persist in thinking of the Prince and that region as theirs. Perhaps they think Haydn himself is also theirs"—he broke off to give a scornful laugh. "I do the best I can." It was making him perspire to speak of it. "Eszterháza is too remote, too out of the way. For another thing, when Nikolaus died, his son, Prince Anton, moved the court back to Eisenstadt, and the family no longer cared about Eszterháza. They permitted that 'miniature Versailles,' as they called it, to rot and decay! Shameful! I would find it impossible now to stage a Haydnfest at Eszterháza. Magnificent as it is, it would require far too much money to restore. And, Madame, it would require far too much tact to manage all those terribly touchy Hungarians. I simply haven't got the time. And I certainly haven't got the patience! Too many other things to worry about." Another laugh.

"I see," murmured Madame.

After more conversation and another cup of chocolate, he seemed less unhappy. It was agreed—I have no idea how—that I would spend a month in Eisenstadt, making myself useful in his office as a clerk, a messenger, and an assistant's assistant in all manner of things. He seemed to accept these requests. But what troubled him was Madame's unshakable insistence that I be a soloist in one of the Haydn concertos.

Dr. von Hornberger noisily expelled a gust of breath. "*Ach,*

Gnädige Frau, Gnädige Frau, you don't realize what you're asking," he protested. "The programs, the contracts are all arranged and drawn up"—he mopped his brow—"who is playing what and when! As I've already explained, much of this is settled for the season. We are not exactly Bayreuth or Salzburg, thank God, but there is still a lot to worry about!" He gathered his things and seemed ready to leave.

Madame took no notice. "I was debating with myself. With which concerto could Master Kapp make his debut—the G major, the F major, or the D major?" Madame directed a charming smile at her guest, as though they were chatting about the weather. "What do you think, Dr. von Hornberger?"

The other shrugged but remained silent, annoyed again.

"You see, Dr. von Hornberger, in most of these concertos, as you know, the orchestra is made up of only strings. The D major concerto, however, includes those beautiful oboes and French horns, and I think that would be most exciting for Master Kapp. He has heard military bands before, but never an orchestra, especially not oboes and French horns. What do you think?"

Dr. von Hornberger remained silent, tapping one shoe on the carpet and looking away.

"I have no doubt about his artistry and technical ability," said Madame, "so perhaps the D Major it is." She leaned toward him with a confiding whisper, which I had no difficulty hearing. "You know, Dr. Hornberger, what finally persuades me about the D Major is the finale." She closed her eyes a moment and smiled at the ceiling. "Not only most pleasing, but as you know, it's also a *Rondo all'Ungherese,* in the Hungarian style, with lively melodies of the gypsies. And Master Kapp, despite his name, is Magyar through and through!" What was she talking about? This was the first I had heard of it. Strange to think of myself as Magyar—or anything else, for that matter. I was Ferenc Kapp—no need for anything else. I held my tongue.

The visitor refused to be charmed and kept looking away.

"And that gives me another wonderful thought," Madame continued. "For the piano trio he will play"—she paused—"why not the one also with a gypsy finale, the G Major? *Two* contributions from Hungary. A graceful compliment to his people, no?"

Later on, when I had lived more years, I came back to that scene and wondered exactly how Dr. von Hornberger was obligated to Madame, that she not only prevailed upon him in that fashion, but permitted me to remain in the parlor during the discussion. I had been allowed to witness an adult stranger's discomfort. I had never seen that before. I had suffered, and would again suffer, my own humiliations. It all seemed to be an essential part of life. You do unto others, and others do unto somebody else. Would I have to pay for what I had witnessed that morning?

✳ ✳ ✳

The upshot was this. I was commanded to prepare a Haydn keyboard concerto, the D Major. And I was actually to be the soloist! I really didn't know what that meant. After all, I had never attended a full concert, didn't comprehend what it meant to join together with a band of musicians. I was to appear in the famous Haydnsaal, together with players from around Europe. Furthermore, I was to appear at one of the chamber music afternoons to perform the Haydn piano trio in G. Of course, it was a tremendous presumption for an inexperienced young fellow. If I'd had any sense at all, I should have locked myself in my room and refused to come out. But I simply had no idea what was in store, nor any idea of the work I had to do. Moreover, I had the distinct impression that, while Madame herself would not make an appearance in Eisenstadt, I was meant to be a kind of representative. Mama tried to explain what was obvious to all but me: I was probably Madame Polkovska's last pupil, and whatever I might do in music would not be a casual event. I was aware that even Mama, who made every effort to keep me from vanity and giving myself airs, was enormously proud.

I still turned up each morning as usual, except Sundays, in the front parlor for my half-hour lesson, followed by no less than three hours now of practice. These days, Madame Polkovska could not manage a step without her cane. She was more bent than when I had first met her, and her hands now shook more than ever. But not when she sat at the piano. Her playing remained strong—as far as I could tell. One thing seemed to have changed. Now and then, in spite of herself, whenever she was pleased with my playing, she couldn't help a faint smile as she listened and watched my fingers at work. If I happened to glance at her, and she noticed, the smile would be instantly replaced by a scowl. The aged housekeeper remained her dour self. She fed me in the kitchen at lunchtime each day without fail. But also without a sign of humanity. What a pair of sour hags.

Mellnicz *úr*, now retired from supervising his department at the tax office, was a constant visitor at Mama's. He spent his mornings at games of chess with cronies, then came over for tea and pastries—which he provided. He also seemed to regard me as his special pride. He was always saying, if he had not brought Madame over to visit, nobody would have known of my gifts and accomplishments. Of course, this cannot be denied. But he never forgot to declare it whenever he was in the house. For some time, I believed that the reason for his almost constant presence was that he wanted to marry Mama. Once, I hotly accused her of plotting behind my back to commit just such an act.

"For a boy who is so talented and intelligent, Ferenc, you can also be quite foolish," she sighed. "Don't you realize that Mellnicz *úr* is over eighty years old? How can you think that I might marry him? He has become a friend, since your dear Papa was lost." Her beautiful blue eyes grew moist. "A friend," she wanted me to understand, "that is all," she repeated. "Alone in the world, like me—but for his cousin, Madame Polkovska. And she, as you well know, is even older than he is." She dabbed at her face with a handkerchief. "Besides," she went on, in a whisper, as though she were telling me something improper, "I believe he is a *Jew*—I think his name is Jewish."

I wanted to rush over to beg forgiveness. But I also resented her for the mere *idea* of my being abandoned for someone else—as I imagined it. Not exactly logical, particularly as the thought had popped in my own mind, not hers. But people said I had a sharp imagination.

Whenever such frictions occurred between us, we developed the habit of giving one another reassuring smiles from across the room. But I had grown tired of doing so. The charm of that practice had been decreasing for me. It now seemed sticky, cloying, and embarrassing. When Mama expected that exchange of looks, I resented it. Too intimate. It was not my task to fulfill. And yet, if I had learned that she expected them from somebody else, the idea would enrage me. I dared believe I might kill him.

She now looked over to me for one of those smiles to assure herself

41

that all was well between us. But I refused to give it. I stared coldly back. I couldn't have felt more guilty as her face crumpled with hurt, and she fled into the kitchen. She slammed the door behind her as I used to do when younger, but I could hear her sobbing. Again, I was torn, bitterly regretting what I had done, but in some strange way, actually enjoying it. Was it possible to relish being bad?

You are going to burn in hell for this, I told myself. I hastily made the sign of the cross and silently begged God's forgiveness. But I did not beg it of Mama at first. When I did, she instantly forgave me, as she always did. It was hard for me to understand. Sometimes, I felt loathsome. Sometimes, I thought I might have to restore balance in the universe by doing myself some kind of harm. But I never did, as you see.

* * *

April arrived in Szombathely; warm breezes streamed over the Carpathian Mountains. Flowers returned, and we could walk about without jackets and scarves. But the world suddenly became frightening. The prices you had to pay for things in the shops went crazy. Our money (no longer the kronen we used during the Empire) didn't seem to mean anything. I could not understand why the loaf of bread that cost five fillér on Saturday would suddenly cost ten fillér the following Monday, fifty on Thursday, and a whole pengö by the next Monday. Crowds gathered outside the bakery, the butcher's, and smashed windows, not caring if our local gendarmerie saw them or not. Mama was frightened by all this. We had rioters in the streets and revolutionaries of all kinds, Communists and people who hated Communists. Mama said nothing made sense anymore. She was running out of hope, but she thanked God that, even though Papa's pension had abruptly dwindled, we would not be thrown out on the streets if she could continue to cook for other people—at least, not that month.

The disturbances did not spill over to Madame's grander street, so my musical education went on. One morning, a dray cart drew up outside her house. Two men lifted off another, smaller piano, trundled it through the front door and into the parlor. I helped make room.

In response to my question, Madame said simply, "It is time to prepare for Eisenstadt, time for you to learn your concerto." I would be at the carved grand piano. Madame would play the orchestral part at the smaller one.

From the first, it was a new regime at Madame's. Gone were the hints of warmth in our lessons. The smiles vanished. In fact, things grew harsh and at times even merciless! But I also saw that Madame was as hard on herself as she was on me. The lessons extended to an hour or more each morning. I could see Madame growing weary as ten o'clock approached.

Once, the elderly servant, bringing Madame her glass of tea, cried out at what she discovered. Madame had stopped playing, was lying back in the armchair she used while at the piano. Her eyes were closed, hand pressed to her bosom as though in pain, her face as white as her hair.

"You are wearing yourself out, Madame!" the servant cried. "You must stop at once and lie down."

She so startled me that I jumped. My eyes and ears were fixed on my solo part. I was unaware that Madame had stopped playing.

Madame opened her eyes, sat up, and glared at her servant. "How dare you disturb us, Agathe," she rasped weakly.

"But, Madame—"

"I am quite angry with you. Thank you for the tea, but I do not need anything else."

The servant vainly attempted to speak.

"Put down the glass and leave," said Madame again. "Woman, are you deaf?" Madame had the strength to stamp her foot. "Go!" The servant finally left.

Madame softened her frown. "It's perfectly all right. I'm not ready to leave the world just yet." She sipped at the hot sweet tea. "There, I feel better already."

"Now," she commanded, her voice stronger, "back to bar 73!" She played two swift chords and immediately cried out in annoyance when I didn't play.

"That was your cue. Where were you?" She shook her fist. "Already you're late!" She thumped the side of the spinet to beat the time. "You begin that rising scale as soon as you hear those chords. Don't wait! You provide the upbeat for the orchestra at that bar. Everybody relies on you at that moment!"

I tried to do better. At the same time, of course, I was preparing the piano trio. I did better with that. One morning, when I arrived at her house for the day's lesson, I found two strangers waiting in the parlor. One was a sweet-faced girl about my own age, seated in a chair, a music stand before her, tuning a violin. The other was an older heavy-set man, holding a cello between his knees, also with a music stand, softly playing scales and occasionally plucking the strings. Madame introduced the strangers, but I paid no attention to their names. I was captivated by the sounds of their instruments, the first time I had seen and heard them. And, again, just as with listening to music itself, I was transfixed. The sounds thrilled me. My eyes darted from one to the other. The girl, in her springtime pale gingham, her quiet face so serious, looked intently into the distance, listening to herself, occasionally tightening a tuning peg. The man with the cello played a series of downward scales, from high up on the fingerboard, continuing down, down, down until he reached and held, with vibrating left hand, a long-drawn-out note, filling the room with a deep sound that made my own stomach vibrate in sympathy. I felt so happy to be there.

Madame, on her parlor armchair, asked me to strike an A on the piano. The girl and the man adjusted their tuning. When the room fell quiet, Madame, with her old vigor, commanded, "Now we begin." The girl and the man immediately sat up, simultaneously put their bows to the strings. I peered intently at my music.

Madame spoke sharply. "Are you quite ready, Master Kapp?" I nodded. "In that case, kindly turn your head to look at this young lady. The solo violin gives the signal to start." The girl smartly dipped her head. We were off.

This was a gracious first movement, not excited like the beginning of the concerto—far from technically difficult, but one had to be alert and accurate. I noticed immediately that my part had many more notes than those of the other two. Madame had schooled me well. I didn't need to worry in the slightest about my fingers and hands. They were in the right place at the right time, doing their runs and trills, and striking their chords. After a while, I dared to take my eyes off my music and notice what the others were doing. We sounded wonderful together. My heart swelled with pleasure. So lovely! I stole a glance at the sweet-faced girl. Her violin sounded beautiful. Occasionally, she would play in unison with me, sometimes a third below my melodic line, sometimes providing a decorative accompaniment. The man with the cello mainly duplicated my left hand, at least a simplified version of it. I felt I was the whole show!

When the first movement ended, Madame nodded. "Not bad at all for a first run-through." She relaxed in her deep armchair and waved for us to continue. The slow movement permitted both the violin and cello to provide lovely melodies, under which I played chords and countermelodies. The Hungarian rondo, with its gypsy flavor, was wild, changed key, changed tempo, and went like a whirlwind, but we got through it more or less at the same time. Madame grunted.

Grinning, I stood up and stretched. I had enjoyed the experience. What else was there to do? I met Madame's eye. "Where are you going? Please, sit down, young Master Kapp. We are by no means finished. In fact, we have barely begun." My grin vanished.

For the next hour, we worked like devils. But I think that time proved the most valuable in my entire musical education. I should admit to having been somewhat worried about my faults being exposed in front of strangers. However, on that morning, the importance of precision, balance, tone, and dynamics was burned into me. I had never seen Madame as pitiless as that.

At the end of an hour, the servant Agathe appeared, balancing a tray of Russian tea and chocolates—never offered during *my* lessons. Now, Madame relaxed and encouraged us to stand up and stretch. She and the cellist, who seemed to be well acquainted, spoke animatedly with each other. The girl stood apart, sipping her glass of tea. She looked shy.

Madame glanced over at us. "Go on, go on," she said to me. "You are permitted to speak to each other. Don't you remember what I told you? You'll be playing this trio at Eisenstadt together with Herr Kabós and his daughter." Why had I not heard the first time? This peculiar mental absence of mine seemed to occur when many things were going on at the same time. But not always. I was interested in the nice, shy girl. So she was the cello player's daughter? We looked at each other from across the room. She blushed, and I felt my face grow warm also.

I found myself next to her. "Hello," I said, blushing deeper, I am certain.

She held out her hand. "How do you do?" she replied. "I am Krisztina Kabós. I am happy to meet you."

I was so horribly clumsy that, when I raised my hand to shake hers, I struck her tea glass out of her hand, knocking it to Madame's thick crimson rug. I was horrified. Madame, engrossed in her conversation with Herr Kabós, had not noticed, but the servant, standing at the side of the room, moved toward me, frowning, painfully got down on her knees, and scrubbed at the stain with a cloth. Krisztina knelt beside her, retrieving the glass from under Madame's big piano.

Miserable, I sat in a corner. Krisztina joined me. I stared straight ahead, full of confusion. "You play beautifully," was all she murmured.

I couldn't tell if she was making fun of me. I dared steal a glance. "And so do you," I said. I turned to her. She was so pleasant to look at, so pretty, her hair so dark and soft—I could look nowhere else.

She blushed again. "Why are you staring at me?" she asked.

I finally blurted, "What are those red marks under your chin?"

I startled her. She immediately laughed, but soon became serious. "Don't you know anything? It comes from playing the violin," she said. After another moment, she added clearly: "One doesn't expect a person one has just met to ask that sort of question." She stood up and returned to the other side of the room.

I wanted to batter my head against the wall. *Clumsy! Clumsy! Clumsy!*

* * *

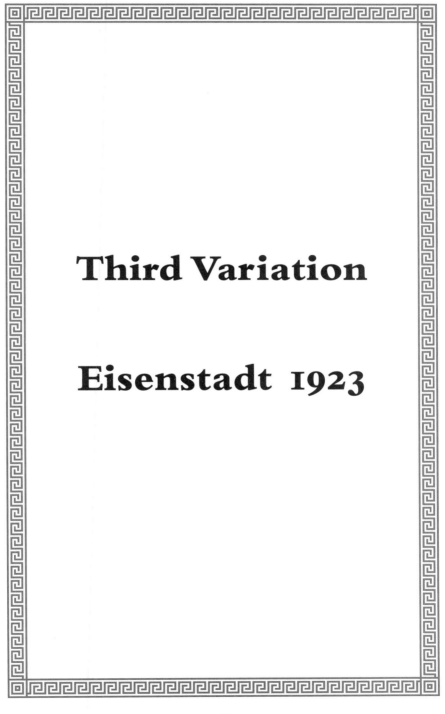

Third Variation

Eisenstadt 1923

On the second of August, I bade farewell to Madame at her house, and later to Mama and Mellnicz *úr* at the railway station. It was high summer and hot. It was to be my first journey away from Szombathely. Not only that, I would travel to a different country, crossing the Austrian border to reach Eisenstadt. I was to do Madame proud. I would spend a month as a general assistant to Dr. von Hornberger, thus paying for my room and board, during which time I was also to prepare for my two performances, the trio and the concerto.

Before I departed Madame's house on the Király út, she asked me to kiss her on the cheek. I did so, but with a mixture of dread and wonder. Her skin was wrinkled and papery. She responded by kissing me on the forehead. I suddenly remembered what Mama had said about Mellnicz *úr*, that he was a Jew. And if he was, wasn't his cousin, Madame Polkovska, also one? I had heard that Jews smelled bad. While I was close to her, I used the opportunity to sniff cautiously. Aged she may have been, but I could smell nothing other than her customary camomile scent. Agathe, the servant, was also in the parlor, with the ever-present disapproval on her face. At the station, tears, of course, from Mama and many hugs. From Mellnicz *úr*, a small bag of *minyons*, the small pastries that I loved. I forgot to smell him.

As he placed the bag in my hands, Mellnicz *úr* winked and grinned mischievously and, making sure that Mama was attending to something or other, put his lips to my ear and whispered loudly: Remember, you are not really going to Eisenstadt. Eisenstadt does not exist. There *is* no Eisenstadt!"

What on earth did he mean?

Mama rejoined us and overheard him. "For shame, for shame, Mellnicz *úr*," she said, looking worried. "What are you saying? Haven't we got enough excitement?"

Mellnicz *úr* widened his eyes in innocence. "I'm only telling the boy the truth," he protested. "Don't you remember, Mrs. Kapp? It was only two years ago. That was part of Hungary." All at once, he startled me when he shouted aloud for everybody to hear, "Part of Hungary! Part of Hungary!" and grew red in the face.

Mama tried to soothe him. "Now, now, Miksa *úr*, you know it's not good for you to become excited—"

Mellnicz *úr* ignored her. He stamped his foot angrily like a child. "Kismarton, Kismarton," he cried again. "That's what the place is called. It's Hungarian! Not Austrian!" He stood, shaking with fury. Mama was aghast. "It's an outrage, is what it is!" he shouted. "How much humiliation can we accept? Everything is stripped from us!"

The train drew into the station with much clanking and hissing. Mama didn't know whom to attend to first. She hastily led me to an open door. I climbed up inside with my one bag and found a window seat, still not understanding what had happened. People knew that the place was called Eisenstadt. It was called Kismarton in Hungarian, also Zeljiezno in Croatian. That was one of the wonderful things about living in the empire under our beloved Ferenc József Császár. You got to learn so much. And then I became sad. We had no more Császár.

The train started off with a tremendous lurch that all but threw me to the floor. I stood at the window, waving goodbye to Mama and Mellnicz *úr*. They didn't wave back. Mama was leading him to a bench. They were soon out of sight around a bend. As the train clattered over a bridge at the end of the high street, I caught a glimpse of crowds forming for another *tüntetés,* one of those noisy demonstrations and window smashings. The price of bread must have gone up again. And here I was, with my bag of *minyons.*

The train puffed along, never working up any speed, and seemed to stop every five minutes. Some of my fellow travelers looked like peasants, with work-stained clothes and sun-reddened faces. There were also gypsies with dark skin, curly hair, gold earrings, silver buttons on their coats, wearing the dilko, a colored scarf, around their necks. They carried makeshift bundles crammed with food. Mama had taught me to be terrified of them because of their dishonest shifty ways, and I didn't take my eyes off them until they got out at one of the stops.

The journey didn't take long, in spite of our unhurried pace. The really exciting part came just soon after we passed Kőszeg. The train stopped at the border. First, two Hungarian officials marched through the car, asking to see our travel papers—after which the train rolled a short distance, and then two Austrian officials did the same, wearing almost the same uniforms, and exactly the same kinds of moustaches and stern expressions.

I glued my face to the window, trying to see whether Austria looked any different from Hungary. I was disappointed. The same green fields, narrow lanes, and dray carts.

A peasant sitting opposite asked me what I was searching for, staring so hard out of the window. When I told him, he gave a twisted, bitter smile.

"I'll ask you a question, young sir. Why do you think the countryside looks the same both sides of the border? What would you say was the reason for that?"

I shook my head, not knowing what to say.

"You really don't know, young sir? With your fine, educated appearance and your clean hands?" I think he was making fun of me, but I wasn't sure. He held up his hands to show me. They were cracked and calloused. I stole a glance down at mine and decided to hold them up too. His eyes grew wide. My fingers were somewhat calloused too, but only at the ends. He seized my right hand, brought them up to his eyes, and wonderingly felt the tips. They were hard and round.

Just as suddenly, he dropped my hand. "I'm sorry, I'm being rude," he said. "But what kind of work is it that you do, young sir, to collect fingers like these?" he asked, newly polite.

"I play the piano," I replied.

"Now that sounds like good fun, that does," the man cried. "I like a good tune myself. I used to play the fiddle when I was younger, and my brother László used to play with me on the zither. Good times of an evening at the tavern!" He leaned forward and tapped me on the knee. "But what work is it that you do to get fingers like that? I've always wanted to speak with an educated young gentleman like yourself, the quality folk, and find out how they live."

"I don't know," I stammered, "I just play the piano." He looked puzzled. "And"—I spoke in a rush—"I don't know why you keep telling me I'm educated or quality, things like that. My mama cooks and does the washing for the real quality. My papa was killed in the war," I ended, feeling at once defiant and sad.

"Was he now, poor young sir?" he said, and crossed himself at least three times. "But how did you get those fingers?" he persisted.

I sighed. Things were becoming tiresome, but the peasant leaned forward, eager to hear.

"Ever since I was six, people said I could play the piano. And ever since then, I've been having lessons and playing the piano and giving concerts, and now I'm on my way to Eisenstadt to play at the concerts there, and I'm going to play a piano trio and a piano concerto and…and…" I let my voice trail away. My companion had not the slightest idea of what I was saying, but he still nodded and smiled.

"And when you play the piano all the time, your fingers get to be like this?" He strained his eyes, peering anew at my hands.

"But you should see Madame's hands—my teacher!" I burst out. "Once, she actually broke a piece of glass just by thumping it with her first finger. It was just as a joke," I added hastily, "and she made me promise not to try it myself. It was only to show me how strong her hands were."

He was puzzled again. "Break a piece of glass? A woman?" he said slowly. "Whatever for?" I said nothing. There was a long pause. I was relieved not to be discussing my fingertips.

He said, "You were asking, I believe, why the fields on this Austrian side look the same as on the Hungarian side. I'll tell you, young sir. But it should be plain as the nose on your face!"

Now it was I who leaned forward.

He looked about him a moment. "It all used to be ours, you know, Magyar land," he whispered. "Let them call it what they like— Burgenland, or whatever bloody name they dug up. It's ours," he hissed fiercely. "It's not right that we lost it, but we'll get it back!"

Funny, I thought. Just what Mellnicz úr had been saying. And this farmer seemed to be as intense as Mellnicz úr had been. Obviously, as a young Hungarian, I ought to have felt indignant about the matter as well. But just then, the train began to slow down. We passed streets and houses, but not many, as we entered the Eisenstadt station.

The train drew to a halt. I said goodbye to my companion, alighted, had my ticket collected, and emerged onto a sun-drenched cobbled square. It was nearly midday, quite hot. I hunted in my jacket pocket for the instructions that Madame had Agathe write out for me. I was to walk to the Schloss Eszterházy and ask for Dr. von Hornberger. By that time, I knew all about Haydn and loved him—almost as much as Beethoven, but not as deeply. Everybody—Mama, Mellnicz úr, and Madame—had given me long lectures: I was to mind my manners, obediently spring to my duties, and be sure not to trip over, squash, or drop anything.

Outside, I asked an aged porter where I might find Schloss Eszterházy. He pointed along a tree-lined avenue, up toward a sprawling yellow building some distance away. Atop its hill, it dominated the view. The largest building I had ever seen, it made even our grand houses in Szombathely—and certainly these quaint houses along the streets of Eisenstadt—look like toys. It made me dizzy to gaze up at it. Whenever I felt that way, I feared I was about to suffer one of my peculiar spells. Happily, it soon passed. I was not only going to perform in this palace but also going to work there for Dr. von Hornberger—and actually stay there. I was going to sleep in a palace for a month!

I took off my wool jacket, which was sticking to me, and started up the broad avenue, named the Rüsterstrasse, because of the elm trees that lined it. When I reached the Schloss, I crossed the imposing square to one of the doors. On either side were posted announcements of the season's programs. I drew close to see if my name was listed. There were so many events—orchestral concerts, chamber music afternoons, solo recitals—it was hard to sort them out. The really grand events, signaled by large letters and heavy printing, seemed to be performances of an opera by Haydn called *Armida,* in the Schloss itself. And there would be an oratorio, *The Creation Mass,* performed in a church. The Haydntage were going to be a crowded ten days. For the first time, I understood something of what Dr. von Hornberger had been complaining about in Madame's front parlor.

The Herr Intendant's office was to be found at the end of a long corridor on the ground floor. I knocked on the heavy doors. No response. I knocked repeatedly. From behind, I could hear muffled bangs and thumps. Finally, I turned the handle and pushed. Inside a large office, beneath an ornate, painted ceiling, four young men in shirtsleeves, but also in collars and cravats, were tearing open enormous wooden packing cases and lifting out piles of booklets, which they stacked on rows of tables around the sides of the airless room. Their faces dripped sweat; the backs of their shirts were soaked.

A fifth man, older, marched rapidly over from the back of the room. He seemed to be in charge. "Are you here to work at last?" he demanded. "You're late!"

Obediently, I went to one of the young men to help unload his box. "No, no," the manager cried in exasperation. "Can't you see he's already working on this one? Get your own box and work on that one."

I tried to do so. But I found the crate to be enormous. I was unable to get my arms around it, let alone lift it to a table. One of the young men closest to me noticed.

"Are you two going to stare at the thing all day?" the manager shouted. "Dummkopf! If it's too heavy for you, why don't you say something?"

Around me, the other young men continued, furiously ripping open their packing cases with dangerous-looking chisels, making stacks of booklets. It was so hot and stuffy there—no air and no good feeling left in me. I wanted to run out of the place.

The manager motioned a young man to approach, and together we heaved the wooden container onto a table and opened it. I seized a handful of the contents, put it down, and reached for another.

"Nein, nein, nein, nein!" The manager was beside himself. "Don't you remember anything? You're just slapping the programs down? Leaving them anywhere?"

I had no idea what he was talking about.

"Look at the date!" He had turned red in the face, reminding me of Mellnicz *úr*, when I had said goodbye to him that morning. "Look at the date," he repeated, grabbing one of the booklets and waving it at me. I was still bewildered. "It clearly says," speaking as though to a fool, "September 12. *September 12!* If you don't carry them to the proper table and put them in the right order, we will never find them." He became, not merely red, but purple.

We were interrupted. A door to an inner office opened. Dr. von Hornberger appeared. "Herr Krebs, is there something wrong?" He seemed mild and kind, unlike the last time I saw him.

The unpleasant manager instantly stopped being nasty, put on a smile, bowed, and rubbed his hands together. "Herr Intendant," he said, "I had to reprimand this incompetent young person. He has remembered nothing of what I told him last week about the orderly arrangement of the daily programs. Nothing!" he sneered. "He has remembered nothing! And as you yourself have made it clear, Herr Intendant, if the daily programs are out of order, this alone could ruin the entire festival! We shall have to send this stupid boy back to where he came from." The head clerk gave Dr. von Hornberger a satisfied smile, which the Intendant, did not return.

"Herr Krebs," said the Intendant, shaking his head, "you have never seen this lad before." As one man, the four clerks halted their furious activity and stopped to listen.

The head clerk's smile faded as he turned to examine my face. "With respect, Herr Intendant, with the greatest respect, I don't know what you mean." He stammered, "I-I instructed him and the others in every aspect of their duties—"

"Please pay attention, Herr Krebs," said the Herr Intendant, speaking as if bored. "I am confident that this boy is just off the train from Szombathely within the past half hour. I repeat, you have never seen him before; ergo, he has had no instructions to forget or misapply. He will assist *me* in various matters, and you, Herr Krebs, will not be in charge of him."

The manager seemed as baffled as I had been moments before.

"In fact, Herr Krebs, this young man has a place on our programs. Twice, in fact. He will perform twice! He is a young musician of great promise." Dr. von Hornberger regarded the head clerk with amusement. "To hear him, I myself journeyed to visit the home of his teacher, the renowned Madame Polkovska of Budapest and Vienna. And he is here at my express invitation to play with us. In fact, Herr Krebs, I am surprised you didn't notice his name while you were unpacking these programs."

Herr Krebs turned to me in apologetic horror. He bowed several times and rubbed his hands together feverishly. He had become gray in the face, eyes popping out of his head. He looked frightened, sick, and ashamed—like me with Madame at times. And yet, surprisingly, he continued to smile. And the smile made him look more sickly.

"A thousand apologies, young sir," he said, speaking in an oily voice. "Believe me, truly a thousand apologies. Can you forgive me?

My mind must have been elsewhere. I have obviously made a dreadful mistake. You must know I would never dream of addressing one of our esteemed artists with disrespect." He bowed yet again. When he straightened up, he noticed the four clerks standing there, mouths open.

"Get back to work!" he screamed.

Dr. von Hornberger motioned me to follow him to the inner office. I did so, once again trying to understand the meaning of this fresh demonstration of the way people treated each other. It was like the way Madame had treated Dr. von Hornberger when he came to hear me play. I knew that grown-ups could treat children with scorn. But why would grown-ups do it to each other? It seemed a dangerous world. I was getting the idea that the best way to avoid unpleasant treatment was to be unpleasant first. I would have to think about that.

Dr. von Hornberger chuckled as he conducted me through the door. "He's a dependable man, Krebs, but needs to be closely supervised."

I looked up at him.

"All Germans do, you know," he said in an offhand way, as though it should have been obvious. "They crave it, leadership, I mean. You'll find out what I'm talking about when you've been here longer. Losing the war did terrible things to us. We were stabbed in the back by traitors. But we did not lose our way, thanks be to God."

Behind the inner doors, there were administrative offices divided up from what I learned had been grand salons, some with gilded walls and painted ceilings. There, Dr. von Hornberger instructed a handsome young man, another of his assistants—I was to be one among many— to guide me to my sleeping quarters. He led me through passages and corridors, up staircases, and across galleries so that I despaired of ever finding my way back. At last, we arrived at a room—it must have been just under the roof—that contained four simple cots and nightstands.

"We are in the old servants' wing of the Schloss Eszterházy," said my guide. "You'll have to take this bed by the door, it's the only one left." I had never had to share a bedroom before. "I should introduce myself." He gave a slight formal bow, just inclining his neck, at the same time clicking his heels. "Graf Konrad von Friesach," he announced. "A privilege to meet one of our distinguished artists."

He was a nobleman! From the stories that Mama and I had read together over the years, I knew all about *nemesség*, the nobility. They were the heroes and the villains of my favorite tales. No matter if Hungarian or German—*Erzherzog* or *főherceg, Baron* or *báró, Fürst, Freiherr, Graf* or *gróf*—I had encountered them all in stories. And here was one in the flesh, extending his hand. To me.

Mama and Madame would have been proud of me. I imitated the Herr Graf. I clicked my heels, gave a terse nod of my head—not like the groveling Herr Krebs—and announced, "Kapp Ferenc-Hermann von Szombathely." He looked impressed.

"Is that in Hungary?" he asked. "Do your people have large estates there? How is the hunting in those parts?"

I instantly lost my poise. "I-I don't know much about that, I'm afraid. I spend most of my time at the piano."

"Oh, yes, of course," replied the Herr Graf. He sounded bored, the way Dr. von Hornberger spoke to Herr Krebs. "To tell the truth, I'm not awfully interested in music myself. And especially not this Haydn fellow. Impossible to dance to, for one thing."

"Then why would the Herr Graf want to work for the Haydntage?"

"To be near Dr. von Hornberger. He is truly an inspiring man." He had dropped his offhand manner and stared directly at me. "Surely, you have felt this yourself." He glanced about him and spoke softly. "There are many of us, working for a new day."

"A new day?" I repeated. "What kind of new day?"

His eyes held mine. "Well, young fellow, I'll let you in on it. You may not be fully grown yet, but you are an aristocrat like myself, and I trust you."

I swallowed and waited.

He brought his face toward mine. I thought for a moment he was going to kiss me. Instead, he whispered, "We are struggling to overturn the shameful treaties of Versailles and St. Germain and Trianon, which ruined all of us. We will do this by any means necessary." He drew back his face and studied mine. He looked pleased to share this. I didn't follow any of it. His smile faded.

"Those unjust treaties," he hissed into my ear.

I shook my head, still not understanding.

"Those treaties that were imposed on us. They meant to destroy us, but *they* must be destroyed!" He seemed in a trance. "Destroy Versailles and St. Germain, and we smash the English, the French, the Bolsheviks, and especially the Jews!"

He was waiting for me to say something back, but all I could think was that the Herr Graf was the third madman I had encountered this day. Mellnicz *úr* was the first, Herr Krebs the second, the young man standing before me was the third—and today was not yet over.

"It is up to us, the nobility and the landholders—what is left of us—to forge unity with all true patriots, no matter from what class, to revive an exciting ancient idea, the idea of a Greater Germany never yet seen! We mean to unite all parts of our fatherland and redeem ourselves from the misery and humiliation we see all around us—the hunger, the fear, crises, inflation, foreign troops poking into our business. We will recover all of Austria, all our lost empire, and reunite all Germans—not forgetting Alsace and Lorraine. And smash that so-called Polish Corridor. Smash the humiliation!" He had begun to raise his voice, but caught himself. "We will astonish the world," he said. "Just watch and see."

He bent toward me again, suddenly clasped the back of my neck with a hot sweaty hand, and drew me against him. I was frightened. He was going to kiss me! I was sure of it. I somehow wriggled free, but there was no escape. He had me in a corner. We stared at each other for a full minute. I was terribly nervous, looking for a gap so I could dash past, but his mocking smile held me captive. Finally, he stood up straight, clicked his heels, gave one of his slight bows, and left.

I had to lean against the wall a few moments. I really had no idea what that had been about. After I had unpacked my few belongings and found my way back, with great difficulty, to the offices on the ground floor, I had regained my appetite. I had not eaten since morning. I was shown to a kind of dining hall, where I was served warmed coffee and a plateful of biscuits by a respectful attendant. It was a pleasant room, with rows of tables, the huge windows open, thankfully, on a hot day like this, overlooking the gardens at the back of the Schloss. I felt awkward to be eating all alone. The servant stood respectfully to one side, watching as I munched my biscuits. It was wonderful.

"Is everything to the Herr Baron's satisfaction?" he asked. "We were told in the kitchens that the young gentleman was a nobleman like the other assistants of Dr. von Hornberger. And an artist too. A double honor." He bowed.

I groaned. It had been only a joke, what I had told the Herr Graf upstairs. Of course, Dr. von Hornberger would soon find out. After my lunch, I reported back to the main office, where Dr. von Hornberger, after regarding me with unsmiling, narrowed eyes—which told me that he was not amused by my presumption—said I was to spend the rest of the afternoon practicing at the keyboard. Such were Madame Polkovska's instructions. Dinner for the general staff was served at seven o'clock. I was to appear at his desk the next morning at 8:00 sharp, ready for any work he might have.

I collected my music books, found a rehearsal room, and got to work. I discovered a curious thing. Even though Madame was not present or in the next room—I think that was the first time I had been away from her—I could imagine her watching and listening, and found that I myself had become strict and exacting as though she were there. In fact, so real was my imagination that I caught myself glancing over my shoulder every so often, and once I even walked around the piano just to make sure. The main thing though was that I worked hard, not only with my performance pieces but also with the exercises, scales, and studies of every kind. I was working for Madame and Mama even though they were back in Szombathely.

When the staff assembled in the gilded eating hall for dinner, Dr. von Hornberger was not there. The room was only half-filled, about twenty-five to thirty occupied places. Some people were chatting and laughing. I noticed an isolated group made up of Herr Krebs and his four assistants. They ate silently and looked sad. There were five young women accompanied by an older one who seemed to be in charge of them. Four of the young women were silent too; in fact, they mostly kept their eyes on their plates, even though Herr Krebs' assistants frequently looked over at them. I noticed the young women stealing glances at the young aristocrats who sat together with the Graf Konrad von Friesach—who ignored their admirers. A fifth young woman openly winked at them.

When he caught sight of me at the door, the Herr Graf summoned me with an imperious wave. I nervously obeyed. His friends looked me up and down with amusement. But they rose to their feet. I had to choke back a laugh because two of them, the same height and dressed alike, had almost identical long ugly scars on the left sides of their faces, making them appear like a pair of weird twins.

"I have the honor to present an extraordinary young man," said the Herr Graf. "Not only one of the distinguished artists but a member of the nobility, one of us. Permit me to present none other than Kapp Ferenc-Hermann von Szombathely." Instantly, the young men roared with laughter, so that the entire dining hall fell silent and stared at us before continuing to eat.

"Look at him, turning all colors," cried one young man, at which they all broke into fresh peals of mirth. I wanted to flee, but couldn't move. It seemed people knew about what I thought had been a harmless joke. Surprisingly, the Herr Graf wished me to join his group. He introduced me to the others—I was too much in a whirl to remember names—but they all seemed to be *von* this and *von* that, with many other titles in evidence, which he took pleasure in reciting at length. He motioned me to sit next to him. I did, but as far away as I could. A waiter placed a dish of roast pork, dumplings, and tiny carrots in front of me. Another waiter, with a questioning look, held up a jug of beer and a bottle of wine. I nodded at the wine. I had never seen food like this, not even at Madame's. I began to dig in.

The Herr Graf leaned over. "I have decided to forgive your deception earlier today," he whispered in my ear. "You have Dr. von Hornberger to thank for pointing out that you are still young and, I hope, unaware of the grave breaches of etiquette such conduct may reveal."

"I am very sorry, Herr Graf," I murmured, swallowing with difficulty.

"But that is only part of the matter," he continued. His companions were ignoring us, having a good time eating and exchanging obviously funny stories. He brought his face close to mine again, just as he had done upstairs in the attic bedroom. Again, he had that almost mad look in his eyes. "It concerns me that I may have revealed intentions in the belief that I was speaking to a fellow patriot and a fellow nobleman."

Intentions? Desperately, I tried to recall exactly what he had said upstairs. As he studied my face, his expression hardened. It occurred to me that if I pretended I didn't remember, it would be a mistake. He would see right through me. How that thought came to me, I cannot say. Perhaps it was from observing Madame Polkovska. Growing old and feeble in the body she may have been, but she was certainly sharp in the mind and could see everything. So I didn't try anything funny with him.

"Oh, yes, Herr Graf," I said brightly, as though he had reminded me of something. "With great respect, Herr Graf, I had been meaning to speak to you of those things again. But I was afraid because of the joke I dared to play on you—that you'd be upset with me."

His eyes narrowed. "What do you wish to say, young man?"

"Just that I-I was interested in what you said about those treaties," I replied.

"What about the treaties?"

"I just wanted to know more about them."

"Oh, yes?" He brought a forkful of food to his mouth and chewed. I tried to do the same but scattered my fork-load back on the plate. My hand was shaking.

"Comrades," he addressed his companions. They instantly paid heed. "Master Kapp here wishes to know something about us." The others sat up. "Even though not strictly one of us, I think he might attend a meeting. What would you say about it?"

"With respect, Herr Graf," said one of the young men with scars on his face, "if you see fit to admit him, no one should object. In Wittenberg, as you know, our meetings were open to anyone who was interested."

"Everybody but—" interjected the other scarred young man, smiling broadly.

"Everybody but?" I piped up, eager to know.

All the young men at the table—except the Herr Graf Konrad— recited in a loud chorus: *Aber Juden haben keinen Eintritt.* Jews are not admitted." They burst into gusts of laughter and slammed their steins onto the table.

The Herr Graf attempted to still them with a forgiving smile. "You are quite correct, meine Herren," he said to the Wittenbergers. To me, he added, "The Baron and his cousin join us from the Reich. They were at the university there, prominent members of the fighting fraternities, where they displayed their indifference to pain, with sabers and rapiers. These are the kinds of men we want."

The two scarred young men from Wittenberg stood up and raised their beer mugs. "Grossdeutschland!" they cried out together, then sat and continued to eat and drink. The other diners peered at them.

It was a bit over my head. If the Herr Graf was no musician, these scarred men seemed even less so. "Are they here to play in the concerts?" I asked the Herr Graf.

Before he could reply, one of the scarred young men put in loudly, "No, I am not a musician." People stared at us again. The Herr Graf frowned. The young man bent his head over the table a moment. When he straightened up, I was astonished to see tears running down his cheeks.

It occurred to me that he could be drunk. I had witnessed Mellnicz *úr* in that condition more than once.

"Do you want to know why I am here and not in Wittenberg? Shall I tell you—"

"Perhaps later," murmured the Herr Graf. Dr. von Hornberger had entered, surveying our noisy group from the doorway. The Herr Graf rose and hurried to join him.

The scarred man resumed, still streaming tears. "The fatherland is finished," he spat. "Socialists, Bolsheviks, Spartacists, Jews! All the criminals in Weimar! All the scum of the world, pouring out of their rat holes! It wasn't enough to stab our soldiers in the back, they have to dance on the grave of the Reich, spit in the face of the Kaiser—" He broke off when he was abruptly seized by two companions and marched out of the room. *What a spectacle.*

"A good lad, but he gets ahead of himself," said the Herr Graf, who had returned to the table. Dr. von Hornberger had vanished.

* * *

The following week, I divided my time between the practice room in the mornings, and in the afternoons mainly carried parcels to and from the post office for Dr. von Hornberger. There were many. Often, I had to wait for Special Delivery and Special Courier items marked Express. They got to know me at the post office and on whose behalf I was acting. I was bowed to, both coming and going. I also did some exploring around Eisenstadt, but there was not really much to see besides the Schloss and some inns and restaurants making ready for visitors during the Haydnfest. Not far from the Schloss, on the same side of the street, in fact, I discovered a whole separate district, with tall, narrow houses and its own graveyard. There were no crosses on the graves or statues of the Holy Mother, but the stones were covered with strange writing. The Herr Graf told me that I had wandered into the worst possible place, the old Jewish ghetto of Eisenstadt, the very fountainhead of wickedness. He said he could not understand why the noble House of Eszterházy would have permitted the Jews to live so close to the Schloss. He could attribute it only to sorcery or, more likely, some kind of financial bondage, which, as the Herr Graf pointed out, was the Jews' particular talent. More immediate to my concerns, however, I found that the pretty young ladies who had caught my eye during dinner that first day would scarcely acknowledge my existence—they were much older than I, anyway—but I particularly wanted to talk to the one who had winked in our direction. They spent their free time mooning over the young noblemen, who—to my great surprise—continued to ignore them, much preferring their own company.

One evening, the Herr Graf told me there would be "a meeting" after dinner that I might attend. It took a moment to remember what he meant. It was held in a beer parlor behind the railway station. There were about fifty or sixty people in attendance—mostly young men. I recognized the waiters from the Schloss and Herr Krebs' assistants. There was a sprinkling of older men too. I found myself a seat near the back and refused the offer of beer. At the front, the Herr Graf sat at a table together with my dinner companions, including the two scarred students from Wittenberg. Tonight, they all wore the same clothing—brown shirts, black ties, and those leather straps that came up from the back, over one shoulder, and down across the chest—like army officers. At about ten o'clock—quite late for me—the Herr Graf got to his feet. Below the waist, he wore black riding breeches tucked into long stockings. Yes, he looked military.

"Kameraden," he began, "I have the great honor and privilege once again to introduce a man whom you all know and respect, a man from whom we have all learned much and who will teach us much in the future."

I thought the Herr Graf looked so handsome and spoke so well. In spite of myself, I was proud to know him, even though he was definitely peculiar. As he spoke, he went over things that I knew about—the treaties of Versailles and Trianon and St. Germain—and the harm they had done, and about the Socialists and the Bolshevik menace and how they had put Austria and the Reich in mortal danger.

"The first humiliation, as everyone knows, was when the Tyrol was torn from us—and we didn't make a murmur." We jumped when he suddenly shouted, "We didn't make a murmur!" He folded his arms and smiled bitterly. "And that was just the first step in our national—humiliation is not strong enough—I should rather say degradation."

The audience broke out into loud applause. I was enjoying this.

After a few minutes more, during which he did not forget the role of the Jews, and having brought the meeting to excitement, he said, "And now, my friends, it is my pleasure to present a truly great man, in fact, the man of the hour. Dr. Bruno von Hornberger."

The audience rose to its feet and began a rhythmic clapping. From behind a curtain at the rear, Dr. von Hornberger appeared. He marched to the front and stood at attention with folded arms, staring at us, waiting for the clapping to stop. Instead, it grew louder, and in time to the rhythm, the crowd broke out into a marching song I did not know, but which everyone sang with spirit.

I thought Dr. von Hornberger looked funny. The Herr Graf and his friends were youthful and athletic. Dr. von Hornberger, in contrast, was fat. Worse, he was crammed into a tight—much too tight for him—pale blue Austrian Army tunic, which made him look fatter—and it was a hot night—high collar buttoned to the neck, a row of medals on his chest, his breeches tucked into highly polished boots. He resembled a huge round ball perched on top of two matchstick legs about to tip over. I had to bite my lips to keep from laughing as Dr. von Hornberger glared at us, not moving a muscle, waiting for the singing to stop. Finally it ended, and the audience sat, still applauding.

Silence fell over the hall. "Kameraden," he began quietly, "as we few keepers of the faith meet amid the shambles and ruins of what we remember and hold dear, we must draw strength from that knowledge—from the sure knowledge—of what we believe."

The crowd leaned forward. "All over the fatherland," he continued, "in the provinces of the Reich—and I speak of all the Reich—whether remaining to us or torn from us, men are keeping the faith. They are picking themselves up—painfully, perhaps—not yet fully conscious, perhaps—but they are picking themselves up." He punched his fist onto his open palm. "We are coming to life again, my friends. There are men—evil men, Jews and Bolsheviks—who ally themselves with world capitalism in order to bring down this *Volk*—these good, honest, hardworking people. This *Volk*, so proud, so generous with its gifts to the world in music and art, industry and science ..."

His voice broke off, and he seemed about to weep; but in a moment he recovered. "This people and this community, I say again, are stumbling among the ruins, dazed, without work, unable to feed their children, unable to prevent their wives from whoring themselves in order to put crusts of bread on the table. But we are coming back to life. That I promise you!"

The crowd applauded again. My neighbors to the left and right were wiping tears from their eyes. I thought Dr. von Hornberger was giving an inspiring speech. I didn't understand that part about going hungry, however. Ever since arriving at the Schloss, I had never enjoyed such good food in my life, and as much as I desired. Besides, you only had to look at Dr. von Hornberger to see that he, at least, didn't suffer from hunger. Again, I had to bite down on my lip to keep looking serious.

"The day is not far off," he resumed, looking stern. "Men, German men, from all over the empire and the Reich, are falling into their old columns, reforming their old battalions, to make ready for the coming struggle. They will rise up in their wrath and cast out the traitors, the aliens, the cowardly backstabbers who have corrupted our beautiful land!"

The crowd became angry—even savage. They stood and shouted agreement. "You know who I mean. You know who I'm talking about!" he shouted back.

He poured water from a carafe and drank while his listeners quieted down. When I remembered how Dr. von Hornberger had appeared when he visited Madame's house in Szombathely, sedate and restrained—and how he behaved now—I was baffled. I imagined telling Madame about it; I knew she would be baffled too. I abandoned that idea instantly. She would never believe it, and I didn't know how to convey my amusement at Dr. von Hornberger's talking about starvation while so fat.

All of a sudden, a man called out from the back of the room. We all swung around. He was an older man with a mustache, wearing a dark suit, with a winged collar and cravat, a pince-nez perched on his nose, waving his arms at the speaker.

"Outrageous, shameful!" he cried. "How can you say these things? We're all in the same boat. We must work together, not fight each other."

The room burst into laughter. The interrupter really looked comical in his indignation, with his mustache and pince-nez. He reminded me of Charlie Chaplin at the local *Kino*. "My friends," he tried to speak over the jeering. He had a funny, high-pitched voice. "How can you listen to this filth, this outrageousness?"

At a sign from Dr. von Hornberger, the two scarred students from Wittenberg rushed past me toward the back and hurled themselves on Charlie Chaplin, knocking him off his feet, punching and kicking him—he cried out in pain—finally picking him from the floor by the arms and slinging him out the front door like a sack of dirty clothes.

I was shaken by the sudden violence but also wished that Dr. von Hornberger had chosen me to join in punishing the intruder. I wanted to belong.

"Comrades," boomed Dr. von Hornberger over the uproar, "comrades"—he held up his hands for silence—"this is exactly what I have been talking about. This is what the enemy looks like—on the surface, harmless and respectable." He was in full voice again. "I see you are not fooled. You all know who they are," he sneered, "I don't have to tell you. While we were at the Front, laying down our lives for *Volk und Vaterland*, these are the vermin who occupied the soft jobs. These are the clerks, the cooks, the medical orderlies, the record keepers, and the registrars of graves. Your graves," he bellowed.

"My friends," he continued, "we have already accomplished great things. Our vigilante irregulars in Bavaria, who have never lost faith, smashed that so-called Soviet Republic, that shameless indecency. And we know who was behind that piece of Socialist-Jewish filth in Weimar, that cursed Rathenau"—he spat the name—"who dragged us to seek accommodation with the Kremlin itself. *SauJude!* Jew pig!"

Another drink of water. "We cannot claim that we weren't warned, my friends," he resumed. "You all know the name of Georg Schönerer, of blessed memory. He correctly identified the Jew as the personification of evil—national, international, political, financial, and moral. I celebrate each anniversary of the day he destroyed the offices of that treasonous rag, the *Neues Wiener Tagblatt,* and its Jew-traitor editors. And you all know the name of another patriot, the former distinguished lord mayor of Vienna, Dr. Karl Lueger. What a noble spirit! He too recognized the Jew for what he was and how he tried to corrupt the Viennese soul. Dr. Lueger saw the threat represented by Bolsheviks, international capitalism, and the insidious temptations offered by the likes of the immoral writer Schnitzler, the Zionist Herzl, and especially the disgusting Dr. Freud and his friends."

He sighed. "Barely a year has passed since Signor Mussolini took the reins of destiny in his hands and liberated his people. Our *own* savior is at hand, not far from us—I don't have to speak his name—you all know who he is. Let the dogs in Weimar tremble—and also those spineless curs who rule in Vienna. Their days are numbered!"

His listeners—myself included—were rapt. Dr. von Hornberger's face was shiny with sweat. He ran a finger around his tight collar and mopped his brow.

"I would like to tell you more," he said, "but it is not yet time. We must be patient. For now, we fill our hearts with courage and we wait. But you should know that, in this year of our Lord 1923, we will witness our deliverance." He raised his right arm in Mussolini's Roman salute. "Heil!" he shouted. "Heil! Heil!"

The crowd got to its feet, cheering and applauding. The group of young aristocrats stood at attention and formed a line to guard the stage from which Dr. von Hornberger gazed at us without expression.

I was exhausted. I stumbled out of the beer parlor and made my way up the hill to the Schloss and back to my bed. I fell asleep almost immediately.

The next morning, I felt like babbling to all my friends about the night before. To my astonishment, I was met with coldness. All the young noblemen, whom I wanted to compliment on their uniforms and their alert response to threats from the audience, refused to let me finish what I had to say, turned on their heels, and abruptly left me.

Finally, one of the scarred students from Wittenberg gripped my shoulder. "Silence!" he hissed. "You were there, you saw, but you will not speak of it!"

Not speak of it? The place had been packed. Who did not know what had happened? He must have spoken to Dr. von Hornberger about this because, fifteen minutes later, I was summoned to his office. The Herr Graf was also there, standing to one side.

"Herr Kapp," said Dr. von Hornberger as soon as I closed the door behind me, "we both understand that you are not here in Eisenstadt for political purposes. But I hope you were inspired by what you saw and heard last night. And"—a fleeting smile—"I hope you can understand why we all feel about things the way we do." His face hardened. "But even though you are too young to be a soldier, now that you are here, the need for loyalty and discipline comes before everything. What you may reveal and what you may not are not up to you. In this, I demand strict obedience. Is that clear?"

I was still lost. "But everybody knows, everybody was there," I pleaded. "How can the Herr Doktor keep it a secret?"

"Everybody will soon know, never fear, but not just yet."

I shook my head again.

"Listen to me," said Dr. von Hornberger, "it's quite simple, once you understand. We here in Eisenstadt know all about it—but, more important, we know each other, and we trust each other. Correct?"

"Correct, Herr Doktor," I murmured.

"In addition," he resumed, "it is an open secret that everybody else in Austria and Germany knows as well. Our friends all over the combined Reich cannot wait for the day. On the other hand, the traitors and our enemies also know it, are also waiting—but they wait in dread. They see it coming, but they cannot do a thing about it. Stupid fools!"—a contemptuous laugh—"imprisoned by their own legal chains, their own stupid legal mentality! As if that would hold us back if the shoe were on the other foot—"

"But I don't know what you mean. What's this *it* you keep talking about, Herr Doktor?"

"Why, the Putsch," he said in mild surprise that I didn't know.

I certainly had not known.

"I understand why you think this may not concern you," he said. "After all, you are Hungarian, and you are young."

"But why?"

"The thing is this—and listen carefully."

I tried to look intelligent and eager.

"Beginning the day after tomorrow, and for the next three weeks, Eisenstadt will be filled with tourists and music lovers. They are going to eat our Wiener Schnitzel mit Grammelknödel and drink our own Braufränkisch and spend money—a lot of money. They will enjoy the music of Haydn to their heart's content. They will dance under the colored lights in the cafés and hold their lovers' hands to the sound of violins. They will walk around the old Unterberg Ghetto and give sentimental sighs. They will take their field glasses and watch the wild birds at the Neusiedler See and have a perfectly wonderful time. We will drench them in good old Austrian warmth and hospitality. We will be so charming—smiling, bowing, kissing the hand of all the ladies. They will leave, awash with memories of music and charm. Afterward, having enriched the souls of our visitors—and filled our own coffers—we shall return to the business of giving the world elementary instruction in the consequences of injustice."

The Herr Graf glowed with admiration. But I was still troubled. I understood Dr. von Hornberger, but it sounded suspiciously easy—like something *I* could make up.

People knew? But pretended they didn't? Even the people Dr. von Hornberger said were our enemies? Whom he said he was going to drive away, or worse? Even they knew? The Jews and the Socialists knew?

Well, later in life, I came into contact with many Jews in Vienna and Germany, before and after the Nazis came to power and before the Anschluss. These Jews were certainly the right sort: intelligent, wealthy, influential—bankers, government officials, artists, scientists, publishers, professors, patrons of the arts, directors of plays, conductors of orchestras—people you would consider farsighted, able to use their large noses to sniff out trouble. But with few exceptions, they paid no attention to warning signs. They took the view that they had been here as long as anyone else and were just as German as the rest. After all, they were not Ostjuden, common East European Jews. They had taste and refinement and spent their Sundays playing in string quartets! Yet, after having been driven from their lecture halls and surgeries, barred from their courtrooms and podiums, they still didn't get the point: it didn't matter whether or not they were the right sort—the whole damned lot of them were simply not wanted. They paraded about, each one brandishing his Iron Cross, crying out that they had shed blood for das Vaterland. But those who tried to leave for other places discovered the rest of the world didn't want them either. So I feel—even though I deplore certain ill-timed and unfortunate excesses—it is really unjust to attribute blame to the entire German and Austrian people.

I tried to do my duty. Dr. von Hornberger had commanded, and I obeyed. I acted as though I knew nothing about the things we all knew. I worked as hard at the piano as I could. The Herr Doktor, for his part, made no further office demands on me.

* * *

It was just as Dr. von Hornberger had said. The hotels and inns were taking in visitors. Up and down the Rüsterstrasse, along the Peargasse and Gartengasse, restaurant owners put out tables and chairs. They strung colored lights between the trees and hung Chinese lanterns. Splendid-looking motorcars crept up and down the leafy avenues. They parked in the square and alongside the Schloss. Elegantly dressed men and women strolled along the avenues, chatting and laughing. Other men and women, more casual, filled the outdoor restaurants, deep in happy conversation, sharing bottles of wine. I noticed several of the waiters who had been among Dr. von Hornberger's audience at the beer hall. They now served at the cafés, smiling, bowing, running back and forth.

The Haydntage were here at last. Inside the Schloss, the staff dining hall became packed. Musicians and singers were all over the place. I had to put my name on lists to get a practice room. Players were to be found standing or squatting—in linen closets, attics, kitchens, lavatories, and passageways—sounding scales, blowing trumpets, tuning violins, singers' voices warming up, high and low. It was thrilling to be alive.

We were no longer served at table—too many of us. Because of the crush, the musicians, singers, and staff workers had to file through the kitchens with trays and point to whatever we wanted, which the chefs served.

One evening, as I was about to dig into a dish of roasted chicken and noodles, I heard my name called from across the room.

"Herr Kapp, Herr Kapp!" It was a tall young man, wearing an open shirt and leather shorts. I stuck up my hand. "Here." He threaded his way to me. "Grüss Gott," he said cheerfully and put out his hand. "I am Fridolin Karl, conductor of some of the concerts, including yours. Now, when and where can we meet?"

"Meet with me?"

"Forgive me if I intrude," he said with a grin, "but I was led to believe that Herr Hermann—or Ferenc—Kapp of Szombathely, a reputed genius of the keyboard, has been engaged to perform the D Major concerto by our dear Papa Haydn. Is that not correct?"

I came back to earth with a bump. For a while, I had thought I was on perpetual holiday. I hastily stood up and shook the offered hand. "That's correct, Herr Kapellmeister." I hoped Madame had taught me the right word.

"I bring you greetings from Madame Polkovska—and from your mother, who hopes you are well and wonders why you haven't written."

I groaned and thought guiltily of the small pile of Mama's letters on my night table upstairs, unopened and unread.

"Well," he continued, "that's really your own affair." He pulled a tiny notebook from a breast pocket and consulted it. "Madame Polkovska informs me that, even though this is your concert debut, she has every confidence that you will be magnificent." I immediately felt uncomfortable. "But you have never played together with an orchestra before?" I nodded, even more uncomfortable. "Why don't we do this," he said. "You are not listed to perform the D Major until Friday evening, five days away. This gives us good opportunities to listen to and get used to each other. But when, is the question."

He flipped rapidly through the notebook. "The problem is," he said with a frown, "there are many groups that require the main auditorium. And I myself am busy with other performances." Then, after more rapid page turning: "I think we should have a short rehearsal by ourselves before we meet the orchestra. It will be good, for example, to see what kinds of tempi you are comfortable with. Agreed?"

"Now?" I asked.

"The sooner the better. There's a lot to do."

He jumped to his feet and sped out of the dining hall. I hadn't finished eating but followed him at a trot through the crowded room, wiping my hands on a napkin.

We found a practice room with two pianos.

"Before we begin," said Herr Karl, "we must agree at least on one thing. You know, it was the general custom in Haydn's day for a keyboard player to play along with the orchestra before he actually entered as a soloist. This was no problem when Haydn's orchestra typically included a harpsichord as part of the ensemble. These days, we're not used to harpsichords, either as solo instruments or as part of the ensemble."

Observing my furrowed brow, he stopped. "Cheer up," he exclaimed, "it's not that difficult. All I'm asking is whether Madame Polkovska prepared you to play the opening bars together with the orchestra or to enter as a true soloist."

"Oh," I said, "is that all? I'm used to sitting and listening to Madame play the introduction for the first page and a half. And then I begin."

So we did the same—except that he asked me once or twice whether *I* approved of how he was playing the orchestra part and whether *I* thought he had paused too long before the recapitulation, questions that Madame never asked. I think he was happy with the first movement, including the cadenza; he beamed at the second, un poco adagio; and he insisted on having me play the last movement, the *Rondo all'Ungherese*, twice!

"That was dazzling," he exclaimed. "What wonderful taste! Your dynamics, so musical! I look upon Madame Polkovska with a new appreciation." I shrugged, not really understanding his warmth—in fact, not understanding why anybody made a fuss. Didn't they know that I could do these things?

He peered at a wristwatch. "It's now a quarter past eight. I know a chorus is still in the Haydnsaal, rehearsing *Armida*. My notes say they should be finished by nine o'clock. If you are willing, I can have the orchestra there—I expect they'll complain and complain—but we could get some work done. And you'll have a chance to try out that quaint Kriegelstein piano that Dr. von Hornberger has unearthed for the festival." He grinned again. "And see whether we can truly stand each other!" He bowed to me, shook my hand, and hurried away.

I liked him. He seemed to like me. He made me smile. At nine, I made my way to the Haydnsaal. The room was flooded with lights, the floors had been polished; the huge frescoes on the ceiling and side panels looked beautiful. The stage, not large at all, was jammed, wall-to-wall, with choristers, who were supposed to march around in certain orderly patterns, but there was not enough room for them, and they were getting things wrong, bumping into one another. Finally, the harassed-looking man in charge shouted that they were hopeless, but the space was needed for other performers. They would try again in the morning.

The singers were replaced by stagehands—I recognized Herr Krebs' assistants among them—who swiftly set up chairs and music stands. A small crowd of men, mostly young, climbed onto the stage, carrying violins, cellos, gleaming curled horns, and other instruments, and seated themselves in semicircles. Each one looked fixedly into the distance and commenced those marvelous jumbles of scales, tootles, and squeals called tuning-up that I already had heard in the Schloss—for me, the best part of a concert.

Amid the hubbub, a piano was pushed to front center stage—not huge like Madame's, but a small grand—with the lid propped open and a stool set in place. Herr Karl appeared out of nowhere and guided me up some steps toward the instrument. I realized that the moment had arrived. At his prompting, I struck an A on the keyboard. The tuning sounds doubled in volume.

The players stared—or perhaps glared. I heard one or two of them snicker. "That kid? He's the soloist? What, another prodigy?"

If he heard them, Herr Karl gave no sign. He merely asked if my stool were at a comfortable height and indicated that I should try the keys before we began. I played a vigorous, rapid series of scales, arpeggios, and chords. I found the action quite looser than I was used to, the sound dry and twangy. This was the Kriegelstein that Dr. von Hornberger had chosen because he said it sounded something like a harpsichord, certainly far from Madame's deep, rich Bösendorfer, but nothing to put me off. I looked around me when I finished my warming up. The snickering had ceased. The players were sitting up in their chairs, looking at me alertly.

The rehearsal was so exciting. I had listened to gramophone records—scratchy and indistinct in those days—but I had never before heard a live orchestra. From the moment Herr Karl swept his baton down and the players sprang to life—a whole group obeying one man—I realized at last that it was possible to feel truly happy. I reveled in the wonderful sounds—violins vigorous with the principal themes, violas scrubbing away with their fill-in chords, cellos and Kontrabassi rhythmically pumping along the bottom. I laughed aloud with pleasure at the thrilling sounds of the oboes, nasally cutting through everybody else. But the horns—my god, the horns were the best—they were golden magic. I loved the look and the sound of them. I was where I belonged.

Now it was almost time to play. I had Madame's two-piano score on my music rack from which I followed things. Then, Herr Karl gave me my cue, and I was off full tilt and headlong. It was a whirlwind. I felt wonderfully alive and even half-crazy. All fell perfectly into place: first theme, bridge passage, second theme, development, recapitulation—all expressed magically in melodies, harmonies, running scales, modulations, and iterated chords. Madame had been right. I had prepared so well that I did not have to think. I was at the keyboard, but I couldn't say that I was playing. For all I knew, the piano was playing *me.* Before I knew it, we were at the cadenza, which I dealt with in a shower of notes. End of the first movement!

I was startled when the players rapped their bows against their music stands. I didn't have time to wonder what it meant, because Herr Karl was beating time for the second movement, adagio, which, I must say, sounded meltingly lovely and sweet. Finally, the rondo was great fun from beginning to end, with abrupt changes of key, from major to minor and back again, and all kinds of unexpected syncopations. Once again, the players rapped their bows on their stands.

Herr Karl came to my side and embraced me. The musicians cheered. I felt like running away. "Give them a bow, why don't you," he said. "They liked it."

I gave an awkward bow to the smiling players but needed to pee badly. I left the stage in urgent need of a toilet and bumped right into Krisztina Kabós, that pretty girl with whom I was to play the Haydn trio. I'd completely forgotten about her. She gazed at me with shining eyes.

"You were wonderful," she said. "I was here the whole time."

"Thank you," I stammered, "but I have to leave."

She drew back, puzzled. If I did not pee within the next two seconds, I would have a shameful accident. I fled up the hall, knowing that Krisztina surely remembered our last meeting, at Madame's, when I had also behaved like a clumsy fool.

That was the Wednesday. On Thursday, the Haydntage officially opened, exciting, with speeches and processions. There were full concerts at the Schloss, chamber music in smaller salons, and the *Creation Mass* at the Bergkirche, in the presence of the tomb of Papa Haydn himself. Dr. von Hornberger unexpectedly decided to attempt something radical, to present the opera *Armida* in the open courtyard of the Schloss under Chinese lanterns.

Herr Karl was busy preparing at least five concerts, so we did not run through my piece again until Friday morning at eleven. Composers other than Haydn were featured. So along with my D Major concerto, he was preparing for the same evening Mozart's Haffner Symphony, which I have loved ever since. Also to be performed was Haydn's 101st Symphony, known as *The Clock* (because of the tick-tocking second movement)—also in D major. It would be a completely D major evening.

I wore my concert costume: a black velvet suit with pantaloons, buckled shoes, and an outsize Eton collar. I looked like a clown. I feared I had lost the hard-won respect of the orchestra. They were grinning again when Herr Karl led me onstage for the performance. But the audience applauded. That cheered me up.

I thought things went well. And if they didn't, I was too much in a daze to care. I played the concerto "brilliantly"—that's what Herr Karl said afterward. To my astonishment, the audience went mad. They demanded an encore. Herr Karl and I, hands linked, smiling and bowing until our backs creaked, knew that I had not prepared an encore. So we repeated the rondo. More long and loud applause. Everybody loved it. I suddenly thought of Mama—and of Madame, despite that awful black velvet suit they had made me wear. They should have been here, even though Mama insisted she couldn't afford the fare—it couldn't have been that much. Dr. von Hornberger came out to the podium to join us, linking hands, bowing and waving to the audience also. He took care always to place me between Herr Karl and himself. He held his hand over his heart as he bowed and dabbed at his eyes as though he himself had played.

"Sehr, sehr, sehr schön," he shouted to me above the applause, shaking his head in admiration. "Such a revelation, such vivacity, such beauty! You know, music is everything to me!"

Finally, after much clapping and my marching back and forth to the stage, Herr Karl appeared without me and raised his stick for the opening bars of the *Haffner* Symphony, at which the audience understood that I would not appear again.

* * *

Because of me, the concert rooms had to be switched around. People must have been stirred up. Consequently, there was an unexpected demand for tickets to my chamber music recital Sunday afternoon. The management had to arrange a larger space. There were long lines; people wouldn't take no for an answer. Once more, I received a message from Dr. von Hornberger, demanding to see me right away.

He sat, as usual, a bulging body behind a desk. On one side stood the Herr Graf Konrad von Friesach. On the other, both scarred students from

Wittenberg. The mood had once again changed. Something told me I should be feeling nervous. To tell the truth, I had not missed the young noblemen's company. It had been a relief not to think about them for the past few days. And it had been a relief not to think about the Treaty of Versailles or the Treaty of Trianon, nor to give myself headaches worrying about Bolsheviks and Jews, but simply to play music together with people who liked me and whom I liked in return.

Dr. von Hornberger frowned as he studied me across his desk. "I am somewhat puzzled by you," he said. "Clearly, you were a great success last night, and we all applaud that." He looked at the others, who nodded in agreement. "This is what we all work for, the power and presence of great music and"—he laid his hand over his heart—"and, may I say, great art." He closed his eyes and turned his large head toward the window, so that he showed himself in profile, sort of like a postage stamp. "In my own humble way, although I play no instrument well, I consider myself an artist too. Mozart, Beethoven, Bach, our own beloved Papa Haydn—I love and revere them all. Just to pronounce their names brings tears to my eyes."

Well, that certainly was true. I had seen him weep over music just last night. I glanced at the others. They were hanging on his every word.

"But," he resumed, "some among us do not behave as members of a community, but regard themselves as privileged. For instance"—he studied a paper on his desk—"we have the figures for extra costs entailed directly because of you. This management recognizes that you have had some enjoyment at our expense, but it *was* at our expense. It adds to our costs if we have to rearrange seating and alter plans because you and the people who encourage you cannot control themselves."

Dr. von Hornberger produced a nasty smile. "I don't blame you so much," he said, "but I certainly do blame Herr Karl." "*Herr Karl,*" he sneered, and the young men sneered together with him. "*Herr Karl,*" he said again, in that unpleasant way. He made my skin crawl.

"What's the matter with Herr Karl?" I asked.

All four burst into laughter.

"What do you think of him?" asked the Herr Graf, trying to keep a straight face.

"I like him," I replied. My answer displeased them. The smiles disappeared.

"Well, I have no particular love for imposters," snapped Dr. von Hornberger.

Imposters? I had never heard the word before.

The Herr Graf chimed in. "People who pretend to be one thing but turn out to be something else."

Was he talking about me?

"We're talking about your precious Herr Karl," said Dr. von Hornberger.

"So young, so handsome, so graceful looking from behind. Surely, all the young ladies are in love with his arse as he conducts!" laughed the Herr Graf.

"He wasn't my choice," said Dr. von Hornberger, "but he draws in the public. He's a good moneymaker. For the time being," he added.

"That's not surprising," broke in one of the scarred students, "considering what he is." The others chuckled.

I looked from one to the other. What *were* they talking about?

"Look," said Dr. von Hornberger, "let's be plain. You remember my speech the other night? When I spoke of the dangers to our nation from the Bolsheviks, the capitalists, and the Jews?"

I still didn't follow.

"I'm sure you remember. You may be young, but you're intelligent. Well, your beloved Herr Karl is one of those enemies I spoke about. He is dangerous precisely because he is so charming and gallant."

I still frowned.

"For God's sake!" Dr. von Hornberger exploded. "You still don't understand? Must I provide diagrams? The truth is he's a Jew! He is a damned Jew! And the members of the Haydn Society in Vienna—fully aware of my feelings on the subject—insisted that I engage him! An outrage! The whole institution is probably riddled with Jews!"

Once again, Dr. von Hornberger was proving himself a man of contrasts. The difference between how he had behaved last night, moved to tears, and the way he was speaking to me now was dismaying. The Herr Graf realized that I was frightened.

"It should be enough for you," the Herr Graf said, "when you understand that your idol has not told you his real name. It is not, and never has been, 'Fridolin Karl.'" The others growled. "The truth is that he covers things up to conceal himself. His real name," he said with disgust, "is Frankl Karl Slonimski—not only a Jew, but from a family of drifters out of Polish Galicia—"

"Oh, but they're insidious and crafty," broke in Dr. von Hornberger, "with their smooth manners and gift for languages—"

"Vagabonds! The Herr Doktor is correct!" The Herr Graf interrupted right back. "They have no home, no loyalty, no allegiances—"

"All they know," said Dr. von Hornberger, "is to settle on our bodies and suck our blood. The nation cannot rest until it rebuilds—until it roots out that vermin!"

The two scarred students from Wittenberg started to march in place, stomping their feet up and down rhythmically on the floor, staring into my eyes, as though they couldn't wait to trample on me. It was becoming a nightmare.

A sudden loud knocking at the door. I jumped. Just when I thought I could bear no more! Raised voices could be heard from the other side. Someone—it seemed to be Herr Krebs, the head assistant—was pleading. "Sir, please, you are not permitted to enter!"

Despite that, the door was thrust open. Four men strode in, three of them in police uniform, all of them wearing tiny moustaches. Dr. von Hornberger rose to his feet.

The visitor in street clothes made a formal bow. "Have I the honor to address Dr. Bruno von Hornberger, Generalintendant of the Haydntage?" he asked.

"You have," replied the other, bowing in return.

"I am Superintendant Renner of the State Security Police," said the visitor. "It is my painful duty to inform you that you are under arrest—you, the Herr Graf Konrad von Friesach, and others among your associates."

"Really!" Dr. von Hornberger smiled. "And what are the charges?"

"The charges are grave," replied the visitor. "The most serious include seditious and treasonous activities injurious to the state, comprising the overthrow of the republic and the constitution."

The Herr Graf turned pale and began to stammer. The two scarred students from Wittenberg sagged against each other as though the air had been let out of them. Dr. von Hornberger merely gave a scornful laugh and held out his hands. "Do you wish to put handcuffs on me?"

"I don't think that will be necessary. I trust, Herr Doktor, that our departure from Eisenstadt will be tranquil."

"And what will be our destination?"

"Vienna, naturally," said the visitor. "I said I was from State Security. What you are accused of goes far beyond activities here in Burgenland."

"Oh, Vienna, to be sure," scoffed Dr. von Hornberger. "There we will be safely surrounded by your Jew Socialist masters." He shook his head in mock pity. "How can you sleep at night serving that scum! Traitors and bloodsuckers the whole damned lot! Come Retribution Day—and, believe me, it will—we will not forget our enemies."

Without a word or change of expression, the three uniformed policemen and the one in street clothes marched Dr. von Hornberger and his young friends away. I followed after them through the outer office and onto the marble front steps, where two large automobiles awaited. The prisoners were locked inside and driven away. Herr Krebs and his young assistants stared with bulging eyes. In later years I was surprised to find that some of the Herr Doktor's theories proved to be true.

$$* * *$$

No outward disturbance resulted from these events. The Haydnfest continued, and with it, the array of symphonies and concertos, and the opera. I played my chamber music trio together with Herr Kabós and his daughter, Krisztina. It turned out well. I don't mind saying that the three of us made lovely music. In particular, I was happy that Krisztina seemed to bear no grudges about my displays of awkwardness.

The closing night's concert was especially thrilling. For the last piece of the season, Herr Karl—or whatever his name was—did a most clever thing. He had the orchestra play what is known as Haydn's Farewell Symphony. First of all, it was written in an unusually strange key, F-sharp minor, which sounded eerie right from the start. The opening allegro was extremely fast. However, it didn't sound happy but breathless and rushed. The second movement, adagio, crawled its way into all kinds of unusual keys, as though it were a prisoner searching for escape. A repeated pattern of grace notes sounded like fits of sobbing. Every so often, the music just stopped, as though it were too exhausted to go on.

The minuet had a definite lilt to it, but was full of tragic-sounding chords; and it didn't end properly, just trailed off again, in mid-phrase. The final movement, presto, started as though the composer had finally found his way. It was still in a minor key, but vigorous and strong. Then, all of a sudden, it too stopped in the middle of nowhere.

Then the most peculiar happening of all. Instead of continuing to lead his men, Herr Karl quietly stepped down from the podium and walked offstage, leaving them to play without him. They commenced a second adagio—strange for a final movement. As they played, the lights in the hall lowered to darkness. We became aware that the musicians had burning candles next to their scores. Then another surprise! Every two or three minutes, one of the players would stop, blow out his candle, and tiptoe away. Finally, all that was left were two violinists, sighing a melancholy air. In a short while, they too stopped, blew out their candles, and silently left. Not a sound could be heard in the darkened Haydnsaal. And then, quite suddenly, the lights glared up again, the orchestra crowded back on, and, headed by Herr Karl, bowed to receive applause and flowers.

Herr Karl told me afterward that, for fun, he had decided to re-enact an event that supposedly had occurred when Haydn was Prince Nikolaus's Kapellmeister. Herr Karl had suggested the idea to Dr. von Hornberger but had been turned down. Now that Dr. von Hornberger had gone, there was no one to object—and it all turned out wonderfully. Everybody congratulated him on it.

The old story was this: All the musicians in the household of Prince Nikolaus had supposedly become impatient because they wanted to go home and spend the summer with their families. But Prince Nikolaus had somehow forgotten. Therefore, the story goes, Haydn wrote this Farewell Symphony to jog the Prince's memory. And they said it worked! Prince Nikolaus took the hint and let the players go home.

It was a wonderful story. "But," I asked Herr Karl, "could a Kapellmeister play such a trick on Prince Nikolaus? Is it true?"

He winked at me. "Well, if it isn't, it ought to be."

Herr Karl put on a party, mostly on my behalf, at a posh outdoor café, attended, I'm sure, by at least fifty people I didn't know, who clapped and even cheered when I walked in. I had no idea what to do or say. Krisztina Kabós sat next to me at the head of the table, her father smiling as he puffed on his pipe somewhere else in the room. Her eyes shone whenever she looked at me. It was a happy evening. Herr Karl put me on the train back to Szombathely when it was all over. As for me, I couldn't stop shaking for weeks. Working too hard, said Mama. Madame thought I had spent too much time away from my studies.

* * *

it was all over. As for me, I couldn't stop shaking for weeks. Working too hard, said Mama. Madame thought I had spent too much time away from my studies.

* * *

Fourth Variation

Vienna 1927

They say life should be a fearless thing when you are seventeen. One should be happy and strong. One should, I suppose, but I didn't always experience it that way. However, the sun shone brightly. From Szombathely, Madame Polkovska sometimes arranged tickets to concerts at the Theater an der Wien and the Staatsoper— most recently for a wonderful performance of *The Marriage of Figaro*. It was overwhelming to be at the opera: the lights, the colors, the costumes, smartly dressed crowds in the lobbies. Inside, the music, the glorious sounds of the orchestra, and those beautiful voices took my breath away. It was just like the first time I played that Beethoven sonata on Madame's grand piano. Even though *The Marriage of Figaro* is a comedy, the piece tore at my heart. I peered down from my hard seat, high up in the top rows of the gallery at the stage far, far below. Most other members of the audience possessed opera glasses, but no one offered to let me have a peep. I strained my eyes until they watered. And then I saw even less. But I could hear.

I remember the words of Cherubino that floated up to me in elegant German. Madame had warned me that Germans and Austrians liked their operas in German, not in the languages in which they were written. Now that I myself have conducted *Le nozze di Figaro* all over the world, I discovered that most of the world prefers to hear it in da Ponte's original Italian. So do I. And, most likely, you do too. You know this piece I talk about as the aria *Non so più cosa son, cosa faccio*, from the first act, in which the ardent young page declares that his emotions are topsy-turvy, and his head is turned by every girl and woman he meets. Each one makes him freeze and burn at the same time; each one makes him blush and tremble.

Vienna was filled with pretty girls who looked boldly at me without shame, right into my eyes—then laughed and darted away if I should attempt to speak. Every one of them made my heart flutter. I had become Cherubino. Every corner I turned brought me face to face with yet another young girl of unspoiled, heart-stopping beauty, of the modest simplicity that I had so come to prize ever since I had to part from Mama. But no matter if she were young or not so young, the sight of practically every pretty woman could render me helpless.

I had been in Vienna for the past year, not a long distance from Szombathely, but a completely different world. Madame Polkovska had generously used her influence to smooth my way to a scholarship and some grants that were just adequate for tuition at the Conservatory and for board and lodging. Vienna was a huge change from home. Here was an exciting city with wide boulevards, gracious parks, bustling taxis, clanging tramcars, throngs of well-dressed—as well as miserably poor—citizens, all mixed together, and those heart-stopping young women of whom I speak.

But there was something else, not so easy to explain, that made me glad not to live in Hungary anymore. After the Great War, we went through dreadful turmoils, like everybody else on the losing side. At first, we were under that insane Béla Kun and his Reds—thankfully soon crushed—but even before I had gone to Eisenstadt, power had been seized by a "regent," Admiral Horthy—standing in for which king? I had no idea. The Dual Monarchy was gone. Austria was a republic, and we Hungarians were separated from it and had our independence. I couldn't tell whether that was a good thing or not. Horthy wouldn't let Archduke Karl, the true heir, be crowned. That upset me. We Hungarians had had only two regents in our past, Hunyadi and Kossuth, giants both of them. For all his imposing appearance on postage stamps, Horthy struck me as no giant—but it would not have been wise to say so. What I found really ridiculous was the fact that he was an admiral in a navy that no longer existed, the navy of the Austro-Hungarian Empire, which used to have seaport bases all up and down the Adriatic. What was left of the empire were the shrunken Austria and Hungary. And the stupid thing was neither had a coastline! The Americans and the English told all the Austro-Hungarian peoples they were free to go, and they lost no time in going—you know, all those people my late Papa ranted about: those Czechs, those Slovaks, those Rumanians, Ruthenians, Bulgarians, Serbs, Bosnians, Dalmatians, Italians, and the rest, all ending up in their bite-sized "nations"—really, a return to the ridiculous duchies of the German Confederation. Fit only for operettas. *La Grande Duchesse de Gerolstein* come to life!

I repeat: the Austria and Hungary that remained had no coastline! And Admiral Horthy clung to his naval rank. It was like being tone-deaf! My soul rebelled at the silliness of being ruled by a head of state who was an admiral of a nonexistent navy. I thought of many coarse jokes that I was unable to share. Too silly for words! On the other hand, people said, the admiral maintained the correct Hungarian attitude toward the Jews: keep them in their place.

So I was thrilled to be in Vienna, at the Conservatory, to be on my own. I was continuing piano studies with an old acquaintance of Madame Polkovska's, one Herr Schneidermann, who turned out to be a difficult man—a torturer, in fact. Not simply demanding like Madame, but truly awful. She had given me a direct recommendation, so I could find no graceful way to withdraw from the arrangement. As far as I could tell, Herr Schneidermann enjoyed the association as little as I. It made me downcast to discover that he didn't think much of my earlier concerts and recitals. He sneered at the idea that I might be ready for a solo appearance—even before my fellow students. Adding to my difficulties was the fact that I was required to learn a second instrument like all other students at the conservatory. I chose the violin, which I found difficult.

When my fellow students weren't practicing or working on their theory exercises, they liked to meet for midmorning snacks at Rosalie's Kaffeehaus, a smoky sandwich-and-pastry bar behind the Conservatory, not far from the parks and grand avenues of the Ringstrasse. The prices were cheap, considering the locale. And there was Rosalie herself, a big, brassy woman. I couldn't tell you how old she was—40? She had bright henna-red hair. Her large breasts bulged over the restraints of her starched shirtwaist, leaving not much to the imagination; and it was around these wonders of nature that the students gathered—and lingered, telling strings of stupid jokes because, if you could move Rosalie to laughter, this would be sufficient to cause those breasts to shake and her nipples to stand, really pop up. I don't know whether

Rosalie was aware why she was the center of such interest. She must have been.

On the other hand, my attention was fixed on her modest, charming daughter. Lotte was seventeen or eighteen—again, I couldn't say—dark haired and shy, almost plain. For me, that was her most endearing quality. I sensed that patrons who dared approach her, guarded by the ever-watchful Rosalie, would be put off by that shyness. Not many would offer to compete for her with me. She carried pastries and the cups of coffee that her mother poured from the huge, hissing urn over to older patrons at their marble-topped tables, reading newspapers borrowed from the racks. I never joined the sniggering ranks in front of Rosalie but always sought a table where I might be blessed—even briefly—with an exclusive moment in Lotte's company. She would pause at my side, await my order with downcast eyes, repeat what I had said in a sweet murmur, and soon return to place before me my coffee and jam tart. She glanced at me fully in the face only when presenting the bill that Rosalie had scrawled. She waited while I counted out the few coins I had in my pocket—which I should have saved to pay for my supper, not squander them at a café like a man of means.

This particular morning, I happened to touch Lotte's hand while handing her a few *groschen*. We both blushed. Then I discovered that I was squeezing her hand. She made no move to withdraw it.

I couldn't think what to say. "You're quite pretty," I managed to murmur. "Have you got time to talk—perhaps after work?"

Lotte's eyes widened in alarm.

The watchful Rosalie's head bobbed up and down. "Lotte!" she called. Her voice sliced through the clatter. "What are you messing about for? I've got five coffees ready for the gentlemen in the corner, and you've got all these tables to clear in the front. Right away, Lotte!"

Lotte darted off. I sank down in my chair in deep shame but amazed by my boldness. I was shaking. After a short while, I was able to bring my cup to my lips without spilling. The Kaffeehaus now overflowed with students, clerks, and working men. Smoke from a hundred cigarettes turned the air blue. Shouted conversations and the clash of plates and cutlery were deafening. It was lunchtime, and new patrons were crowding in by the moment. Menacing eyes surveyed me at my solitary table.

I now felt steady enough to make my way out. As I passed Rosalie, she gazed at me with deep disapproval. Just before I reached the heavy glass doors, Lotte passed me and, without saying a word, pressed a small piece of paper into my hand. I was outside the café before I realized it. When I unfolded the slip, it read simply, "Five o'clock. Back door." I stared at it.

The rest of the afternoon was a turmoil of emotion. From two o'clock until three, I was in a practice room at the conservatory, preparing for my dreaded Tuesday lesson with Herr Schneidermann. I was working on two of the Opus 90 Schubert impromptus, the second one in E-flat and the fourth in A-flat minor—at least that's how it starts before it switches to the major key. Neither was technically difficult.

What troubled me was the way Herr Schneidermann made exasperated noises and actually rapped my knuckles with a ruler, crying out, "Lighter! Lighter! Lighter! Schubert is not Wagner! You are not in Fafner's cave!"

I was shocked the first time he did that. After all, I was seventeen years old. I felt that only Madame Polkovska had the right to be harsh with me. And she had never touched me when irritated. Especially not on the hands! But I knew that other students at the conservatory had been struck by some of the professors. It was the way of things. Even though I felt humiliated when Herr Schneidermann hit me, I recognized what he was after—something different in a different kind of music. Madame knew her Bach, Beethoven, and Brahms. I think she was uneasy with Schubert. She never played his sonatas; she never played the impromptus, and she wouldn't touch Chopin—also disapproved, as you know, of Debussy. She would lump them all into one category.

"All that insubstantial showy fluff," she would sniff, adding, "You know, my revered teacher, Franz Liszt, was a true hero as a performer at the piano. As a pianist. But I never really liked his compositions. All that insubstantial showy fluff!" she would repeat. "All that thundering up and down the keyboard."

You certainly could not mention Ravel to her, let alone Stravinsky!

I had come not to care about that. By that time, I had experienced more than a couple of music teachers. Each one seemed to be a passionate lover of this composer and a violent hater of that one. It didn't matter whether the composer were alive or how long he had been dead; the faces of those who argued about them turned just as red, and the veins in their necks got just as swollen, as if the battles had just broken out.

Just the day before, I had persuaded Rudi, my friend at the Conservatory, to come into the practice room to listen to me. Rudi was a composition student and not terribly interested in piano technique. But he listened as I tried to play the Schubert pieces as swiftly and lightly as I could.

"You're playing too rapidly," he said at last, "blurring the notes. Clever of you, mein Lieber, to do that. Nobody can tell whether you're light enough or not."

In despair, I turned to face him. He was tall, pale, and thin featured. His hands and fingers were long and delicate. Mine were short and thick.

"Why aren't you the piano player?" I said bitterly. "You've got the hands for it. Everybody says so." I brandished my stubby fingers. "What can I do with *these*?"

"I don't know what you're talking about. What's wrong with your hands? They've worked for you so far." He seemed astonished. "You're making entirely too much of your silly fingers, darling. Just bad nerves and looking for an excuse."

I scowled and then he resumed on a more serious note.

"Did I mention that I earned three whole *schillings* last night, working as an usher at a piano recital by that darling Artur Schnabel? And I noticed something interesting, my dear. I was working in the stalls, but after all the people were in their seats, I managed to grab one for myself way down in the front row on the keyboard side. And what I noticed was that Herr Schnabel's hands looked even thicker, shorter, and stubbier than yours. What do you think of that, my dear?"

I made an impatient gesture. He had no idea how upset I was.

"Oh, now he's pouting, poor darling." He tried to place a comforting hand on my shoulder. Angrily, I shrugged it off. "No, you should have been there and seen his pudgy fingers racing up and down the keyboard while playing the *Appassionata*. Just like a handful of Vienna sausages!" He chuckled.

"You damned skinny fairy," I scowled. "Why do I waste my time around you?"

"Why?" he smiled. "Because nobody else but me will talk to you, you threadbare penniless bastard. And I mean that last word literally."

I sighed. It was all true: not only forever poor, but it seemed—how, I don't know—that knowledge of my birth had become known to some.

And yes, I was unhappy with my hands. I had been troubled about my fingers for years now—not to Madame Polkovska, of course. I knew better than that. She would have had no time for it. But to Mama I would regularly complain. And she, misguided, unappreciated soul that she was, thought she was comforting me by telling me that in the fingers, at least, I took after my father. I did not rejoice at the news but never lost an opportunity to pull at my fingers, stretch them every which way in the belief that they could be made longer.

This day's lesson turned out most uncomfortably. Herr Schneidermann broke my reverie when he entered the practice room, a short, stout, bearded man who breathed noisily, wearing a tight winged collar and a cravat.

There was no greeting other than a snappish, "You have been working on the Schubert impromptus, Herr Kapp?"

"Yes, Herr Professor," I murmured.

"Well, let's hear, let's hear." He was annoyed before I had even begun.

I took my seat at the piano. Herr Schneidermann stood behind me, rocking up and down on his heels. I began with the A-flat impromptu. I was unable to please him, even though I tried to vary things—one way slower, one way faster, with rubato, without rubato. He unnerved me by pacing back and forth, back and forth. Nothing would do. In fact, my playing elicited a mounting crescendo of complaints.

"Ach, du lieber Gott!" he shouted at last. "What are you doing? What are you thinking?" He slammed his hand on the piano. "This is not a Schubert impromptu. This is absolute nonsense!" He strode over to me. "Get up!"

I did as he said in haste. He sat down in my place, breathing hard with fatness and exertion, and began to play. Like Artur Schnabel, as in my friend Rudi's story, Herr Schneidermann had short, stubby fingers—just like stubby pork sausages too—but even I got an idea of what he was looking for. The way he played the impromptu shimmered like silk. Indeed, he did not seem to be causing hammers to strike piano wires. He looked like a devil, but at the keys he sounded angelic. As I say, like silk. Not until I had the good fortune to hear Walter Gieseking, some years later, would I catch something comparable.

I knew he despised me, but I couldn't help smiling in admiration. His playing was wonderful. I received no smile in return. He rose and ordered me back to the piano stool. I was painfully eager to emulate what I had heard.

I did not succeed. But when Herr Schneidermann tried to strike at my fingers with the ruler that he used to beat time, he did not succeed. I knew what was likely to happen. I whipped my hands off the keyboard just in time. Instead, he struck the D and the D-sharp keys above middle C with such force that he dislodged the ivories and sent them flying across the room.

"Dummkopf, dummkopf, dummkopf!" he shouted. His face was red above his high starched collar. "You have not got it right! You didn't get it right at the last lesson—nor the one before that." He glared at me, the left side of his face twitching. "Never, never have I had the misfortune to be given a stupid, clumsy goat such as you." He strode to the door. "And to think that Madame Polkovska herself recommended you!" He laughed bitterly. "She must be getting weak in the mind!"

Flinging open the door of the practice room, he paused only to add, "I shall report this to the rector. You are no longer my piano student. He can do with you as he likes." I listened to his furious footsteps stomp down the corridor.

There was a small mirror by the door. My face was pale, but it wore a broad lunatic grin. How was it possible, I wondered, that a man who could play as beautifully as Herr Schneidermann could also be such a brute? My hands were shaking.

Rudi appeared. "What the devil have you been doing, Liebchen, to cause Herr Schneidermann to roar in this fashion?" he asked, sounding impressed. "The whole third floor has heard it and they're standing in their doorways, dying to find out."

I thought I was about to faint, I needed air. I summoned some strength and managed to stagger down the stairs and out of the building, out to the columned temples of the Ringstrasse, where I collapsed on a park bench in one of the gardens. After a while, I could think clearly again. I tried to make sense of what had happened. Herr Schneidermann had behaved like a madman—that was plain enough. But, my god, what would this mean for me? Surely, this meant the end of any hopes I had to become a musician. Surely, I had lost my scholarship and the stipend that came with it. What would Mama say when she heard of it? Herr Schneidermann had thrown me out. What about Herr von Amerling, who taught composition; Herr Ferdinand, my professor for theory; and Dr. Böhm, the professor in conducting? Could Herr Schneidermann in fact have me thrown out of the Conservatory all by himself?

I groaned. Some of my classmates had developed the habit—young as they were—of drinking too much when their cheap gaiety girlfriends refused to see them anymore. I now regarded them with a certain sympathy. Thinking about my piano professor was giving me a bad headache. I wished to get drunk too.

Thrusting my hands into my jacket pocket, I discovered the folded piece of paper that the charming Lotte had given me. I smoothed it out and read its message again. "Five o'clock. Back door." I would be there.

I had no watch. I could afford neither those impressive turnips that gentlemen of means kept in their waistcoat pockets, nor the wrist-watches that had become so popular since the war. Luckily, there were many grand buildings around the great curves of the Ringstrasse—many of them bearing clocks. One of them struck a quarter to five. Immediately, I leapt to my feet and hurried off to Rosalie's café, two cobbled streets down.

I was happy again. On the way, I thought to buy a solitary red rose from one of the street sellers. I really couldn't afford to buy flowers, but I thought it the right thing to do. When I arrived at the tinted-glass front doors, nothing seemed amiss. Patrons were bustling in and out as usual. After a few moments of watching, I casually slipped down the narrow alley that led behind the building. It was chilly and gloomy. Spring had been late this year. I shivered and shrank down into my jacket collar.

After a while, I heard at least three clocks chime five. A sound came from behind the back door. I smartened up and walked eager-ly toward the steps, proffering my red rose, a smile on my face, full of expectation.

A key turned in a lock. The door opened. And there stood Rosalie—one hand on her hip! A cigarette dangled from the side of her mouth.

"Grüss Gott, young sir," she said. "You were expecting somebody?" She looked at me with amused contempt.

Confusion swept over me. Words strangled in my throat. At last, I found my voice. "Bitte," I began timidly, "I-I wanted to speak with Fräulein Lotte, if I might be permitted the honor—"

Rosalie interrupted with an unpleasantly raucous laugh, which turned into violent coughing on her cigarette smoke. "Young sir," she said when she had recovered, "what kind of gentleman would sneak around a back door when calling on a young lady?" Her eyebrows raised, she maintained her sneer.

I must have turned all kinds of colors. "I-I—" I began again.

Rosalie broke in once more, her laughter louder than ever. "Listen to me, you young fool. You think I don't know why you're creeping around back alleys? You think I was born yesterday? You've got the smell of fresh meat in your nostrils. Yes, you have. I can tell!" Rosalie laughed even more loudly. My confusion doubled. I lifted up my poor, solitary red rose to demonstrate my honest intentions.

Her smile vanished. "Listen, I didn't bring up my young Lotte to amuse the likes of you," she said. "Look at you—your shabby clothes, your arms sticking out of your sleeves, your boots with worn heels, that grubby shirt and cravat—don't make me laugh! I haven't been slaving over coffee urns for my health, you know. Lotte's going to have someone better than you, someone respectable, not a penniless nobody, giving himself airs, pretending to be an artist—"

It was like being stripped naked. I felt defenseless. Suddenly, the door behind Rosalie opened. Lotte appeared, wearing a long coat over her dress, a small suitcase in her hand. Rosalie was taken by surprise. I was too. Before either of us could move, Lotte had jumped down the three steps and seized me firmly by the hand.

"Lotte, are you crazy or stupid?" Rosalie shouted. "What do you think you're doing? Let go of his hand and come back inside!"

Instead of answering her mother, Lotte turned to me. "Take me away this instant."

If you think I had been shocked by Rosalie's tirade, now I was dumbfounded.

"What? Take you where?"

Without answering me or her mother, Lotte strode off down the alley toward the street, pulling me by the hand, Rosalie continuing to scream at us. We emerged out of the gloom and paused.

"Which way to your lodgings?" asked Lotte. "We must hurry. She will follow."

I was utterly bewildered.

"At least, we must get away from the café." Lotte wore a new expression on her face, different from what I was used to. No modest look now, no downcast eyes. She stared boldly at me and handed me her small suitcase. Silently, I took it. "Come," she said.

Hand in hand, we quickly crossed over the broad avenue, dodging the trams, taxis, and horse-carts, and disappeared into one of the parks. I was aware that, behind us, Rosalie had appeared on the front steps of the café and was calling out to us. Apparently, she didn't see us as we hurried into the gardens.

We walked quickly northward toward the Danube, past the Johann Strauss monument, taking care to stay mostly inside the parks, and settled on a wooden bench within a secluded area. At last, I had a chance to catch my breath. Lotte had not let go of my hand. That new expression on her face was still there. In fact, it was even bolder. In fact, I realized in shock, it was becoming intimate and downright inviting. The evening drew in; it was growing darker. The lamps were being turned on, but the walkways were almost deserted. It was still too chilly to stroll in the evenings. We were alone.

Under the lights, Lotte studied me. "You're a nice-looking young gentleman, you are." She stretched her face up to mine and closed her eyes. "Kiss me," she breathed and, clasping the back of my head, drew it to her.

What about Rosalie? I was thinking. But it was my first kiss—at least from a female who was not my mother or one of my mother's friends. It was unbelievable! Lotte clung to me, seeming to yield and grant at the same time! I became electric and breathless. This seemed like the true passion I had heard about. I was stirred. I wanted to do *more*. I had read novels by Schnitzler and poems by Mallarmé, who strongly suggested that much more could be done—to say nothing of those alarming, exciting, downright indecent paintings of Kokoschka and Klimt, filled with lascivious embraces and breasts, before which I had spent hours in the museum. Much more. But how to begin? Or what could be accomplished on a park bench?

After long seconds into that kiss, Lotte drew her head back and gazed into my eyes. I thought her expression not merely bold, but combined with her conduct ever since I had turned up at her door—her running off with me, her defiance of Rosalie, and all the rest—it occurred to me that her behavior was so shocking I could not imagine what might happen next. Decidedly, there was a wild and lunatic look to her.

All at once, she burst into raucous laughter, sounding uncomfortably like her mother. "What's your name?" she demanded.

I jumped. "What?"

"Your name, silly. I don't know what it is."

"You don't?"

"Of course I don't, why should I?" She leaned forward and kissed me again as she had before, long and deep.

I gulped. "No, of course. Why should you know? We were never introduced." Suddenly, Lotte's face seemed sweet now. Gone was that wild and lunatic aspect—for the moment. Demure again, she was all welcome and affection. My heart warmed anew. Her behavior may have been strange in a young girl, but heaven knows, I had been acquainted with strange and peculiar people myself ever since childhood—including my own father; Madame Polkovska; my friend Rudi, who said he was not interested in girls; and last, but not least, the terrifying and dangerous Herr Schneidermann.

"Go on," she giggled. "What's your name? You already know mine."

That was an undoubted fact. I rose to my feet and gave a polite, formal bow. "It's Hermann Kapp," I said. More giggles.

"What's the matter?"

"You know what your name means, don't you?" she said.

"Yes, of course I know. It means a cap or a hood. What's wrong?"

Lotte positively squealed with laughter. She looked crazed again. She clapped both hands over her mouth to quiet herself and tried to be serious, without success.

"You don't know what *Kapp* means here on the street? I don't believe you." I still looked blank.

"When a girl's with a man and she doesn't want to get in the family way, she makes sure he wears a *Kapp*. You see what I mean?" She watched me intently, her eyes dancing, eager to share secrets. I shook my head.

She meant for me to understand, no matter how long it took. She pronounced an impressively long word, slowly, syllable by syllable: "Eine Empfängnisverhütung?" A contraceptive.

I frowned. I'd never heard the word before.

"Never heard of a contraceptive?" she asked.

Another long pause. It was dawning on me that, while I may have been a young pianist of much talent, Lotte was quite accomplished in her own way. Far from the modest maiden of downcast eye, she was turning out to be a wild one. Whatever cocky composure I thought I possessed as a seventeen-year-old man about town, on his own in a great cosmopolitan city, I could muster not a trace of it.

Right then and there, I resolved never to let Lotte out of my sight, although she frightened the life out of me. I meant to possess her. Once having tasted her kisses, I could not do without them. Whatever more lay ahead with her, I wanted it. At the same time, I was terrified, knowing I would regret it.

Lotte and I resumed our progress through the early evening. We came to the waterside quays and crossed the Kanal by the Aspernbrücke, from the center of the city to my own humbler part of town, Leopoldstadt, in the Second District. It was a devil of a walk, but I couldn't afford tram fare for the two of us. We said little to each other on the way. We frequently smiled at each other, but my heart was anything but easy. I was carrying her suitcase, alternating between intoxication and terror at the enormity of what we were doing. I had actually persuaded a girl, not only to walk by my side, but also—

I abruptly stopped walking and forced myself to cease this clearly delusional way of thinking—probably induced by my proximity to Lotte. I had *not* persuaded her to walk with me. Quite the contrary. She had chosen me. Why? Again, I had no idea.

"What's the matter? Why have we stopped?" asked Lotte with another of her loud giggles. She sounded almost hysterical. What had happened, I wondered again, to the silent girl I had worshipped?

"Lotte, where are we going?" I asked.

"To your lodgings. That's what you said."

"And what will happen when we get there?"

She flung her arms about my neck in glee and jumped up and down, still clinging, almost causing me to drop her suitcase. "We will live together and be happy and forget all about Rosalie," she said.

"But she's your mother and she'll worry about you, won't she?" Lotte struck my face with a slap that stung. "Rosalie is not my mother," she shouted. "Come," she said and set off furiously down the street. I was stunned. After a moment, I followed.

We walked at a rapid pace in silence, which gave me a chance to reflect on what I was going to do. Part of my mind clearly told me I had picked up a live red-hot coal that I should immediately drop. I was most reluctant to have Lotte join Herr Schneidermann as one of the people who screamed at me, as seemed likely. She appeared to share Herr Schneidermann's ability to exhibit rage just like that. And since I already had many examples in that sphere, I was not inclined to encourage more.

On the other hand, on the other hand…the sensations of Lotte's mouth against mine and her caresses on the back of my neck were fresh and not easily thrust aside. While we were kissing, I had pressed her to me. That had led to a series of marvelous revelations—the way her hips swelled out from her waist and, when she shifted position, the way her limbs seemed to undulate, the scent that rose from her thick, full hair, the softness I sensed from the bosom close to mine, which I had not dared to touch. Was I ready to renounce all this?

Another matter. Although Lotte was clearly furious with me, she had not abandoned me. We were now deep in the Leopoldstadt district, where I was obliged to lodge among the peddlers and street hawkers—all Jews—she slightly ahead, I following, and it was clear that we were together. If that was so, what was I to do with her? I lived on the top floor of a mean, rickety building on the Malzgasse, right close to a synagogue. The owner of my lodgings was the aging but vain Frau Malteser, who tried to make up for the terrible food she served at supper by colorful stories about husbands and lovers who, she claimed, had been drawn to her because of her exotic dark features.

"My name tells the whole story," she would tell boarders. "My grandfather said he was from Malta. At other times he said it was Turkey. But wherever it was, he passed his name and good looks on to me." She would chuckle coyly. I could barely keep from shuddering when she said things like that. I never thought her remotely good-looking. She was just an ordinary ugly woman. She smelled bad too. People said that was the way Jews smelled. You could tell them by the smell. Also too dark in the complexion for my taste. I was accustomed to people from all over Austria-Hungary—gypsies, Bosnians, Italians, whatever. Some darkness in the face was all right, but Frau Malteser's was too much. And besides, I was convinced that she really was a Jew, like nearly everybody else in Leopoldstadt.

We paused in front of a shabby building. It was completely dark by now, but not late—about seven o'clock. Even so, it was quiet. Those Jew vendors and sellers of junk, I knew, were already asleep because they had to get up before dawn to scramble for a place at some street corner until the police made them move on. Here in Leopoldstadt we didn't yet have electric lights. Me, I preferred gaslight anyway, softer and yet brighter. One of those lamps, hanging from its ornate standard, cast a pool of light on Lotte. Her face was happy once more, I was glad to see, the spasm of rage at an end.

"Is this the house? Is this the house?" She was excited. I nodded but was unable to think of what to do next. At the end of a long and crowded day, I felt weary and apprehensive. *What was next?*

Lotte seized her small suitcase from my hand and, to my horror, resolutely marched up to the front door and pulled the bell. After a few minutes, Frau Malteser swung open the door and screwed up her eyes, peering out into the dark.

Lotte bobbed in tiny curtsy and offered her hand, which the bemused Frau Malteser automatically took.

"Grüss Gott, *Gnädige Frau,* I am so happy to meet you." Lotte curtsied again.

"Grüss Gott," Frau Malteser responded. She peered into the gloom. "Who is it? What do you want?"

Instead of an answer, Lotte stepped to one side, revealing me.

"Herr Kapp," said Frau Malteser in surprise, "is that you?" I gave a weak smile.

Frau Malteser gave me a lewd, knowing look. "Herr Kapp, I never would have thought you'd try to smuggle young ladies into the house. You know my rules."

"He is not trying to smuggle anyone anywhere," Lotte said with great sweetness. "Didn't you know? Hermann and I are married. I have just arrived from Graz for a visit, and I thought there would be no harm if we stayed together until I went back—"

I thought that I would drop to the cobblestones in shock.

"Married?" Frau Malteser gave a scornful laugh. "You're not married. You're no more than a child." She gestured at me. "And so is he!"

"I'm eighteen years old, and Hermann is twenty-one," Lotte said defiantly. She held up her left hand. On its third finger was a plain gold band I had not seen before. "And," added Lotte, now dabbing at her eyes with a small handkerchief and speaking in a breaking voice, "if you want to see our marriage certificate, I've got it right here in my bag and I'll show it to you." Real tears ran down her face.

I must have turned white. You simply didn't challenge Frau Malteser like that. She was entirely capable of demanding to see the birthmark on your arse if she thought it necessary. But Lotte's tears affected her. I had never seen Frau Malteser at a loss for words before. I knew that she had a vast experience dealing with grafters, grifters, and swindlers of every sort—a whole host of late rent-payers, non-rent-payers, liars and thieves, scoundrels, and blackguards—she had met and vanquished the lot.

After a long moment, I was astonished to watch Frau Malteser stretch her hand out to touch Lotte's tear-stained cheek. "There, there, *Puppchen*, poor thing," she murmured. "Don't be upset with me. These days one can't be too careful. But I know Herr Kapp. He's a nice, respectable young man. But"—she wagged her finger at me—"he's a sly one, isn't he, not to tell me he was married!"

Frau Malteser stepped to one side, inviting us to enter. "Of course, you may stay," she said. "I will not charge you too much. Just something to pay for the meals—nothing extra for the room."

We stepped into the hallway. "Perhaps Frau Kapp would care for some hot chocolate or perhaps something to eat before she goes up to bed?" With complete aplomb, Lotte consented to be shown into the room where we ate, the Speisezimmer, just off the hall. I was unable to speak; my head was spinning.

After a bowl of Frau Malteser's watery, tasteless *Goulasch,* not a bit like Mama's rich *gulyás,* she offered us each a glass of *Schnaps* in celebration of our "marriage." But just as Lotte and I were about to climb the stairs to my humble room, Frau Malteser asked us to wait another moment. She led us into a private back room that I had never known about, carefully closed the door, and unlocked a small cabinet. Wearing a smile of complicity, she withdrew from it a shallow flat box covered in dusty red silk. Like a woman before a shrine, she opened it. It contained just two objects. On the left was a faded sepia-tinted wedding photograph. On the right was a large bright gold coin.

"Can you recognize the picture?" asked Frau Malteser, sounding roguish.

Lotte cried out in delight. "It's you, Madame, it's you!"

I peered more closely at the faded print. True enough. Frau Malteser peered back at me from the photo with a coy, simpering grin, younger certainly, but not young, no more pleasant looking than she was now. By her side, a stony-faced man in a soldier's uniform stared out at me. I couldn't help shuddering. He reminded me of Papa.

"Very good, *Puppchen*." Frau Malteser was completely won over, but her face wore a sad smile. "Yes, this was me and my poor Bobo, taken when we were married in the summer of 1916." She sniffled. "The next week, my poor Bobo had to go back to the Front. He was killed by the Italians—I hate those *Schweine*…" Her voice trailed away in a moan.

By the Italians! The way my own Papa had died.

Lotte rushed over to embrace her, making soothing noises, for all the world as though she were her mother. I was just an onlooker, nothing to do with it.

After a few moments, Frau Malteser had collected herself and turned her attention to the large coin. "And here is my most precious memento. Feel the weight of it."

She actually permitted me to hold it in my palm. It was a large, heavy four-ducat gold piece, brilliant, elegant—quite dazzling. For some reason, nobody wanted the empire's gold money these days—people preferred banknotes. Strange! Obviously, that wasn't true of Frau Malteser. One side of the gold piece was almost completely filled by an image of our late emperor, Ferenc Jószef Császár—or rather, Kaiser Franz-Josef, I should say, now that I was in Vienna—wearing a laurel wreath like a Roman conqueror. I was struck by strange emotions as I read his titles circled about the rim: "By the Grace of God, Emperor of Austria, King of Hungary, Bohemia, Galicia, etc." On the back were the imperial coat of arms, the imperial crown, and also the crowned double-headed eagle, clutching in its talons the sword and scepter of imperial mastery. Young, modern, and a thoroughgoing skeptic, I had believed the trappings of lost empire to be without meaning.

I felt my eyes sting with tears. I couldn't have imagined it: that coin aroused emotions of which I had been unaware. Suddenly, I felt that, without our Kaiser, I was without substance. At that moment, I felt diminished by not having him, that I was fatherless in more than one way. I felt depressed and stifled—almost choking, struggling for air. I felt just as I had when Herr Schneidermann had so brutally flung me away. Had I been asleep for years and was only just waking up? My country had lost the war! Almost forgotten memories of my poor dead Papa came back to me. Of course, he had admired Kaiser Wilhelm.

But I missed our kindly, fatherly Kaiser Franz-Josef. The two emperors had been brothers-in-arms, and they had both lost. I had lost too. Why did the image of Dr. von Hornberger suddenly come to mind? Even though he had been sneering and unpleasant, hadn't he spoken of our losses in the war? All at once, I was reminded of those losses. All this required some sorting out. I decided to keep it to myself for the time being. Who would have understood? I certainly didn't.

I realized with a start that Frau Malteser had fallen silent and was holding out her hand for the coin. I silently gave it back.

"It was the first year of the new Kaiser's reign, in 1916," she said. "I'm talking about Emperor Karl, you know," she added loftily. "He presented this four-ducat piece himself, struck in memory of his father, the Kaiser Franz-Josef." She sighed. "It was so beautiful, that day at the Schloss Schönbrunn, when he presented it to my Bobo and me, together with the other soldiers and sailors who got married that week." Again her eyes grew moist. "The most precious thing I own, and I wanted to show it to you fine young people, at the beginning of your married lives." We watched as she carefully replaced it in the box, together with the picture, and locked it in the cabinet.

"After my Bobo was lost, I could not bear to be called by his name as a married woman is. It sounds strange, and I cannot explain it. But that's how it is. And I have been Frau Malteser ever since. I used to be *Fräulein* Malteser, but I am *Frau* Malteser now." She drew herself up and looked us boldly in the face. Now she seemed once more to be the shrewd woman I was used to. "My father's name is a good name." She still looked—and smelled—like an ugly old Jewess.

She led us to the foot of the rickety stairs, embraced Lotte once again, shook my hand, and bade us good night.

Lotte and I climbed the five flights to my room. I struck a match and applied it to the gaslight mantel. It gave a slight pop and grew into a soft glow. She spun delightedly around, surveying my desk, the faded, peeling wallpaper, the grimy curtains, my shabby upright practice piano, piles of books, music, and clothing scattered across my cot, upon which she collapsed with a tiny scream.

"I'm so tired, I could sleep for a year," she exclaimed. There was barely room on the cot for me. She closed her eyes as she spoke. "My mother practically kicks me out of bed every morning at five. I have to put the chairs on the tables, sweep out the café, put the chairs back on the floor around the tables, pour water in the coffee urns, light the gas under them, unlock the doors, and begin serving—while Miss Rosalie takes her time dolling herself up—"

"You said Rosalie wasn't your mother," I broke in.

"When did I say that?"

"You know, before, when you were angry with me."

Lotte shrugged.

"You know," I persisted, "when you slapped my face."

Lotte opened her eyes and looked over at me. "Where's the *pissoir*?" she demanded without a blush. I blushed enough for us both. After a moment, she said, more loudly, "I haven't gone to the you-know-what for the longest time. I have to go badly. At least, have you got a *Nachttopf*? I'm going to burst if I don't go!"

I dragged out my chipped enamel chamber pot from under the cot and held it out.

She placed it on the floor at her feet. "Thank God," she cried. "You have saved my life!" She raised her skirts and made ready to squat right in front of me.

I gazed at her in horror. "Should I go outside, leave you by yourself?"

She smiled at me. "No need." There came the sound of a mighty hiss.

My face ablaze, I whirled about and stared hard at a patch of peeling wallpaper, wishing I had clapped my hands over my ears.

After what seemed an awfully long time, the hissing ceased.

"You can turn around now," said Lotte. She held out the chamber pot, now clearly filled and heavy. "What do you do with this?"

"The Klosett is at the end of the corridor," I said. She didn't stir. It was up to me.

"You'd better empty that before you spill it," she commanded.

In a daze, I did what I was told.

When I returned to the room, Lotte had made herself comfortable under my blankets. Her blouse and dirndl were draped over the back of my wooden chair. She held out her naked arms to me in invitation. They glowed pink in the gaslight, pink and rounded, with black tufts in the armpits. That was unexpected.

"It's late, little husband," she giggled. "Time to come to bed."

I gulped but moved toward her. She drew back the covers. I gasped. The rest of her was as naked as her arms and looked equally round and soft. There was a shocking bush of black hair at the bottom of her belly. I had never seen a live naked girl before, and I was not prepared for that. I was not completely ignorant. My friends and I used to pass around those dirty pictures from Berlin, what we students called "wicked Weimar-Berlin," not the Berlin in the guidebooks. So scandalous! You know, scenes from the wicked naked bars and the Kabarette they have there. These pictures were not so easy to come across in our more respectable Vienna. I was glad that Kaiser Wilhelm was in exile, unable to see what Berlin had become. But now, it was startling to be face-to-face, so to speak, with the thick black hair of Lotte's bush.

"Little husband," she pouted, "I'm getting cold like this. Come to bed."

About to swoon, I sat on the cot, not knowing what to do, still fully dressed. Lotte wasn't having any of that. She energetically pried me out of my shoes and stockings, then tore off my shirt and long combinations, flung them across the room, turned me onto my back, as easily as though I were a child, and with a blissful smile lay on top of me, full length, effectively pinning me down with all that intoxicating smooth, soft body, pressed on me without a hint of shyness—quite the contrary.

She giggled again. "Little husband," she whispered in my ear, "am I too heavy?"

I lay there, eyes closed, motionless.

"Little husband," Lotte said again in a pleading child's voice, "pull the blanket over us." I reached down to one side, found it, and did so. "Now, do you think you could put your arms around me and rub my back? I'm still cold."

I placed my hands on her. Her back was cool, smooth, and silken, but it felt like flame. My hands were seared with sensation. I gasped. At the same time, she raised her body slightly and permitted her breasts, which had been squashed between us, to blossom into large round apples. I couldn't hide the fact that my *Pistole* had become hard as a rock. It was too much for me, much too much. I gasped again, shuddered—and shame upon shame—for the first time suffered the humiliation of bursting into a climax of the highest pleasure, in the presence of a stranger.

Lotte shrieked with laughter like an alley girl. "So quick? We haven't done anything yet. What a mess! It's all over me." She laughed again.

I was a regular tangle of emotion. There was deep embarrassment.

104

But at the same time, I couldn't help feeling wonderfully happy, warm, and at ease—despite my rapidly cooling wet body. Lotte wiped both of us down with my shirt and drew close to me and was still. I sighed and closed my eyes. I had also had a long day. I had indeed entered the world of *Le Nozze di Figaro*. I had indeed become Cherubino. I had achieved the Susanna of my dreams, but this Susanna was not always trying to slip away, did not have to be wooed and conquered. This Susanna was all mine. I fell into a deep sleep.

$$* \; * \; *$$

A thunderous pounding on the door burst into my slumber. When I opened my eyes, I was blinded by dazzling sunlight, right on my face. That pounding again! I pulled myself upright, dazed, my head spinning. I needed to piss badly—just like Lotte last night. I glanced about the room for her. I was alone. Still more pounding. I found my trousers and put them on. I had no time to look for my underwear.

I swung open the door, gasped, and stepped back. Frau Malteser stood there together with an enormous mustachioed policeman.

"That's one of them, don't let him get away," she cried, stepping past me into the room. "Where is she, your whore?" The policeman seized me by the arm. Frau Malteser's voice was a hysterical screech. "Where is she?" she repeated. "And where is my four-ducat gold piece?"

"Come down with me," ordered the policeman.

I was completely lost. Frau Malteser stopped shouting long enough for me to ask if I could put some clothes on and then, when she had stepped outside to permit me to dress, I asked the policeman for permission to piss, which he granted—in his presence—a bizarre reenactment of last night with Lotte. And where indeed was she?

The policeman frog-marched me downstairs into Frau Malteser's parlor. I was horrified to see broken pieces of her cabinet strewn across the floor. It looked like someone had taken a hatchet to it. On a table were the remains of the red silk box. It had been wrenched in half. My landlady's wedding portrait lay crumpled. Of the four-ducat gold piece there was no sign.

Frau Malteser broke into loud, hoarse sobs at my appearance. "Give me back my gold coin!" she screamed.

"Better do what she says if you know what's good for you," the policeman said.

"I haven't got it," I stammered, "I swear it."

"So you know what we're talking about, do you, my lad?" The policeman indicated with a broad smile that he would not be fooled.

I could only wave my arms about in sheer fright.

"It'll go better for you if you confess and return the lady's gold piece," he said.

"I haven't got it," I repeated.

Frau Malteser screamed again. Her gray hair was awry, her face almost dead white, from which glared red-rimmed eyes. "Can't you tell he's lying? Where is the other one, that lying whore? That stinking liar," she spat, "that filthy shit, pretending to be so sorry for me!" She threw her kerchief over her head and sobbed loudly.

I was led away and taken to the local Polizeiamt, accompanied by Frau Malteser, who made her accusations to the examining officer with great indignation. It was rapidly established that Lotte was not my wife—Frau Malteser was outraged afresh. Further, that she was the same as the missing daughter of one Frau Rosalie Schratt, proprietor of Rosalie's Kaffeehaus, who had reported the vanishing of her sixteen-year-old, last seen in the company of an unknown young man—believed to be a music student at the Conservatory—together with roughly one hundred *schillings* of Frau Schratt's hard-earned money. It was not immediately clear whether the young man was himself a thief and an abductor. This information the examining officers sought to determine with enormous thoroughness.

It was also established that I and Fräulein Lotte Schratt's cofugitive and cocriminal were one and the same. But it required an additional twelve hours to persuade the detectives, first, that I had not abducted anyone—the opposite was more likely—and, second, that I was innocent of any charges of robbery. I understood that the detectives, however much they gave me stern and disapproving looks, disliked Frau Malteser even more and quickly tired of her noisy weeping and wailing.

"*Das verdammte Jüdische schlabberei!* That damned Jew-slobbering makes me sick!" I heard one say. She had gone home long before I was released.

It was eleven o'clock at night as I stumbled out of the police station, exhausted and hungry. When I arrived back at my lodgings in the Malzgasse, the street was deserted and silent. I broke down and cried. My belongings had been stuffed into my two shabby suitcases and left on the doorstep. Mercifully, nobody had made off with them. There was a scrawled note, ordering me to have my practice piano removed from my room right away if I wanted to see it again. I was not to reappear at the house. What a spiteful thing to do! I savagely cursed the ugly old Jew bitch for putting me through all this torment—and nothing had been my fault! I hoped everybody understood that.

It turned out to be a sharp but short-lived problem. Yes, I thought I was going to have to tear my hair out by the roots in order to have my piano removed from Frau Malteser's, find new lodgings, clear up the dangers created by the horrible Herr Schneidermann, and stop thinking about the mare's nest left behind by the dangerous but oh-so-bewitching Lotte.

If I started out deep in panic, it was my queer friend Rudi who saved me. I really didn't want to turn to him because the way he was made me nervous—not that he ever tried anything funny with me. Surprisingly, he revealed an astonishing capacity for organization and solving problems.

But I was in near hysterics as I dragged my two suitcases through the wretched streets to where he lived. Not too far, it was in the next district to the north, the Twentieth, known as Brigittenau, on the old quays of the Danube. It was almost midnight, and I passed all kinds of raucous low-class bars and one brothel after another. First, I tried Rudi's boardinghouse. He wasn't there, which upset me more. I tried to calm myself and think. What about the places along the docks? I found him drinking with three others of his kind at a dimly lighted homosexual bar, which I ordinarily would not dream of entering but for my feeling half-crazed. I found them sitting near the doors at a rough table. The establishment was half-filled with young and not-so-young men. The not-so-young men were in formal business suits and starched collars; their companions more colorful, some of them rouged and wearing mascara.

Rudi looked startled as I barged through the doors and dropped my cases.

"What are you doing here, *Liebling*? What has happened to you?"

I was unable to answer. I collapsed onto a chair and began to sob.

Immediately, Rudi and his companions gathered around me, stroking my back and making soothing sounds, even though they didn't know me. But I couldn't seem to stop sobbing. It was hard to catch my breath. It was like another of those strange "attacks" that occurred when things got too much. I thought I was about to faint.

"*Ach, Liebling, Liebling*, what has happened?" Rudi said again. He placed his glass of *Schnaps* in front of me and urged me to drink. When I finished it, they gave me another. And a third.

The *Schnaps* steadied me. The room stopped swimming. During swallows, I managed to give a stumbling account of the previous twenty-four hours. The recital both enthralled and horrified them. I was able to notice Rudi's friends. For all their kind intentions, I could make no sense of them. They didn't seem to belong with each other. One of them looked like a ballet dancer, tall, lissom, and graceful—like Rudi himself. Of the other two, one looked like a Danube dockworker—a squat, burly, hairy gorilla—the other like a prim, buttoned-down civil servant. To my surprise, the graceful young man in the party was not Rudi's special companion, as I thought. Rather, it was the hairy gorilla, whose name was Johann. I couldn't help noticing that Rudi's hand lingered on Johann's shoulder. After I calmed down, they carried my bags up to Rudi's flat, wrenched off my boots, pushed me down on Rudi's spare couch—which alarmed me somewhat—but threw a blanket over me and left. I was exhausted. I think I was asleep before the door closed.

I could not tell how long I slept. I was abruptly awakened by five or six heavy thumps and the loud jangling of piano wires. It was still night. Rudi and his friends were back and in high spirits, to judge from the way they could not stop talking at the top of their voices and screaming with laughter—even the civil servant. Through their half-drunken splatter, I managed to understand that these men had actually wakened Frau Malteser in the dead of night, invaded the house, brushed aside her protests and calls for help, manhandled my piano down five rickety flights of stairs, got hold of a horse-cart, and transported it through the streets, from Leopoldstadt to Brigittenau, and trundled it over to Rudi's place. And here it stood. Rudi told me to consider his place as my own until I could get a new room.

But my troubles were not over. That morning, when I managed to return to the Conservatory, I discovered fresh challenges. Even though

Herr Schneidermann had put my piano studies into question, I was marked down for a violin-section rehearsal of the beginners' orchestra at 2:00 p.m. I also found a notice in my message box summoning me to a proctors' committee, for possible disciplinary action, to be convened at 11 a.m.

It was like being back at the police station all over again. I sat on a solitary chair in the middle of a room that smelled strongly of furniture polish, which, together with my hungover condition and throbbing headache, made me feel like throwing up. I faced a committee of three bearded proctors. The chairman was Dr. Hannover. They were seated side-by-side at a table with the windows behind them, so that the light glared into my eyes and made my head feel worse. Thank heaven, they knew nothing of Frau Malteser, Rosalie, or Lotte. And, thank heaven, I quickly sensed that nothing drastic was being considered. Herr Schneidermann's feelings were not to be trifled with, but it was clear the committee was thinking of another teacher for me, not punishment. Not expulsion.

Sensing that I was not facing the worst, I relaxed and permitted my mind to wander. Mind you, I still sat up straight in my chair and stared contritely at the proctors. I urgently wanted to know why this string of disasters had happened to me. What had caused them? Was it all accident and coincidence? Some of it, I thought, could not be helped. Herr Schneidermann, for example, was a kind of natural disaster. For all the world, I could not imagine what might satisfy him. The mess with Lotte, on the other hand, together with all its painful consequences—including the loss of my lodgings—I could make some sense of that.

I had behaved like an absolute idiot. It wasn't pleasant to admit, but it was true. All I knew about girls had been gained from *kolporteurnovelle,* cheap, stupid idealized romances, fairy tales, and going to the *Kino.* But better novels, by Schnitzler for instance, and those Klimt and Kokoschka paintings, crammed with stark sensuality and lush enigma, even though they made me shudder, suggested a different kind of reality—evil, betrayal, and double-dealing—shamelessly saying one thing but meaning another. Even though I had sufferered this past night, it had been somehow purifying. If I could only keep that in my mind, I could rise above the humiliation. I could learn to master it. From my seventeen-year-old point of view, people like Lotte, Rosalie, Herr Schneidermann, and Frau Malteser—with their ruthlessness and cruelty—seemed to have the answers. Cherubino belonged in the opera. The world belonged to the swine, not to the meek.

Dr. von Hornberger came to mind again. In contrast to my own craven demeanor just yesterday at the Polizeiamt, Dr. von Hornberger had been contemptuous and defiant. I heard that he had been released after a three-week detention—only promptly to set about organizing a Putsch in Salzburg, to coincide with Hitler's in Munich. Both uprisings failed. Hitler went to jail; Dr. von Hornberger fled the country.

Now, Dr. von Hornberger seemed to have a special message for me, reaching across the years. Although hard for me to admit, I was too easily frightened. On the one hand, people told me I was a young musician of unusual talent. On the other hand, too many were treating me like filth—belittling, demeaning, and insulting me. My immediate recent experiences with Lotte, Rosalie, Herr Schneidermann, and Frau Malteser had shaken me badly. They had all treated me like a despised enemy. Dr. von Hornberger's speech in the beer hall came back vividly. He claimed he had been speaking to the crushed and the despised. Well, I was one of those. And you had only to read the daily newspapers to know that panic and riot were around every corner. It was just as he had said: the Jew-Bolshevik-Socialists would not rest until everything we knew and loved was smashed.

The conclusion was obvious. There was nothing to be gained from being a simpleton. A conviction took shape. If I could not ally myself with somebody like Dr. von Hornberger, somebody who could lend me strength, I would be lost.

I remained seated before the droning proctors, appearing to listen respectfully. However, in one hideous day and night, I had grown up. I determined not to be such a fool. In order to survive and prosper, I was going to have to become different. But it would not do merely to emulate my tormentors. I would do better by far.

With a start, I noticed that the meeting seemed to be coming to a close. The proctors were gathering their papers and getting to their feet, pushing their chairs back with loud scraping sounds. They smiled and beckoned me to approach. I hastily did so and, bowing, shook all three outstretched hands. Dr. Hannover was saying that I would be transferred to Professor Karl Starker for my piano studies that same day, and he hoped that my progress thereafter would be marked by smoothness and success. No further action would be taken, and nothing would be noted on my records. I had the idea that Herr Schneidermann and his tantrums were well known. Good riddance to him! I would not have been surprised to learn he was another Jew.

* * *

Fifth Variation

Vienna 1928

You cannot imagine how things change in a few short months. The previous summer, I was practically friendless—if you don't count those pariahs and perverts with whom I had been obliged to associate. And then things started to happen. The world turned upside down double-quick. In fact, I thought it might end, so tumultuous did Vienna become. And, I have to say, I encountered a few setbacks of my own.

It all started last year in provincial Burgenland, at a town near Eisenstadt, funnily enough. People said it was entirely the fault of the Jews and the Socialists. While I was still reeling from the effects of the business with Lotte and Herr Schneidermann, the newspapers alleged that three honest lads, upright Austrian patriots, had murdered a couple of local Jew Bolsheviks. All three were put on trial but found not guilty. The Jews had made up their minds the lads were guilty. They went crazy. Troublemakers spread all over. In Vienna, the streets were filled with rioters. The police and militia put up barricades of wood and barbed wire. The demonstrators pulled them down and built barricades of their own. They invaded the Conservatory and the University and tried to disrupt lectures. They refused to obey officials. They marched on the Palace of Justice itself and actually burned it to the ground. They screamed insults at the police and called them Fascists, Nazis, and swine. All this upset law-abiding citizens. Finally, the police got rough and started shooting. When order was finally restored, eighty-five of the scum were dead and more than eight hundred wounded. That quieted them down!

After that, we became accustomed to battalions of students marching through the streets. They were members of the Young Nationalist Patriots League doing their bit to maintain order. They were an inevitable consequence of the Jew-Bolshevik outrages. I recognized some fellow members of the Conservatory among them, but people said they were principally law and faculty of arts students. They made a stirring sight as they strode along with perfect discipline, singing and chanting slogans. Those troublemakers I mentioned tried to disrupt the marchers with rotten fruit and insults, but the Young Patriots had no problem fighting back and bloodying noses.

Professor Starker, my new piano teacher, and I got along well. He was more pleasant and understanding than Madame Polkovska, but I would say, just as exacting. He certainly was as different from Herr Schneidermann as a bright day is from a nightmare. In fact, it was Professor Starker who helped me to find a new place to live, two clean, decent rooms off a tiny courtyard near the Old General Hospital in the Ninth District. I was now on the correct side of the Danube, happy to be removed from my former Jewish neighbors and the homosexual haunts of the dockside taverns. Best of all, it was not far from that part of town that contained the Conservatory, the Staatsoper, and the Musikverein. Easy walking distance.

With Professor Starker, I felt I was growing, not being stifled. He understood right away, unlike Herr Schneidermann, that my musical temperament at that moment was not suited to Schubert impromptus, beautiful as they might be. The wilder Schubert sonatas perhaps, but not the impromptus. He recognized that I would not do well either with Chopin nocturnes and waltzes, charming though they might be. He recognized that at this stage it was Beethoven, Mozart, and Bach for me, and he let me have my way. He was confident that, in due time, I would discover Brahms, Schumann, Schubert, Ravel, Poulenc, Stravinsky, and Chopin's ballades and the *Berceuse* all by myself.

"You may be a quiet and amiable fellow," he said one day, "but something tells me that you want to be stern and pure. The way you sit at the piano and play the instrument reflects that drive and purity. Out with sentiment! You must be muscular and virile!"

In a way, he was correct. I was now eighteen and determined never to slide back into the despicable weakness that had made me, for example, Lotte's victim. In fact, he said he was prescribing—as if he were a physician—a diet of Beethoven, Mozart, and Bach, and only those three for the time being, to purge my soul of "impurities." At times, he seemed to echo Madame. I needed Bach for the intellect, Mozart to recognize both innocence and the tragic, and Beethoven to experience the immense. And all three, moreover, for tenderness and passion. To ready my fingers and hands, he called upon my old friend Carl Czerny, with his volumes of rigorous exercise.

"Czerny will prepare your hands and soul for the mighty statements you crave," he told me one day. "It doesn't matter whether you know what I am talking about," he said. "You've got the right gifts, and you have me to teach you. These are sufficient for now."

Stirring words. But it was at such times that my mind wandered. Not just to the disturbances in the Vienna streets, but back to my disasters of the year before—to the humiliating business with Lotte and the way she had simply toyed with my body and my hopes. Disgusting! What kind of sixteen-year-old girl would know such things? And then, Frau Malteser and Herr Schneidermann—curses on them both! I bitterly regretted having had to depend on Rudi and his queer friends. That really brought home my humiliation. Even though I continued to see Rudi in the hallways of the Conservatory, I pretended I hadn't. He and his companions made my flesh crawl.

Life resumed. I did as little violin playing in the Beginners' orchestra as possible. I didn't have the time. Similarly, I paid no attention to my composition courses. Most of my hours were spent at the keyboard. But my interest in Dr. Böhm's conducting class was burgeoning. Sometimes, fellow students got to lead the Second orchestra, sometimes even the First. But not I. Not yet.

Some student instrumentalists—violinists, cellists, and clarinetists—were excellent. You could tell they were on their way to joining good orchestras or becoming soloists. At the same time, I thought most of my fellow conducting students to be dreadful: no sense of rhythm, tonal balance, or whether the orchestra was even playing in tune. It was unbelievable! Sometimes, I could barely keep from laughing out loud. I wondered whether Dr. Böhm himself, an intense short man, had not come down with Beethoven's own ailment—deafness. He didn't seem to hear a thing.

Under Professor Starker's guidance, I was preparing a series of short programs suitable for student recitals. But I rarely got to perform outside the practice room. One particular reason was another pianist, a year or so older than I, close to his diploma. Everybody seemed to adore him. He was Eduard van Vleiman from Amsterdam, originally named Yudl Fleischmann! His appearance was puzzling. Far from resembling a typical Jew-boy, with a huge nose and oily ringlets, he was tall and thin and looked fastidious. In fact, he resembled portraits of Chopin. He reminded me of Rudi—not at all like those hilarious caricatures of Jews you used to see in *Kikeriki* and other satirical papers. I remembered Dr. von Hornberger's remarks about the Jewish talent for adaptation and could understand how Yudl Fleischmann could turn himself into Eduard van Vleiman, a "true Hollander." Just the way Frankl Karl Slonimski had transformed himself into Fridolin Karl back in Eisenstadt.

But, I had to admit, van Vleiman played the piano like a god. He had performed at four student assemblies and had been stormily applauded each time. He could, if he chose, provide the full range of a traditional recital. He could begin with Scarlatti, then move on to Mozart, Beethoven, Schumann, Bach-Busoni, and Moussorgsky—and play Chopin wonderfully besides. I recognized that he was dazzling. His hands were huge and strong. It seemed there was nothing he could not do. I joined the other piano students who crowded around him in fear and envy.

I complained to Professor Starker.

"What is the point of trying?" I said. "Why does Eduard van Vleiman need the Vienna Conservatory? Why does he need any of us?" I got up from the piano and stamped about angrily.

Professor Starker smiled. "What's the matter?" he asked. "Are we not all proud of Herr van Vleiman? Why should mention of his name cause you to perspire?"

I dared scowl.

"I assure you," he said, "there is room on God's earth for both of you!"

At his command, I returned to Beethoven's *Diabelli Variations*. I was working on no. 23 of the set, the allegro assai. This was the stuff for which Carl Czerny's *School of Velocity* had prepared me, not only extremely fast but also thrilling, abrupt changes from loud to soft. Professor Starker had me play through it twice. He nodded slowly. "Sehr schön," he said. "You handle fire with distinction, but what about less savage matters?"

I knew what he meant. Near the beginning of the entire set, the second and third variations were mysteries to me. Oh, the notes were not difficult—quite easy, as a matter of fact. The second was formed of alternating chords shared between the right and left hands. It called for subtlety and gradation. But the third variation—ah, the third— what a monster! No, that is the wrong word. It presented no technical difficulty. It was a quiet progression of notes. I'd think I'd grasped it— but then I hadn't. At the next to the last line, it is as though the world suspends. It is mysterious, elusive. That was how Professor Starker described it. I could feel in my heart how it should sound, but I could not produce it. Was this really Beethoven? Was he really deaf when he wrote it? Could he hear what I could not play? Still, I worked to pre- pare recitals that I knew I would have no chance of playing as long as van Vleiman was on the scene.

* * *

The following week in Dr. Böhm's conducting class, I finally had a chance to take up the baton. We had practiced beating double time, three-quarter time, six-eight time, and all kinds of subdivided meters in between while Dr. Böhm played at the piano. We attempted the sec- ond movement of Tschaikovsky's Sixth Symphony, the *Pathétique*, the one that resembles a waltz in three-quarter time, but then turns out to be a tricky and unusual five-four time.

My fellow students? One tone-deaf fool after another. Dr. Böhm signaled the first to step to the podium. He was Gunther Jutlander, a tall blond-haired idiot—handsome, but stupid. All he could talk about was the superiority he felt he derived from his Viking ancestors. We were to conduct the second movement of Beethoven's First Symphony, the andante cantabile. Gunther had no idea what to do. He provided the upbeat to start things off, but it soon became clear that he was fol- lowing the players rather than leading them. He ignored the most ele- mentary things. Melodic lines were softer than the accompanying fig- ures, so that they could barely be heard. He had no sense of dynamics but displayed everything on the same dreary level of sound, no *fortes*, no *pianos*, no gradations between. It was as though he had no ears. He did not even have the players tune up before they started, and the intonation was disgusting. Gunther had the good looks I would have killed for, but good looks don't beat time.

Dr. Böhm allowed the wretched Gunther fifteen minutes. Before he stepped down, Gunther actually turned around and bowed gravely to us, his fellow students, even though our arms were firmly folded. No hint of applause for that dismal rubbish. It had been painful. He was followed by two other equally hopeless people. I couldn't believe how awful it was to listen to indifferently presented music. What's more, in a conservatory? Now it was my turn. At first, I hadn't been interested in conducting. It was merely a course requirement, a change from my driving concentration on the piano. Now, what with the dismal performances we had just heard, I was aware of something new stirring in my heart.

I stepped up to the platform and looked out at the orchestra. It was a fair-sized group of about forty or fifty. I had to repress an urge to giggle. Nerves. But I had studied the music—committed it to memory, in fact—so I didn't need the score. I raised my baton and my eyebrows at the second violins and, indicating the tempo with a silent "free bar," gathered them into the opening.

The sound of the violins, whose playing I had caused, so entranced me that I stopped beating time. The wonder of it! My arm was raised but motionless. Obediently, when I stopped, most of the second violins stopped too. One or two straggled on for a bar or so, but they fell silent also. They may not have been tuned up, but they were alert and watching me. The dozen or so conducting students behind me, paying jealous attention, burst into laughter. I was furious. Those tone-deaf idiots were making fun of me? The student players also laughed.

"Herr Kapp!" Dr. Böhm called from the back of the room. Face on fire, I whirled around. "Herr Kapp." He was smiling. "It is not sufficient that you merely indicate the beginning of the piece and then watch. You must continue to wave your arms. The players like it, even though they don't need you in order to play. It makes them happy to see that they are not the only ones at work."

My fellow students in the hall and the orchestra onstage roared. Was I so generally disliked? There had to be a reckoning. I had no idea what. But at that moment, it was the only thing that kept me there. I discovered that loathing others could provide a remedy for shame.

I discovered something else. I saw a familiar face. She was a pretty young woman, and she alone did not laugh. There were not many girls at the Conservatory then. If there were, they tended to study harp or perhaps piano. There would be few other opportunities for them in orchestras. I was still angry, which probably didn't help me to place her. I continued to scan the laughing faces—

"*Ruhe, stille!*" Dr. Böhm called in a surprisingly deep voice. He ordered me to begin again. I had heard Beethoven's First a number of times at concerts. It was also a favorite of the student orchestras. But I must confess, it was not until this moment, when I was leading this play-through, that I really heard it. I mentioned before that I was not particularly interested in composition. Well, this might not have been composition in the strictest sense, but you couldn't tell me I was not creating music. And the players, who just now had laughed, would respond. I would make them.

Again, we began with the second violins. It was much better. They managed to shape the phrase almost as I wanted, with that rise and fall in sound I wanted. In the sixth bar, the violas, cellos, and double-basses joined in, a fourth below—in a suggestion of a fugue. In the tenth bar, I signaled the bassoons and horns to enter, and finally, in the thirteenth, the first violins, the flutes, oboes, and clarinets. They all had their eyes on me and simultaneously read their parts in the way that orchestra players do. And they were responding. It was wonderful, truly wonderful! In bar 54 began that magical section where the kettledrum beats a slow, quiet tattoo—like the beating of my own heart— *ta-dum, ta-dum, ta-dum, ta-dum.* I had to stop the timpanist at that point—he just wasn't getting it right. No mystery to it. I saw, or rather heard, the trouble. The felt on his sticks was too hard. They sounded almost metallic.

"*Herr Paukenschläger!*" I called, "haven't you got softer sticks? The ones you're using sound too hard."

He looked up from his stool at the back of the orchestra. "Er, yes," he replied, "I've got softer ones." He held up some sets. "One pair is very soft," he said. "Do you want me to use those?"

"No, no, *not* the softest," I called back, "they'll sound muffled. I want to hear distinct beats, yes, but not to sound metallic, the way you played it." He tried another pair. Much better. Now, you may ask, how did I know this? I have no idea. I must have stumbled on it, even though I had never heard it. Is such a thing possible?

We tried the soft tattoo on the timpani again, together with the flute and the first violins weaving a staccato embroidery in triple-time. I couldn't have described it properly while it was happening. But that is how it was. The feeling was unforgettable, joy and a kind of pain at the same time, the thing that I sought to create at the piano, only much larger. I would seek it again and again throughout my life.

We ended the movement with Beethoven's three tranquil chords. A moment or two of rapt silence. I was startled when the orchestra beat their bows against their music stands; some stamped their feet like the orchestra in Eisenstadt. My head was spinning. I now greedily wanted to play the third movement, Beethoven's mad scherzo.

But Dr. Böhm was on his feet, consulting a large pocket watch. "Unhappily, we must stop for now," he said. "Herr Kapp," he added, "that was an interesting effort, but we must leave until next time a discussion of its good and not-so-good points."

I was instantly cast down. Not-so-good points? It had been incredibly good! Especially compared with the rest of the class. The orchestra and the conducting students drifted off in chattering groups. Dr. Böhm summoned me. I hastened over.

"What I find remarkable," he said, "is that, even though you have not faced this orchestra before—or any orchestra at all as far as I know, you seemed to know what to do. How?"

I had no idea. "Of course, I attend many concerts and the opera, and I've listened to the other students. But to tell the truth, Dr. Böhm, I don't know—"

Dr. Böhm put his head back and emitted a series of dry sounds, between laughs and coughs. "You listened to the other students and decided to do exactly the opposite. Impudent! Shameless!" But he didn't sound angry.

After Dr. Böhm left, I was alone but for one other person, the young woman I had noticed during the rehearsal. She walked toward me slowly, a slender, graceful figure, carrying her violin and bow, a shy smile on her face.

Now I recognized her. "Krisztina! Krisztina Kabós," I cried. "Krisztina from Eisenstadt. What are you doing here in Vienna? Have you been here all the time?"

She blushed and nodded. I remembered that she had had such a sweet face. Now, she had become beautiful.

"I have been here at the Conservatory since September," she said.

"And I remember those times we were together, yes—"

"I'm glad that you do."

"Why?" I asked.

She hesitated and blushed anew. "I don't know. You always seemed angry with me, or with something I said …" Her voice trailed away. She was silent for a moment. "Except for the time we played the Haydn trio in Eisenstadt and the lovely dinner with Herr Karl afterward. That was so nice—"

"You actually remember that, so long ago?" I must have been wearing the biggest and most foolish grin in the world.

"Not so long ago," she said. "Only five years."

"Only five years," I agreed.

"Well, were you?"

"Was I what?" I asked in return.

"Angry with me."

I groaned. All my acts of clumsy awkwardness came back to me. I shook my head. "No, of course not. Only stupid and shy."

"You? Shy?" She laughed. "My god, you had us playing so well this morning. Nothing shy about you."

Side by side, talking with each other, as though there had been no interruption in our acquaintance, we walked down to the main doors and out onto the fresh, sunny Ringstrasse as the honking autos and tramcars swept back and forth along the broad, curving boulevard. It was an unusually bright day for October. We stood on the steps of the Conservatory, with its ornately carved windows and crenellated spires, completely absorbed in each other.

I was ravenously hungry. I was made so tense by my impending appearance before the student orchestra that I had been unable to eat supper last night or breakfast in the morning. I was exhausted, felt suddenly weak, and sagged back against the wall. Krisztina gave a small cry.

"It's all right," I said. "I'd been worrying about the class. I think I forgot to eat." I tried to smile. "It's happened like this before."

"Are you able to walk?" she asked. "May I go with you to a café where you could have something? Not far and not expensive?"

She took me by the arm and led me to a quiet, dark-paneled *Beisl* on the Josefsgasse, where, with a worried eye, she made sure, first, that I drank a large cup of milky coffee, and then munched on bread wrapped around Bratwurst and mustard. I think such a combination would be indigestible for me today, but I thought it delicious at the time, and it made me feel immediately better. Being with Krisztina completed the happiness. We talked about the old days for an hour or more, without the slightest difficulty or hesitation. And, wonder of wonders, we could speak in Hungarian, the blessed mother tongue, as well as in German. In my completely agreeable mood, I forgot that there was no room in my abstemious budget for such extravagance as lunch in a *Beisl*. I would not afford meat until Sunday. Back to earth with a bump when the waiter presented the bill. Not enough money.

To my profound embarrassment, Krisztina seized the check, opened her purse, and counted out some coins.

"You look as if you need someone to take care of you at the moment," she said cheerfully. "I'll make sure you pay for me if we see each other again."

I was humiliated by her gesture. I wanted to rush out of that cheerful, chattering place and leave her there. Foolishness seemed second nature with me. For once, I restrained myself from behaving stupidly with Krisztina. But for several minutes, I could not speak.

After a while, we walked out of the *Beisl*, blinking in the sunshine.

"Would you like me to accompany you home?" I asked.

"It's not really necessary," she said, suddenly shy. "It's not really far away—I mean, I have to take the tramcar to the Klausgasse, near the sports fields. If it's a fine day, I usually walk."

"Have you got your own room? Has your family come to Vienna with you? Are you perhaps staying with relatives? Have you—" The questions came in an anxious rush.

"The answers are no, no, and no," she said twinkling. I looked blank. "I mean I haven't got my own room. I live with a roommate in a residence. My family did not come to Vienna. My father had to find a new first violin for his string quartet. And I am not staying with relatives, although I have an aunt and uncle here in Vienna who keep an eye on me and with whom I occasionally go to church and have dinner on Sundays."

That was the wonderful thing about living in a big city, and not a provincial town like Szombathely. The anonymity of it all. In Szombathely, I would never have been able to have a conversation in public with a beautiful girl. People would have stood and stared, making all kinds of comments, making sure "accidentally" to bump into one's parents and guardians, eagerly looking for scandal, if not actually creating it. But this was Vienna, the city of riots and shootings. It occurred to me that most of my scandalous doings last year had taken place under cover of darkness—the business with Lotte and my piano being trundled through the streets. The Viennese don't accept everything calmly, but certainly more calmly than people in the provinces.

"And where do you stay?" asked Krisztina.

"Not far, near the Old General Hospital." I was torn between wanting this conversation to continue and a sudden hunger to return to my piano and practice.

She sensed my unease. "I should be going," she said cheerfully. "It's three o' clock. I have my chamber music class. We'll see each other again. How can we not?"

I reversed myself. Now, I didn't want her to go. I felt completely mixed up. "Chamber music? What sort of stuff are you doing?"

"Beethoven," she said with a smile so open and lovely that it made me gasp. "The fifteenth quartet, the Opus 132." She assumed a mock-serious expression. "Profound," she uttered in a deep voice. "But so long and exhausting. That slow movement! I feel like taking a cure afterward." Then reverting to her usual face: "That's what my father would say. But it's so beautiful. Now, I must run."

"Yes, yes," I stammered, awkward again, reverting to German. "*Auf Wiedersehen*, or—" I dared something warmer "—as the Viennese tell their friends, *Servus!*"

"Or, as the Viennese say to special friends, *Tschüs!*" She turned away and marched off with healthy, quick steps, leaving me in a state of delight. I was quite captivated. But at the same time, I couldn't deny that I was relieved that she had left. Strange, strange, my desire for opposites.

* * *

Back at my piano, I began as usual with my scales, chords, and arpeggios. I tried to apply what Professor Starker had been demonstrating

125

about good posture at the piano. I tried to be poised and relaxed at the same time, so as somehow not to use all my energy and stamina in my first piece.

"You are young now and probably don't fully understand," Professor Starker had said, "but one expends an awful lot of energy when playing. A serious musician cannot afford to consume himself like that. I take it you look forward to a career that lasts longer than six months."

It was hard to learn new ways, but I persevered. It helped. As I worked at the *Diabelli*, it was hard to keep my mind fixed. It alighted on Krisztina, the student orchestra, and back to Krisztina again. The morning had been packed with events. I think I had fallen in love. Krisztina was so beautiful, her smile so lovely. She had not changed a bit in that regard since Eisenstadt. And she had been so open, had immediately reinvited me into her acquaintanceship. My mind returned to the rehearsal, where—with small knowledge of how an orchestra worked—I had created a performance of the Beethoven movement. It had been good. I knew it in my blood.

What should be my next step? I craved suddenly both the piano and the podium. Was it possible to possess both? I certainly desired both. To make the tension go away, I plunged into one of the fast and furious *Diabelli* variations, not thinking of Professor Starker's advice about relaxation. Instead, the long, sensitive face of my "rival," the so-called van Vleiman, filled my mind. I decided that I detested those features of his, the soulful eyes and the hollowed-out cheeks. He still reminded me of Rudi, for one thing, and while I tried to ignore his "Jewish condition," it nevertheless nagged at me—as it would whenever I felt unsettled. However, the main trouble was that he alone stood in my way. Nobody mentioned me and him in the same breath. That angered me. I could never win the First Piano Prize and play the senior recital while van Vleiman was dazzling everybody.

What I was thinking made me tense. I had to stop playing. My hands and fingers were so stiff that they cramped. So much for Professor Starker's urging me to relax!

While I frantically kneaded my fingers, I tried to think. One way or another, I was going to have the First Piano Prize *and* become a Kapellmeister at the same time. How? I couldn't say right off. I was going to work hard at the piano and drive myself to insurmountable levels of proficiency. No one should be able to say that I was a fraud. Next, somehow I had to become known among the conducting faculty, concentrating my efforts on Dr. Böhm, but also making myself familiar to his colleagues so that they could not help but accept me.

In addition, I needed something else. Trying one's hardest didn't ensure a thing. Among the company of hacks and timeservers that formed the bulk of my fellow students, there were some exceptionally talented people—some incredibly gifted, in my opinion. But I needed something else. Ability would not be sufficient.

Something popped up in my mind. I remembered that frightening thing that had occurred during Dr. von Hornberger's speech back in Eisenstadt—frightening but exciting at the time. Once more, I saw the two students from Wittenberg with the long scars on their cheeks, watched as they hurled themselves upon the meek, inoffensive man who had dared interrupt Dr. von Hornberger. They beat him and threw him out like a sack of old bedding. I wished for the courage to do a thing like that. You know, just to take things into one's own hands, if one had to, and no one daring to object. *Would I actually wish to beat someone senseless?* Being in charge was what I wanted. Making someone listen to me—or having him pay the consequences—was the thing. Controlling the orchestra this morning had been like that. Coming to the end of a long, difficult Beethoven sonata, with everything working just right, raising one's eyes to meet the gaze of an audience, their eyes filled with admiration and awe—that was like it too. If only I could have those things, I might not have to beat someone senseless. These thoughts quite wore me out. I had to leave the piano and throw myself on my bed.

* * *

Next morning, I didn't feel like dropping into my usual café. I bought a mug of coffee at a curbside stall outside the General Hospital, near my rooms. I was on my way to another piano lesson with Professor Starker. I leaned against the stall, sipping at the hot, strong brew, trying to clear my head of cobwebs. I hoped that Krisztina might happen by, although I knew her tramcar traveled along the Gablenzgasse, a completely different route. But, wonder of wonders, someone else who was on my mind did appear—the so-called Eduard van Vleiman himself. As usual, pale, thin, and nervous, he had just walked out of the main hospital building and attempted to slink along the pavement without being noticed. I called out to him. He jumped and pretended to see me for the first time.

"Eduard!" I called again. I had to shout to be heard above the traffic and the screech of tramcars. "Have you been visiting somebody this time of day? Is anybody ill?"

He shifted uncomfortably from foot to foot, looking up and down the Lazarettgasse, avoiding my gaze. "No, it's nothing like that." He was anxious to be off.

What he was able to do at the piano both fascinated me and increased my hatred of him and his cool, precise fingers. I made a flippant remark, revealing my thoughts more than I intended.

"Have you come to the hospital because of yourself, Eduard?"

He stared at me for several moments. "Can I trust you?" he said in a low voice.

Was he about to confide in me? Was he more of a helpless innocent than I was? Had he not the faintest idea what I thought of him?

"You see, you see," he stammered, "I was preparing a recital—I don't know if you've heard—as part of a faculty concert to be given at the end of term." I had heard. I had not been invited to play. "The thing is, the thing is ..." van Vleiman spoke in an agitated way. He splayed out his fingers in front of me, his long, powerful fingers. "Look at them," he said, "can you see anything?"

I peered down. "What am I supposed to see?"

"Take hold of my hand and squeeze," he begged.

I did so. I felt the large hand attempt to squeeze back, but it was unable to. I looked up. "My goodness, Eduard, what's wrong? Are you crying?"

Van Vleiman sagged against a lamppost and wept silently. I watched him, the student I most envied and feared, standing at this roadside together with me, quite in pieces.

"I can't feel a thing with them. Not a thing," he moaned.

"When I took your hand just now, it looked all right to me. You can't feel with either of them? When did this happen?"

"I don't know, I don't know," he moaned. "I noticed something funny two weeks ago. I thought it would go away, but it got worse. I've just spent five hours at the hospital. I had to come here at three in the morning, I was so frightened. Nobody paid attention to me for the first two hours, but I've been seeing doctors since then. Nobody has any idea what could be wrong. I had to wait until seven o'clock for a specialist to arrive. I was with him more than an hour. He doesn't know what the matter is. He thinks I've been playing the piano too long, too hard, too—too—much." He looked wildly up and down the street. "It's true, I have, I have!" He began to sob aloud.

Passersby looked at us with curiosity but continued to hurry along. This, after all, was Vienna. But the toothless old woman who owned the curbside stall came over and offered Eduard a free mug of coffee. Free, I noted bitterly, while I, poor as a church mouse, had to pay.

"If I can't feel the keys, I can't play, can I!" he wailed. "One of the doctors said this might be the first step to complete paralysis!" His voice shook, the long, aristocratic nose dripped. I shuddered and, without thinking, handed him my own handkerchief. Whoever that doctor was, I didn't know whether to be grateful to him, because I wanted to see Eduard discomforted—or make the hospital get rid of him. I could be the next pianist to whom he said something as stupid as that. Heaven knows, I played and practiced as relentlessly, as obsessively as I believe Eduard did.

Eduard vigorously blew into my handkerchief. I indicated that he keep it.

"I think I might go away for a few days," he said. "I've got an aunt and uncle in Linz that I can stay with. Perhaps," he resumed, with a pleading look, as though I were in charge of his case, "having a rest, not playing for a few days, not doing anything, will help." He shook his head. "One of my teachers always noticed the way I sat and used my hands. He used to tell me that I was too rigid and tense." He grimaced. "I suppose he was right. But I'm really frightened, you know?" He looked at me hesitantly. "Would you be kind enough to do me a tremendous favor?" he asked.

"Of course," was my immediate reply. "How can I help?"

Eduard gave a tentative smile, the first I had seen that morning. "I wouldn't want anyone to know about this, not the Conservatory and not Dr. Sonnenlicht"—he named his piano professor. "If you could somehow tell people that I had to return to Amsterdam for a few days—family trouble, or something like that. If you could tell them that I will certainly return to resume my studies, and of course play the senior recital, and so forth and so on." His voice trailed off; his eyes, like a puppy's, shone in wet gratitude.

"Of course, I will, Eduard. Of course," I said.

He tried to grasp my hand. His hand was massive, but felt flabby, could exert no pressure.

"Many thanks, many thanks," he said over and over.

"That's really all right, Eduard," I replied. Another grateful look.

"As a matter of fact," I said, "I've been hoping so much to meet you and talk about music and the piano and what you like to play and how you manage fingering and other things."

"Really? I had no idea." He unsuccessfully tried to grasp my hand again while speaking in a rush. "It's all my fault, really. I don't mix with people much—I'm too shy, I suppose. I come out of my room only when I have a lesson or to play the piano somewhere. I suppose that's true. When I'm playing, I forget everything else." He emitted a sudden high-pitched laugh.

I kept telling him that it was nothing, I was happy to help, I had admired his playing for so long, and I was glad to have met him at last—not under these unhappy circumstances but glad nonetheless.

As we walked in the direction of the Conservatory, he continued to speak nonstop in that high-pitched Dutch accent of his—which sounded vulgar. "I think I have been too busy and self-absorbed to meet people and make friends," he said. He spoke like one who has been silent a long time, all bottled up. When he looked at me, he trembled like an anxious, overfriendly dog.

How looks can deceive. He had seemed such a snob, so superior, so fastidious. It occurred to me that, precisely because he was so innocent, he had no way of sizing up the people around him. Not an innocent exactly, but perhaps a fool. I was also getting used to the idea that simply having enormous talent, even becoming a *dazzling* artist—that was what people said about him—did not mean he knew what was going on in the world. One thing seemed to have nothing to do with the other.

Take myself, for instance. Myself! I abruptly halted. Eduard, in his nonstop chatter, did not notice and kept on walking. I prided myself on being an exceptional pianist, perhaps on the way to greatness. But look at where he was—and where I was! What was wrong with being jealous and fearful? The way life and others had treated me left me with the conviction that I was in constant danger. Mother had slaved for me, with piles of other people's laundry and dirt. I shuddered to think of her constant anxiety to maintain us. We staggered from crisis to crisis. A new inflation threatened. We had barely survived the last one. What would Mama do now? What could help? Madame Polkovska was always insisting that art and music made us better people. Well, what about Professor Schneidermann? Nothing but a despicable monster! And what about Dr. von Hornberger? I had mixed thoughts about him. At least he offered something. I had lived through the riots and street-fighting just outside my door. Why should I be expected to be better than those people, to be noble? Because I was an artist? My fellow men ought to be grateful for Bach, Beethoven, and Mozart. I could give them something of value in the career I looked forward to, and I looked forward to being well recompensed, and why not?

Eduard wished to leave me at the door of the Conservatory. He made to shake hands once more. Now, he was not able even to clasp mine properly. In this condition, how would he be able to play? But he smiled bravely.

"I won't come into the building," he said. "I don't want to see anybody I know. I just have to collect my bag from my lodgings and go straight to the station. I'll be safely in Linz with my relatives before long." He gave me another moist look. "You are a good friend." He moved to embrace me, but I stepped back. I was having none of that.

"Remember, dear Hermann, please say nothing." He turned and left.

With Professor Starker, I returned to my work on the *Diabelli*. I attacked it with zest. "You are certainly filled with fire this morning," he said, looking at me over his spectacles. Professor Starker was correct. I had just finished the whirlwind variation 23 again, to his partial satisfaction. He was never completely satisfied, mind you, but he never slapped my fingers with a ruler. A great advance.

"Not bad, not bad at all," he said. "Since you're in a mood to slay dragons, let's go right to the fugue."

I was happier and happier. I was in the right spirit for that ferocious fugue. I felt reckless and dangerous. Things were surely coming together. I knew how to get Eduard out of my way. The fugue expressed savage joy.

I had been working on it for some time. It was the culmination of the entire set of variations. When that stupid Herr Diabelli had approached the divine Beethoven with his condescending request for just one variation on his insignificant waltz, he never realized what he was in for. Diabelli meant to publish a collection made up of one variation each from composers of the day. People said it was supposed to be a joke or to raise funds for some charity. But the master had responded with superb contempt. He wrote, not one, but thirty-three variations and thus twisted his finger in the pretentious Herr Diabelli's eye. When I played this fugue, I would stand at Beethoven's side, sneering at the sneerers. I was about to strike the E-flat that begins the piece. Professor Starker stopped me. "You should begin with variation 31, the largo right before it, and *then* lead into the fugue. They belong together."

He startled me. I scrambled two pages back in the score. I was not on comfortable terms with variation 31. Like variations 2 and 3, which I have mentioned before, I found it mysterious and not easy to grasp. In particular, it called for languor and the sensual, seemed to mock regularity and strictness—seductive and feminine with its festoons of decorations and trills. It didn't seem quite German. It reminded me of Lotte. My god, where had she come from? I saw her clearly before me. I had become sexually aroused while playing Beethoven!

Professor Starker noticed that I was not at ease. "Perhaps we can return to this later," he said. "Perhaps you need to know this better." I could breathe again. "But," he went on, "the two variations belong to each other—you must realize this. And not only because the last note of one leads directly to the other. But also because they are somewhat mirrors of each other. One is all feminine softness"—*Did he know of my embarrassment?*—"but, in its truth, it is like steel. And the fugue that follows is rigorous and masculine, but also, strangely, possesses tenderness." When he talked like that, it was hard to follow what he meant.

"Look," he said kindly, "this is a great and complex piece of music, the kind you will study all your life. And you will make discoveries throughout your life—may it be long and healthy! So don't worry if you don't get to see heaven on the first day."

"If you please, Herr Professor, I would like to say—" I wanted to tell him all about Eduard's infirmity. But I was nervous about taking that step.

"No, forgive me for interrupting you," he said, "but I just want to add this. When you practice the fugue at home—and we are about at the end of our lesson—it would be a mistake to ignore those...feminine aspects. The music *is* fierce and masculine, but not savage. You will see, following bar 71, and at other places, you can dare to be lyrical. You may be playing a *Hammerklavier*, but please, you don't have to hammer!"

He rose. The lesson was over. We would see each other in three days. My next duty was to play violin in the Beginners' orchestra, made up of those obliged to fulfill the curricular requirement. Few wanted to be there. Most were unable to produce much more than strangled howls—a company of cats being murdered. I sawed away with the rest, allegedly playing the slow movement of *Eine Kleine Nachtmusik*. It was hideous. The senior conducting student who led us waved his arms with a blissful smile on his face, as though he were before the heavenly band itself. It gave me time to think. I would not have an opportunity to inform fellow piano students until later. But I intended to spread word of Eduard's condition. I had no other choice. I did not make the rules. If one couldn't play, he couldn't play. It was that simple. The ordeal of the Beginners' orchestra mercifully ended at three, having achieved no noticeable improvement.

* * *

On my way out of rehearsal, I ran into another of Professor Starker's piano students, Gustl Wiedner, an amiable sort, with a pale, bleary face and cropped blond hair. He was said to spend as much time as he could with young ladies, to drink too much, and consequently to neglect the piano. He was said to face expulsion if he did not mend his ways. I had nothing in particular to do with him. But he grabbed my arm in passing.

"Hermann," he said urgently, "I'm glad to see you." I paused. "Listen," he said, "I think we can do each other a big favor, but you have to agree right away. There's no time for messing about."

"What is it?" He looked like a wreck—red-rimmed eyes bulging from his pasty face. He clearly had been doing too much of something.

Gustl told me. The rumors were true. Professor Starker had

133

threatened to drop him because he was not studying or practicing enough—and Professor Starker, unlike Herr Schneidermann, was a kind, gentle soul. So what had Gustl done to bring this about?

He explained what was already well known. He had a job playing the piano in some café. He was there every night from nine till three in the morning, with no more than three or four hours of sleep. He was to be seen stumbling around with shaking hands and puffy eyes. He had indeed been threatened with expulsion for neglecting his studies and poor performance. He feared his father might disown him if he were expelled.

"Hermann, you've got to help me," he pleaded. Two such requests in a single day! What on earth was going on? He gripped my lapels. "You've *got* to fill in for me at the Café Gonzaga—tomorrow night, and the next night. Those two nights. Somebody else will take over, but he can't start until Friday. You've *got* to say yes! An emergency!"

"You're insane," I shouted. "I haven't the slightest idea how to play piano in a nightclub. I wouldn't know the first thing." I moved back so that he released my lapels. "I understand that you spend six hours there each night. I wouldn't know how to fill six minutes with that kind of music, let alone six hours!" The whole thing was absurd. "Café Gonzaga?" I snorted.

I turned to leave, but Gustl blocked me. "Listen," he hissed. "Will you just listen a minute!" Other students were bustling by in the echoing corridor. Some looked curiously at us; most paid no attention.

"I don't know what you imagine you'd have to play at the Gonzaga," he said, "but it's not ragtime or show tunes, or anything like that. The owner doesn't expect that kind of music. That's why I can do it, and that's why I know you can too."

I laughed. "You mean you play Bach, Beethoven, and Brahms all night?"

"Not the really heavy stuff, not all night long," he said seriously. "You can do some of that, but mainly they expect the kind of music you'd play for encores."

I was becoming interested. "Exactly what kind of place is the Gonzaga? Is it a dance hall or a nightclub or something like that?"

"No, no, no, nothing like that," he replied. He had caught me. "The Gonzaga is one of those smart, intimate clubs in the *Innere Stadt*." I knew the old, historic town center of Vienna. "It's a place where a rich married man can bring his little *Schatzie*. They sip champagne, look at the candles, and listen to you play Brahms's Lullaby and the *Liebestraum* all night. For all they care, you can play them over and over. The place is high class and quiet; there's practically no talk. The girls are usually beautiful, and their heads are usually empty—they have nothing to say, and it doesn't matter. They're not there for conversation. The lights are dim, and the waiters tiptoe about. Nobody bothers you. You just play slowly and softly to fill the silence, to…to create a wonderful, cozy atmosphere. The only thing is that you have to be there—with occasional breaks—for six hours."

"For just two nights?"

"For just two nights."

"Brahms's Lullaby and the *Liebestraum* for six hours."

"No, no, be serious. But they like music of that kind—restful. You don't want to get these rich, old codgers excited and cause heart attacks. Leave that to the girls. You get paid only twelve *schillings* a night, but the old codgers tip well—very well."

"Why choose me?"

"Well"—Gustl studied my face—"don't be offended," he said, "but you always look as though you could use some extra funds. You give the appearance of being desperate in the money department. I hope I'm wrong—"

"No," I sighed, "you're not wrong." His well-tailored jacket was rumpled as though he slept in it, but clearly looked expensive. That reminded me.

"What about clothes? This Gonzaga place sounds like I couldn't play there dressed like this." I indicated my own barely presentable garb.

"That's nothing." Delighted by my interest, he grinned. "We're almost the same height and size. That's another reason I thought of you. I'll lend you a dinner jacket and a wing collar and teach you how to tie a cravat." I hesitated. "Say you'll do it. Please. Only two nights! I know you take your studies seriously, and it's an enormous favor. But only for two nights!"

"What happens after that?"

"I already told you. I've arranged for Nicki Fassbinder—do you know him?—to handle everything after that. But the problem is, he cannot start until Friday. And, after that, you wouldn't have to worry about it anymore."

For two nights? I couldn't see much wrong with that. After a moment, I nodded.

"Wunderbar!" he cried and wrung my hand. He hastily scribbled an address. "Look, this is where I live, not far. Why don't you drop in—say, eight o'clock this evening. You can try on the dinner jacket, and then we'll walk over to the Gonzagagasse—there *is* such a street, believe me—and I'll introduce you to the owner, Herr Zuckerweiss. He's a Jew, of course, but a decent type. I'll recommend you—praise you to the skies. There'll be no trouble at all, and Herr Zuckerweiss will thank us both for solving his problem." Suddenly happy, he spun around to leave with a cheery wave.

This was turning out to be an exhausting day. I felt that I had lived two lives already. I had a sudden yearning to see Krisztina. It would comfort me. After searching and checking various locations, I spotted her through the glass panel of a small rehearsal hall up on the fourth floor. I crept in and sat at the darkened back of the room. At the front, bathed in light, Krisztina was playing first violin. Grouped around her were another young woman on second violin and two young men on viola and cello. At that moment, they were indeed rehearsing the slow movement of Beethoven's fifteenth quartet. I had read up on it in a zeal to find out all I could about Beethoven. It was described as a hymn of thanks after illness—*Heiliger Dankgesang eines Genesenen*—written in the Lydian mode. To watch them, you might have thought Krisztina and her companions were priests serving at a holy rite, their faces fixed in concentration, the music solemn, sustained, and deliberate. You could almost see their stretched-out nerves. Their professor sat to one side, head bowed. Krisztina's face bore an expression of exalted suffering. In spite of my scorn for holy things, I was touched, close to the spirit of the music. The movement drew to its close and finally died away, the players keeping their bows on their strings, sustaining their tones right into silence.

All at once, it was over. They put down their instruments and heaved great sighs—laughed in relief. The viola player stood up and stretched. "Isn't it possible for us to go to dinner after that long, long *molto, molto adagio* and finish the quartet after we eat? I'm exhausted. I have to lie down."

The professor ignored him. Perhaps he had heard it before. "I want to tell all of you that you are playing magnificently, even Herr Tauber"—nodding at the viola player—"who evidently would prefer a life in comic opera." He stood. "Until we meet at the next rehearsal, dear students."

I didn't want Krisztina to know that I had been watching her. I quietly slipped downstairs, and waited outside the great doors of the Conservatory. Another demonstration by the Young Nationalist Patriots League was in progress, usual around that time of day. They marched without bugles, just to the beat of a solitary drum. It was stirring to see their disciplined, determined faces. It made you feel secure. The policemen directing traffic cleared the road for them, watching with smiles of approval. They knew who their friends were.

"What a nice surprise," I exclaimed when, within minutes, Krisztina appeared.

"Just *nice*?" she asked and then blushed.

"No, not just nice," I said. "*Very* nice." We giggled like silly people. And then, before I knew how it happened, I was clasping her, kissing her mouth. She held me with one arm, the other clinging to her violin case. I jumped back, startled at my audacity. She seemed not at all displeased. Just then, Dr. Böhm walked down the steps with his rapid pace, wagging his forefinger in mock disapproval.

"Ah, Vienna, Vienna, thou immodest Vienna," he said but continued to smile as he proceeded to the corner of the Ringstrasse.

Krisztina and I both blushed and began talking at the same time.

"Would you like to have a—" I had to break off my invitation. I'd forgotten I had no money to pay for coffee. I had no wish to repeat the embarrassment of her paying for me.

Instead, we strolled and talked. We sat on a bench in the Volksgarten. The air was cool and fresh. The trees shielded us somewhat from the traffic noises. As before, I was entranced. She was charming and friendly, so pretty and wholesome-looking. I couldn't take my eyes off her. She seemed such a contrast to the unwholesome ideas passing through my head. One time, when we embraced again, we had to jump apart when others appeared. I looked at her in wonder. I couldn't help remembering my horrible episode with Lotte just a year before. Lotte had seemed sweet and demure at first. And then, you know how that ended. I think part of me was on the alert, waiting for something disturbing. But this was truly different. She and I talked about many things: differences between Hungarians and

Austrians, for instance, lots of laughter there; between Vienna and Budapest, where she had been born—Budapest was more beautiful. What was better? To live in a republic or under the empire? Or what was worse than being ruled by an admiral without a navy? She had never thought about that before. Much merriment. And, of course, what we had been doing all these years since Eisenstadt.

"I will never forget that serious boy in the black velvet suit and the large white collar! Looking so determined, sure of himself, and cocky. It was wonderful!" She sighed. "I've never stopped thinking about it—and also the music we played together." She chattered on.

I enjoyed listening, but uncomfortable thoughts remained. Once again, I was in a public park with an attractive and amiable girl. And she had used a somewhat vulgar word—cocky. Not terrible, I suppose, but unexpected from her. And I was still poor, without substance, therefore vulnerable.

Krisztina fell silent and stared at the neatly tended flowerbeds. "Do you know what those are?" she asked, nodding toward some autumn blooms. I shook my head, suddenly gloomy. A clock chimed five times. The same hour I had met Lotte.

Abruptly, Krisztina got to her feet. "I'm hungry," she said cheerfully. "Aren't you?" This was the dreaded moment. I would have to confess—if she hadn't already guessed—my poverty.

"I suppose you're going to your lodgings," I said, trying to be brave.

"Eventually," she smiled, "but it's still early. Why don't we eat something?"

I made a despairing gesture. "I haven't got enough money to pay for us both. You've already paid for my lunch—"

She laid her hand on my mouth. "That's enough about money, Ferenc. Shouldn't one Magyar help another?" she said. "I'm only doing what you would if I needed it."

"No, no. You misunderstand me, Krisztina. I can pay for myself—"

"But you cannot pay for me," she broke in. "All right then," she said with determination. "I'm still hungry—now more than ever—and I mean to eat. So I'll pay for my meal, and you'll pay for yours. Is that all right?"

It seemed every last humiliating detail was revealed. I could not afford another *Beisl* or café this month. I usually bought bread and cooked meat, which I would munch at my own table, together with coffee I made on a spirit stove. I told Krisztina all this. She was not in the slightest dismayed. She promptly accompanied me and bought the identical bread, boiled beef, pickled onions, and apples that I did. She added a jar of mustard and a half bottle of wine. I would never have thought of those. And to my mingled horror and delight, she walked with me to my rooms. This time, there was no Frau Malteser. We were alone and safe in my rooms off the courtyard. Krisztina cleared my table, cautiously inspected my dishes, and laid out food. We ate, drank wine, talked, and laughed. I had not felt this easy since Herr Karl's banquet at Eisenstadt.

We fell silent. It was still light outside. I rose awkwardly and walked around the table. She watched me with a hint of a smile. "Yes?" she said. Everything was still. I dropped to my knees before her and put my head next to hers. She held it gently and began to hum. In the half light, the world was hushed and far away. I kissed her, interrupting the melody. She kissed me back, a long, sweetly drawn-out kiss. I drew back and put out my hand to touch her breast. She was startled, her eyes grew wide, but she did not move back or push my hand away. I felt so daring, but she stayed where she was. Emboldened, I cupped her breast fully in my hand and caressed it. It felt wondrously soft and firm at the same time. Neither of us seemed able to breathe.

"Is it all right with you?" I finally murmured.

She looked at me earnestly. "*Je suis contente.*"

We couldn't stop. Everything was sweet. We kissed and kissed until we almost died. My hands roved all over. She did not resist. I was now the experienced one. I pushed aside and pulled down clothing, my fingers discovered a soft wet center. I plunged into such unbearable sweetness. I cried out, my cry matched by hers.

When I came to myself, we were on my bed, Krisztina and I side by side, quite still. I raised myself. It was completely dark. A lamp had turned itself on outside in the courtyard and gleamed through the window. There were tears on her face.

"It hurt," she said. "It was the first time."

I was stricken with remorse. "I'm sorry," I said. "I'm so truly sorry."

Krisztina winced as she stirred but drew me back to her. "No, I'm sorry to make such a fuss," she said. She kissed me again. "It was beautiful. I am so happy to be here with you." I rolled onto my back and sighed.

"You are easy in your heart—for the first time since I've known you," she said. "I can tell. Ever since Szombathely."

It was true. I could lie there, not a troubling thought in my head.

Krisztina stirred. "I must use your Klosett," she said shyly. "I think I'm bleeding." She gasped as she raised herself and looked down at the bed. "I'm terribly sorry—I've made such a mess. They tell me this is what happens." I had to get off the bed so that she could gather up the cover sheet to wash.

My new flat included a private bathroom. Krisztina disappeared, and I heard splashing water. In a while, she reappeared, not angry, I was relieved to see. She had removed her dress, presumably to wash it too.

"I hung up the sheet," she said. "No harm, it will dry." She lay down next to me in her slip, sighed, and kissed me on the cheek. I put my arm about her shoulders. We were together, side by side. "I think I have"—she paused—"liked you for a long time, you know, since we played that trio together in your teacher's parlor. You're wonderful at the piano—I've heard lots of players, but you are really, really good. So sensitive and strong." She took my hand and pressed it to her bosom.

I sighed again, contented; but as we lay there, listening to the ticking of my alarm clock, I wondered what her frank open gaze might expect from me. After that wonderful thing that had happened between us, I was feeling not so urgent. I had run out of things to say for the time being. She was smiling bravely at me, I think still in some pain, but clearly content as well. Don't mistake me—I was happy— but restless, thinking that it would not disturb me were she to go home soon. We could see each other, say, tomorrow or the next day. *Would it be awful if I were to say that?*

My eyes happened to catch the clock face, illuminated by the lamp outside. A quarter to eight! I had just fifteen minutes to meet Gustl! I would be late! I jumped off the bed and scrambled for clothes and shoes.

"Look," I was frantic. "I've got to meet someone, right away. Now, as a matter of fact!" I cursed as I struggled with knots in my bootlaces. Krisztina sat up, alarmed.

"It's all right," I panted as I rushed about. "You don't have to hurry.

Just leave when your dress is dry. I'm sorry I can't take you to your tramcar, but you know how to get to it—you turn to your right, follow the avenue to the Ringstrasse—and you'll know where you are."

"Are you leaving now, like this?" In the gloom, I could make out that she had her hand to her face. "When can we speak?"

The ticking clock told me I had a scant ten minutes. I would be terribly late. "I'll see you tomorrow," I shouted, "sometime at the Conservatory—somewhere, I'm sure." I rushed to the door and opened it. "When you go, just close it behind you. It will be all right like that. Sorry, sorry!" I began to run as hard as I could.

* * *

I arrived at Gustl's rooms fifteen minutes late. "I thought you might have backed out," he grinned out of his bloodshot eyes. I had run my guts out on the way over, and it was hard to speak. When I had recovered, Gustl ordered me to take off my shirt. I did so and replaced it with a starched one of his. He helped me with the collar studs. I put on his spare dinner jacket. "Almost a perfect fit," he declared. "Now the cravat." He stood behind me and demonstrated the bow tie—the folding, the tucking, the endless adjusting.

"*Voilà!*" he cried. "You did it! What do you think?"

I stared at my reflection in his bureau mirror. From the waist up, I looked quite the swell. It was better yet after I had smoothed my hair. In spite of my haggard appearance, having just run almost two kilometers, I looked presentable. Krisztina would have been proud to see me like this. But I had just fled from her in a panic. *Why in heaven had I done that?* I had never been terribly interested in Gustl's idiotic enterprise in the first place, but I could not remain in that room with Krisztina after we had been so close. I had to have a break after the things we had done.

Would she still be at my rooms? Should I return now? After all, we had just done this frightening and beautiful thing together. I should not have run off like that. But I was afraid of what she might expect. Would we just stare at each other? I released some pent-up breath. I was rattling myself over nothing. Of course, we would see each other later. I donned Gustl's extra pair of black trousers and, complete in my borrowed evening wear, walked with him to the *Innere Stadt*, to the Café Gonzaga.

He had described the place pretty well. Once past the nondescript entrance, the interior was dark red luxury—carpets, walls, tablecloths, lampshades—everything dark red. Waiters were arranging ashtrays and glasses—they were red too. To one side, upon a raised platform, stood a mahogany grand piano, elegantly carved, the lid raised. At one of the tables, smoking an enormous cigar, sat a small fat man, almost completely round—Gustl's Jew. Gustl nudged me forward.

"Herr Zuckerweiss," he said with a bow. "Bitte, permit me to introduce that accomplished colleague of mine at the Conservatory."

The owner regarded me with an unblinking stare out of bulging, heavy-lidded eyes. He said nothing but twisted the huge cigar in his mouth. After a while, he made a circular motion with his hand.

"Herr Zuckerweiss wishes you to turn around," Gustl whispered. "He wants to see you front and back."

I obeyed. "Slowly, slowly," Gustl murmured. Apparently I passed that test.

Herr Zuckerweiss murmured something. "The Herr Patron wishes you to play." I hadn't anticipated that. I had brought no music.

Herr Zuckerweiss was waiting. I was frozen. "For God's sake," hissed Gustl, "play something!" He gave me a sharp push.

I stumbled toward the daïs, sat, and began to play the *Liebestraum*. I knew it by heart. The piano was a wonderfully mellow old Blüthner—the first time I'd been at one. I played, if I might say, beautifully and apparently produced the desired atmosphere.

Herr Zuckerweiss seemed pleased. He grunted something else that I could not make out. I looked at Gustl. "The Herr Patron graciously invites you to spend an hour or two this evening as his guest and watch what happens here."

I was startled. "Tonight?" I asked.

"Why not?" said Gustl. "You're here, you're wearing the right clothes. It will be a wonderful opportunity. You'll get used to things—without a cover charge."

Herr Zuckerweiss grunted again and puffed out a plume of fragrant smoke.

"The Herr Patron approves of you," said Gustl, bowing toward the table, "and is pleased to have you in his establishment." How on earth Gustl could understand all that from two grunts and one puff of smoke, I had no idea. We backed away from the Herr Patron, bowing as though in a royal presence. Herr Zuckerweiss nodded and gave a gracious wave.

Gustl showed me to a tiny dressing room, separated from the passageway by only a curtain, where he was able to remove his jacket and relax every forty-five minutes or so. No sooner had we sat down than one of the ancient waiters tapped on the wall outside, drew back the curtain, and entered with a tray bearing sandwiches, two small glasses of *Schnaps*, and two mugs of beer. "With the compliments of the Herr Patron," he said before leaving.

Gustl whistled. "I told you, he has *definitely* taken a fancy to you," he said. "He's never sent *me* sandwiches. Only beer and some brandy." He lifted the bread and whistled again. "What luck! Paprika sausage. Dig in, my boy!"

The sausage was delicious. It wasn't until my second mouthful that I remembered that I had already eaten, no more than two hours before—and with whom I had eaten. It didn't prevent me from enjoying this meal. I really wished that Krisztina were here now. I had conquered all my qualms. I was impatient to see her. She would have enjoyed the whole mad chain of events. We would have a good laugh together later.

At nine o'clock, Gustl went out to the piano and began to play. I sat at a tiny table to one side, prepared to watch and listen. It was just as Gustl had said. The place was half-filled with couples, most of the men looking somewhat like Herr Zuckerweiss: fat and bald, all elderly and in evening clothes. The women were much younger, much more slender, and some I thought cheap-looking—heavy lipstick, tons of blue eyeshadow, cigarettes in ridiculously long holders. Krisztina, with her honesty, would roar with laughter and put these silly women to shame.

I needed to emulate Gustl, so I paid close attention. He didn't so much play as caress the keys while the men at the tables murmured to the young women. The women stared into the eyes of the men and held their hands while sipping champagne. The bent waiters crept back and forth, bringing more wine and tiny dishes of chocolates and fruits. It was Gustl, gently stroking the Blüthner, who bound the whole thing together. He looked so spiritual and poetic. The romantic gloom of the place concealed his pallor, his awful red eyes, and his belches—we had so relished our *Debreziner* sandwiches! I could see that it didn't really matter what he played. Any melodious tinkling would have served. I could kick myself for hesitating when first asked.

Now I had time to peer more closely at the young women. Some seemed vulgar and sluttish. But there were others who looked elegant and beautiful, as far as I could tell in that light. I tried not to stare openly. One young woman took my breath away—so beautiful! She sat a few tables off to the side, half-embracing her elderly gentleman. Her short black hair covered her forehead and was cut in a straight line just above heavily shadowed eyes. She looked directly at me over her escort's shoulder. As she stroked his plump neck, I could swear that she gave me a wink. I started and turned my attention back to Gustl. After a moment or two, I sneaked another glance her way. She got to her feet, leaned down, and kissed the man atop his hairless head. He handed her money.

She wore a long black gown covered with tiny beads. *Oh yes*, I thought, *this was a vamp right out of a film from America.* She had done her best to look like Theda Bara. She stepped daintily out into the dim rosy light on her way, I supposed, to the powder room. As she passed me, her purse slipped from her hand. In an instant, I was on it and gave it back to her. I don't believe anyone noticed.

"Danke," she said sweetly and continued on her way.

I had the overwhelming feeling that I should follow her. But I didn't. Fifteen minutes later, she returned. I stared expectantly at her but received not a glance in return. She resumed her seat next to her companion, placed her head next to his, as she had done before, and only now, looked straight at me again—while continuing to stroke his cheek.

The heavily draped, rich room with its subdued crimson lighting, the ugly, wealthy men carelessly placing wads of money on the waiters' trays, the exciting, beautiful young women murmuring in their gentlemen's ears, Gustl's soft piano—I found all this arousing. This really was the high life, a long way from Szombathely and Frau Malteser's garret. I belonged in places like this. At the same time, I sorely missed Krisztina. That young woman could stare at me as long as she wished. Krisztina was a hundred times better!

After about forty-five minutes, Gustl took a break. I joined him in his dressing room. "Well, how do you like things so far?" he asked with a too-broad smile. A waiter brought a glass. More *Schnaps*. "You think you can take over tomorrow night?"

"I think so," I replied.

"What do you make of all these glamorous girls? Have you ever seen such a crowd of lovelies in one spot?" Gustl gave a heavy wink. "You know," he said, "these old-timers can't take all the drinking and the late hours. I'll get invited by one or another of these peculiar couples to see them safely to their *pieds-à-terre*. We get the old geezer's shoes off and his collar loosened and leave him snoring on the couch. Then"—another wink—"the little *Schatzie* and I can have fun together."

"Really!" I hadn't dared imagine that.

"Really and truly!" Gustl laughed.

"How often does this happen?" I asked. "When do you sleep?"

"Almost never. Why do you think I look like this?" He laughed again.

I couldn't disagree. He did look like hell. And I was feeling the hours. I told Gustl, over his protests, that I was going home right then.

"Damn shame," he complained. "You're a rotten sport," he said, but he still wore his foolish grin. "You can take the evening clothes home with you, so you'll be ready for tomorrow night." He wrung my hand and thanked me again for helping him.

On my way out, I paused at Herr Zuckerweiss's table to say good night. He was puffing on a fresh cigar and nodded back in his royal fashion as I bowed. Neither the beautiful young woman in the black beaded gown nor her companion was to be seen.

I hurried as quickly as I could back to my rooms, by way of the Schottenring. I was excited and couldn't wait to show Krisztina what I looked like in Gustl's dinner jacket. She would laugh, of course, but she would be impressed by what I had to tell her.

When I unlatched the door, I was surprised that she didn't answer my hello. I stalked through the two rooms. The table where we had eaten still bore our dirty dishes and pieces of bread and meat. The jar of pickles was uncapped, the half-bottle of white wine uncorked. The bed was a chaos of rumpled sheets. I tried the bathroom. The coverlet hung there silently, a large damp circle at its center. She had really been there, tended to me—and then had left. I was close to tears. But I was exhausted. I remembered to strip off Gustl's evening clothes before falling on the bed and closing my eyes.

The next morning, it was back to Dr. Böhm's class. I would see Krisztina. I arrived before the class began. I bounded up onstage and saw her seated among the first violins. I waved cheerfully, but she ignored me—stared right through me.

Dr. Böhm entered. "Is Herr Kapp present?" he called out. Reluctantly, I jumped down and approached him. He drew me aside and handed me an orchestral score. It was the Brahms Second Symphony. "Here," he said. "I want you to study this and be prepared to rehearse the orchestra. At least two movements, probably the second and fourth. If you do well with it, perhaps the whole work." He moved to take his accustomed chair.

I followed him. "By when, Herr Professor? How much time have I got?" I knew next to nothing about the Brahms symphonies.

"Oh, two or three weeks, perhaps," he replied. "I want you to be thorough because I think you can do something with it." He hesitated, peering at me over his spectacles. "You remind me of a fine young man who studied here at the Conservatory a year or so ago. When he was done with his studies, Bruno Walter snapped him up to assist him at Salzburg. Leinsdorf was his name. Do you know him? Erich Leinsdorf? You remind me of him somewhat. You have the same kind of feel, the same approach that he had. You tackle things in a similar way."

He put me into shock. First, the praise, *but where was I to find the time?* Agreed, I may have been brilliant on my first try with the baton, but I was slaving over the *Diabelli Variations*, polishing up a virtuoso level of performance—a gravely serious priority. I was sure all would be well once I told Krisztina my news. She would understand why I had to rush away.

The conducting lesson was endless. Dr. Böhm did not call on me to lead that day. I was obliged to listen to various fellow students massacre portions of the Beethoven First Symphony. Excruciating! They had no ear—too many of them—no sense of time, rhythm, dynamics! To say nothing of how things might fit together. In the Vienna Conservatory yet! They made me ill. Besides, I was developing an uneasy feeling in my stomach about Krisztina. This stony indifference was not like her. I had quickly become used to her admiration and her healthy good sense. Just as I had felt peculiar about her after we had been so wonderfully close and had not known how to face her, she on her part might have had her own qualms. Yes, that must be the case. Surely, all was well.

The class went on and on. Again, I had to endure one numbskull after another. *Why was Dr. Böhm so courteous and polite to these hopeless drudges? It was too painful.* Finally, the orchestra was dismissed, and I eagerly got to my feet. I could see Krisztina smiling and talking to others, which made me sigh in relief. She seemed in good humor again. She put away her violin and bow and walked down the steps beside the stage, chatting with friends.

When I stepped toward her, she simply walked around me without a glance. I was dumbfounded. It was humiliating. After a moment, I rushed and caught up with her at the landing. Again, she pretended not to notice. I plunged into the middle of her group and seized her by the arm. The cheerful talk around us died away. She turned pale. For my part, I could not speak, full of bewilderment.

"Why—why—" I stammered.

Quite deliberately, Krisztina plucked my hand from her arm and dropped it as though it were a loathsome object. She continued down the main staircase together with her friends.

I was badly frightened and ran to the railing. "Krisztina," I cried down to her. She neither looked up nor responded. "Krisztina," I called again, "may I not speak with you?" The only response was a burst of laughter from her group, now out of sight. I sagged over the balustrade, feeling faint.

Dr. Böhm paused as he walked by. "Didn't I see you and that young lady together the other day?"

I nodded miserably.

"Yesterday, or whenever it was, you gave me the impression of complete happiness together, and now I witness this." He heaved a great sigh. "I suppose I'm getting old. I couldn't put up with this kind of *Sturm und Drang*." He smiled kindly. "These days, I confine my passions to music and art. In my personal life, I desire only the emotional equivalent of serenades: calm and tranquillity. You young people, I don't know where you get the energy for these tempests!" He chuckled, shaking his head, as he walked to the staircase.

"Herr Professor," I wailed, without shame, "will she forgive me and come back?"

He stopped a moment. "How can one tell such a thing?" he said.

"At least," he continued, "the finality with which she rejects you sure-ly matches the fire with which she may have been drawn to you in the first place." He stopped when I groaned and made a gesture of despair.

"Yes, yes," he said. "I understand. You are not interested in just any woman. You want only Fräulein Kabós—with whose family in Budapest I happen to be well acquainted." *That was unsettling to hear.* "But I do not interfere in my students' affairs of the heart. They have a way of sorting themselves out. At your age, one young lady friend will soon be replaced by another." I groaned again.

"No, no, I assure you, Herr Kapp, it will happen."

All at once, he looked severe. "The only time I feel compelled to intervene in what my students do is if I should learn of the existence of cruelty and vice. Those are much too uncivilized to be tolerated." He softened his tone. "Go with God, young Herr Kapp. Try to be happy. Win the charming Fräulein Kabós back, if you can. If you can-not, make peace with it. And *do* set about getting the Brahms ready. That's truly important." He gave me a pleasant bow. "Auf Wiedersehen, Herr Kapp." He pattered down the broad, echoing stairs.

Outside, the Young Nationalist Patriots League, accompanied by its usual solitary drumbeat, was holding its daily march.

"Death to the Jews," they chanted.

✳ ✳ ✳

Sixth Variation

Vienna 1929

1929 proved to be a year of depression, restlessness, and chaos. The scent of death was everywhere. Turmoil in Europe broke out all over. But let me not get ahead of myself. I spent the rest of that afternoon in misery, dashing from place to place, trying to find Krisztina. I looked for her in the commons and the library. I loitered outside the studio of her violin professor and attempted to interrogate her friends. They refused to talk to me. I tried to remember where she lived—she had talked of taking a tramcar to near the university sports fields—too vague for me to remember. No humiliation is excessive when you fight for life.

In my throes, I committed stupid acts. I forgot to meet Professor Starker for my lesson. I smacked myself on the head when I remembered. I seemed to be coming to pieces. I even forgot for a time my grand scheme of eliminating my "menacing rival," Eduard, who had turned out instead to be a pathetic, contemptible specimen. Not surprising, given who he was. After almost a day of pointless wandering, not having practiced my piano, not having studied at all, I returned to my courtyard flat.

It was just as I had left it that morning. For one moment, I hoped that Krisztina had returned. But when I opened the door, there were the remains of our supper—rock-hard crusts of bread; dried pieces of meat, now abuzz with flies; dishes caked with grease. I needed a drink. I lifted up the wine bottle, still a third full, peered inside, and shuddered. The surface was covered with dead flies. I had been too rushed last night to straighten things. Now I cleared the mess and put the plates in my sink. But ugh! I didn't like the flies. Mama had purchased special sticky paper in the summertime; I would have to do the same.

Deprived of the greasy dishes, the flies darted in angles under my hanging lamp. Krisztina had not come back. I could only try to catch her in the Conservatory corridors or wait until next week's conducting class. I collapsed on "our bed." The pillow retained hints of her scent. I wore myself out sniffing and hunting for other traces, remembering that we had kissed and clasped each other on that bed just yesterday.

I must have dozed off. When next I opened my eyes, it was dark— just like this time last night. Again, I felt empty, thinking about Krisztina. When I chanced to glance at my clock, I jumped. 8:15! The Café Gonzaga! Once again, I had to rush.

Now I was really frantic. I remembered coming home last night, wearing Gustl's evening clothes. But I couldn't find them. This was insane! My place was not large at all, but for the life of me, I could not unearth that dinner jacket. With mounting terror, the time running away, I tore through the Klosett and dug into my trunk and small wardrobe. Nothing. Finally, I thought of looking under the bed. It was there, neatly laid out, the shirt and cravat too. I had absolutely no memory of my putting them there.

A mad dash to wash and clean myself up. With shaking fingers, I inserted collar studs and tied my black bow, and not quite as pressed for time as last night, set out for the *Innere Stadt*. On my way, I reflected that, if I experienced more unhappy days like this, I would be well on my way to looking just like Gustl.

I arrived at the Gonzaga in plenty of time, took off my shabby overcoat, smoothed my hair, and paused at the table of Herr Zuckerweiss to give obsequious greeting. "Herr Patron," I said and bowed. As before, the full moon of his plump round face contained a large cigar at its center, which he removed as he acknowledged my presence with a nod.

In the tiny curtained dressing room, I almost wept again, thankfully this time, as I discovered another plate of sandwiches and a bottle of beer. I hadn't realized that I was starving. I had been too rushed to eat. Pretty decent of Herr Zuckerweiss, even if a Jew.

Feeling much better with food inside me, I emerged into the dimly lighted main room and took my seat at the Blüthner. Herr Zuckerweiss, at his front table, was no longer alone. He had been joined by a thin dark-haired young woman. When they glanced my way, I saw that she was the one whose purse I had retrieved the night before. I looked to see if her gentleman friend was there. He was not—at least so far. She wore something different tonight—not beads, but black velvet. She still looked beautiful, too impossibly remote for me to approach. I was happy to see that she was *not* caressing Herr Zuckerweiss.

As I began to play, the place filled almost magically. Just as before, the glamorous young women with long cigarette holders glided in, accompanied by their prosperous-looking, decidedly unglamorous escorts. The bent old waiters again passed back and forth with flutes of champagne, chocolates, and liqueurs. Again, the room seemed to exhale sighs of contentment as two dozen slender hands fondled as many fat necks. Bliss was in the air. I alone was miserable.

Within twenty minutes, I had played the Brahms Lullaby twice and Liszt's *Liebestraum* three times—not that I think anyone noticed. I simply couldn't stand to play them anymore that night—or ever again! I sat immobile, not knowing what I should do. After a while, I saw Herr Zuckerweiss staring at me, raising his upturned palms in a silent question. The young woman at his side laughed. With a start, I began to play again. Absolutely by themselves, my fingers found Satie's *Gymnopédies*, those "lovely meditations," as Professor Starker called them—quite in keeping with the mood of the evening. Of course, the Satie pieces are far from my usual Teutonic tastes, but at times, they suited me. They are quiet but don't make me feel uneasy. There are three of them, which I played without a break—their mood is similar: solemn, sweet, and sad—but when I next looked out into the room, all conversation had ceased. The young women and their gentlemen were looking at me. I was nonplused. There was even a smattering of applause. Surely, that was not supposed to happen. This was not a concert. I turned anxiously toward Herr Zuckerweiss. The young woman next to him was one of those lightly clapping. The Herr Patron, with impassive face, was nodding and rotating his hand in a gesture that clearly said, "Continue!"

Liberated from the bonds of Brahms and Liszt, I attempted music, I'm sure, never before heard at the Gonzaga. I simply played as many slow movements from Mozart and Beethoven sonatas as I could remember. They were all beautiful and—to the indifferent listener—restful. I gave them the andante to Mozart's third sonata in C, the adagio of his fifteenth sonata in D, and the allegretto of Beethoven's Opus 10 No. 2. They worked remarkably well, I thought, and my idea to offer them brilliant beyond description. Besides the occasional applause, more than one of those bizarre couples ascended my podium to murmur words of appreciation. One of the women, who frankly looked ghastly, with her heavy mascara and almost jet-black lipstick, took my hand in hers and thanked me, eyes shining, for taking her back to her childhood when she too had played those pieces. Her gentleman friend tucked money in my jacket pocket. When I managed to glance at it, I saw that it equaled my pay for the whole night.

After about forty-five minutes, I was ready for a break. I needed, first, to pee and, second, to drink something. Before I could leave the dais, however, Herr Zuckerweiss beckoned to me, inviting me to sit on the other side of the young woman in black. He removed the cigar from his mouth, cleared his throat, and patted me on the arm.

"Fräulein Klara," he said in his blurry fashion, "likes your playing a great deal." I began to stammer thanks. He cut me off with a wave.

"She thinks you should play here all the time," he continued.

The young woman gazed at me steadily, eyes gleaming, but said nothing.

"For a while, I thought all that more serious, classical stuff would ruin everything," he said reflectively, "but I was wrong, I was wrong." The young woman leaned in to wipe a dot of tobacco from the corner of his mouth. "Yes, Max Zuckerweiss did not get where he is by refusing to admit a mistake."

Hidden beneath the tablecloth, Fräulein Klara slowly massaged my knee. I looked up, startled. "And I agree with her, absolutely agree," Herr Zuckerweiss went on, unaware. "Who is this unknown replacement that your friend, Herr August, wants me to hire? I have never met him. I have never heard him. But I've heard you. And I like you. Fräulein Klara likes you too. What do you say?" The Herr Patron spoke and looked at me, as usual, completely without expression.

Fräulein Klara's hand under the tablecloth left my knee and took up residence along my upper thigh and squeezed. I jumped. Her eyes were fixed on the Herr Patron.

"So you would not merely tinkle pretty tunes," he added, "but play real music. It would be an added attraction. Fräulein Klara says so."

The young woman smiled at me in friendly fashion. Out of sight, her hand lurched upward. Again, just as in Eisenstadt, an interesting social encounter was threatened by an urgent need for a *Pissoir*. I stood up hastily. "Bitte, Herr Patron, would you kindly excuse me for a few minutes." I fled, followed by Fräulein Klara's laughter.

When I was through with the Klo and back behind the dressing room curtain, I found a tumbler of brandy waiting for me. Without thinking, I drank it down in one gulp. Indeed, I was coming to understand why Gustl looked so destroyed. Easy access to brandy and these women—both more than somewhat lethal—would do the trick. Still, the Herr Patron had made a fascinating proposal, and I didn't know what to do.

I gazed angrily at my reflection in the looking glass. "It is a foolish and stupid idea and will only make trouble for me," I said loudly. "Of course, I must say no!"

The curtain was abruptly pushed aside. Fräulein Klara entered and pulled it to behind her. "I heard you talking and couldn't wait to join the conversation."

Shocked, I instantly got to my feet. She calmly occupied my chair and sipped from the large champagne glass she carried. Although she smiled sweetly and her voice was charming, I knew I might be in danger.

"Instead, I find you completely alone," she said, speaking as though to a child. "Are you always in the habit of talking to yourself?"

I shook my head. How quickly could I get her to leave? "Forgive me, Fräulein, I didn't realize I was speaking aloud. Does the Fräulein require anything?"

She laughed softly. "Does the Fräulein require anything?" she repeated. "The Fräulein requires perhaps many things." She took another sip. "But what were you saying just now, you handsome and talented young man—and with such fire in your voice?" She made her eyes large, still questioning as she might a child.

She was making fun of me, but as glamorous and out of reach as she was, also angering me. Lotte had been like that—certainly not high class, but she had treated me as a plaything. I didn't like it. I didn't want to be treated like that when everything had become so serious. Krisztina would never speak to me that way. I sagged against the wall when I remembered that Krisztina was not speaking to me at all.

"I see that I make you nervous," said Fräulein Klara, "and perhaps you wish to be by yourself on your breaks." She studied her reflection in the mirror and smoothed her hair. When she returned her gaze to me, her eyes were dancing, but she made no move to leave.

"Why did you touch me?" I blurted.

"Did I touch you?" she asked.

I refused to take any more of this stupidity. I began to shake with rage. I took a step to her side in the tiny room and grasped her naked arms. "Yes, you touched me," I raised my voice. "You know you touched me. Nobody else touched me."

"You're sure it wasn't Herr Zuckerweiss?" she asked coyly.

A man's voice came from just outside the curtain—Herr Zuckerweiss had come to find us. "Is everything all right there?"

I leaped back. There were angry red blotches on Klara's arms. "Yes," I called, "everything's all right." She opened her mouth wide in a silent laugh. It maddened me. I was actually about to strike her.

"You could show yourself again, Herr Kapp," said Herr Zuckerweiss from outside the curtain. He sounded as calm as always. "It could be time for more music." The corridor outside was too heavily carpeted to tell if he had walked away.

Klara looked down at her bruised arms, then at me. She shook her head in mock reproach. "Bitte," she said as sweetly as ever and waited for me to pull the curtain aside. Outside, Herr Zuckerweiss indeed stood there, ready to escort her back to the table. I bowed to him. He bowed back. I missed Krisztina with all my heart.

I seated myself back at the keyboard. All the ladies and gentlemen welcomed the "new music." Whatever Herr Zuckerweiss thought about Klara and me, he kept to himself. She had disappeared. If I happened to glance at him from the piano, he would nod slowly at me, his eyes without expression. I played, I took my breaks. The hours passed. Then I was aware that the Gonzaga was emptying. The old waiters in their ill-fitting clothes were cleaning up, removing wine glasses, and folding tablecloths. Here and there, the last few glamorous ladies were being helped into their expensive wraps.

I was bone-tired. Within four or five hours, I was due to present a respectable version of the *Diabelli Variations* for Professor Starker's approval and explain why I had been absent from the previous day's lesson. He had been mentioning—nothing definite, mind you—the possibility of my performing Beethoven's Fifth Piano Concerto—the "Emperor"—in the spring. If I managed to be absolutely fantastic in the concerto—and why shouldn't I.?—I could reasonably expect to

outshine even the likes of Eduard van Vleiman. But I was also expected to have mastered the full score of the Brahms Second Symphony for
Dr. Böhm—learned it, made notes on it, and be prepared also to master the Second student orchestra and make it respond the way it had
when we played the Beethoven symphony.

I went to say good night to Herr Zuckerweiss. He silently handed
me some folded banknotes, fifteen *schillings*, instead of the twelve I
had expected. Generous. I bowed and thanked him. In addition, the
gentlemen friends of the young ladies had been stuffing money in my
pockets all night long. I hadn't counted any of that yet.

"What about making the Gonzaga your home all the time?" he
grunted.

"May I give you my answer tomorrow night, Herr Patron?"

He narrowed his eyes. "Sorry, no. I'm afraid you may not," he said,
rolling the cigar between his lips.

"Why ever not, Herr Patron? It would mean just one more day.
Forgive me"—I assumed a sincere expression—"but I thought you
liked the way I played tonight and for that reason you might give me
extra time to consider."

Herr Zuckerweiss's lips twitched with amusement. "Of course, I
like the way you play. I wouldn't be talking to you now if I didn't.
We're discussing replacing Herr August's replacement—if you remember. That other friend of his who was originally to take his place. If you
intend to join us, that young man has to be told as soon as possible, so
that he can make other arrangements. If not, he need not be disturbed.
This may be business, but we try to be decent about it."

I couldn't believe my ears. The Herr Patron was running practically a high-class bawdy house, filled every night with rich aging dirty
dogs and their *schatzen*—and he spoke to me of decency?

"Sit down a moment. I want to say something to you, mein
Junge." He carefully tapped cigar ash onto a plate. "I know what you
think," he said mildly. "You think the Gonzaga is a whorehouse and
that I am the brothel keeper."

I rose to my feet in alarm. Was I so transparent? I didn't want to anger
a Jew, especially a rich and influential one like Herr Zuckerweiss. They
could be so touchy.

He motioned me to resume my seat. "Look," he said, "we are not
children. We all know that the Gonzaga is not a kindergarten."

I suppose not, I thought.

"Yes," the Herr Patron continued, "the Gonzaga is unsavory, it violates the licensing laws, it countenances immorality and helps ruin marriages that are already doomed. Nevertheless, I forbid violence, cocaine, and underage girls. As for the rest of it"—the Herr Patron shrugged—"we are famous throughout Europe. The tourists can't wait to visit. The police are well aware of us and share handsomely in our profits."

Another twist of his cigar. "We may not be virtuous—but we don't have to be evil. It's as the doctors say—'do no harm.' Perhaps they do not cure everything, but at least they try not to make things worse!

"So, Herr Kapp, tell me, will you stay with us? I must let the other piano player know." I looked away. "Why do you not speak, mein Junge? I will not be angry if you refuse. Whatever you say, you still have the job for tomorrow." He dropped one of his heavy eyelids in a wink. "By the way, how much did you earn tonight? I will not betray you to the Bureau of Taxes."

I placed on the table the fifteen *schillings* he had just paid me. Next, I retrieved all the crumpled bank notes that the elderly gentlemen had stuffed in my various pockets. When they were smoothed out and counted, they amounted to ninety-four *schillings*. For a moment or two, I was unable to breathe. This was more than I permitted myself for two months of existence. No wonder people rioted in the streets! Those curbside orators had not been lying. The differences between rich and poor were criminal.

Herr Zuckerweiss blew three consecutive smoke rings. "That is a most gratifying concert fee. But I still need to know what you have decided."

A terrible rage seized me. For a moment, I wanted to grab Herr Zuckerweiss by his fat neck and squeeze the life out of him. This disgusting old *SauJude*, and the others, fondling and poking their fingers into all those young girls at the Gonzaga, swilling brandy and champagne, throwing around all that money! All over Austria and all over Hungary, people didn't have enough to eat. I was covered in shame, thinking of Mama, who struggled every day, while I lolled about in the presence of men like Herr Zuckerweiss. I had read the Communist pamphlets. The Bolsheviks had it right, but only partly. They wanted to sweep away corruption, all right. But those same Bolsheviks insisted on everyone's being on the same level. That didn't sit well with me.

I certainly was not the equal of a pig like Herr Zuckerweiss—he had admitted his corruption to me not two minutes before. I resented it. I was young, strong, and vigorous. I wanted to be among others like me—and I didn't mean that bunch of incompetents, my fellow students at the Conservatory, nor necessarily the National Young Patriots League, who resembled those imitation storm troopers who consorted with Dr. von Hornberger at Eisenstadt.

Herr Zuckerweiss still waited. I smiled at him. I had made up my mind. I would appear tomorrow night at the Gonzaga. But only tomorrow night. The money was good. But it would be madness to make myself insane—to end up looking like Gustl—in order to cast away my career for a shameful cesspool like the Gonzaga. I owed Herr Zuckerweiss nothing.

"Yes, I accept the position," I said. "Please tell the person it's filled."

Herr Zuckerweiss smiled back. He closed and opened his eyes in assent. "All right then, we're agreed." He patted my arm. I did my best to hide my distaste.

Next morning, I staggered out of bed to leave a message for Gustl, saying simply that I would be using his dinner jacket again. Then I hurried off to Professor Starker's studio to make my peace with him. We had a rigorous session with the *Diabelli*. He had news for me concerning Eduard. It seemed that the poor lad had written to his own piano professor, withdrawing from the Conservatory, date of return unknown, because of what were described as severe medical problems. His hands were damaged. No one could say how or why. The doctors were baffled.

"What do you think of this?" asked Professor Starker, shaking his head. "I hope you have been paying attention to my concerns about possible muscular damage or degeneration of the nerves. It is a genuine hazard of our profession. It is the reason that I often talk about correct posture, spinal damage, and care of the hands and fingers."

I was seized by a severe fit of coughing. Professor Starker, alarmed, approached with a glass of water. I received it gratefully and drank. In reality I had been laughing. I was grateful to be relieved of the burden of planning some sort of calamity for Eduard. Just what I might have done, I had no idea. Nothing serious, of course, but at times I wondered if I would be able to hurl him down the stairs or, perhaps, in front of a tramcar. The problem was how to get away afterward. Such thoughts had crossed my mind. But surely the good angels that my Mama had invoked for my protection had taken care of the task for me. Of course, I am speaking tongue-in-cheek. I don't mean to blaspheme, but what a stroke of luck! This meant there would be no impediments to my winning the major piano prizes, playing the senior recital, or appearing with the First student orchestra in the "Emperor" Concerto next year. The future was without limit!

That whole day was lived at top speed, from one thing to another. Before I had a chance to breathe, it was time to return for my second night at the Gonzaga. Herr Zuckerweiss was in his customary place in front. I bowed to him on my way to the cubicle. He merely raised his cigar as I passed. Once behind the curtain, I slumped in my seat, too tired even to eat my sandwiches.

The curtain parted. Klara, again dressed in black. I had dreaded another meeting. She took a step toward me and, without speaking, put her arms about my neck. To keep from falling backward, I put my arms around her shoulders. She pressed against me. I kissed her, or she kissed me—I cannot tell which. But her waist and back felt so amazingly supple and pliant, as though there were no bones at all, no ribs, no spine. She might melt right into me. Definitely not like Lotte, who had felt solid and muscular with all her hard work in the café. And quite different from beloved Krisztina—she had strength from her years at the violin, but as I well knew, also quiet and yielding. Klara was different, like…like—don't laugh at me—like a flowing river, of the infinitely deep and treacherous kind.

She drew back from that long inflaming kiss and left as she had entered, without a word. I drained my tumbler of brandy in one gulp and straightened my jacket, ready for my evening's work.

Outside, at the keyboard, I resumed my progress through the succession of slow movements and meditations that people had enjoyed the night before. Once again, as before, the young women and their gentlemen "friends" sipped at their glasses, caressed necks, discreetly touched bosoms in public, and punctuated my playing with quiet applause. As before, couples paused on their way somewhere to utter complimentary words and tuck banknotes in my pockets. The hours proceeded. I took my breaks. In vain, I scanned the room for a glimpse of Klara. It was already one or two in the morning.

At last, I spotted her—she may not have been there all the time.

She was some distance away, at a table to the rear. She was in the embrace of an elderly admirer.

I was immediately enraged. Why should that have been, given what went on at the Gonzaga? I have now somewhat come to recognize the disparate parts of my temperament. But remember, I was then nineteen and far less skilled in the arts of self-control.

I became crazed. I stood up, and with all my strength, smashed my fists onto the keys, jolting everyone awake. I did it over and over. The sudden cacophony caused one of the ancient waiters to drop his tray with a crash. At the front tables, I saw at least two monocles drop from startled eyes—and one wizened gentleman in full evening dress clutch at his heart. Herr Zuckerweiss stood up in alarm, but before he could move, I bounded over to Klara's table and jerked her savagely to her feet. When her venerable escort protested, I pushed him roughly so that he sprawled backward onto the carpet. I didn't care whether he was hurt or not.

Two burly men appeared from out of nowhere, grabbed me by the arms, and marched me rapidly into the kitchens, Herr Zuckerweiss following close behind. The whole thing had happened in a flash. My captors were breathing hard, but the Herr Patron regarded me with a sad smile, slowly shaking his head.

"Should we just throw the little shit out," growled one of the tough-looking men, "or first punch some sense into him?"

"The bastard needs a lesson in behavior. This is a respectable place!" said the other, bunching his fist.

"No, no, gentlemen," said Herr Zuckerweiss in a soothing voice, "that will not be necessary." He smoothed my rumpled lapels and gestured for my captors to release me. "Herr Kapp, you know, is quite a distinguished artist. And artists are well known for their uncertain temperaments, *nicht war?*"

I couldn't stop trembling.

"There, there, Herr Kapp. You must be quite upset. But you will forgive my friends for their vigilance. From time to time, we might have disturbances, but I'm grateful to have the assistance of civic-minded members of the Polizei, who look after us. Off-duty, of course, and at no cost to the public." I groaned. So my guards were policemen. I was already known to the police because of the horrible Frau Malteser.

"But what are we to do about this matter?" Herr Zuckerweiss

mused sorrowfully. "Obviously, we have to reconsider our arrangements," he said. "We have a discreet establishment, Herr Kapp. We cannot have riots breaking out just like that."

One of the off-duty policemen spoke. "Are you sure, Herr Patron, we shouldn't teach him a lesson?"

Herr Zuckerweiss made no answer but only shrugged. "Really, Herr Kapp," he said. "You leave me no choice. You have to go. Such a pity," he added. "But let us part without bitterness," he said, placing some banknotes in my hand. "There, you have played well, and are entitled to your earnings—and something extra." Typical of his oily kind, I thought, trying to ingratiate himself. "Please be careful," he said to the policemen. "Don't hurt his hands as you show him out."

He bowed and abruptly left. The bodyguards threw my coat at me, marched me through the kitchens, thrust me into the alley outside, and slammed the door behind me.

The night was cold and dark. I needed a minute or two to collect myself. Despite these immediate alarming events, things had turned out strangely well. For the second time this day, I had got what I wanted—with no effort on my part or blame. Eduard was disabled and no longer a threat, and I had just extricated myself, without really intending to, from the Café Gonzaga. Perhaps I was the *Übermensch* I'd heard mentioned in my required philosophy course. Perhaps not. Perhaps it was sufficient just to be lucky.

I stumbled from the alley to the street, ready to walk home. Now it was *really* cold. I made out at the corner, beneath a lamppost, a cream-colored Bugatti sports car, its lights on, but its top and canvas flaps buttoned down. As I drew level, a door swung open. Klara grinned at me from the driver's seat. I regarded her with mingled disgust and fear. She said not a word. After a long moment, I got in. She roared off, drove to the north, made some turns, and soon squealed to a halt outside a modest-sized but smart-looking building.

"This is my flat," she said. I didn't move at first. "Would you like to come in?" Her face dimpled when she smiled. I was out of the car, following her to the house. I now understand something about mental pathology, but at the time, I couldn't tell you why I obeyed.

The modest entrance hall seemed rich yet tasteful, covered in dark mauve and red fabric rather than just wallpaper. Klara's flat was on the second floor. We had to pass a sleepy concierge. Upstairs, I found the same unusual colors as in the foyer. But Klara's walls were also covered with art—drawings and paintings of naked lovers. They outdid in daring the Klimts and the Egon Schieles that had so excited me and drawn me again and again in furtive delight to the museums. Klara poured glasses of an amber liqueur for us and curled up next to me on a soft black leather sofa.

For a long while, she watched me, dipping her tongue into her liqueur, lapping like a cat. At last, she looked down and spoke quietly. "Do you care for me?"

I burst into a loud, bitter laugh. She was not to be believed. Then I became infuriated. Didn't she know, after what had happened this night, her question was insane and designed to make me crazed? But no, this maddening girl—young woman—seemed perfectly oblivious.

I threw my drink down on the dark red carpet and seized her arm, at the same time snatching her glass and hurling it across the room, where it shattered.

"You disgusting whore," I shouted. Klara turned white. "What a pig you are! One minute, in my arms, kissing me and—and—making me think that you're my very own"—I couldn't help breaking into the language of my rubbishy novels—"the next minute, you're slobbering over that disgusting old man. In front of everybody! Disgusting!" I slapped her face.

There was a horrified silence. A red blotch spread across Klara's cheek. This was the second time I had bruised her. I wanted to leave. I tried to get up from that deep sofa, but my feet became entangled in something. I stumbled and fell. I must have cut my hand on some broken glass—not badly—but all at once, Klara was down on the floor with me, sobbing, licking the blood off my hand.

"I am so sorry, I am so sorry!" she moaned over and over, so cravenly, as if she were addressing a music professor. "Please don't go," she sobbed. "I'll be better in a short while. Just stay with me, please!"

We sat on the carpet amid fragments of glass, drinking out of a bottle that we passed between us like a pair of derelicts, clinging to one another. Holding her had the same effect on me as when we kissed in my dressing room earlier this night. Again, she felt so soft and melting, as though she were blending into me. At my age, I don't have to tell you, a man becomes easily excited. Nevertheless, I behaved correctly. My hands did not rove. Perhaps a half hour passed. I was unable to move and grew numb. When I tried to stir, I discovered that Klara had fallen asleep. But I couldn't remain where I was. I struggled to stand—she still clung to me—and dragged her toward what I hoped was her bedroom. When I managed to drop her on the bed, I was so exhausted myself that I fell beside her—and I couldn't keep my eyes open.

When I next stirred, I couldn't tell how much time had passed, but I was emerging from a lurid and exciting dream. I was back in Eisenstadt. But the rooms of the Schloss did not resemble what I remembered when I was there—cut up into cubicles and offices. Instead, I saw them as they appeared in the tourists' guidebooks—in all their glory, lavishly gilded, furnished with golden draperies and satin divans. In the dream, I was reclining on such a divan, being kissed and fondled, fed rare and wonderful fruits by beautiful young girls. I was so unwilling to wake from that dream! But some kind of urgent excitement was thrusting me back into the world. And when I opened my eyes, many things remained the same. By the morning light that struggled through Klara's heavy curtains, I saw that I was naked below the waist. I beheld the top of Klara's head, buried in my privates. Her mouth engulfed, and was being loving to, my *Schwanz*. With her soft hands, she caressed my belly and thighs. What a way to wake up! I was in the power of a witch or a genius. I had heard talk of such activities but had refused to credit them. Entirely fantastic. No decent, beautiful girl would do such a thing. However, I was instantly converted to belief. It was true enough! One had to experience the electricity for himself. I could only lie there in mounting excitement and eventually explode.

After a few moments, the world stopped spinning. Klara, completely naked, crawled up and clung to me with a fond smile. I was frozen in shock. I mean to say, she had actually swallowed me! She didn't seem to care *what* she took into her mouth. Last night, it was my bleeding hand, and this morning, it was—*me!* She wrapped herself cozily around me and drew up the covers. Next, she actually kissed me on the mouth! I was horrified.

Rolling away from her, restless and uneasy, I sat up and studied my left hand, the one that had been cut. The wound didn't appear deep, didn't seem infected, didn't throb or ache. A pianist has to take such things seriously.

Klara propped up on one elbow. "Are you going so soon, *Liebchen?*"

she asked. She looked beautiful and defenseless, with her tousled black hair, her thin naked shoulders, and her dark-topped sweet small tits. But I couldn't help shuddering at what she could do. She had taken me to heights—or depths, call it what you like—of sensation. But, like Lotte, she insisted on being a law to herself. I understood her. She would do as she pleased. I hoped I had enough sense to save myself.

I sat on the side of the bed and began pulling on my clothes. Klara shrugged in disappointment. "You're leaving? What will you do now, Herr Kapp?" she said in a child's voice. "Poor young man, he's lost his job. Who will stuff his pockets with *schillings* and supply him with free brandy? Just for strumming the piano a few hours a night."

"You need not worry about me," I said. With every article of clothing I pulled on, I felt stronger, more encased. Within minutes, I would be gone.

She chuckled and collapsed back on the bed, gazing up at me. "You may be *sure* that I won't worry about you. Even if I did, it wouldn't be any use."

I paused in my dressing. That sounded nasty. "What do you mean by that?" I hesitated a moment. "Whore!"

She raised her eyebrows. "Oh, yes, you are correct," she said evenly. "I know I am a whore. The question is, do you know who *you* are?"

"What do you mean?"

She raised herself on an elbow again. "You really want to know? I'll tell you."

I made a gesture of impatience and continued dressing.

"I've met men like you before—they may be older and richer than you—but they're the same. Some are quiet, and some talk a lot, but they all have one thing in common. They all think they're big men, too big for disasters. They take foolish risks. Some of them make fortunes—and lose them the next day. They may not care, but sometimes they ruin a lot of people who depend on them."

I shook my head. "I don't know what you're talking about. I don't know anybody like that. I'm just a piano student at the Conservatory."

"The moment you appeared at the Gonzaga, you looked like one of the men I'm talking about. Even though you wore clothes that didn't fit you, you behaved as though you owned the place. You wanted things your own way. You played the music you wanted. You argued with Herr Zuckerweiss—oh, in the nicest and politest way. You got him to overturn all his plans and offer you a permanent place—and profitable it would have been too. I was extremely impressed," she grinned. "So young and so masterly!"

"And what's the matter with that?"

"What's the matter with that?" She laughed. "The matter is—with all your intelligence—you've still got no brains!"

"And you're still a whore!"

She laughed again. "Yes, I've already agreed with you on that. Oh, but, Herr Kapp, you must never bother a whore while she's earning her living. Never!"

"Are you talking about when I lost my temper? But that was your fault! If I hadn't seen you with that man, that disgusting old man—"

"But, Herr Kapp, we agree, I am a whore," she said softly.

I sat on the bed, tired and defeated. "Then what was this all about, what just happened between *us*?" I snarled but on the verge of tears.

She reached to the night table for a cigarette, struck a match, and lighted it. "Look," she said, "when you so gallantly leaped over tables and chairs like a wild horse and attacked that poor old gentleman, you put us all in great danger."

"What do you mean?"

She sighed and rolled her eyes. "What do you mean, what do you mean! This is what I mean. That old man is the minister for war, that's all! And the only reason that I, Herr Zuckerweiss, all the staff—including you—are not lying in a dungeon at this moment is that Herr Zuckerweiss, whom I know you despise—pure young man that you are!—has passed around a great deal of money to smooth things over." She drew in a mouthful of smoke. "For a moment, we thought you had caused him a heart attack! We were lucky. But everybody saw it. I suppose we were also lucky that he was worried about his own scandal, about being seen at the Gonzaga, I mean."

I was silent. Klara was a whore, but she was most expert at it. Under her fingers and mouth I had experienced great wonders, not easily forgotten. I turned to her with a smile. "Couldn't we, perhaps, talk things over—"

She interrupted me. "I don't know what you want. Anyway, it's too late. Our moment has passed. You have ceased to be amusing. I don't think I'm interested." She lit another cigarette. "In fact, there's something about you that much disturbs me."

I was becoming angry again. "But you don't know what I'm going to say."

"Look, Herr Kapp," she sighed. "You are young and good-looking. You are obviously talented. Perhaps you are audacious and may go far in life. The trouble is, you are also dangerous. You haven't sorted out when to be intelligent and when you can't help being stupid. I don't know whether you can tell the difference. That's going to mean a lot of trouble for yourself and for the people near you."

"What are you talking about?"

"I mean that you're too reckless and dangerous even for me. In fact, you are *eine Katastrophe,* a bringer of disaster!" She spoke matter-of-factly.

I didn't understand. "But you said that you knew all that last night. And this morning, while we were together, it didn't seem to bother you until this minute."

"That's true," she said. "I thought we could have had a good time with each other—we are somewhat alike!" I didn't have time to be offended by that. "But when you didn't even have the brains to hang onto your cushy job at the Gonzaga—"

"No, no, you're wrong about that, Fräulein," I said eagerly. "I had arranged the whole thing. Even Gustl believed I was going to stay for only two nights. And then I would be gone. I did it only to do Gustl a favor. I never meant to stay—"

"And so you lied to Herr Zuckerweiss?"

"*Ach,* that Jew!" I grinned. "What does he matter?"

Klara did not smile back. She drew the covers up to her neck so that her body was hidden. "Herr Zuckerweiss has always been considerate to his employees."

"What are you talking about now?" I chuckled. "It was only a joke!"

"I don't want to listen to jokes about Jews. I am one also."

That explained a lot. Jewish girls—when young—were known for their passionate natures. Before they became old and fat. Yes, that explained a lot. It occurred to me that if I couldn't continue to visit Klara, I would be deprived of a wonderful and magical world she could share with me. She had much to teach.

"Yes, I am Jewish," she said, looking me in the eye. "I just called you *eine Katastrophe.* There is another word that suits you—ein Unglück—a misfortune. There is a Yiddish word that's close to it, but it's got a meaning all its own. You're not only ein Unglück in German, but also ein imglick in Yiddish!—a misfortune, not only for himself and the people around him. There's something more. At the same time he's pitiful—ridiculous and absurd!" She laughed again. The laughter hurt me much more than what she said.

"There is nothing amusing, Fräulein, about your disgusting insults," I said as haughtily as I could. She laughed harder. I rushed out of her flat and slammed the door as loudly as I could.

* * *

The following days were hectic and breathless. Professor Starker was working me harder than ever on the *Diabelli* and had put me down to play at the first student recital in February, about nine weeks away. In addition, he seemed to have abandoned the idea of my learning the "Emperor" Concerto first, substituting instead Beethoven's Fourth concerto. I had been so looking forward to playing the "Emperor"—so heroic and manly. One can make a glorious noise with it—granted, the middle movement is solemn and poetic. Professor Starker knew I felt at home producing blazing sounds. The Fourth, on the other hand, would require of me constant poetry. He knew how uncertain I was about tackling those mysterious-sounding sections of the *Diabelli*. I had to revise my entire practice plan. Thank God, Christmas break was almost here. Time to breathe.

At the same time, Dr. Böhm unexpectedly canceled our conducting class. He had been summoned to Leipzig to lead performances of Mozart's *Zauberflöte*. A colleague had become ill. I had a temporary reprieve from my obligation to prepare the Brahms. By the same token, if the student orchestra did not meet, I was robbed of a chance to see Krisztina. It had been three weeks already. Where had the time flown? I was having to dash from one thing to another. But now, things were falling into place, and I could see clearly that Krisztina was the one for me, a true love, honest and sincere. All the nonsense that had occurred in these three weeks—Gustl, Herr Zuckerweiss, the Gonzaga, and especially Klara—had all been stupid, nightmarish distractions. Now, I had awakened and was secure in my path.

I practiced for my recital as diligently as I could. Professor Starker was full of praise and encouragement for my performance of the *bravura* variations. But I was aware, in playing what he called "more sensitive" music, that I was still disappointing him. And I didn't entirely understand his comments. I observed all the indicated dynamics, played *piano* and *forte* where it said—faster and slower where noted, held pauses, and so forth and so on. Still, Professor Starker withheld his really deep smiles.

"You know what the matter may be, Herr Kapp?" he observed after a particularly baffling half hour. "In the slow movements, where you need to occupy space and time, you seem—I don't know—*impatient* may be the word. What do you think?"

I had heard something like that before. Herr Schneidermann—that maniac—had criticized my Schubert impromptus in a similar way.

"You see, Herr Kapp, you are without doubt heroic in allegro sections—brilliant and exciting. But what about andantes and adagios? Have no other teachers made similar comments?" He scratched his head. "And why have I not noticed? Perhaps my attention was caught by other things." I felt resentment stirring.

I planted a pleasant smile on my face. "I think I understand, Herr Professor," I said. "I'll try harder to please you. I'll work harder—"

"Please, Herr Kapp," he interrupted. "It is not a question of working harder or longer. It may be a question of the heart, what you feel."

I stared at him. I didn't follow. Something suddenly came to mind, something I had read in the newspapers. It was a review from Milan on the work of the reigning Italian Kapellmeister—Maestro, they called him there. Signor Toscanini had sneered when critics objected to his "mechanical precision" and what they called the "pitiless clarity" of his performances. They complained about his supposed lack of heart. They looked in vain for soul and compassion.

The Maestro had exploded in contempt. "What the devil do you mean when you say I have no 'soul'? I don't recognize 'souls.' I don't recognize 'feelings.' I don't acknowledge 'auras' or 'sensitivities.' They mean nothing to me!"

"Then what do you recognize?" asked the journalists.

"I recognize *allegro con brio*," the Maestro snapped, entering the backseat of his open car. "I know what it means, and I know what to do with it."

I had read this account about a year ago, and it had rung true for me. But now, even though I had come to trust Professor Starker in most things, my mind had focused independently from his. It wasn't simply a case of my being brash or stupid. Like the Maestro, I had a point of view. *Allegro con brio* meant exactly what it said. I would know what to do with it. In the meantime, if Professor Starker required "sensitivity," *ritards*, hesitations, and *accelerandos* in slow movements, I would give them to him. And bide my time.

"Bravo, bravo," he cried when I once more attempted the second and third of the *Diabelli* variations. "Excellent," he added. "Now you're getting the idea. More flexibility, more air. That's the balance your forcefulness requires!" Yes, I knew what he was talking about, but I didn't agree. I had Signor Toscanini to back me up. I wondered whether I could manage a trip to Milan.

When I left Professor Starker's studio, it came to me that I was in for a lonely holiday. Workmen were decorating the grand public buildings with festive wreaths and lining the Ringstrasse with Christmas trees, with a truly tremendous one opposite the Burgtheater. Mothers, fathers, and children of all ages paraded along the broad avenues, chattering and laughing, dressed in furs and wraps, buying roasted chestnuts and sausage, first, blowing to cool, and then munching as they marched rapidly along. I missed having people to talk to. For some reason, I yearned for the Café Gonzaga. I had completely forgotten that the Conservatory would be closed for the holidays and that it wouldn't have mattered whether or not I played at Herr Zuckerweiss's establishment. I kicked myself. *What a fool!* I could have been earning more than a hundred *schillings* a night during this time. And I might have been enjoying a good time with Klara to boot! So there was no Klara and no easy money. Everybody I knew seemed angry with me. Even with my Café Gonzaga earnings, I felt desolate.

As I turned into the courtyard outside my lodgings, to my amazement, I saw Krisztina huddled at the door, obviously waiting for me. She had so successfully avoided a meeting, I feared she might have even left Vienna. I had given up hope.

I rushed over and seized her hands. "My god, where have you been?" I cried. "I've looked all over for you. You haven't been at the Conservatory, and I didn't know where you lived."

She removed her hands from my grasp. "May we get out of the cold?"

Inside, I hastily turned on a light and started my small spirit stove to take away the chill and heat water for coffee. Krisztina kept her coat on and remained standing. I was shocked to see her looking pale and thin.

"What's happened to you? Have you been ill?" I asked.

"What do you think has happened to me?"

"I don't know, I don't know," I said, "but I'm so glad to see you again"—I brightened up—"and I have lots of exciting things to tell you. You cannot imagine the incredible adventures that I've had—I don't know where to begin—"

"Later, Ferenc," she said. "I don't know where to begin either." She gazed into my eyes. "Can you guess why I'm here?"

"All I know is that I'm so happy to see you. I've been thinking about lots of things." I seized her hands again. "What I want to tell you is that I love you so much. I've been so miserable and unhappy since you...vanished." Tears came to my eyes.

She smiled faintly and touched my cheek. "Thank you for saying those beautiful things. It makes it easier."

I had no idea what she was talking about.

"I'm pregnant—at least, I'm pretty sure of it," she said.

I was dizzy, unable to breathe.

"You've turned white. Have you seen a ghost?" she asked wryly. "Are *you* feeling all right?" I mumbled, trying to find something to say.

"Are you really happy to see me? You don't look happy."

I could only make futile gestures. "Are you certain?" I asked. "And are you sure that it's...because of me?"

The disgust that flashed across her face appalled me. "I'm quite sure," she said. "And I'm quite certain you are the one. You should know that well yourself." She tilted her head to one side, but she looked serious. No smile.

"Would you like to marry me?" she asked in a level voice.

I groaned. "Please, Krisztina, I cannot do that. I cannot marry anybody. That would be terrible. I haven't got the money, I haven't got the time. I can't have a wife or a family. I've got too many things to do. I'm supposed to make a career."

"So much for love," she said.

Her calm was frightening. "What will you do?" I asked.

"You know, your precious career isn't the only thing at stake! What I'll have to do," she said, "is commit a mortal sin. Are you a believer?

Do you go to Mass? Do you go to Confession? If you do, when was the last time?"

"Would you return to Budapest?"

"Is that what you hope?" she snapped. "You don't understand anything, do you! If I go home like this, it will break my father's heart. Even if you begged me now, I would not marry you. It would be a terrible mistake. I curse myself for thinking good things about you." She sat on the bed—our bed—and covered her face, weeping quietly. After a few minutes of this, during which I could only wring my hands, she calmed herself, got to her feet, and blew her nose.

"I'm sorry, I'm sorry," she said. She straightened herself. "It's my own fault. I'm sorry. I thought you had grown up since Szombathely." She smiled faintly again and shook her head. "You're still the charming, gifted boy who took Eisenstadt by storm, aren't you?" She walked to the door.

"Goodbye," she said. I must have looked stricken and miserable. "Cheer up, don't worry. After next week, there will be no baby. Some of the women where I live have been helping me. Thank God for women. At least, some of them know what life is about." Her eyes blazed. "If we should see each other next term, please, Ferenc, do not speak to me. Ever again."

I tried to go to her, but she waved me off. "I suppose it's not all your fault, but I've found great troubles through you. This is the worst thing I could ever imagine happening to me." She left, closing the door behind her. I was sad for awhile but then the *Diabelli Variations* pushed into my mind. I was still worrying about the fingering.

* * *

The days that followed were cold and drab. I received a welcome present from Mama, a pair of soft thick gloves, and from Madame, a fine silk scarf—which I exchanged for a more practical woolen one. I also received the news that Superintendent Mellnicz had died. He was eighty-eight years old. I did not dare to inquire after the health of Madame, nor did Mama tell me. It had long been incredible to me that she still clung to life, shaking, tottering, and infirm as she was. I suppose she was a marvel in her way.

Professor Starker had gone to Palermo for Christmas. He was finding the Vienna winters difficult to endure. Dr. Böhm kindly sent Christmas greetings from Leipzig and reminded me about having the Brahms symphony ready for the new term. My pleasure at his card and my excitement at the prospect of conducting the Second student orchestra were dashed when I remembered that Krisztina had forbidden me to speak to her. Outside, the avenues were crowded with smartly dressed, as well as humble, merrymakers alike. The theaters were packed. The Musikverein, the Singakademie, and the Staatsoper were putting on their Christmas and New Year gala performances. I spent most of my so-called holiday time in a practice room at the Conservatory. One of the staff permitted me entrance a few hours a day—the pianos there were far better than my own, and besides, the place was heated.

A few days later, the first week of January 1929, I found an envelope in my message box at the Conservatory. The new term had not yet begun, but students were returning, and the corridors echoed with musical noise. The message was from Dr. Böhm, newly returned from Leipzig. He wanted to know if I had seen Krisztina. Her father in Budapest had communicated with him. He was worried because he had not received her usual weekly letter. I responded that I had not seen her either.

That same evening, there came a loud knock at the door of my lodgings. A plain-looking woman, in her thirties perhaps, wearing a severe hat and dark coat stood on the step.

"Herr Kapp?" I nodded.

"Forgive me for intruding. I am Fräulein Gerigk. We don't know each other, but I share a flat with Krisztina Kabós—perhaps she has mentioned me—"

"Is something the matter?" I asked.

"How perceptive you are!" she exclaimed. "Yes, you might say that. And I might say I have reason to believe that you are involved. May I come in?"

She had the air of an avenging angel. I stepped aside for her to enter and sit. "This is the thing," she said briskly. "Your young friend, Krisztina Kabós, finding herself expecting a child—a child that would be a profound misfortune at this unmarried stage of her life—insisted, against all reason, on asking around for an abortionist." She gave me a sharp look. "You know what I mean, young man?"

"Yes, I think so," I muttered.

"Oh, good for you," said Fräulein Gerigk. "You're up on the latest information. Just like the stupid fool who found the abortionist for her in the first place! I tried my best to stop her. She refused to hear of it. She only talked about doing away with the shame for her family. And this is the strangest thing of all: the young idiot who got her into this predicament—she refused to involve him, even to let him know. Unbelievable! And that, I take it, would be you, Herr Kapp?" She was most unpleasant.

All I could manage was a terrified stare.

"You men, you make me sick, the whole lot of you! The bad ones and the so-called good ones. No difference! All it requires to create mischief is beastly men and gullible women. At least, women are not the criminals here. Thank God for women!"

I gaped. *Was she one of those women who loved women? Was Krisztina?*

Fräulein Gerigk rapped sharply on the table. "I'll tell you why I'm here," she said. "When Krisztina came back from the abortionist, it was clear that things were not good. But we hoped she would get better. Now, after twenty-four hours, things are worse. Krisztina is a beautiful and brave girl, but her optimism is not working. I think she has an infection. She needs a hospital."

"Where's the infection?" I asked lamely.

"Where do you think?" she snapped. "Where you tampered with her. In those regions down below."

"What can I do about it? Why didn't you take her to the hospital?"

"There is a slight problem with such a step," said Fräulein Gerigk. "You obviously have not heard that abortions are illegal in Austria—not only illegal, but also a grave offense to the Almighty," she added. "Our worthy republic, with all it has to worry about, seems to reserve its greatest wrath for punishing abortion—but surely, you have heard that!"

She was mocking me.

"And because abortion is illegal, I do not want to draw any attention to it in any way. I have quite enough trouble with the police as it is, because they know how I prefer to live and with whom. They already hound me day and night. I don't want to invite more unwanted notice. Do you understand what I mean? I cannot summon an ambulance to my premises or have Krisztina transported to a hospital."

"But why not just take her to hospital now? If you say you're her friend—"

"Stupid, stupid, like all men and their regulations!" Fräulein Gerigk was angry. "You haven't heard me? If women made the laws, the world wouldn't be as mad as it is. Look here, I'm writing down our address. You will come as quickly as possible. You will remove her to the hospital, which I understand is quite close to here. You take her in. You answer all the awkward questions and fill out the forms. I must have nothing to do with it. I'm truly sorry, but it has to be done this way. Is that quite clear?"

She swept out, leaving me shaken. Everything was crumbling. The worst had happened. I felt paralyzed. People would turn from me in revulsion. Wasn't Fräulein Gerigk truly the callous one?

All at once, I thought of the one person I could tell. I flung on my coat and, once again, ran madly through the chilly nighttime streets of Vienna. Within ten minutes, I had arrived at Klara's flat, phoned from the concierge's desk, and been permitted upstairs. She greeted me with a wary expression. She was as I had last seen her, clad in a flowered silk wrapper, pale, completely without makeup.

I blurted out my story, at the top of my voice, without drawing breath. She listened, astonished. "What am I to do? People are going to blame me."

Klara lit a cigarette, shaking her head. "Do you remember what I told you, *Liebchen*? Indeed, you are *eine Katastrophe*, the bringer of disasters!"

I couldn't stand it. I began to sob.

"Wait for me here," she said. She soon emerged from the bedroom wearing a coat over trousers and a thick wool jersey. "Come along, we will have to hurry. And please, stop that damned blubbering. Nobody cares about your tears."

"Where are we going?" I was steeped in misery.

"To take your unfortunate Krisztina to the hospital. Come on. Don't dawdle! Have you got the address?"

I couldn't believe it. "But why, Fräulein? Why should you want to help?" We were already in the Bugatti, pulling out into night traffic, heading for the Gablenzgasse amid honking and exhaust fumes.

"Because it sounds serious," she said, intent on the other cars. She muttered a curse as a policeman halted us to permit a cross-stream of traffic to proceed.

She turned to me, her face eerily pale in the reflected light of many headlamps. "And because I have been in a similar situation."

I was aghast. "You have? What happened?"

The policeman signaled us forward. "I almost died." My teeth started chattering. "After that, I saw life differently. For instance, love and the promises of men don't mean a damn thing. I almost died because I didn't understand that. I do now." She laughed.

It was a world horrifyingly removed from Mama's goodness and from the purity of music. "I cannot believe that," I said. "If there is no love—"

"There is no love," she declared. "I have been left stranded, pregnant, and believing in promises. I was fifteen, and my handsome boy-lover was terrified, as you are now." She turned to me. "His parents packed him off to America. I was taken to a butcher of an abortionist and left there. It was in a frightful alley or slum. He could not stop the bleeding, but at least, he himself got me to a hospital. When it was all over, I had no insides. I would have no children. My father refused to visit. My mother came once to leave a bag of clothes. I had offended God, she said, and deserved everything that happened to me. I found friends who showed me kindness. When I became stronger and more interested in life, they taught me how to dress, how to behave, how to flatter men—how to make money from them—the only truth on God's earth. The same God I had offended."

I shuddered at the blasphemy.

"And that is why I drop everything to help a poor stupid girl who has been taken in by an equally stupid young man." We halted by a tenement in the Pilgerimgasse. "I think this is the place," she said. We got out of the car. "The only difference is that the stupid young man dances on, free and clear. The stupid girl ends up dead or broken in pieces." She slammed the car door.

Fräulein Gerigk showed me into a sparely furnished flat. I think she was surprised to see me accompanied by an elegant young woman.

Krisztina was dressed, waiting in a chair for me. Her face was flushed and sweaty. Her eyes were bloodshot, she was breathing rapidly. But she broke into such a sweet smile when she saw me. "Hello, Ferenc," she whispered. "I'm sorry that I'm putting you to such trouble. It's all stupid, I know." When she caught sight of Klara, her smile vanished, and her eyes filled with tears. "Is it your new lady friend?" She sank back in her chair.

"I think she's becoming funny in the head," said Fräulein Gerigk. "The sooner you bring her to the hospital, the better."

Klara and I helped Krisztina to the car. It was something of a tight squeeze, but we managed. She was truly hot and feverish. She didn't make sense when she spoke. In less than twenty minutes, we arrived at the Old General Hospital, really just around the corner from where I lived. As we took Krisztina inside, we happened to encounter two young doctors in long white coats pacing along a corridor. By then, she was moaning and noticeably trembling, barely able to stand. One of the doctors immediately sat her down on a bench and was about to place a thermometer in her mouth when she cried out in pain and apparently had a violent attack of diarrhea right there. Thank God it hadn't occurred in Klara's car. The doctor leapt back with a curse and shouted for orderlies and nurses. The smell was really foul. The attendants began to clean Krisztina even as they wheeled her out. Others set about furiously scrubbing that corner of the waiting area, replacing the smell of feces with strong carbolic.

"I am Dr. Volkmann. Now what do you know about all this?" asked the doctor. "Who is she? Where is her family? Are you related to her? This is a most unusual admission. Do you know what has happened to her? She seems to be a refined young lady. I don't enjoy mysteries!"

I was paralyzed again. I turned to Klara for help, but she had vanished during the excitement. I would have to speak alone. I was frightened and worn out. I had no stamina to make up a story. I told the doctor what I knew. As far as I was aware—which was the truth—the young lady had had an illegal operation, an abortion in fact. She had not been doing well, and friends had helped me bring her to this hospital. That was all.

"Are you the father of the child?" he asked. "Else, what are you doing here?"

I hesitated. It was a complicated story.

"In the absence of a denial, I will assume the answer is yes." I made a helpless gesture. "And as such, you have been complicit in the procurement and commission of an illegal act. Anyway"—he shrugged—"the police will look into that."

"What's going to happen to her?" I begged. "Will she get better?" I suppose it was heartless, but I couldn't help thinking of myself. I was about to be buried under a mounting scandal that would ruin my life—my hopes for a career, Mama's happiness, and Madame's dream of my brilliant future.

A nurse approached. She exchanged quiet words with the doctor. When she left, he sat down next to me. "We have put the young lady in the gynecological ward. She gives indications of having contracted a severe septicemia, perhaps puerperal fever."

I didn't understand.

He addressed me as though in a lecture hall. "We would lose horrifying numbers of women in childbirth because of puerperal fever. No one understood it—they talked about the will of God, bad air, evil spirits. It seemed a curse on the event that should ensure happiness. Finally, in the mid-1800s, Dr. Semmelweis—at this hospital, in fact—had the right idea." He cocked his head brightly at me. "You know what it was?" I could only stare at him.

He couldn't stop chuckling. "It was the medical staff themselves! Unbelievable ignorance! You know, people hadn't the vaguest idea of hygiene, sepsis, or the germ theory—anything like that. Doctors would examine and treat patients, one after another on the wards, without washing their hands. In fact, sometimes, they would proceed from working with cadavers to handling patients—also without washing. They refused to—they were such proud men! They persisted in refusing, even after they'd collected evidence. Finally, the truth sank in. Doctors attending women in labor began washing their hands in soap and water or antiseptics. And, wonder of wonders, mortality rates plunged! Now, I would never say that childbirth is a pure pleasure for the ladies, but it is much more safe now. Physicians are no longer transmitting toxins from patient to patient."

I groaned with fatigue. I was not interested. *What had this to do with Krisztina? She was not going to have a baby.*

The doctor's smile faded. "Now, as I understand the problem with your young lady friend—she has undergone a surgical procedure most likely not performed in a sterile environment. In fact, she is unable to tell us what that environment was."

He gave me a look. I could say nothing.

"But the general effect is the same as in the story I just told you," he said. "All signs are that she indeed has an acute septicemia, most likely puerperal fever. The best defense would have been scrupulous attention to cleanliness on the part of the practitioner—doubly required for one who deals with the female urogenital system. Extremely vulnerable to infection."

"But can't she be given some kind of medicine, Herr Doktor? Some drug?"

He shook his head. "We don't much know what could help. The researchers are reporting interesting results with sulfonamides, but so far"—he shook his head again—"things would be much too new, much too experimental."

I felt hopeless. I would be held responsible. "So what are you going to do, Herr Doktor?"

"We wait for the fever to run its course. We try to feed her and hope that she has the stamina to resist the infection." He sighed and actually clapped me on the shoulder before rising to leave.

"Can I see her?" I called after him.

He turned. "Too soon. She wouldn't have passed the crisis yet."

I decided to stay. I remained on the waiting room bench all night. It was quiet and lonely. I must have drawn my feet up and slept full-length because the next thing I knew I was shaken awake by morning sweepers who plainly disapproved. *Streng verboten!* they hissed as they worked. "You may not lie down!"

I blinked at the clock on the wall. A quarter to six. It was still dark outside. Suddenly, the waiting room was crowded with nurses in cloaks, caps, and kerchiefs streaming in through the doors from the outside. Fifteen minutes later, another group of cloaked nurses—the night staff—was on its way home. When the bustle calmed down, I was surprised to see Klara. She had just come from the Gonzaga, dressed as I had first seen her—evening wear, black furs and wraps, elaborately made-up.

"I came as soon as I could—after my wicked work—to see how the innocent Fräulein Krisztina might be faring," she said. "I have inquired at the desk. We will be permitted to see her for a short while. Come on, if you want to."

Gynecology was on the second floor, around several twists and turns. But they had moved Krisztina to a small private room. They said she was no longer strictly a gynecological patient but suffering rather from acute toxemia—and besides, she was disturbing other patients with her constant talking and crying out. They warned us that they didn't like the look of things. They said that we should perhaps summon her parents, no matter how we might wish to protect them from unpleasant news as to why she was in hospital.

It was all profoundly depressing. When I caught sight of Krisztina's face, I became truly frightened. First of all, she didn't recognize me, and she didn't realize that Klara was with me. In fact, she wasn't aware of anything. She was talking to herself, alternately frowning and laughing. A nurse in the room put wet cold cloths on her forehead, but Krisztina didn't seem to notice. Her face looked red and hot. The nurse invited us to sit, all the while staring at Klara's long black evening clothes. The perfume she wore was not defeated by the antiseptic hospital smells. We remained there for a half hour, I think. Not once did Krisztina cease from her chatter and giggling. At times, she sang. I recognized Hungarian nursery songs that Mama used to sing to me in Szombathely. The doctor who had talked to me in the morning looked in and said he wanted to examine the patient. He asked us to wait outside. He suggested that we visit the commissary and buy something to eat. I hadn't realized how hungry I was.

In the corridor, Klara yawned and stretched. "I simply must sleep," she said. "It feels as though it's been weeks. And, of course, I have to go back to work tonight."

"Can I come with you? I need to sleep too—just to sleep," I added hastily because of the look she gave me. The sight of her in her Gonzaga finery really stirred me up. Even in Krisztina's hospital room, even though I knew I was a heartless beast, I wanted to be with Klara again.

She laughed. "Absolutely not."

"Why not?" I complained. "I don't want to be alone. I'm also tired—I can't even stand up. I've been running around from here to there without a stop."

"I know," said Klara. "I've been at your side for much of it." Her laughter vanished. "You know, Herr Kapp, you completely take my breath away—and I don't mean that kindly. It would be good if you stopped thinking about yourself. Here is this poor girl, raving—out of her mind. You seem to have no idea it was your fault."

That wasn't fair. She kept harping on it. She had not been there the night it happened. She didn't know that Krisztina had joined in willingly, if not gladly. But it was no use. I would be blamed.

"I've been trying to help," I said.

"What do you know about women? About abortions? What do you know about your Krisztina?"

"What do you mean?"

"Apparently she loved you." Her mouth twitched in disgust. "I'll try to come again this evening, before I return to work. By the way," she continued, "aren't you the least bit curious about the man you battled with so bravely at the Gonzaga, whom you so gallantly dashed to the ground—my companion of the evening, His Excellency, the minister for war?" I could barely remember.

"He is dead," said Klara, pulling on her gloves.

"Because of me?"

"No, of course not. Don't puff yourself up! He was a sweet old man but in poor health—ready to go at any time. I shall miss him. His encounter with you was one excitement too many. I was correct to think of you as *eine Katastrophe*, right?" She turned and left. I remained outside Krisztina's room all day, slumped in a chair. I couldn't bear to watch her, although I could hear her talking and singing away. At about three in the afternoon, she fell silent. A doctor was sent for. He emerged after several minutes accompanied by the nurse, who pointed me out to him.

"Are you the patient's friend?" Alarmed, I nodded. "Nothing immediate to worry about, but I think the crisis is at hand. She is maintaining quite a high temperature, but she's sleeping at the moment. Dr. Volkmann, whom I believe you met, is on call. I am summoning him for a consultation. Please be so good as to wait out here."

When Dr. Volkmann appeared, he nodded to me as he hurried by into Krisztina's room. In spite of instructions, I followed him. The doctors were murmuring together. They looked annoyed to see me. Dr. Volkmann motioned me to follow him back outside.

"Nothing particularly new," he said. "The poor girl's exhausted and dehydrated. She has developed skin lesions consistent with septicemia. If she can get through this night with her strength intact, she might have a chance. In any case, there would be a lengthy convalescence. Has her family been informed? They should. It's strange to see an obviously well-bred young lady all alone, except for one young male visitor."

We were interrupted by a cry from within. Krisztina had awakened and was crying out again. I followed Dr. Volkmann inside. Another doctor and nurse hastened to join us. Even though deep in fever, Krisztina was pale, with angry red blotches on her face and about her eyes. Her hair was wild. She looked thin and wasted. She would not stop shouting.

"What is she trying to say? What is she shouting?" The doctors and nurses looked at each other in bewilderment. And to me, "Can you understand her?" Indeed, I could. It was all perfectly comprehensible Hungarian. "Ferenc, Ferenc, my handsome young man!" At the top of her voice, the endearments sounded unbearably freakish. "I've loved you…ever since I first saw you." Her eyes stared wide open, though she saw nothing. Other doctors and nurses were drawn by the noise. I was overcome by terror, lest someone discover that it was me she was howling at. "I love your beautiful hands," she screamed. "When you play. When you touch me."

The doctors and nurses grimaced and shrugged, not even trying to understand. *"Ungarisch!"* they told each other, tapping their heads, implying that being Hungarian and crazy were the same thing.

Krisztina's voice became scratchy and ragged. Soon, all that was left were hoarseness and pathetic wheezing. But still she did not fall silent. She filled the room with loud insane whispers, just as crushing to hear as when she screamed. It almost killed me to hear those declarations I fervently wished not to hear, especially not in that place. It was an unbearable mockery.

Mercifully, out of sheer exhaustion, she fell asleep, although her breathing remained rapid and shallow. I had to rest as well. I announced to the room that I was going home and would return in a few hours. Nobody looked up. As you know, by coincidence, my lodgings were just around the corner. Krisztina was going through her ordeal right on my doorstep. When I emerged on the Lazarettgasse, it was snowing—about three inches had fallen. I could take no joy in it. Once home, I fell onto my bed without taking off my muddy boots.

I returned to the hospital before nine o'clock that night. An elderly couple were seated in the room, Krisztina's Viennese aunt and uncle. Fräulein Gerigk must have informed them. They stared at Krisztina. Her face was drawn, chalk white, eyes closed, panting.

The uncle stood and murmured his name. I was too distracted to catch it. The aunt clutched rosary beads. To the uncle's questioning glance, I mumbled that I was an old friend from Szombathely. They smiled when they heard the Magyar.

"Do you know what has happened to her?" the uncle pleaded. "The people here say they don't know anything."

I listened, stricken. "I am just a friend from the Conservatory," I said.

"We don't know Krisztina's friends. It's kind that you should take the trouble to visit." I heaved a sigh of relief. They were unaware of my existence. "We have telegraphed her father in Budapest, begging him to come as soon as possible," said the aunt. "Whatever is wrong with her, it looks bad." I closed my eyes tight. I would not be able to meet Krisztina's father again.

We were all silent. The only sounds were Krisztina's rapid breathing. A nurse continued to apply cold wet cloths. She shook her head. "The poor girl is burning up." At about eleven o'clock that night, Dr. Volkmann put in another appearance. He saw no change. Just as he was about to leave, Krisztina suddenly sprang awake and sat up. She began to shout more loudly than she had that morning. Again, although her eyes were open, it was evident that she saw nothing. Also evident, she was wracked by waves of agony. The aunt and uncle clung to one another at the spectacle.

"We've been giving her opium for the pain," said Dr. Volkmann, "not that it's helped much."

"Ferenc, Ferenc!" she screamed. I rushed to the bed, even though the doctor tried to prevent me. "*Szeretlek*, Ferenc—I love you!" she screamed again and fell back on the pillows, exhausted. I bent over her. She seemed to recognize me.

"Ferenc," she breathed, barely able to pronounce my name. Her face had grown softer, calmed from the fury of this terrible day. She actually smiled at me. "Ferenc," she murmured again. Then her eyes closed. There was a long sigh, and then no more breathing.

A full minute passed. I heard Dr. Volkmann. "I think she's gone."

I was stunned. I couldn't believe it. The aunt began to wail. Full of terror, I turned to bolt from the room. Dr. Volkmann held out his arms to stop me.

"You can't leave before you sterilize your hands," he shouted. "You've been exposed to toxins of the worst kind. I warned you not to approach her!"

I broke from his grasp and ran through the corridors, frantically trying to remember whether I had given anyone at the hospital my address.

* * *

For two whole days, I sat huddled in a corner in my Klo, not eating a thing, too terrified to move. I played chess with huge dead water beetles on the checkered tile floor. I expected a visit from the police. Nothing like that happened. I ventured into the streets. As far as I could tell, I was not being watched. Piano lessons resumed with Professor Starker. He confirmed that I was to play the *Diabelli Variations* in February and, in early April, Beethoven's Fourth Concerto. He declared that, since Eduard van Vleiman had disappeared, I had emerged as the Conservatory's stellar piano pupil. Dr. Böhm had returned from Leipzig. When I entered his study, he ignored my outstretched hand, at the same time ignoring my respectful questions about his performances of *Zauberflöte*.

"Before returning to Vienna," he began, "I took a side journey to Budapest at the urgent request of my old friend, Herr Kabós." He peered over his spectacles at me. "It was his daughter with whom you were acquainted here in Vienna?" My blood froze.

"Herr Kabós was plunged in grief, quite devastated. His daughter is dead—only eighteen years old—beautiful, gifted, and charming. It happened just last week! He performed the sad task of bringing her home." He paused again. "And nobody has the slightest idea of what happened. Or nobody will say. Ill one day, dead the next."

I clamped my jaws shut. I remembered how my teeth had chattered in fright when Klara had spoken of her abortion in the car. And the name that she had called me—*Katastrophe!* So unfair. My eyes filled with tears.

"What do you know about this terrible thing?" he asked.

"Nothing," I replied, swallowing hard.

"That is curious. Have the police been in touch?" I shook my head. "That too is curious. The sister and brother-in-law of Herr Kabós said that a young fellow student at the Conservatory had visited her in the hospital and spoken to them in Hungarian. You resemble their description. They heard Fräulein Kabós address that young man by the name of Ferenc. But your name is Hermann, isn't it?"

My teeth began to chatter.

"I do not know what might have occurred between you and

Fräulein Kabós, but I can imagine many things." He stood and walked over to me from his desk. "I confess that I am torn, Herr Kapp. I think of you as a young man of great promise—I would stake my reputation on it. How one comes to possess such a gift—whether one is born with it or somehow develops it—is one of the great enigmas. I still don't know you well, but I feel in my bones that you possess the makings of a great career. I sense that you really grasp music—the design, the sweep, the power of it. Of course, you need training, but it might have been the most rewarding training I could impart."

"Might have, Herr Professor?" I stammered.

"You know that Professor Starker has the highest opinion of your talents. But I wonder, what exactly do you express when you play?"

I could only hang my head.

"Is it possible that you don't understand me? Is this the first you hear that musicians communicate something? Well, I ask again. What do you presume to say when you make music? When you are at the keyboard? Or while you stood before the orchestra in my class and seemed instinctively to understand the meanings behind tempo, balance, and dynamics? Was it a mere technical feat? Did it have no connection to humanity? Or to the great souls who created that music?" I had nothing to say.

"Perhaps you recall my saying that I could never abide cruelty and vice?"

Something terrible was about to happen. I knew it.

"Yes, I am torn," he said again. "Because I also feel in my bones that, even though she apparently renounced you, you committed some grave harm—"

"I didn't do anything to her," I burst out. "What did she tell you?"

"She and I have never spoken," he said sadly. "But just as I am sure you could be a great Kapellmeister, I am more than reasonably sure that you harmed that child!"

The injustice of it! My mind began to race. We were alone together. Had anyone seen me enter? Perhaps I could do something. Dr. Böhm saw my eyes flicker over a large marble paperweight at the edge of his desk. He smiled.

"You will, of course, resign from my class," he said.

Wearily, I inclined my head.

"I have no wish to impede your brilliant career. But for all your talent and appeal, I think there is something"—he searched for a word—"*schrecklich* about you. Something frightful." I gasped. He had all but slapped me across the face.

Dr. Böhm stroked his chin, lost in thought. He brightened. "No, not so much *schrecklich*. A better word would be *ekelhaft*. Yes, loathsome is far better!"

I stumbled out of his study, my face burning. The terrible words that had been hurled at me—*Katastrophe, Ekelhaft, Unglücklich, Schrecklich*. I had not behaved in the best way. But I had truly loved Krisztina. Perhaps I should have immediately offered to marry her— she had given me no chance to think! People were just not being fair. I certainly had not wanted things to turn out this way. Another thing—even if I were driven from the Conservatory, would it bring Krisztina back?

For Professor Starker, I was the piano genius of the year. In addition to the *Diabelli*, he set me in earnest to rigorous work on the Beethoven Fourth, which I was to play in June. To my horror, I was to be accompanied by the Second student orchestra. Dr. Böhm refused to have anything to do with the enterprise.

"I don't understand," Professor Starker commented to me. "He gave me the impression that he was one of your enthusiasts, that he saw enormous promise in you. Now"—he raised his hands in incomprehension—"when he knows I want to talk about you, I get no chance to begin. He simply walks away. What is in the man's mind?"

I could only shake my head and continue to practice. The whole matter was playing hell with my nerves, interfering with my concentration. Of course, I was most thankful that Dr. Böhm had not made a public issue of it. I had no idea why not. But the fact that he had not was worse than if he had. I couldn't stop thinking about him, asking myself why he was keeping my involvement with Krisztina— and its awful consequence—a secret. Not even telling her father. It was taking me forever to fall asleep at night. And when I succeeded, I dreamed of him and Krisztina. Usually, they stood side by side, staring at me. Strangely, Professor Starker said I was playing far better than ever he remembered.

"Good, good, good," he nodded. "The Variations are coming along wonderfully. The bravura sections are, as usual, working well."

He gave me a puzzled look. "I detect something different. Are things all right with you? I've just noticed the way you play those quiet, introspective sections, for instance." I was unable to meet his gaze.

Professor Starker cocked his head to one side. "Yes," he said, "your face is thinner, you've developed circles under your eyes. Have you been ill? You must forgive me for not asking sooner. When music is playing, I'm a lost cause—hard for me to think of other things."

My heart was so burdened that I almost was tempted to tell him all about it. Just in time, I remembered that I also had thought of Dr. Böhm as a friend. The business with Krisztina was not to be shared. I had anxieties enough. I needed to lean on Professor Starker, not turn him into another disapproving presence.

The day of my recital arrived. In the first half, I was to play two sets of Beethoven's *bagatelles*, all seven in Opus 33 and the eleven in Opus 119. Both Professor Starker and I thought them a suitable hors d'œuvre to the Diabelli—provocative, charming, with an edge of violence. I had wanted to include the six *bagatelles* in Opus 126. But Professor Starker said that would be too much. What a shame. There never could be enough Beethoven!

I was trying to do my best to avoid running into Dr. Böhm—using certain unaccustomed entrances and staircases. But I spotted another person whom I didn't want to see. I cursed under my breath in disbelief. It was none other than Eduard van Vleiman. Professor Starker had assured me that he was out of the picture for good.

When he spotted me, he called out and gave a cheery wave from the landing above, pointing to his afflicted hand, announcing that everything was better.

"Hermann!" he bubbled with happiness. "Glad to see you, so glad to see you again! You've been a true friend," he added. "You kept my secret! I've been home, seen the best doctors in Amsterdam and London. They all told me nothing was physically wrong with my hands. I actually had to come back to Vienna, to see Dr. Freud. I'm a hysteric—not paralyzed at all!" He giggled like a gleeful child.

He had arrived at my landing and was advancing toward me with a huge, pleased smile on his face. Hurrying down just behind him were four young men who wore military-style tunics, breeches, and high polished boots. That was nothing unusual these days. But they must have been following Eduard, for as he paused, they suddenly rushed toward him, seized him, three of them thrusting him violently against the balustrade. Eduard cried out. They almost threw him over.

The leader of the four advanced on me, wearing an ugly expression. "You a friend of this Jew?" he sneered. Eduard bleated in terror.

I didn't know what to say. They had appeared so abruptly.

The leader stuck his face right into mine. "If you are, you'll get the same."

"But what's happened?" I managed. "What has he done?"

The leader put a comradely hand on my shoulder and smiled. "If it's nothing to do with you, count yourself lucky. All you need to know is three things about him. Number one, he's a dirty Jew. Number two, he's a filthy Communist. And number three, he's a foreigner! Isn't that enough? Kindly step aside and let us get on with it."

They didn't care who might see them. One pinned Eduard's hands behind his back. The others took turns punching his head. When Eduard dropped to the floor, they kicked his body. Eduard screamed in pain, his face covered with blood. After a while, he made no sound. His attackers drew back, breathing hard after their exertions.

"That's that then," grinned the leader. In spite of my shock, I recognized him. He was the handsome youth who led the Young Nationalist Patriots League on its daily marches through the streets—said to be in his final term at the school of law. Two of his companions seized Eduard by the legs and dragged him down the stairs. His head made a hollow thump on every step.

They left me shaking in fright, staring at a puddle of blood. It had all happened so quickly. You will say that I have heard of this sort of thing before. I had, but never seen it, never imagined what it was like. I *knew* Eduard—didn't care for him a bit—but I *knew* him. I had wished for something like this to happen but only in the abstract! To witness it was entirely different. *Should I have protested, said something, done something?*

I felt faint. Was I really playing Beethoven this day? My head was swimming. My legs refused to hold me. I slumped to the floor and threw up. I began to sob and must have lain for a good half hour, smeared with vomit and Eduard's blood.

* * *

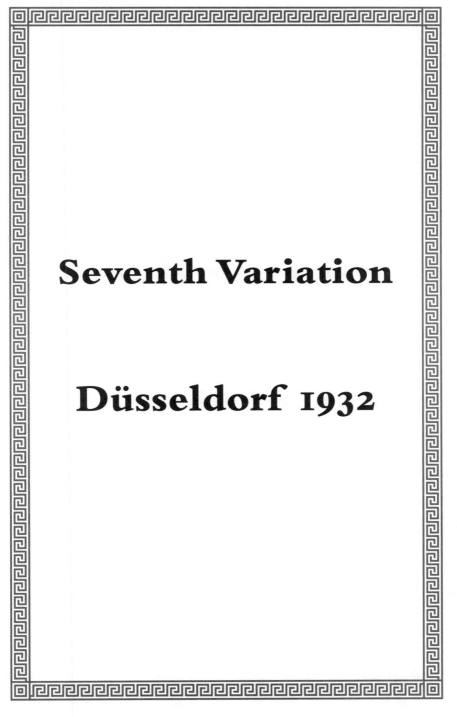

Seventh Variation

Düsseldorf 1932

Franz Liebermann would say he was a genial tyrant, that his bark was worse than his bite. But that was only his side of it. As Generalmusikdirektor of the Westfälische Staatsoper of Düsseldorf, he had complete control of the following forces: an orchestra and chorus; a resident company of singers and voice coaches, as well as touring soloists, who dropped in for a couple of weeks at a time, and thought they could ask for anything they pleased (rarely granted); a corps de ballet, choreographers, and a ballet master; stage directors; set designers; lighting designers—and the workmen who carried out their wishes. This was a community of perpetually discontented people who believed they belonged in Berlin or New York and took it for granted that they were right and everyone else was wrong. Presiding over this unruly collection was Herr Liebermann, lofty and mostly silent, except when he exploded in terrible rage, enormously irritated by what he called "that pretentious band of poseurs."

I should have been grateful to Herr Liebermann for providing a refuge after I was obliged to quit my studies in Vienna. But why did I always have to fall into the hands of Jews? It demonstrates the grip of those rootless wanderers upon the soul of German art. I echoed only what many people were saying.

Soon after my arrival in Düsseldorf, I managed to sneak into a speech given by Adolf Hitler, the up-and-coming political leader. He had come to address a meeting of Ruhr Valley millionaires on the topic of connections between racial purity and the state of the economy. But his audience was worried about the words Socialist and Workers in his organization's name, the National-Socialist German Workers' Party. They feared that, like the Bolsheviks, he meant to confiscate their industries if he came to power. He soon set their minds at ease. The first word in his party's title, National, was the one that counted. He was a German first, last, and always. He added that we were all workers in the task of Germany's revival. Stormy applause! And what a magnetic speaker! He put into perspective what Dr. von Hornberger had pointed out back in Eisenstadt as the causes of our misery, the twin evils of international Bolshevism and international Jewry. He had a wonderfully sarcastic sense of humor. He put us into stitches when he denounced the Weimar Parliament as the "headquarters of stupidity!"

He aroused us to indignation when recalling for us the recent history of Düsseldorf, particularly the imposition by the French of a Black-Colonial Army of Occupation in the Rhineland. Herr Hitler said the Allies could not have failed to predict the humiliating outcome: Rheinlandbastarde—the countless black offspring of these abominable unions. He spoke for hours, but people didn't notice the time and hung on every word. And he made sense even for my particular problems. The awful circumstances under which I was obliged to leave the Conservatory were precipitated, you might say, by a Jew and were no fault of my own. Now, three years later, it was hard to forget.

The whole thing was ironic because I detested the thought of Eduard van Vleiman. What had happened to him was dreadful, of course, but the consequences for me were almost as bad. For some unknown reason, I could not bring myself ever again to play as a soloist in public after what I had witnessed. And you must not forget my agonized meeting with Eduard's parents—they had rushed to Vienna from Amsterdam. They insisted on seeing me, weeping, pleading for explanations—in the presence of the police—as if I could have helped. It was indeed too much. Of course, I could never reveal the identity of his attackers. It wouldn't have been prudent. Don't mistake me. The Young Nationalist Patriots League were no doubt extreme in what they did; but on the whole, people agreed with their aims. Their violence was upsetting, but you have to admit they never fiddled about. They decided, and they acted. I couldn't help admiring them for that—so different from my own spineless indecision. Things with them were simple, clear, and direct.

But that day, I had to flee the Conservatory building, could not set foot in it again, and besides, discovered that something unnamable prevented my appearing as a solo performer. In addition, Professor Starker lost his sense of understanding and refused to communicate with me for a whole week, after which he either shouted at me in utter incomprehension or else stared at me in silence, shaking his head.

"What will become of us?" he asked over and over. "One piano prodigy is beaten to death within the Conservatory itself. The same day, another refuses to play at what would surely prove to be his triumph. Things are upside-down. The streets are full of ruffians and hooligans. They threaten everybody—the police, the government, the president of the republic himself! I fear the worst. What will become of us?"

To make a long story short, the rector decided that he had heard enough about me and my problems. He reminded me that he had already switched me from Herr Schneidermann to Professor Starker and that he had "indulged" me sufficiently. He pointed out that, while he was not interested in harming my career, he and the Vienna Conservatory had gone as far as they could to advance it. I would have to look elsewhere. Professor Starker agreed that I possessed a remarkable talent; but as I seemed unable to prepare for a concert career, his hands would be tied. These unhappy events might have spelled the end of the story. But I turned out still to have friends. Professor Starker remained as one. He enlisted the aid of Herr Fridolin Karl of Eisenstadt. Another was Madame Polkovska—now bedridden and surely more ancient than ancient. The ironic thing was that they were Jewish (or so I was led to believe). They must have communicated with all the Jews they knew throughout Austria and the Weimar Republic— they are, as everybody knows, not only notoriously clannish but industrious. They wanted to know, if I "refused" to play concertos and solo recitals, would I be willing to work as an accompanist? If so, situations might be found. I agreed. Sighs of relief must have been heard all the way from Hungary to the Rhine. For my part, I didn't much care and couldn't comprehend why it mattered so much to them.

So there I was in Düsseldorf, working as *répétiteur,* a rehearsal coach, and musical odd-job man for Herr Liebermann. All I had to do was be ready to sight-read any piano score at a moment's notice—never a problem for me. I was awed by my new home. The Westfälische Staatsoper occupies—or rather, occupied—what had been an ornate eighteenth-century baroque building, not far from the Königsallee. Unhappily, it was destroyed in 1942 by RAF night bombers, in one of those barbaric wartime attacks. When I knew it, however, I was most charmed. Never overwhelming, it never failed to impress. Four tiers of dark red plush boxes reached from floor to ceiling, circling the auditorium. At the rear, on the second level, decorated with his coat of arms, was the Elector's Box. Each of the other boxes was decorated with sculptured nymphs and *putti*. From the cream and gilded ceiling, which depicted mythological courtly scenes, hung an immense crystal chandelier. I belonged in a place such as this.

I worked with soloists and small groups of singers, drilling them, passage by passage—sometimes note by note. Most were decent musicians, but a few, even though they had voices and had appeared in many roles, couldn't read music—or not well—which astounded me. I worked with them at the piano, banging out phrases, over and over, which they would attempt to reproduce, until I had pounded the stuff into their heads. They were not permitted on stage unless they were note-perfect. Herr Liebermann would have skinned me alive. Among them, by the way, were some pretty young women who made eyes and simpered when I was near; but I had no appetite for them—there was a heaviness in my heart. Besides, most of them thought they were too good for me—absolute snobs. They gave me dazzling smiles when signaling their readiness to sing, but I learned the smiles were only for show. Their hearts belonged to the latest greasy touring tenor. I was lonely. I missed Krisztina. I grieved for her and was bitter at her absence.

Yes, Herr Liebermann could be an impatient tyrant. You'd think he was being civil, listening to what you had to say, but that was also for show. There was a young assistant conductor in the company—in his late twenties—Manfred von Krefeld. For some reason, he felt compelled constantly to show off, to demonstrate that he was a real musician. He would pester Herr Liebermann at the most inopportune times. Our Kapellmeister clearly found him irrelevant, irritating—often infuriating.

"Not now," Herr Liebermann would growl. "Not now, Herr...Herr..." He could rarely think of the young man's name while working.

Unaware of danger, Herr von Krefeld would persist in babbling before the whole company. "Don't you think, Herr Kapellmeister, at the end of the third act prelude, you might hold the orchestra still for about a minute before the curtain goes up."

Herr Liebermann closed his eyes. "Why should I want to do that?"

"Why, to let the audience sit with the ravishing memory of that prelude, to let it linger in their minds and have time to be astonished by the modulation that follows." I shook my head. Even I would know when to stop.

Herr Liebermann would give a great bellow. "Herr von Krefeld! Shut your trap and try to learn something! Most important, be quiet until I ask for your help." The unfortunate young man would finally sit down with a sickly smile, but it seemed hard for him to understand. Unearned wealth, I heard, might have been responsible. Herr Liebermann's rages could be provoked by anything. Once he went crazy because his eleven o'clock coffee was not only four minutes late but also cold.

On another occasion, he went insane because the aging contralto, with whom he was rehearsing *Carmen*, sang her mocking act 2 melody, where she accompanies herself with castanets, in her own eccentric way—off-tempo, off-pitch, and with much vocal scooping and sliding about. He had already endured in silence the same levels of perform-ance in the *Seguidilla* and *Habanera* in act 1. Now, Herr Liebermann had had enough. He emitted a great howl, slamming his open palms loudly on the score, stopping the rehearsal. The players put down their instruments and watched, perhaps relieved that, this time, they were not the objects of displeasure.

"What do you think you're doing, Madame Honoret?" he demanded. She was on loan from the Opéra-Comique. Still in charac-ter, clicking her castanets, she swayed and pirouetted to the front of the stage from the midst of the chorus, who, when in costume, would be bandits and wenches at the tavern of Lillas Pastia.

She gave Herr Liebermann a large wink and a roguish smile. "*Chéri*," she announced huskily, "when I sing a role, I don't just sing notes. I don't just play Carmen. I *am* Carmen—seductive, treacher-ous—*irrésistible*." She squeezed her eyes tight and embraced herself in ecstasy. I thought Herr Liebermann would explode. He stared at her a moment and then screamed my name. I scampered forward from my seat in the middle of the hall.

"Herr Kapp," he shouted, "is this the way you went over act 2 with Madame Honoret?"

"Oh, Herr Liebermann, *chéri*, do not be angry with this young man," she chided, with the same fatuous smile. "He tried to be strict and exact with me. I'm sure he drilled me according to your wishes. Ah, but"—she broke off, rolled her eyes, and shook her ample hips— "but this is Carmen. *Carmen!*"

Herr Liebermann was trembling. "Madame Honoret," he began quietly. "I well know the character you are attempting to sing. You may slump about the stage all you wish, but you still find it impossible to keep correct time and to stay on pitch—"

"But," Madame Honoret broke in again, "this is the way I create a character," she wheedled. "You have heard of Sir Thomas Beecham, *chéri*? This is the way he and I worked out the role together at Covent Garden. I have sung the part this way at the Opéra-Comique for the past twenty years."

Herr Liebermann stunned us with a scream. "Then it may be time for you to retire, Madame! To the devil with Sir Thomas Beecham! Don't inflict this lazy caterwauling on me. Are you trying to rewrite Bizet? At least, he knew what he was doing. Which is more than I will say for you!"

He seized his massive conductor's score and attempted to rip it in two, but it was too large. Instead, he hurled it to the floor and stamped on it. Then he turned and stormed from the orchestra pit. Madame Honoret, looking dismayed, promptly followed. The orchestra, I was interested to see, kept their places. Someone replaced the score on his desk. After about fifteen minutes, the pair reappeared arm in arm, chuckling—she taking her place onstage amid the chorus, he once more in the pit.

"Back to the damned castanets," he commanded.

They began again, as though nothing had happened. But this time, Madame Honoret sang scrupulously in time, on pitch, with the appropriate phrasing, clicking her castanets correctly on the beat. She kept her eye on Herr Liebermann, who signaled all the seductive hesitations and *rallentandos* one might wish for. The offstage bugles of *La Retraite* blended precisely on cue. It was perfect, and I was impressed with both of them. Herr Liebermann, stopped the music just before the next section, Carmen's fury at Don José for heeding the bugles' summons, and tapped the desk with his baton in approval. The orchestra tapped bows and stamped their feet. Madame Honoret, at first frozen in a dramatic gesture, castanets held above her head, curtseyed deeply and granted Herr Liebermann a ravishing smile. I couldn't help wondering if there might not have been something going on between them when they were younger. Perhaps it was still going on. I knew that a Frau Liebermann existed at a swanky house on the Hofgartenufer, said to overlook both the Rhine and the Elector's Gardens. How I envied the idea of that splendid house.

Herr Liebermann meant to be in charge. He demanded perfection—in the Westfälische Staatsoper, of all places—not one of your first-rate opera companies. He reminded me something of myself in front of the student orchestra in Vienna—straining for perfection from the imperfect. It would have done no good to point out that Westphalia was not as wealthy as Berlin and could not command the talent. Herr Liebermann knew that as well as I. Nor as rich as Dresden, Munich, or Vienna. In fact, someone once tried to say this, but Herr Liebermann shouted with scorn that, nowadays, everybody in Germany was destitute. Money didn't mean anything anymore; but at least, we could share a rich tradition, great music, and great art. In later years, I remembered what he had said and how he had presumed—this Jew—to lump himself as a sharer in the German patrimony!

As a matter of fact, because of those *Carmen* rehearsals, the whole question of music, women, and Jews came together for me. Let me try to explain. While I was watching Madame Honoret swish and sway, she reminded me of Lotte and Klara. Like them, Carmen is shameless and unclean. She makes fools of men, tantalizes them, turns them upside down. If she were to tempt you, it would be to your destruction. Carmen is a gypsy—my mother had warned me about them. I didn't see any great difference between Carmen and Klara. And Lotte might well have been their sister. The Conservatory always buzzed with rumors of students being ruined because of women. After a day spent in classes or practicing, they went out on the town at night, got drunk, and woke up in the morning with some whore or other. These revelers often developed nasty rashes in their private parts—or were certain to come down with syphilis, a terrifying, slow-developing disease from which they either visibly rotted or went mad and died. Girls could actually destroy you, not merely make you feel horrible. When I thought of girls, it was with both yearning and terror.

And what about these girls? And what about Krisztina? The memory of her pale, fading face filled me with sorrow, panic, and longing. My private parts and the wonderful way they made me feel could actually lead to death. One moment erect and excited, the next shrunken and afraid. I couldn't understand it. *And what about Carmen?* She mocked men because she knew what they hungered for. And she destroyed them until she was destroyed in turn. But then, she was a gypsy—dark, dishonest, and unclean—an alien enemy. I was succeeding in putting my thoughts together. When the Young Nationalist Patriots League beat Eduard van Vleiman to death, they certainly went too far, as I've said, but just as certainly, they identified the unclean enemy—Jews, Bolsheviks, gypsies, and mocking women. They corrupted honest, decent men. The League was too violent and too simplistic in its approach to complicated matters, but you could not accuse them of indifference. Their instinct for clean, decisive action was most appealing, straightforward, and above all, virile. I found the same kind of approach in that speech of Herr Hitler's, especially in his appeal for unity and racially healthy thought, as opposed to what these Jews tended to—anarchic individualism. I never dared express or share these observations.

* * *

After Herr Liebermann had observed my coaching the singers for some months, he asked if I would also like to drill various sections of the orchestra—the strings, the woodwinds, the brass. That surprised me. The programs listed Herr von Krefeld as Herr Liebermann's assistant conductor.

"They hate each other's guts," a voice hissed in my ear. "You know that."

It was Herr Kalandrelli, the archivist and librarian, the dried-up lanky man responsible for putting out and collecting the orchestral parts for the players. "The problem is," he continued with a sneer, "Herr von Krefeld is the grandson of Frau Augustina von Krefeld, the generous and well-nourished patroness and benefactress of the Westfälische Staatsoper. The state government hardly provides enough. You might say that we all work for her—including Herr Liebermann!"

He continued whispering all kinds of nonsense. I drew back in distaste. He was a skinny stick of a man with bad breath. "The Herr Kapellmeister wants as little to do with Herr von Krefeld as possible. His grandmother may have secured the post for him, but Herr Liebermann will not let him wave the stick."

I asked why. "Who knows? Perhaps he's too stupid." Chuckling, Herr Kalandrelli finished placing music on stands. As he passed me on his way from the pit, he muttered, "If he doesn't like it, he could always go home, yes?"

Herr von Krefeld watched with a scowl as I prepared to go over with the brass section their parts in *La Bohème*, in particular the fanfares that begin and end the second act, and the timing of the onstage military band at its close.

I was delighted by these duties. I didn't care how much work was piled on me. The more, the better. Anything to take my mind off the insults and disappointments of my years in Vienna. And how fortunate for me—it was precisely the work I craved. I couldn't get enough of it. By the end of my first season in Düsseldorf, I knew I was receiving the best musical education in the world. I learned entire repertoires and how an orchestra and opera house function. Within a short time, I ceased to regard myself as a hapless derelict, a charity case. I was actually earning my keep. One of the singers reported to me what Herr Liebermann had told him—that my work was full of credibility—that he trusted me. I was dazzled by that but waited in vain for a direct word of praise. I also hoped in vain for an opportunity to conduct an actual performance, but first, Herr Liebermann was keeping a tight hold on that sphere and, second, I would somehow have had to dispose of Herr von Krefeld.

My success with the student orchestra in Vienna had been no accident. Callow and unsure in many areas of life I may have been, but I knew in my guts how an orchestra must sound. Perhaps it was the memory of what Herr Fridolin Karl had done with me in Eisenstadt. Or it was perhaps the operas and concerts I had the good fortune to attend in Vienna. From high up in the gallery, I had witnessed the conducting of men like Hindemith, Knappertsbusch, Weingartner, and Pfitzner. An assembly of gods! So far, I had not seen Toscanini, the Maestro I had read about. For some reason, his Duce, Signor Mussolini, now disapproved of him. But like him, I knew what *allegro con brio* meant, and I knew what to do with it. After I had met the Staatsoper orchestra a few times, it was obvious that they took me seriously.

The plain fact was that I was not a musical scholar in those days. And I never grew into one. You know the sort of person I mean, who is not happy unless he discusses, dissects, and analyzes, drones on about structure and modulation, and writes treatises on ways to express Geist—spirit and genius. Such a one builds his career on a foundation of weighty lectures and tomes. That's the kind of thing Herr von Krefeld liked, as if that had anything to do with how a piece should sound, for God's sake! With all the parts falling into place—so that it becomes inevitable. Not what it might mean, not what it might signify, but how it should sound! Somehow I discovered that. And I discovered how I might wrest what I wanted from other musicians. Another strange matter—I was fearless in front of all those players whom I faced every day. In fact, I had no respect for them. I didn't think of them as decent players—in spite of all Herr Liebermann's noise. He wasn't getting the best out of them.

What did we perform in that first season, the winter of 1929? The New York Stock Exchange had just collapsed—bringing down all other bourses at the same time. This was the ultimate blow. Now, we Austrians and Germans would never pull ourselves up from our mutual catastrophe—the lost war and our hopeless lives. On the other hand, in Düsseldorf, we were living in musical luxury. We put on Beethoven's *Fidelio*, Mozart's *Abduction from the Seraglio*, Verdi's *La forza del destino*, Weber's *Der Freischütz,* and *La Bohème.* All these were holdovers from previous years. We were also preparing new productions, *Carmen* for the current season and *Die Walküre* for the next—if we could secure the funds. The Bizet was a sheer delight. On the other hand, the Wagner stirred me with that mingled pleasure and pain. I absorbed it on gramophone records, was made almost ill by its unbearable beauty, relentless drive, and daring plot—the incestuous love between brother and sister.

"Wait until he hears *Tristan*!" Herr Liebermann is supposed to have said.

Outside the elaborate façade of the Staatsoper, the world was grim. Once again, inflation was ruining people. No one could afford anything. There was no work. Shops and businesses went under right and left. Respectable young women sold themselves on the streets for their daily bread. We heard, from Munich and Berlin, about armies of desperate men who carried the red banner of the Bolsheviks. They battled almost daily with armies of other desperate men who carried the swastika. The police, as usual, were helpless. Gutters ran with blood, and the melancholy sirens of ambulances sounded day and night. And yet the seats of the Staatsoper were filled. Gentlemen in evening clothes bowed and kissed the hands of ladies in tiaras, emeralds, and pearls, and after performances, swept them off to caviar and champagne. I could not fail to note obscene resemblances to life at the Café Gonzaga in Vienna. There too, behind closed doors, all had been luxury and opulence, while I struggled to survive. Here in Düsseldorf, it was a hundred times worse. The Bolsheviks claimed we were witnessing the death agonies of capitalism. Our salvation would come when we swept aside, once and for all, that exhausted system and returned to the people the fruits of their labor.

The problem I had with such an idea was, where did it leave me? And where did it leave the Germans with whom I increasingly identified? I couldn't understand what good it would do us to abandon who we were and sink our identity in some anonymous, untidy concept known as "the masses." I was the son of Wilhelm Kapp, after all. I felt pain at our having lost the Austria and Germany of yesterday. At the same time, I was frightened by the Nazis. The memories of Eduard and the Young Nationalist Patriots League were ever fresh. The League would have laughed at my timidity. You'd have to choose one or the other. And they would have been right. The League and the Nazis defined themselves through unapologetic action. I did not have the courage for that, even though I believed them to be correct.

* * *

Months passed. Preparations for *Die Walküre* had been under way for some time. Herr Liebermann wanted a production that would make the Bayreuth people sit up and take notice. He invited me to join meetings at which we walked around scale models of stage sets and discussed lighting, direction, and the merits of various singers. Some contracts had been signed; others were under negotiation. I was proud to be included in the conversations.

"Those singers' agents are disgusting," grumbled Herr Liebermann one morning. "They practically run auctions with their singers, playing one opera house off another. They don't care if they ruin us or our work!" Later, I discovered that opera houses did precisely the same with the singers.

It was an immense and expensive enterprise. Frau Augustina von Krefeld must have made her fellow patrons dig deep, for I was unaware of any lack of money. It was whispered that, for the sake of "his" opera house, Herr Liebermann was prepared to do almost anything—even spend nights in the bedroom of the same Frau Augustina, a revolting thought. At least, Madame Honoret, our Carmen, had possessed vivacity. But Frau von Krefeld? That's a Jew for you, the Nazis would say—anything for money! Herr Kalandrelli informed me that, *if* Herr Liebermann were indeed spending his nights with Frau von Krefeld, it was a noble sacrifice that maintained all our jobs. That observation was too sordid for words. It defiled both art and music.

The *Walküre* singers had to be of heroic dimension. The opera is long and demanding. They had to be first class. No, world class!—the kinds of singers Düsseldorf could ill afford. Even so, we cast our nets world-wide to find our Siegmund, Sieglinde, Hunding, Wotan, Brünnhilde, and Fricka. All had to possess phenomenal voices and endurance. In addition to Brünnhilde, there were eight sister Valkyries. Moreover, we required an enormously swollen orchestra. Herr Liebermann insisted on carrying out Wagner's requirements to the letter. Anything smaller would insult the spirit of the master himself.

Our customary eight first and second violins were not enough. There had to be sixteen of each, as Wagner demands. Twelve violas and cellos instead of our six. Eight double basses instead of our four. In woodwinds, there had to be three or four of everything—including piccolos, cor anglais, bass clarinets, and contrabassoon. The brass required eight French horns, two tenor and two bass tubas, three trombones, and a double-bass trombone. The percussion battery was not unusual, but Wagner calls for no fewer than six harps. Before the end of summer, workmen were tearing out the front rows of the stalls—expensive, income-producing seats—to make extra room for the orchestra. Our patroness swooned when she heard of it. The director of the Budget for the State of Westphalia insisted on a crisis meeting.

By September 1932, Herr Liebermann was eating and breathing *Die Walküre*, immersed in countless details of production and design. He ignored almost all else. He was oblivious to the turmoil in the streets.

These were not as severe as the street battles between Communists and Nazis in Berlin and Munich, but intrusive enough. You would think he might have noticed the brown-shirted swastika-wearers rattling their collection boxes.

"Buy the Jews a one-way ticket to Palestine!" they howled, laughing. Herr Liebermann stalked past them. Even when they jeered him by name, he said nothing. "Hey, Liebermann, you Yid!" they called. "We're talking to you! How dare you conduct Wagner. He's not for you. He's a German!"

Walküre was to have its premiere on February 3, 1933, a Saturday night. Four of our eight Valkyries; our Fricka, the wife of Wotan, ruler of the gods; and our Hunding, the captor-husband of Sieglinde, were already contracted members of the company. Other stellar roles had to be imported: Siegmund, twin brother and lover of Sieglinde, was not due to arrive until mid-January, true also for our Brünnhilde, Wotan, and Sieglinde. Herr Liebermann was impatient to see them. In the meantime, because of the sheer amount of work, he had to relinquish portions of the repertoire to Herr von Krefeld, namely *La forza del destino* and *Der Freischütz.*

"What else could I do?" he grumbled to me. We were alone in his cluttered office one morning, peering once again at stage designs and costume sketches. "I have to conserve my energies—I can't do everything. His damned grandmother was pestering me night and day without mercy." He mimicked her voice. "Why can't you give the lad his chance? Why, why, oh why?" he wailed in mockery.

It was uncomfortable to listen to such confidences. Herr Liebermann might turn on me one day.

"The thought of that young butcher, von Krefeld, playing fast and loose with my orchestra and my company makes my blood run cold." He cast a wary eye on me. "At least, you seem to have a reliable ear, and you don't drive me crazy with stupid public pronouncements on the meaning of art!"

Wary myself, I kept silent.

"As a matter of fact," he said, "I was thinking of involving you more actively in *Walküre*." He studied me a moment, rocking up and down on his heels. "Herr Kapp," he said, "if I were to require you not only to drill the singers but also to take some responsibility for preparing the orchestra, could you do that?"

My eyes opened wide. Lights began to flash around me. I felt electric.

205

I tried to speak calmly. "How might I be of assistance, Herr Kapellmeister?"

"First, I need you to integrate the new players. The musicians we have now can be relied on to perform at their customary second-class level." *Indeed? He knew how bad they were.* "They can't even play in tune, poor devils." He barked out a short, humorless laugh. "I've ripped my bowels out trying to make them play like professionals! I don't anticipate with pleasure the effort of blending them with new-comers." He favored me with a wintry smile. "That, dear boy, is a task I prefer to leave to you. Agreed?"

"At your command, Herr Kapellmeister." I dared to salute and snap to attention, like a common soldier receiving orders. I grinned broadly. I could not have been happier. Clearly, Herr Liebermann did-n't think highly of my attempt at familiarity. He dismissed me with a wave. Like our conductor, I too immersed myself in *Walküre.* I pored over the pages of the score anew; I spent entire nights at the piano, try-ing passages one way, then another, seeking to ingest the music. I was determined to penetrate each nuance of Wagner's intentions and sniff out all his wishes.

The plan was this. I would work with the orchestra for an hour and a half each morning. After a break, Herr Liebermann or Manfred von Krefeld would work with them on the performance for that evening. It would be grueling for the musicians: two separate rehearsals and an opera at night, to be repeated six days a week, in addition to a matinée. On the other hand, I didn't pity them. They should have been grateful to have jobs, even for their two hundred marks a month. The orchestra committee, that bunch of Bolsheviks, would have noth-ing to say.

The next morning, my first with the full orchestra, a vast assembly of players awaited me. I was taken aback by how many there were. The front rows of the auditorium had been removed, the barrier moved back. Before me, on either side, was desk after desk of violins, violas, cellos, and double basses. Behind them were hosts of woodwinds, brass, and an entire battery of percussion. Even with the additional room, they were jammed against each other. You could see the dust stirred up by the workmen hanging in the air, clinging to every surface. The musicians continually wiped their instruments as they chatted with one another.

I marched up to the conductor's stand. Talking ceased, and I became the object of stares. Many of the players already knew me, of course. Many did not.

"Gentlemen," I said, "it is a warm morning. Why don't you remove your jackets?" There was an appreciative buzz as most followed my invitation.

"And now, gentlemen, although you may have already tuned up, please be so good as to tune your instruments in my presence, beginning with"—I turned to my left—"first violins."

They all looked shocked. After a moment, the concertmaster raised his hand.

"Herr Dirigent," he said, "with great respect, we are all experienced musicians. You already know many of us. You might understand that we know our jobs; and of course, you would not oblige us to tune up in front of you, as though we were—"

"Humiliating!" someone declared from among the body of players. There was a growl of agreement.

"As a matter of fact, and again, with great respect, Herr Dirigent," the concertmaster continued, "you are suggesting a radical change in procedures and practices of which, I'm sure, Herr Liebermann knows nothing and on which the orchestra committee has not yet had a chance to debate."

I took fright and was tempted to flee. The entire orchestra leaned forward. Some were smiling in anticipation of my own humiliation. In a second, I managed to conceal my fear behind fury. I would be damned if I gave them the pleasure. I did what I had seen my father, Herr Liebermann, Herr Schneidermann, and that idiot head clerk in Eisenstadt do, and that was to scream my head off.

"In the absence of Herr Dr. Liebermann, must I endure this ignorant, damned insubordination?" They sat up, eyes bulging. "You think, because Herr Liebermann's not here, it's your opportunity to be slovenly?" I drew in a shaky breath. "Let me inform you, gentlemen, your intonation is dreadful! And one reason is that you don't tune your instruments properly—"

Someone among the cellos interrupted. "Herr Liebermann doesn't complain in this rude way!" I wheeled around but was unable to locate the culprit.

"That's because he's probably given up trying," I snapped. "But I've listened to you for a couple of years now—and I want our newcomers to pay attention! You could be a decent orchestra, if you weren't so careless. Sloppy and careless! I heard Herr Liebermann himself say this, just the other day. He also said that you were a second-class bunch." I glared at them. "The whole shameful lot of you. Second class! Shameful, and you ought to be ashamed."

Some turned white, some red. But for some reason, they all sat there. I had forgotten about the orchestra committee. Never mind, I would worry about that later. I was shaking, not so much with rage, but at my own temerity. *What held them there?* Lack of work elsewhere? But also, when you think about it, they were used to it. For many, it was the German way to behave. We scream, and we are screamed at. We are a disciplined, obedient people. Order us to line up and march: we march!

There I was, at the age of twenty-three, berating some hundred and ten musicians, all older and far more experienced than I, shouting out from the terrors and frustrations of my own young life. I had become a madman. Workers, cleaning women, designers, lighting technicians: all stopped working and gaped. I could make this kind of demonstration only once. I stood, arms folded, trembling, staring into their faces.

After a long silence, the concertmaster looked away, raised his fiddle to his chin, and lifted his bow. The rest of the first violins followed suit. I signaled to the oboe for the A. Of course, their tuning had been atrocious for years. I suspected that Herr Liebermann's own ears were not serving him well. We did not touch *Walküre* that morning. I took my time and was relentless about the tuning and intonation. When I was done with the strings, I turned my attention to the brass. They were also badly out of tune and required major alignment. The next morning, when we all assembled again, first, the orchestra rose to greet me. That was intoxicating. Second, everybody seemed to be in perfect tune. It had worked. I gave thanks to heaven for that trait in the German character that commands perfect obedience when someone screams loudly enough.

We began in earnest with act 1 of *Die Walküre*. In addition to my own study of the score, I called on the memory of a terrible performance I had attended in Vienna, led by one Vaclav Kladno, a Czech conductor. At that time, I recognized the power of the music, but Herr Kladno had been so sluggish that, first, I became bored and, second, enraged by his conducting. Whatever he had done, I now took care to avoid. This opening music of *Walküre* had to be as urgent and impetuous as I could make it. For God's sake, it was about storm, terror, disaster, and passion of the wildest degree.

I fixed the orchestra with a stern eye and swept down my baton. The second violins and violas commenced their tremolos on the D, while the cellos and basses began their restless, striding scales. The difference in sheer volume of sound between this enlarged orchestra and what we were used to was at once apparent. Almost immediately, I stopped them. They were fighting me. The pace was flabby, they were not together—it was sluggish—Vaclav Kladno all over again. In addition, I wanted the violins and violas to play more *sul ponticello*—*am Steg*, as we Germans say, nearer the bridge—to produce the tense, reedy sound that I remembered from gramophone records. The cellos and basses could remain full-throated.

"Keep your eyes on me," I commanded. "Follow the beat, and don't make me waste time! The tempo is marked Rapidly, with Violence. Give me that, if you please!"

I plunged the baton down again. It was better and smarter. At least, they were keeping time. But almost immediately, we ran into more trouble. Whatever the cause—unfamiliarity or hostility—they were slovenly with the dynamics, their heads buried in their parts, not looking at me. I stopped them once again. It was just like Dr. Böhm's conducting class back at the conservatory. You could almost taste the resentment and stupidity.

"Terribly sorry to trouble you again, gentlemen," I began, "you are giving me the notes, but you are ignoring the dynamics—those instructions are just as important!" The players refused to look at me. I slammed my open palm down on my conductor's score in emulation of Herr Liebermann. They jerked their heads up.

"You observe that we begin *forte* and then reduce immediately to *piano*, only to build back to *forte* by the third bar, soften to *piano* again—alternating back and forth up to bar 37—when the winds join in. You see that?"

Heads were nodding as faces peered at music stands.

"I am relieved," I said. "I was coming to believe that my score was the only source of those markings." Some nervous laughter. "That not being the case," I continued, "I must insist that your playing reflect the composer's wishes. And that you keep an eye on me. No dynamics, no meaning! I will signal the dynamics with my hands. But I shall shout if all else fails."

I spoke to them as though they were children, this throng who outnumbered me and could outperform me. Why? Because they were childish in their resentment. That Germanic upbringing again. From my father down to certain of my teachers, the message was plain. In order to exact obedience, one had to crush opposition. That was the task of the Kapellmeister. One had to be ruthless in order to create art. Some few individuals from among the horde were destined to become leaders. I had no doubt that I was some kind of Nietzschean figure. *Wasn't it übermenschlich of me to dominate Herr Liebermann's orchestra?*

We started over again. Wonder of wonders, they responded. I didn't need to shout. I grimaced, I glowered, I stamped my foot; I swayed, I crouched, I leapt in the air. And, wonder of wonders, they responded! Restlessly, alternating between loud and soft, the music began to express the turmoil I was seeking. Soon they were swept up in it and actually began to communicate strength and motion. They had got it! Now, it would have been too easy just to wave my arms, move to the music, and enjoy myself. But I couldn't fall into that trap. This orchestra would follow me, not the other way around.

By bar 37, when the winds and horns enter, Herr Liebermann would not have recognized his orchestra. They were transformed, playing with spirit and fire. The score called for even more agitation, the phrases breaking up, becoming fragmented, as we neared the point for the curtain to rise. The stage was occupied by painters working silently on a sun-splashed bullring for *Carmen*, but I was able to conjure in my mind a gloomy interior, house of the villainous Hunding, dominated by the trunk of a huge ash tree. A climax of sound. Then the orchestra abruptly fell silent. This was the cue for the exhausted Siegmund to stagger onstage.

In the absence of the cast, I could not refrain from croaking out Siegmund's first words myself: *"Wes Herd dies auch sei, hier muss ich rasten* (Whoever owns this hearth, here must I rest)."

To my astonishment, the orchestra cheered. *My god,* I thought, *why don't they hate me?* The concertmaster rose to shake my hand.

"Herr Dirigent, you know how to make music," he said. I was more startled when I realized that Herr Liebermann had been sitting in the seats behind me, watching.

"Gentlemen, well played," he called out as he strode forward to the proscenium. He was actually smiling. "Yes, well played indeed. You could take your break now. Those of you not needed for tonight's performance may leave now. We shall see you tomorrow at the same hour for more *Walküre*. The rest will reassemble in fifteen minutes for act 4 of *Carmen*." His smile vanished as he turned to me. "To my office—now, please!" he muttered.

What could be wrong? The orchestra had never sounded so good. I had rarely heard playing so responsive and subtle, certainly not from these musicians.

Once the door had closed, Herr Liebermann turned to me. "Herr Kapp," he began, "I confess I am at a loss. On one hand, you are drilling our players well. The sound they produce harmonizes with what I imagined. I cannot quarrel with that. On the other hand, the contempt and disrespect with which you address them, as though I had died, with you appointed Generalmusikdirektor in my place—and a wretched caricature of me at that—cannot pass without comment." He placed himself directly in front of me. "When you behave in this fashion, it is the utmost disrespect toward me. Do you understand that?"

He had not raised his voice, but it was as though he were scourging my flesh with wires. I refused to meet his eyes and stared straight ahead. All I had done was to behave exactly the way he had. Herr Liebermann ranted and raved, and I had followed his example.

"Herr Kapp, you are presumptuous! You cannot treat people like this—you haven't earned the right. Will you believe me when I say that the Kapellmeister I admire most is Herr Bruno Walter of the Leipzig Gewandhaus? A saintly man—far better than both of us—a gentle man of infinite patience, he never raises his voice." He paced about for a moment. "You are young and possessed of an impressive talent. I urge you not to follow in the steps of the insufferable Herr von Krefeld, that weight around my neck, who fancies himself my successor. I beg you not to be so foolish. I must put up with him because of his family. I am not bound to you in the same way!"

He abruptly turned to his desk and handed me a large envelope. "I want you personally to deliver this to my wife. She's waiting for you now at my home. It's the guest list for the gala reception after the opening of *Walküre*."

I gasped. I couldn't believe it. No praise, but only grudging comments, a stinging reprimand, and an instant conversion from Kapellmeister to messenger boy!

Herr Liebermann immediately became lost in his notes and papers but finally noticed that I had not left. He waved at me in irritation. "Still here, wasting time, Herr Kapp? I said that Frau Liebermann is waiting for you at the house."

My eyes actually filled with tears. It took all the will I had to stop myself from slamming the door. As I was leaving the building, Manfred von Krefeld, who had taken my place at the podium, struck up the boisterous opening to act 4 of *Carmen*. I felt anything but boisterous myself as I made my way toward the Hofgartenufer. How could Herr Liebermann have said those things to me after I had transformed his orchestra? After I had created from nothing such a sensitive, responsive ensemble? Damnable and abominable so it was! And he had the gall to claim he admired the saintly Bruno Walter? I was so angry that I was tempted to rip his stupid envelope into shreds and throw them into the Rhine.

I deliberately took the long way to his house to calm myself, but I remained angry. Herr Liebermann was nothing but a damned Jew, less than human, to say what he had. I was angry, but I didn't want to lose my head or do something stupid. On my way, other thoughts intruded. I passed kiosks, signboards, and men walking around carrying placards covered with election posters. Chaos and disturbance were all around us. We had national elections every five minutes, it seemed. People were really fed up with the government. Weimar had failed us again and again. People yearned for something stronger, more defined and stable. Now, the entire band of fools was trying again. Vote for the Communists. Vote for the Social Democrats. Vote for the German Nationalists. Vote for the Catholic Centrists. Vote for the Iron Front. And, of course, vote for the NSDAP, the Nazis.

It was hard to avoid the Nazis. They were superbly organized and all over the place, marching, singing, rallying, aggressively shaking their collection boxes in people's faces. They were leading in both state and Reichstag elections. They would make people like Herr Liebermann sit up and take notice, perhaps even behave decently.

But as you know, they also had that outrageous side to them. Earlier this year Reich Chancellor Brüning had outlawed the Nazi militias, the SS and the SA. However, our canny Reich President von Hindenburg neatly responded by getting rid of Brüning and replacing him with Franz von Papen, a dignified aristocrat. Von Papen lifted the ban on the militias, but he couldn't solve problems and managed only to disappoint people. He was soon replaced by the no-nonsense General von Schleicher. But all continued up in the air—in other words, a profound mess. At least, the Nazis were promising what we badly needed, and what they had a catchphrase for. Election posters proclaimed Law and Order on every corner. The Nazis were exactly like a sewage system or, better yet, a purgative. We all need a thorough cleaning-out once in a while, but I, for one, prefer not to know how it happens.

I walked up the marble steps of Herr Liebermann's imposing house and rang the bell. I was shown into a downstairs library by a maid and asked to wait. I could hear the riverboats steaming up and down the Rhine just outside, engines chugging and whistles sounding. Soon there was a rapid click of high heels in the vestibule. I whirled around to see a remarkably beautiful young woman enter and approach me across the carpet.

"Guten Tag," she said with a charming smile and in a cultivated Berlin accent. "I am Frau Liebermann. I have heard of you, but I don't think, after all this time, we have met before."

This was Herr Liebermann's wife? This exquisite blonde creature, in a fashionable dark gray tea gown that set off her green eyes, with pearls in her ears and at her throat? So young and attractive—my heart melted. How old was she? Inevitably, I raced to compare her to her husband, whom I had left not a half hour before. He, ugly, short, bald, thick-waisted, evil-tempered, in every regard most disagreeable. And here was his wife, so sweet, so young, gracious, subtly perfumed, with perfect blond hair, and those unforgettable green eyes. What a vision stood before me. I was dumbfounded. I could only stammer and stare.

She held out an elegantly braceleted hand. "I am happy to greet you at long last. My husband speaks highly of you," she said. "I cannot understand why he has not brought you round before."

I murmured something in reply. After a few moments of silence, she nodded at the large envelope I was holding. "I believe you have something for me?"

I was so mixed up that I extended my empty hand rather than the envelope. As she smiled in response, I realized the root of my dilemma. It was not only the fact that the wife was so young and beautiful— and the husband so repulsive. It was also that this Frau Liebermann clearly and unmistakably did not look Jewish but was a veritable Aryan blond beauty, if I ever saw one. The Nazis were always making noise about how the Jews not only corrupted our daily lives, but also polluted our Aryan race by seducing German women. The Nazis would describe women like Frau Liebermann as Judenliebchen, Jew lovers, hardly a compliment! I had paid scant attention to claims like those, but I was in such a bad mood that they struck me with new force. *If the Jews grabbed the beautiful German girls for themselves, how would I get my share?* It was a pretty fundamental question. How could this rare beauty have joined herself to an aged ox like Liebermann? The answer was obvious to anybody to see. It must have been his money. Just like Klara in Vienna. It had been the money. My mother in Szombathely used to sing a sad song: "Love makes the world go round, but it's so hard to find." I knew better. It's money that does the trick. The only problem was that the Jews seemed to have their hands on most of it.

I suppose I became crazed in a way. The whole thing felt Wagnerian—a beautiful young bride trapped by an ugly dwarf, wildly sinful love affairs, sweeping emotional instability arising from unfixed, mutating harmonies! The room began to spin. I feared one of my fits. Memories swept over me that I had believed safely buried—but so vivid and real, it was frightening. I saw Lotte again, the mocking Lotte, and next to her, the mocking Klara. There was much talk of hypnosis and hallucination in those days. In actual fact, I was in Frau Liebermann's library, speaking with her, but I plainly saw Lotte and Klara together with her, side by side, laughing at me. At the same time, thoughts of poor Krisztina flooded into my mind—what I had lost and would never have again. Familiar, searing sensations overcame me, as they did when I was younger, flooded as I was by jangled memories too untidy to sort out. I surely had a sickness. To my horror and embarrassment, my legs refused to hold me up. I sagged to my knees. Frau Liebermann cried out and knelt beside me.

"Herr Kapp, what's the matter? Are you all right?" By sheer effort of will, I managed not to sprawl on the floor. But the room continued to revolve. I was certain I was going to be sick and vomit all over that rich carpet. I could not permit that.

"Please don't try to get up," she said. "I will ring for help." I stared at her. She reached out a hand to feel my brow. I avoided her touch. "Let me get you some water."

Without reason, I laughed. Her eyes widened in alarm. Magically, her reaction cleared my mind. I no longer felt intimidated. The room steadied. I could look at Frau Liebermann with the indifference she merited—even contempt. She had betrayed herself by marrying a Jew, at the same time inevitably rejecting and betraying someone like me. Contempt, I discovered, was a powerful cure for the soul. I felt much better. I was able to get to my feet. I bowed, did not take the hand she offered, left the envelope with its stupid details of a reception to which I expected no invitation, turned, and departed.

Thankfully, I was able to bury myself in work, and there was much to do. I had to accept that *Walküre* was not really mine; nevertheless, I had to go on shaping and molding that magnificent, terrible, fate-driven music. I worked like a slave. All of a sudden, I lifted my head and the New Year was here. Strange, no one invited me as a guest for Christmas dinner nor had me over to toast the New Year. I never expected anything from the society swells who hung around the Liebermanns. But I was disappointed that none of the orchestra asked me.

* * *

It was mid-January 1933, and barely two weeks to the opening of *Walküre*. Things became feverish. Soloists arrived from all around the world: tenors, contraltos, baritones, basses. And especially sopranos, with lungs of leather and of impressive girth—floorboards creaked wherever they trod. They assumed the stature of gods themselves. Herr Liebermann now took over the rehearsals. He stood on the podium, evoking the sounds I had fashioned. The illicit love between Siegmund and Sieglinde, the jealous rage of Fricka, the death of Hunding, the demented ride of the Valkyries, the passionate farewell of Wotan to his daughter Brünnhilde before he cloaks her in magic fire—he employed the orchestral textures I had created.

The turmoil in *Walküre* matched the rage in my heart—and also that in the streets, where things had stretched to the breaking point. Everybody could see where things were headed. Last summer, it had been touch and go whether Germany would go Bolshevik or Nazi. There seemed nothing in between. In the final days of Weimar, a woman, if you please, got to be president of the Reichstag. Of course, to make the upside-down nature of things complete, she was a Communist! You could tell that people had had enough when she was abruptly replaced by the war hero, Hermann Göring. There was constant juggling of votes and influence among the parties. The scandal sheets produced much enjoyment as they described people who, in public, swore eternal enmity to each other, but, behind the scenes, wheedled each other for cabinet posts. In the streets, Communists and Nazis were still breaking each others' heads. Within only two months of his becoming Reich Chancellor, people were sick of General von Schleicher. He had resolved nothing. The nation was going from bad to worse. The Great Inflation. No work. People thrown out of jobs and homes. Soup kitchens. Cellars full of cold, hungry children. Limbless ex-soldiers from the war. People needed action, but von Schleicher seemed helpless. I thanked God daily for the food in my belly. I actually felt ashamed for existing without having to sell myself.

Von Papen was scheming to return to power—it was no secret. He believed he could use Hitler's popularity to boost himself, and then dump him when he became Reich Chancellor again. People *were* put off by the Nazis' street brawling, but their daily paper, *Völkischer Beobachter,* assured us that Hitler would never seek power by unconstitutional means. There was no need for that. Everybody could see that the Nazis had achieved their majorities in open elections, that there was no insurgency. Germans were *voting* for the Nazis. Who could argue with it?

Opening night for *Walküre* was almost upon us. Out of nowhere, Herr Kalandrelli came out with the depressing observation that, because the Westfälische Staatsoper had never before attempted a Ring Cycle opera, we would fail miserably. The whole thing was beyond us financially and artistically.

"Did Liebermann imagine he was in Bayreuth?" Herr Kalandrelli wanted to know. "This is Düsseldorf, for pity's sake. Surrounded by Ruhr millionaires, but not an ounce of culture among the lot of them—except for Thyssen, perhaps, buying modern art on the cheap."

As usual, I tried to get away from him, not only because of the bad breath, but because I still had some regard for Herr Liebermann's musicianship. Jew or not, he was an able Kapellmeister. He could keep things going.

"Of course, Herr Liebermann is going to fail," Herr Kalandrelli went on, seizing my arm in a fierce clutch and drawing me close. I thought for a moment he had gone mad and that I was going to have to fight free. But he only meant to whisper in my ear. *Lord, his breath was foul!*

"I must tell you something, Herr Kapp. I know Wagner. I've heard the best conductors. As a young man, I heard von Bülow—Mahler adored him, you know—as well as our own beloved Bruno Walter. Von Bülow was a regular show-off in front of the orchestra—lots of flamboyance, lots of waving the arms and so forth. And so difficult—temperamental outbursts, madness—the whole lot. Many a Kapellmeister condemned him. But they were just jealous. He made music so well!"

Despite the breath, I wanted to hear more. "I never saw von Bülow conduct Wagner at Bayreuth, much to my sorrow," he went on, "but I did hear him in Berlin and Vienna and Meiningen—and right here in Düsseldorf. His Wagner and Beethoven were tremendous. And his Brahms!" Herr Kalandrelli paused to kiss his fingertips. "I can say the same of Nikisch—I heard him in Leipzig at the Gewandhaus. The way *he* conducted Brahms and Beethoven, Wagner and Mahler—not to be believed! It was all emotion and electricity."

His eyes glared, lips drawn back from his teeth in a devilish grin.

"I tell you all this because you—*you*—should be conducting *Walküre* on Saturday night, not Liebermann."

I flinched and looked around. If Herr Liebermann should overhear, my life in Düsseldorf would be finished. The ground beneath me was already shaky.

His grip on my arm tightened. "Don't worry, many here agree with me." That alarmed me further. "I mention von Bülow, Nikisch, and Mahler," he continued, "because you remind me of them. Those weeks that you rehearsed the orchestra"—Herr Kalandrelli uttered a short, bitter laugh—"Herr Liebermann is probably smacking himself on the head for asking you to do that. It was the most stupid thing he could have done. I don't know how, but you have accomplished things with that orchestra. When you handed them back to Liebermann, they sounded as though they belonged in Leipzig or Vienna themselves! Has he expressed a single word of appreciation?"

"He has not," I muttered, uncomfortable.

"Well," said the other, "if I were you, I would be packing my things and booking myself a railway ticket to some other city and to some other opera company."

"Are you serious?" I was aghast.

"Of course," he grinned. "Can you imagine that Herr Liebermann enjoys knowing that you make music better than he does?"

If the allegation were true about my musical talent being slighted, and on such petty grounds, it was time to take things into my own hands, no matter the cost. A wave of terrible anger swept over me. I had to speak to Herr Liebermann.

I broke free of Herr Kalandrelli's grasp and rushed upstairs to the Kapellmeister's office. I would have the whole thing out with him. Once and for all. He was not there! Not to be found in the entire building. So incensed was I that I ran right out of the opera house and made for his residence without pausing for my overcoat. It was a bleak late-January afternoon. A damp frigid wind blew from the west across the Rhine. Soon, I was shivering badly. I ran all the way; it was too cold to walk.

The front door of Herr Liebermann's house was wide open, all the lights blazing. People were coming and going up and down the marble steps. A large black Mercedes limousine stood in the driveway. All four of its doors were open too, as was the trunk. A manservant struggled to load suitcases.

Just inside the foyer, Herr Liebermann was shouting instructions into a telephone. Too intent to notice me, he was talking to someone in a bank, instructing him what to do with various accounts—close some, transfer others. When he finished that call, he straightaway clicked the receiver, demanding to be put through to the Hamburg-Amerika Shipping Company. Finally, he looked up.

"What the devil are you doing here?"

I began to speak, but my words were lost in the general commotion, shouting, and clatter. The telephone rang while he was holding it. A pair of manservants passed me, struggling with a steamer trunk. The caller managed to satisfy Herr Liebermann. He would be sailing on the *Bremen*. Steamship tickets for New York were assured for his party the next day. *He was leaving? All this luggage? When would he return? What about our opera?*

My rage dissolved into puzzlement. "What's happening, Herr Kapellmeister? What about our *Walküre?*"

"'Our' *Walküre?*" Herr Liebermann asked with a twisted grin. "Will you just listen to the boy! He takes the breath away."

Frau Liebermann made an appearance, hurriedly crossing the foyer, wearing a black lambskin coat loosely thrown over her shoulders. She started when she saw me.

"*Ach*, Herr Kapp, have you come to say goodbye? Are you feeling better than the last time we met? Where is your overcoat? You must be freezing." She had tears in her eyes. My dislike of her rekindled.

Herr Liebermann was irritated. "For God's sake, *Liebchen*, I don't know why he's here. I didn't ask him." He turned to give instructions to a servant carrying another bag out to the car. Herr Liebermann followed him.

The beautiful Frau Liebermann began to cry again. I gazed at her without expression. "It's so terrible," she said, dabbing at her eyes. "Everything is upside-down."

"But what *is* it that's happened, *Gnädige Frau?*"

She sat down abruptly on a chair and stared earnestly at me with a moist gaze. *My god, she was really beautiful!* Again, I didn't in the slightest comprehend what she was doing with Herr Liebermann. She attempted to speak once or twice. "Can we trust you, my husband and I?"

"Most assuredly," I replied and laid my hand on my heart. She glanced nervously at the open front door. Perhaps Herr Liebermann would prefer her not to speak to me about his matters. "It's this business with Hitler," she said.

"Hitler," I repeated. "What about Hitler? What's he got to do with it?"

"Franzl—I mean my husband, Herr Liebermann—received extremely disturbing news this morning." She covered her face with her hands a moment. "No, not disturbing. Devastating! And he's decided to act right away."

"Oh?" I said with a sympathetic smile. "News from whom?"

"From close, dear friends. Of course, he has absolutely no interest in politics. But we're actually leaving Germany because of politics—"

She broke off as Herr Liebermann suddenly reappeared. "Are you still here, Herr Kapp? We mustn't keep him, must we, my dear?" He hurried past her upstairs.

I was startled. "You are leaving? Why now, of all times? Will you be back for the opening of *Walküre*?" This occasioned more tears.

She calmed herself. "You have heard of Rudolf Ullstein?" Indeed, I had. *Völkischer Beobachter* attacked him daily. He was one of the most notorious Jews in the country, fostering disloyalty through his chain of newspapers.

"Herr Ullstein told us, on reliable authority, right from the top," she continued. "Reich Chancellor von Schleicher has given up—after only seven weeks in office. Reich President von Hindenburg fears everything is falling to pieces, that the country is on the brink of ruin. He insists that Germany must have a strong government"—she lowered her voice—"this is strictly confidential. There will be new elections in March—"

I whistled at the news. This would be the eighth election in only a couple of years. The rest of Europe would be laughing at us.

"Herr Ullstein told us that Hitler and von Papen are fighting over which of them will be the new Reich Chancellor—as crazy as that sounds: one has already made an utter fool of himself, while the other is a dangerous criminal. But with von Hindenburg's support, one of them will succeed."

She looked at me pleadingly, as though I might help. "But I still don't understand, Madame," I said, "this sense of emergency—"

She stood up and stamped her foot. "You don't understand? You don't understand? If Hitler becomes Chancellor, life for us becomes impossible. The Nazis have made no secret of that. My husband has said many times publicly that he will not live in a country ruled by that madman. And if von Papen succeeds, Hitler would not permit him to survive. Either way, we would have the maniac and his bullyboys."

That was hardly a respectful way to speak. I couldn't understand why she was making such a fuss. What did these new elections matter as long as the music could continue?

"Right after Herr Ullstein phoned," she said, "we heard from our dear friend, Otto—Klemperer, I mean. He was looking forward to being here Saturday night for *Walküre*. Now, that is impossible. He's worried about his own position in Berlin. Hermann Göring imagines himself a patron

of the arts. He will appoint himself Intendant of the Berlin opera houses." She uttered a hysterical laugh. "Can you believe that? Göring is
already throwing his weight around—complaining that the Jews are ruining German life." She shook her head. "Surely you're aware they've been
vilifying Otto all these years. He upsets them by playing Hindemith and
Schoenberg, all these so-called degenerates. And for being a Jew. That side
of things is so unimportant to him—I think his father was religious—but
I believe Otto converted some time ago."

I couldn't stand Schoenberg myself. "If you'll permit me," I ventured, "I wonder whether the situation is as hopeless as you think." She
looked up at me. "The Nazis do a lot of shouting about Jews. But surely these demonstrations are only for show—to wake people up—"

"By uprooting the lives of our most distinguished artists? Men and
women whose every gesture honors Germany? This you call waking
people up? What danger are we in that couldn't be cured by throwing
out that maniac?"

What a splendid picture Frau Liebermann presented! Her face
flushed with emotion, her glistening emerald eyes, her beautiful blond
hair—she quite ravished my heart.

"Forgive me for speaking frankly, *Gnädige Frau,* but surely, you are
not directly affected by your husband's wishes, are you?"

"What do you mean?" she whispered.

I swallowed hard. "I mean—that is, everyone can see—"

"What can everyone see?"

I smiled warmly. "Why, *Gnädige Frau,* it's plain to see that you
yourself are not Jewish." I leaned forward. "Now, if Herr Liebermann
thinks it necessary to leave the country for a while, that should not
affect you. All this excitement will quickly blow over. People are saying that Herr Hitler would be rendered harmless. He would be surrounded by people who would restrain him, like von Papen and
General von Blomberg. They would make quite sure—"

"For someone who says he does not follow politics, you seem to
know a lot."

"What I am suggesting, Madame," I tried to soothe, "is that, if
Herr Liebermann leaves, it would not be for long. You could remain
behind in safety…"

I was unable to complete my remarks. Frau Liebermann began to
scream at me. She placed her hands about her ears and howled. I had

heard nothing like it since I was in the hospital with Krisztina. The foyer rang with it. The tall grandfather clock to the side resounded. Herr Liebermann came running downstairs. Two manservants bustled in from the outside.

"You disgusting beast! You utter swine!" she screamed. "Monster! Disgusting monster! Utter filth!" The last time I had heard language like that directed at me had been in Dr. Böhm's study in Vienna. I had no idea what she was carrying on about. *Hadn't I just suggested something that might help?*

Frau Liebermann flung herself in her husband's arms. "If you heard the things he said—this piece of filth!" she sobbed. "He actually said that you should run away alone, go abroad, and I should remain behind."

It was Herr Liebermann's turn to stare at me.

"He said that nothing would happen to me because I wasn't Jewish, but we'd have to separate. He actually said that!"

Herr Liebermann marched right up to me and slapped me hard on the face. Twice.

It hurt like hell, but I didn't flinch and even smiled.

One of the servants spoke. "Shall I throw him out, Herr Kapellmeister?"

"I'll do it," Herr Liebermann growled. He grasped me by the neck and one arm. I was unable to move. "You know, I never liked you, you impudent snotnose!"

It was no use trying to break free. He was too strong.

"I do not understand you—you are a good musician, but I would not trust you with two *pfennigs*," he spat. His hands were closing around my neck. I managed to loosen his hold, but still he held me.

"Herr Kapellmeister," I protested, "haven't I behaved the same way you did? I have literally sat at your feet, watching how you wave the stick, what you listen for, how you signal for certain effects—I was never more honored than to become your orchestra coach."

Herr Liebermann paused but did not loosen his grip. "Yes, it's true I can be arrogant. But I've earned the right. I've been around the world many times. I've conducted from Riga to Yokohama, from Lima to Omsk. I have struggled always to create art, to create beauty—if I was lucky—not exercise power for its own sake."

I had him there. "But, Herr Kapellmeister, wasn't I after the same thing? You said yourself that you were pleased with the orchestra after I had prepared them."

He released me. I was able to massage my neck. "Yes, I was satisfied with your music," he said quietly. "But—am I perhaps jealous as well?" He thought a moment. "What I'm saying, Herr Kapp, is that your own lack of balance—perhaps lack of reason—makes you presumptuous and lose control." He shook his head. "God knows, I've become accustomed over the years to arrogant prodigies without number. But you outdo them all."

Despite the cold, I was perspiring. "On one hand, you appear humble and respectful," he went on. "On the other, it turns out that you are really arrogant and hateful—without having earned the right. I've seen it myself. Nobody likes you—are you aware of that? At whose home did you eat Christmas dinner? How many invitations did you receive?" In spite of my brave show, I shuddered. "Everybody knows you, but nobody wants you. Quite an achievement!"

"Believe me, Herr Kapellmeister, I meant no disrespect. But one cannot ignore facts. We should be thinking about Frau Liebermann. She could indeed remain behind and watch over things. As I say, I think she'd be perfectly safe—nobody would touch *her*. And when things were quieter, you would return and—"

"Will you shut your stupid, ignorant mouth while you still have teeth?" He had somehow become enraged again. "Who cares what you think! My life in Germany is over. I can't stand to breathe the air. I choke on it, it's poisoned. I know what's in store. The show has already closed down. I don't know why others, like Bruno Walter and Klemperer, are still hanging on. I'm not waiting to find out."

I tried, without success, to speak.

"I only wish I knew yesterday about your latest impertinence," he said with loathing. "I would have taken pleasure in dismissing you on the spot—throwing you out of the Staatsoper completely. I would have taken pleasure in writing to your piano teacher, Professor Starker, and to your unbelievably patient, much-deluded Madame Polkovska. It is not true that you suffer from bad luck, young man. What you suffer from is a malicious and selfish heart. Your outrageous suggestion to Frau Liebermann demonstrates that. You and the new Germany deserve each other!"

He reached out and pushed me violently toward the door. I almost fell but was able to recover my balance. I gave Herr and Frau Liebermann a deep bow.

"Bon voyage," I said. "Are there any instructions for the company before you leave?" Herr Liebermann advanced on me. I retreated. He slammed the door behind me.

In great excitement, I ran all the way back to the opera house. Night had fallen, and the wind had grown even more sharp and bitter. It was a Sunday evening, and most people were at home, preparing for early bed, to be rested for their jobs on Monday—that is, those who had them. The Staatsoper was dark; we rarely had performances on Sundays. But backstage was humming. People had somehow found out that Herr Liebermann had suddenly quit, leaving us stranded. Manfred von Krefeld, of all people, was attempting to throw his weight around, using expressions like *disgraceful, treacherous,* and *cowardly*. The chairman of the orchestra committee, who was listening, said nothing; nor did the concertmaster, the chorus master, the head designer, the chief choreographer—and Herr Kalandrelli. They were gathered around a table set up onstage.

"Aha, our hardworking *répétiteur*," Herr von Krefeld cried as he caught sight of me. "Perhaps you have not heard, but our esteemed Kapellmeister has mysteriously and unexpectedly decided to abandon his post—without a word to anyone, except for a last-minute telephone call to my grandmother. At least he had the decency to do that!" He chuckled. "Who would have thought that our fire-breathing Kapellmeister would turn out to be so timid."

Herr Kalandrelli, the chorus master, the head designer, and the chief choreographer looked serious. "But was this so unexpected?" asked Herr von Krefeld. "We all know how things have suddenly become, shall I say, shaky for certain people in Germany—"

"Well, I for one, can't blame Herr Liebermann," said the concertmaster, "but I agree he has been somewhat hasty. I mean, whatever happens in Berlin, the nation as a whole is not about to become unbalanced. This is still Germany, for heaven's sake. The storm troopers may be running around Berlin and Munich like hooligans, but they will ultimately have to obey the law like everybody else. If our Kapellmeister has really abandoned us, we have to worry—"

"We have to worry about the rest of the season, won't we?" sneered

Herr von Krefeld. "Typical that he blusters at the top of his voice but could not face us like a man! I happen to know that his being a Jew was not the whole story. If that weren't bad enough, I know he has been heavily involved with the Socialists—perhaps the Communists as well! So he would be in difficulties on more than one account." He smiled.

In the silence that greeted this, it was plain that Herr von Krefeld had become awfully cocky. *What could be the explanation?* In a flash, I had it. Herr Liebermann probably wasn't the only one secretly political. It was not hard to guess that Herr von Krefeld had a storm trooper's uniform in his closet. You know I was no friend of Herr Liebermann, but Herr von Krefeld clearly had plans and ambitions that would get in the way of mine. I knew what he was after. He was as dangerous to me as Herr Liebermann had been.

The concertmaster turned to me. "How do you think we should proceed, Herr Kapp?"

"Well," I said, "shouldn't the board of directors decide such matters?"

"When you talk about the board of directors, you're talking about my grandmother," Herr von Krefeld broke in, "and you may rest assured that, on matters of repertoire and presentation, my grandmother will follow my suggestions."

Herr Kalandrelli murmured in my ear. "But she could never get Liebermann to make the boy his official conducting assistant." I grunted in agreement.

Everybody looked at everybody else. "What do you think your grandmother and the board—of course, following your advice—will recommend?" asked the concertmaster. "We have about six weeks to go; the repertoire is established for now—"

"But the permanent conductorship is not," said Herr von Krefeld. "And besides, we have to think of next season." He beamed. "For instance, I have a wonderful idea. I don't think this house has ever presented Lortzing's *Zar und Zimmermann*. It's a marvelous piece, extremely popular; and I'm ready to plan for it."

An even longer silence. The concertmaster cleared his throat. "But, Herr von Krefeld, with respect, aren't we forgetting something more urgent than the next season?"

Herr von Krefeld raised his brow. "What do you mean?" he asked.

The other looked up at the ceiling. "We've got an opening this Saturday night, if I'm not mistaken," he said. "Our much-anticipated and carefully prepared *Walküre*."

Herr von Krefeld laughed gently. "There's nothing to worry about, meine Herren. I shall, of course, take charge of conducting the work."

A further long silence. Then, "You will permit us, the department heads, a few minutes to discuss this?" asked the concertmaster.

Herr von Krefeld looked bemused. "What is there to discuss? This is preposterous. We have a crisis, and I have offered to see us through it. Not everyone would be able—"

"Again, with respect, Herr von Krefeld, this is an ambitious, expensive production featuring prominent singers. We cannot have such a presentation handled by someone—forgive me for saying this— by someone of whom nobody has heard."

There were nods around the table.

Herr von Krefeld threw his arms in the air. "So what should we do? Should we send telegrams to Berlin and Leipzig, to Klemperer and Kleiber? Drop everything. Rush to Düsseldorf. Save our *Walküre*. You have five days." He sneered. "If I know anything about those gentlemen, they may be already packing to leave the country as well. They suffer from the same affliction as our own lamented former conductor. They're all Jews." He ended in a mock-serious whisper.

Herr L'Orénoque, the head designer, rarely spoke. He was a large bearded man, with huge hairy arms, which we were able to see since he liked to roll up his sleeves and work together with his crew, constructing and dismantling stage sets. He looked like Karl Marx—a massive head and a flat nose, resembling a gorilla. Now he stirred.

"What the concertmaster is talking about should not be taken lightly," he rumbled in a deep voice. "After all, the reputations and fortunes of the whole company are at stake. There is an entire world outside Düsseldorf, and we have to survive in it. Not everyone comes from a prosperous family."

Herr von Krefeld was indignant. "Exactly how would my leadership of the company threaten those reputations?"

Herr L'Orénoque roared with laughter. "Your what? Your leadership, did you say? Listen, young man, don't you think you're the slightest bit unripe to take on a job like *Walküre*?" Herr von Krefeld turned red. "You're a known quantity here. We're all aware of what you can

226

and cannot do," he went on. "For instance, you're not too bad with *Carmen*." He shook his large head. "But *Walküre*? No, no, no, and no! As I say, we know you, and by the Living God, you are not the Kapellmeister for *Walküre*. If you intend to conduct it Saturday night, I for one, will hand in my resignation on the spot."

Everybody around the table looked shocked. "That would be easy for you, wouldn't it, Herr L'Orénoque?" said Herr von Krefeld. "After all, the design work and construction are completed, and if I'm not mistaken, your own contracts for that project are largely settled. So forgive my own frankness, but you speak at no possible risk to yourself."

A long pause. Finally, the concertmaster again. "I agree with Herr L'Orénoque," he said. We looked up in surprise. He was generally a quiet man but known to be firm and reliable. "For you, Herr von Krefeld, to conduct our premiere of *Walküre* would be a profound mistake. To be polite, you lack certain essential qualities. I could not be party to it. I'm not certain what the orchestra committee may decide— that would be up to them—but I will do my best to persuade them to agree with me."

"So what do you suggest, meine Herren, cancel the performance? Cancel the rest of the season?" Herr von Krefeld got to his feet and stamped noisily up and down the stage. "Are you all interested in committing financial suicide?"

Herr L'Orénoque also rose. Because of his bulk, it was an impressive sight. "Herr von Krefeld," he called, "I want you to be good enough to sit down and hear what I'm going to suggest." The other, perhaps noting his size, complied. "Look," said Herr L'Orénoque, "we are faced with deep problems here but few solutions. I suggest we do our best to complete the season with honor. And if we are to survive, try not to make idiots of ourselves. I don't want even to think about new productions at this point—forget about *Zar und Zimmermann*, for god's sake!"

Herr von Krefeld looked appalled.

"And the obvious thing is to have Herr Kapp conduct *Walküre* Saturday night and as much of the repertoire as he can handle at this short notice—"

Herr von Krefeld began shouting, red in the face again. I could not hear what he was saying because people were talking at the same time, banging on the table.

"Are you all completely out of your minds?" Herr von Krefeld broke through the tumult. "First of all, doesn't the comment you made about me apply to him as well? Nobody has heard of him either! Second of all, isn't he"—jerking his finger at me—"the one person nobody can stand?" The group fell silent. "I remember what you all said at Christmas time, that you refused to have him in your homes!" He was vehement. "Herr Kapp is grasping and obnoxious. That's what you all said, do you remember? He is arrogant and disrespectful. He gives himself airs. He thinks he is God's gift to music. He is ruthless and tramples on people's feelings. And again, since you raise my lack of fame, who in the world has heard of him? What sort of attraction for the public is he?"

The usually taciturn concertmaster broke in. "We are wasting time, meine Herren. Herr L'Orénoque is absolutely correct. Herr Kapp is obviously the man for us. I vote for him!"

I was amazed. I had not believed such a thing might happen. Surely, the concertmaster had been my enemy. Herr Liebermann had confirmed it.

Nein, nein, nein! Herr von Krefeld was beside himself. "The concertmaster positively has no authority to decide such a thing. It is a matter for the board—"

Herr L'Orénoque's huge voice drowned Herr von Krefeld's. "Herr Kapp, do you think you can handle the task?"

Herr von Krefeld howled. "He's got nothing to do with it! *I* am the official assistant conductor, not he. My grandmother, Frau Augustina von Krefeld, is, I remind you, chief patron and benefactress of the Westfälische Staatsoper—"

"And she would be horrified to think that Herr Liebermann's sudden departure would result in the collapse of her company." Herr L'Orénoque marched up close to Herr von Krefeld, laid two huge hands on his shoulders and stared into his eyes, a move that reminded me of Herr Liebermann and myself an hour before.

Herr von Krefeld was the first to look away. "All right," he muttered as though chewing broken glass.

"All right what?" asked Herr L'Orénoque.

"Herr Kapp conducts *Walküre* Saturday night," said Herr von Krefeld and made to leave.

"And?" Herr L'Orénoque held him in place.

"And the other five performances—"

"And?" persisted Herr L'Orénoque.

"And whatever items in the repertoire he wishes to handle."

"And you will be sure to convey this agreement to the *Gnädige Frau,* your grandmother, for ratification by the other members of the board. They may rest assured that the company have responded in a most inspired way to the emergency presented by the sudden departure of our Generalmusikdirektor."

Herr von Krefeld must have been out of his mind with rage, but the thing was settled.

The whole day had been sheer dizziness. My fortunes had plunged and risen with such rapidity that I was thoroughly bewildered. It was no surprise to discover that Herr Liebermann thoroughly disliked me, but its depth shook me. However, it was astonishing that I had so impressed my colleagues with my work that they were willing to overcome their own massive distaste, to stake their reputations and livelihoods on me. Our committee got to their feet and applauded—the concertmaster, the head designer, the chorus master, the chief choreographer. Even Herr Kalandrelli!

Herr L'Orénoque now marched up to me and laid massive paws on *my* shoulders. "Herr Kapp," he said solemnly, "we put ourselves into your hands." I nodded, terrified. "What do you want me to do?" I whispered.

"Why, nothing less than be magnificent. Sweet-natured at the same time." I didn't know what to say. His eyes bored into mine. All of a sudden, he roared gusts of deep laughter, swept me to him in a stifling embrace, and held me against him for a long, long time. I fought not to faint! The others cheered and slapped me on the back.

"What are your wishes, Herr Kapellmeister?" They were happy that someone other than themselves was responsible, but I was aware of too many things to worry about. Herr von Krefeld stood with folded arms, watching me. So many things had happened this day. I was exhausted. I collected myself sufficiently to dismiss the company for the night and called for them to reassemble the next morning at 9, a Monday, the beginning of a new week.

Wrapped up in these turmoils, I had taken my eyes off the political excitement. Frau Liebermann's news had been startling, that Hitler might be on the brink of power. But Monday morning happened to be January 30, 1933. I stepped out of my lodgings on a chilly gray morning and purchased a copy of the local Nazi *Westdeutscher Beobachter* from a grinning storm trooper. I shook it open and whistled. It blared in huge letters: REICHSKANZLER HITLER! *How had he pulled it off?*

The most recent Reichstag elections had shown the Nazis actually losing seats and the Communists gaining. Nevertheless, during the night, President Hindenburg had done precisely what that Jew publisher Ullstein had predicted. He had appointed Hitler chancellor. Papen was vice-chancellor and Göring prime minister of Prussia. As Ullstein had said, Papen, War Minister Blomberg, and the moderate nationalist Hugenberg were there to see that Hitler didn't become too extreme. The *Westdeutscher Beobachter* said nothing about these restraints.

As I walked over to the Staatsoper that morning, I thought about certain interesting parallels. Like Hitler, I was taking over an enterprise with people around me, watchful lest I become too extreme. But, you know, once one achieves a position, if he satisfies most people—and doesn't make too many mistakes—I believe he'd be difficult to remove. I had not followed the career of Herr Hitler that closely, but I knew he did audacious things, yet maintained an air of respectability. In my own sphere, I knew I could produce audacious and thrilling effects. My past setbacks, I could see now, were the results of ignoring that other vital component. I was apparently upsetting too many people. I truly didn't understand how. As far back as I could remember, I was always astonished by how many I would seem to offend. I would have to see about that. I did not think of myself as an evil person.

The week passed in a hideous blur. That Monday, the soloists in *Walküre*, assembled from around the world, clutched their heads in dismay when they learned the news about Herr Liebermann. But when they heard good reports about my music making from the concertmaster and others, not one declined to appear. True, our Brünnhilde from Copenhagen, Anna Maria Zille, put up an initial fuss that first Monday morning's rehearsal, but after observing how I handled act 1, in which she does not appear, she became sweet.

"*Sehr gut, sehr schön, junge Kapellmeister,*" she murmured. "I think I trust you."

I flashed her a grateful look and turned back to Señor Ramón García from Buenos Aires, our Siegmund, and Fräulein Celestina Schlageter, our Sieglinde, who, together with Mr. Montgomery Lewis, our Hunding from Chicago, were stalking each other about the stage, alternately snarling and being passionate—accompanied by surges of that incredible music. The orchestra was magnificently responsive and truly mine.

And the singers were mine too, their eyes now on each other, now on Herr Kalandrelli, who served in the prompter's box, most of all, on me. I couldn't avoid—though I resisted—awareness of how sexual was this act 1 of *Walküre*. It was nothing less than an enormous exercise in sex—and forbidden sex at that. It was yet another instance of my being aroused while performing music. I couldn't help blushing. Sieglinde has drugged her abductor-husband, Hunding, leaving the magical night to her and her long-lost twin brother, Siegmund. They become increasingly fascinated and passionate with each other.

The situation becomes more inflamed. Siegmund discovers his father's sword buried to the hilt in the massive ash tree and plucks it out, demonstrating that he is the true hero. The pair realize that they are brother and sister, but that they long for each other, *not* as brother and sister. They cast to the winds the laws of men and the gods in their embrace. Cries Siegmund in triumph:

Be bride and sister to your brother—
so flourishes the Wälsung Blood...

All terribly, thrillingly wicked!

Finally, two hours of massive labor ended. Other members of the cast, Fräulein Zille, together with our Wotan, our Fricke, and the eight other Valkyries—the painters, carpenters, even the cleaning women—erupted in spontaneous applause as I swept my arms down for the thunderous final chord of act 1. Grateful for their generosity, I grinned from ear to ear, though soaked in perspiration. I wondered if I could survive. At least three-and-a-half hours of music remained.

"This is definitely going to work. Definitely!" The concertmaster was pumping my arm up and down in uncharacteristic enthusiasm. After all that strain and uncertainty, I relished the approval. All I did— in spite of the almost painful pleasure that the music invoked in me— was to make sure that things sounded right, were in perfect tune, in balance, made dramatic sense. All I did was forgo my personal ecstasy and exercise control. It wasn't easy. Apparently, the audience was with me. People said I had an unforgiving ear, whatever that means, that I would not let the slightest thing past me if I didn't like it. Well, as you know, I possess perfect pitch.

After a break, Von Krefeld had to run through possible problems for that night's performance, *Forza del destino*. We would have to divide the rest of the week between us. Tuesday was *Carmen*, Wednesday *Freischütz*, Thursday *Bohème*, Friday *Seraglio*. On Saturday, there would be no matinée so that we would have some breathing room before the big premiere. We did as best we could and tried not to collapse in hysterics—we had quite a bit of those—and fatigue.

I have no clear memory of the performance itself. After a final run-through on Saturday morning, during which I had to bite down hard to stop myself from giving voice to many dissatisfactions, I went back to my lodgings for a nap. I must have been exhausted because, when I failed to arrive at the opera house at six, one of the workmen was sent to find me. He said he had been pounding on the door for some time before I answered. I managed to dress, hurry over, and appear backstage only a scant fifteen minutes before the opening. The house was packed and glittering, depression or no depression. Everybody was curious about the rumored coup at the Westfälische Staatsoper and the quality of the new Kapellmeister—not a word said about Hitler.

I wanted to have a moment in my dressing room before making my appearance. I needed to catch my breath, but even this brief respite was denied. A messenger with a telegram from Mama awaited me. Madame Polkovska was dead. She had passed away peacefully in her sleep at the age of 101! The funeral would take place five days hence. Mama said I should be there. If I left immediately, I should have no trouble reaching Szombathely in time.

I stared at the flimsy piece of paper. Madame was dead. I owed her much, but leaving now or the next day—or the next month—was impossible. I had too much to do. Madame would have understood. It was she who had instilled in me the dictum that we were all servants of art. I scribbled my regrets and handed the note to the waiting messenger.

At precisely seven at o'clock, I stood at the front of the hushed, darkened auditorium and swept down my arms. Five hours later, Wotan had cast Brünnhilde into a deep sleep atop her mountain, covered her with her own shield, and sung his haunting Farewell. The people in charge of sound and lighting effects surpassed themselves and joined the orchestra to create Loge's Magic Fire, which surrounded Brünnhilde with leaping flames. In those final pages, shimmering arpeggios in the strings, matched by all six harps, swept gently against drawn-out chords from hushed woodwinds and brass. I almost swooned with the beauty of it myself. The music slowly died into silence. No one stirred; every man's eye was fixed on me. Finally, I lowered my arms, which by now shook with fatigue. The players put down their instruments. The applause began. Tentative at first, it swelled, continued, and ultimately became deafening. The singers appeared before the great curtains, singly or two by two. Eventually, the entire cast beckoned me onstage, to be met by such a roar!

I was supremely happy, though exhausted and again drenched with sweat. And even though emotionally and physically wracked, the thing I feared most in such a situation—one of my peculiar attacks—did not occur. The reason was my triumph. Exhausted yes, but not strained or stressed. That was the difference.

Herr Kalandrelli chose that precise moment to show me poster proofs. For the first time, I saw my own name prominently displayed, but the sight did not please me.

"Do you approve, Herr Kapellmeister?" Barely able to stand, unable—because of the throngs about me—to make my way to the dressing room, I had to sit on a chair in the wings to catch my breath. Kalandrelli would not go away. From another direction, I caught sight of Frau Augustina von Krefeld approaching. I threw my head back, silently begging heaven for relief. I saw only vast, soaring spaces behind the proscenium arch, many ropes and weights, gangways suspended high in the air. God was not there.

"I say again, do you approve of the new posters, Herr Kapellmeister?" Kalandrelli repeated. The printers have to know right away."

In a rage, I seized the proofs, about to rip the sheets. But surrounded by well-wishers, I caught myself. I suddenly understood what disturbed me. It was my own name. I had never really liked it. There was no music in it. It was even ugly. *Kapp, Kapp!* It sounded like a barking dog or someone choking! In Vienna, the jeering Lotte had reminded me, it was slang for contraceptives. Also, I didn't think it sufficiently impressive. Because of my stay in Düsseldorf, I had considered appending the name of that city to my own—*Kapp-Düsseldorfer.* That combination was ungainly. On the other hand, I had also enjoyed visits to nearby Dortmund. That name appealed.

Kalandrelli held out a black crayon. Under the word Dirigent was my name, Hermann Kapp. I added a hyphen and then scrawled *Dortmunder.* That was to be my new name, Kapp-Dortmunder. *Hermann Kapp-Dortmunder.* Even though not a native of Dortmund, I wanted it. It sounded good. I had always striven for good sounds. I stood and held up the amended poster for the throng. The crowd cheered. I could do no wrong. Frau Augustina von Krefeld beamed and nodded. *Was it possible, with Madame Polkovska gone, I had acquired a new patron?*

* * *

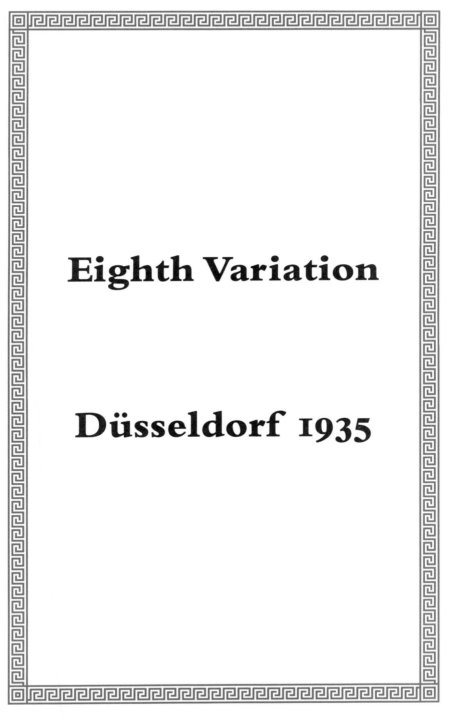

Eighth Variation

Düsseldorf 1935

It was time for me to marry. Not altogether what I wanted—not when I wanted, but it was time to prove my respectability. I decided I would marry. I was twenty-five and, in all but name, ruler of the Westfälische Staatsoper. After my tremendous success in *Walküre*, I had become the toast of Düsseldorf. People were breathless to meet me, particularly women. From a nonentity, I sprang to fame. Everybody asked where I had come from. Why had they not heard of me before? It was such sweetness to see Manfred von Krefeld jostled by reporters and photographers as they pushed past him to besiege me.

My rise to prominence coincided with Herr Hitler's. Even the hard-headed Ruhr industrialists, from whom I expected better sense, made much of that. They were actually superstitious, declaring that the simultaneous happening was an omen, a sign from heaven. There were two chief consequences. One was an immediate increase in the opera's subscription list. The second, local ranks of the exclusive circle known as the Friends of Adolf Hitler almost doubled, as did contributions to the party. The district Gauleiter attended some of my performances, even though he was a stupid *Schwein*, a particularly dull and illiterate functionary. But it did no harm to be esteemed in party circles. At the opera house, I was given practically *carte blanche*. I received a most gratifying increase in salary as well as a pretty free hand in running the whole show. For a young man, it was heady. But while I ruled the ship firmly, I learned not to overdo it. Things worked better when I didn't shout as much.

Among other benefits that accrued were young women. All at once, I had no lack of lady friends, especially among resident singers of the company. Before my *éclat*, I had hungered after the good-looking ones, only to be regularly snubbed. As a nobody, I hadn't been able to interest them. Of course, the plain women sought to engage me in earnest conversations on abstruse subjects—that's what plain women do. Now the most attractive women found excuses to talk to me. They sought my advice—on their musical training, their plans for the future, on their own affairs of the heart. It was laughably transparent. I never forgot how cruelly they shunned me when I was lonely. On another plane, my new prominence put me in touch with an entirely different class of women, elegant and rich, from the nobility and great families of Ruhr millionaires. The older, like Frau Augustina von Krefeld, tended to be stately and busy themselves supporting the opera, the local symphony, or the institute of art. Many of the younger gave me looks that indicated interest. But these veered more to political affiliation, forming ladies' auxiliaries of various party organizations, providing the local Nazis with society credentials. Some of these women wore uniform, even when not attending meetings. But whatever they wore, most sported swastika pins and brooches on their bosoms and lapels. They were too doctrinaire for me. I had no trouble with the flighty ones, but was made uneasy by the wealthy. They seemed too independent, respected no one, and potentially could make me suffer. It was a good move when the party encouraged women to give up their jobs, resign their professions, and devote themselves to their husbands and children. It seemed the *völkisch* thing to do. What I sought, if you want to know, was another Krisztina.

As I say, after *Walküre*, I did not become rich; but my circumstances improved dramatically. When that season at the Staatsoper ended, I was helped by my society ladies to inaugurate a summer guest conductorship with the Düsseldorf Symphony, which was most satisfying. I was able to conduct orchestral works of Mozart, Beethoven, and Brahms without the aid of Dr. Böhm of Vienna. People remarked that my interpretations were fresh, insightful, and blended with the temper of the new Germany. I was able to afford a small Opel, so that, on Sundays, I could tour the beautiful Rhineland countryside and vineyards. Best of all, I moved from my threadbare quarters, out of Düsseldorf completely, to a tasteful flat in Neuss, on the west bank of the Rhine, about a twenty-minute drive from Düsseldorf. Neuss is a picturesque old town dating back to Roman times, full of buildings from the Middle Ages. Later, of course, it suffered from the bombing. After the war, attempts were made to reconstruct, but the town became engulfed by the sprawl of industrial Düsseldorf. When I knew it, however, it had much charm.

To Neuss then, to my quiet, comfortable apartment, I brought a succession of pretty young women. I remembered the Gonzaga Café in Vienna, with its distinctive, seductive lighting, dimmed and tinted red. I had the same kind of lighting installed in my place. The young women came to drink wine, then a cozy dinner at the Café Quirinus next door, and after, back to the flat for the night. Sometimes, we had no chance to go out. The wine and the passion were sufficient.

Those women turned out to be unimaginable enchantments. I cannot describe how I trembled as I watched them slide out of their dresses and blouses, camisoles or slips, knickers and stockings—those pretenses to modesty, which never failed to provoke—and transform themselves into objects of flaming sensuality.

Sometimes, they were reluctant to disrobe. We would kiss. I would nuzzle an ear, a delicate neck, caress a youthful back, move daringly to a breast—I could feel a beating heart—and then things would stop. She would draw back, attempt to rebutton. But having come this far, how could she stop? If I encountered genuine resistance, I suppose I would cease my advances, but that never happened. As soon as they accepted my invitation, the ladies understood what was what. If they tried to hold on to their garments, I would move to slide them off. The soft cries of the hesitant were the most exciting of all. Every young woman, without exception, concealed fire beneath her clothing. I could never get enough of their sleek limbs, unloosed hair, breasts, bellies, rounded bottoms, skin smooth as silk. Never enough! Like a starving child, I plunged into all that. I suckled, feasted, but was never satisfied. I said I had virtually no need to pursue. Women now followed me with adoring eyes, only too happy to be asked, eager to accept. They were modern women, well conditioned by the naughtiness of Weimar. The party may have had its ideas about the place of women; I had my own. Not *Kinder, Kirche, Küche,* but rather the plunging in and bliss in the bedroom!

After such a rapturous night, a young woman might relax. Now, she believed that I was all hers. She could trust me. For my part, I could permit myself to stretch out and sleep, cradled against the breast of my lover, who would stroke my hair and fondly watch me. Early next morning, after strong black coffee, we would drive back into Düsseldorf. I would drop her at some convenient, discreet corner and politely wish her a good day. Invariably, I divined an unspoken question, which I never permitted to be uttered, on the order of "Will I see you again?" If a particular young lady were actually to say this, I would be ready with a reply: "Why, of course, my dear, in about three hours, at our rehearsal later this morning!" A warm and grateful smile, and I would drive off. Yet search as I might, I could never find another Krisztina.

Kapellmeister at the Westfälische Staatsoper I may have been, but whenever I brought up translating that title into Generalmusikdirektor at meetings of the board, there was nervous clearing of throats. Even Frau Augustina von Krefeld found it hard to meet my eye. But I certainly carried the duties of the higher post. I conducted many works in the repertoire. Staging, costumes, décor, and lighting—all would have to undergo my judgment and approval. Herr L'Orénoque, Herr Kalandrelli, the concertmaster, and the rest appeared every morning at nine thirty for our conferences. Herr von Krefeld was there as well, my "loyal" associate. But I didn't trust him for a second. I couldn't stand him, and we had nothing in common. I despised his musical judgments. Only his grandmother, Frau Augustina, kept him there. Another curiosity: he seemed to have no lady friends. I would see him striding about with robust, manly-looking Brownshirts—party colleagues, I assumed. I had never seen him in uniform. *But were they simply colleagues? Never any women. What could it mean?* The Staatsoper had many a *pédéraste* in its ranks—dancers, designers, singers, even scene-shifters. It no longer meant much—except less competition for the women. But Herr von Krefeld was different. He was a perpetual irritant, particularly because he was protected. On the other hand, certain party branches, particularly the Brownshirts, were said to harbor such perverse creatures.

But why could I not advance? I exulted in my work by day and reveled with my ladies by night. One activity refreshed me for the other. The only disappointment was that I seemed to be stuck. I deemed it a slur when board members refused yet another request for promotion.

The problem was my impatience, they said.

"At twenty-five, why must he be Generalmusikdirektor? *Ach,* why such a hurry?" Frau Augustina was delegated to deliver their response.

"The board extends its profound gratitude for all your services, but—"

I strode up and down her drawing room carpet. "But what is it, *Gnädige Frau*? Which of my abilities awaits further demonstration?"

She watched me from her brocaded chair. "Your abilities? You do nothing but please us with your abilities. I am first to applaud your music, your gift for organization, your training of the orchestra and singers." She hesitated. "One or two members of the board take exception to your lack of academic credentials, the absence of a doctorate, which makes some of them unhappy. There is even a question of whether or not you were properly graduated from the Vienna Conservatory." Such talk made me uneasy. "But," she continued, "I have always refused to listen to such nonsense."

I looked at her. Had she brought up these matters as weapons she might use?

After a moment, she said, "May I be direct?" I nodded. She smiled, wishing to put me at ease. "I wish I were a man," she said. "I think a man would be more comfortable with what I want to say." She cleared her throat. "Herr Kapp-Dortmunder, since your great success here— that unforgettable *Walküre*, and those equally memorable other productions—you have made me and the Westfälische Staatsoper extremely proud. But—" Again *but*.

"To be Generalmusikdirektor, the position for which you yearn, demands a man of impeccable respectability, maturity, and good judgment." Far from calming, her smile alarmed me. I was accustomed to Madame Polkovska's bluntness.

"The fact is, Herr Dirigent, that there have been rumors, disquieting rumors …" She broke off. "Need I continue? Oh, I do wish my husband were alive. He would have known how to speak to another man about these matters."

"Rumors? Concerning what, may I ask?"

She blushed and dabbed at her brow with a tiny handkerchief. "Rumors concerning an immoral…way of life—debauchery, drink, women. I refuse to believe such things. But they are talked about."

I requested permission to smoke, removed a cigarette from my silver case, tapped it, snapped on my lighter, and applied the flame. I needed to be careful. At the same time, I felt lightheaded and reckless, liable to utter the oddest things. That's the way my temperament works.

"By whom are these rumors spread, and by how many?"

She rose to her feet, looking unhappy. "Believe me, Herr Dirigent, this is of the least importance," she said. "What matters is whether the rumors are true or not."

Did she imagine that a young man could live like a monk? I worked hard to suppress laughter.

I let out a slow trail of smoke. "There is not a word of truth in these rumors," I said. "They're all lies, terrible lies." I suspected that the source of the tales would likely be Frau Augustina's grandson. "As a matter of fact," I continued, "what makes these rumors painful is that it was my intention to announce my engagement to a certain young lady of good family. I had not meant to reveal this yet, but I feel sure you will approve when you learn who she is."

Frau Augustina turned pale. "Herr Dirigent," she said, "is this really so? What have I done? Can you forgive my presumption?"

"Permit me to ask if you have shared these rumors with others."

"No, no," she hastened to say. "In fact, this unpleasantness has been discussed in confidence between myself and only one other person." I had guessed correctly. That spiteful bastard, Frau Augustina's grandson, had not given up trying to destroy me. Surely, my counterattack would serve not only to clear things up but also—if Frau Augustina were sufficiently remorseful—to deprive him of his inheritance. I needed to accomplish my marriage quickly. Young von Krefeld was too persistent a pest. He had to be dealt with. I thought it interesting, the rabid way he had become obsessed with my dalliances. Could this righteous purity be masking something? *What if I discovered an illicit lover in his life? If there were one, I suspected it might well be a male.*

Last year, the authorities had publicized the homosexual scandals surrounding SA Chief of Staff Ernst Röhm, former head of the Brownshirts—the bullyboy branch of the party to which von Krefeld belonged. Both the Führer and Dr. Goebbels had condemned their public brawling. It was an embarrassment, they said—never mind that they had gained power because of it! Moreover, they declared, their shameless perversity was destructive to the ideals of German morality.

Röhm had paid with his life, not only for his immorality but also for his treachery to our Führer. Homosexuality was condemned by the party. But, my god, what could any man find attractive among ranks of the SA? So many looked like street toughs, uncouth louts with faces like apes, not at all like the SS, who numbered in their ranks many a Herr Doktor, many refined intellectuals—scholars, lawyers, scientists, government officials. Would it be of benefit if I were to join the SS as well? For now, I would wait and see.

The next morning was a Sunday. I found myself in the grip of a crisis. According to Frau Augustina, my career stood in danger. I would have to be careful. I made a large mug of coffee and sipped while taking notes. I wrote down the names of all the pretty young women in the Staatsoper with whom I had, as they so quaintly say, *slept.* I studied those names. Exciting for the night as they had been, I laughed at the notion of a week together—let alone a life. Yes, perhaps a week, but *never* a lifetime! My mind drifted to other faces, the stylish young women, those with money, position, influence, and good breeding—the women whose assurance I found unsettling, whom I was reluctant to approach. The trouble with those was that not one of them stirred my heart. Not one. More than one opera girl would murmur, during my wildest throes of passion: "Hush, hush! Why so savage? Why so rough?" I could not tell them I hated them for not being Krisztina. I poured another cup of coffee and pulled myself together. The opera girls were simply not eligible. I had promised Frau Augustina a bride from a good family.

* * *

Besides my regular duties, I was immersed in a new production of *Der Rosenkavalier.* The following Tuesday evening—free from a conducting assignment—I had agreed to present a talk on some Mozart operas, illustrated by slides and singers, I at the piano. The sponsor was the organization known as Glaube und Schönheit (Faith and Beauty), the young adult division of the Bund deutscher Mädel (League of German Girls). The GuS wished to develop cultural and spiritual awareness among female party members. The party was eager to counter false impressions overseas that brutality was its stock in trade. It was time to remind the world that Germany was the home of culture—music, art, literature, and philosophy.

I was glad to do my bit, having been approached by Fräulein Margarethe von Hassel, the leader of the local GuS, who managed to excite me by appearing to be both innocent and sensual. On the surface, however, she was the kind of well-brought-up young woman whose hand one kisses.

Fräulein Margarethe looked to be in her early twenties: slender, shapely, blond-haired, blue-eyed, and demure. She had softly tapped at my dressing room door after a performance of *Marriage of Figaro*. When I heard the *von* in her name, I bowed, indeed kissed her hand, showed her to a chair, and offered a glass of champagne. During a necessarily brief conversation—I was as usual drenched with perspiration and needed to change—she expressed three ideas. First was her admiration for the performance she had just attended. Second was her wish—dare she voice it?—that I visit the local branch of GuS and talk to her girls about Mozart. Third, and most important, she believed passionately in the work of our Führer, Adolf Hitler, and what he was achieving for the nation. She wished to aid that work in every way, one of which was for me to speak before her girls.

Fräulein Margarethe interested me, both her charm and her appearance. I noted intimations of the voluptuous. The mouth was full, the blue eyes large and appealing, and the kind of figure that I preferred, not too much, not too little. She would have been among the fruit I might pluck. But that *von* intimidated me. The images it conjured—wealth, hunting estates, servants, and possessions—drove me back to my humble origins. I would have to overcome those fears. I knew nothing about Fräulein Margarethe, and it didn't matter. I was going to marry her. Or someone like her.

On Tuesday evening, I was led by Fräulein Margarethe to the front of a meeting hall in the Brown House in Düsseldorf, local party headquarters. Thirty or so young girls between fourteen and eighteen, identically dressed in pinafores and tunics, hair in braids, sat waiting in orderly rows. They rose to their feet as I entered, together with Herr Tenner and Fräulein Neudeck-Lippe, who were to sing selections from the operas. At the back of the room was a brownshirted slide-projectionist, ready for my cues.

The whole thing went wonderfully well. I outlined scenes from *Figaro*, *Zauberflöte*, and *Così fan tutte*, illustrated with slides of costumes and scenes. Occasionally, I walked to the piano to accompany the singers in an aria or duet. I really didn't have to speak that much; the selections and the slides filled most of the time. Afterward, the girls surrounded me, Herr Tenner, and Fräulein Neudeck-Lippe, seeking autographs, eager and excited, but in a most polite and well-bred way, their open, fair faces shining with pleasure. If the new Germany produced specimens like these, it was doing well.

Shining also was the countenance of Fräulein Margarethe, my hostess. "I hope the evening hasn't been too tiring for you, Herr Kapp-Dortmunder." Before I had a chance to deny it, she clapped her hands for silence and requested the girls to line up and thank me personally, one by one. I laughingly put a stop to that awkward maneuver. Fräulein Margarethe relented, but only after I agreed to listen to her girls sing verses from Friedrich Zilcher's setting of *Die Lorelei*, which they did passably well. But I was puzzled. Surely, she knew that the words were by the onetime Düsseldorf Jew, Heinrich Heine—not only a Jew but also notorious for loving Bolsheviks. I kept my questions to myself. Later, I discovered that quite a few Jewish works like *Die Lorelei* were deemed too precious to abandon. Nazi thinkers hit upon a brilliant solution. They kept the poem but discarded the Jew. They retained *Die Lorelei* in the canon of cherished works but now attributed them to "Anonymous." After *Die Lorelei*, Fräulein Margarethe insisted that I be her guest for a light supper at a nearby café. It would, she said, be pitiful recompense for the wonderful evening I had given her girls. She didn't realize that a chance to be alone with her was what I had been hoping for.

"You have a gift for making opera and the stage easy to understand, Herr Kapp-Dortmunder," she said. The waiter opened and poured a pleasant *Qualitätswein*. "It seemed so effortless. My understanding was so deepened. I look forward to more events like this. It is how I imagined the perfect cultural program for my girls would be. Dare I impose upon you to listen to other ideas I have in mind?"

"If you have other such ideas," I said with a bow, "and we are to have other conversations such as this, then, dear Fräulein Margarethe, permit me to suggest that we not be so formal with each other. I would be honored if you would address me by my given name, Hermann."

She blushed and, in confusion, covered her face for a moment. I stared at her, astonished at how easy everything was. I also grimly commended myself for not revealing my true name, Ferenc. Only Mama and poor Krisztina had had the privilege of calling me that.

"Hermann," breathed Fräulein Margarethe, "the same name as that of our joyous, confident hero, General Göring, who stands at the right hand of our beloved Führer." Her eyes were shining again. We must have talked for hours. She seemed truly well-bred and quite intelligent. In due time, I would have my hands on her breasts.

"Has the Fräulein attended university?" I asked. With all I had achieved, I still envied the products of universities.

She laughed. "My goodness, no. The girls in my family do not do that. We go to finishing schools in Paris or Switzerland. We are supposed to acquire graces and ladylike accomplishments—needlework, embroidery, playing the harp and the piano—but not to be a real musician like you." She blushed again. "I would say that I had been brought up to manage servants and a household, to be agreeable, to entertain, to look forward to marriage and motherhood."

I was ready to laugh with her, but she was perfectly serious.

"It is the practice of the class I was born into," she said. "My father, Gustav von Hassel, was a wonderful man, though I hardly remember him. He was Colonel of the Fourth Westphalian Grenadiers, killed in 1916, leading his men into battle—"

"That is terrible to hear," I broke in. "So was mine. Killed in Italy."

"Was he?" She touched my hand. "Was he also a leader of men?"

"Yes," I said.

"I felt that was so." She blushed yet again as she pronounced my name. "Hermann, you bear your loss bravely. I see that, like a general, you lead and inspire your musicians. This is a rare quality that men acquire from their fathers, whether they have a *von* in their names or not." She squeezed my hand, her mouth trembling, on the brink of weeping.

"After my father's death, my mother never completely recovered. She somehow retired from the enjoyment of things. I have become used to looking after myself," she said with a brave smile. "My leadership of this local group of GuS—I was inspired to it by a call to duty from our beloved Führer. I bury loneliness in service to the nation."

I was on the right path, I knew it. Fräulein Margarethe was certainly given to sentimental posturing, but she was not stupid. Could I take her seriously? *It didn't matter, I was going to marry her.*

246

I rose to my feet and kissed her hand. "Fräulein Margarethe," I said, "the hour is late, and we should bring this delightful evening to a close. Would you honor me"—I had not released her hand—"by being my guest at tomorrow evening's premiere of *Rosenkavalier*? I should say this evening's premiere—it's past midnight. I shall be conducting. It will be a gala presentation. It would mean so much were you to be there."

She hesitated. "I don't know. What a generous offer. But on Wednesday afternoons, I always sew with my mother. It is usual for our time together to stretch into the evening. It's a tradition of ours. At this stage, she prefers life to be predictable."

Better and better. "Then may I beg that you break tradition, this once, and bring the *Gnädige Frau*, your mother, along to the performance," I asked. "I am so proud of this production. I'm sure it will please you both."

Beaming, she rose to her feet and reached for my hand again. "That is so charming, Herr *Hermann*!" The expression of warmth occasioned a startlingly loud giggle. The wine? "And you should call me Gretl. 'Fräulein Margarethe' sounds too grand for me." *These young women were all the same, both the ones you knew were accessible and these high-flown aristocrats. All one had to do was to pierce the reserve.*

"I shall have to speak with my dear Mutti and see," she said. "She is really set in her ways. On the other hand, she loves music, she loves opera. She told me she always went together with my father. It may take some persuasion. Will it be convenient if I telephone you at the Staatsoper at about eleven o'clock tomorrow morning? Would that be sufficient notice?"

"Absolutely. Entirely sufficient! You do me great honor, Fräulein Margarethe—*Gretl*, I should say." And I bent to kiss her hand once more.

Abruptly, she broke away and hurried to the door. For a moment, I thought I might have offended her. I caught fright. I had an impulse to rush after her, to apologize, buy her a spray of violets from the aged crone at the door, to see that a taxi be found. I was relieved when, just as she stepped out, she turned and gave a cheerful wave. I had a moment to reflect. Once again, I had veered crazily between supreme confidence and abject anxiety. *Was there no middle way?*

VARIATIONS ON THE BEAST

✳ ✳ ✳

As usual with a premiere, the next day was filled with endless last-minute troubles—people having hysterics, singers claiming to come down with laryngitis, costumes that didn't fit, collapsing scenery. Amidst all this, Fräulein Margarethe telephoned to say that she and her Mutti would be delighted to come. I had already made arrangements for them to have the Elector's Box—reserved, as you may imagine, for special occasions. Naturally, I would be occupied in the orchestra pit, so I had instructed one of the staff to attend to their every wish—champagne, refreshments, and the like.

At about two in the afternoon came another telephone call. Herr Kopsch, the house manager, dared burst onstage in great excitement, disrupting and making a shambles of the most lyrical section of *Rosenkavalier*—the act 3 trio, featuring Sophie, Oktavian, and the Marschallin. The composer, Richard Strauss himself, had just telephoned. I almost fainted when I heard. He apologized for leaving things to the last minute, but as he was traveling in the area, he wished to attend tonight's performance. Would it be a terrible inconvenience to find seats for him, his wife, his son, and his daughter-in-law?

In best Franz Liebermann fashion, I howled in exasperation and terror, sweeping the score to the ground. I had been slaving for the better part of an hour to pull things together, to imbue the orchestra with the desired tenderness—fighting to keep out the mawkish and saccharine. The Marschallin has to express an older woman's acceptance that she has lost her young lover, Oktavian. On the other hand, Sophie (quite innocent) and Oktavian (not so innocent) celebrate the birth of love with their discovery of one another. Everything has to be completely enchanting without descending into syrup—the voices pure, the orchestral textures transparent—accented by pungent glints from flutes, harps, and celesta, the motif of the Rosenkavalier himself—the Knight of the Silver Rose. Even my detractors kept silent at such moments.

What awful battles I had undergone two years before, when I was first seized with the idea of putting on *Rosenkavalier*. The most bitter of them, of course, with Herr von Krefeld. He had organized quite a rebellion.

"We've never done *Rosenkavalier* in this house before," was one contribution. Another was: "Our Kappi may be good with violent and boisterous works like *Walküre* or *Fidelio*, but what can he know about the refinements of eighteenth-century Vienna? The ways of the court? The subtleties of satire?"

I confounded them with the notes I had assembled before approaching them. What kind of fool did they think I was? Not only did I talk about general plans, I had brought along sketches for stage design, decor, lighting, and costumes. I had ideas on whom I wanted in the cast. I reminded them that Richard Strauss was a contemporary composer and that something was going on besides a mere reproduction of eighteenth-century Vienna. This was not another version of *Marriage of Figaro*! The comedic acid in Mozart was quite different from that in Strauss. But there were similarities. Both men sensed violent change around the corner: the French Revolution for Mozart, the Great War and bloody chaos for Strauss. I saw almost the whole thing as drenched in sex—trysts, affairs, improper liaisons, lechery. Not everything, of course. There is also delicacy, refinement, and rapture. But that overture, with its raw, bawdy, thrusting horns could not be more obvious.

Finally, I reminded them that I had lived in Vienna and had spent many hours basking in the magnificence of the Schloss Schönbrunn, the Belvedere, the Kinsky, and other palaces. I persuaded them that I was steeped in the spirit of two hundred years ago. Of course, I was nothing of the kind, but I am a quick study. They watched and listened with fascination—and one at least with active dislike. Despite his youth, they said of me, he has astonishing wisdom. Say what you like about his filthy temper, he knows what he's doing—he understands the period, these characters' hearts, the delicacy of their feelings, the robustness of the comedy.

I had worked hard on that third act trio—and the duet between Oktavian and Sophie that follows. The orchestra responded almost exactly as I wished. It was coming to sound ethereal, otherworldly. I was on the brink of magic. One or two details remained—not exactly details, but rather certain touches, the mishandling of which would spell the difference between wonder and kitsch. The Marschallin understands the growing fascination between her lover, the young Oktavian, and Sophie. She leaves the pair by themselves and accepts that the dalliance between herself and Oktavian—sung by a woman, just like Cherubino in *Figaro*—is over. After a while, she reappears together with Faninal, Sophie's father. He fondly observes the young people and sings,

"Sind halt aso, die jungen Leut!" (That's how young people behave.) The Marschallin responds quite simply, *"Ja, ja."*

I had to turn myself inside-out to get Frau Ebenhauser, my Marschallin, to do it correctly. She offered, first, melodramatic exaggeration, second, a plebeian shrug. In response to my frown, she tried in turn girlish giggles, sarcasm, reproofs, and haughtiness. None was what I wanted.

Frau Ebenhauser came down to the edge of the stage. "Herr Kapellmeister, I don't know what you want," she wailed. "Is she unhappy or isn't she? Just tell me and I'll try my best. It's past two o'clock, and we have a premiere. If we don't stop soon and give me a chance for a nap, I shall be in no condition to sing tonight."

I ran up onto the stage. "Listen, it's not difficult. The Marschallin cares about losing her lover, especially to a young thing like Sophie. But it's not the end. She's not a hag. She's only 32. Her husband neglects her, but there will be other lovers." Frau Ebenhauser looked happier. "She must sing '*Ja, ja,*' not in anger, scorn, or despair, but with dignity. She accepts. She is a noblewoman and, at the same time, a noble woman." I squeezed Frau Ebenhauser's hand. She said she would try.

I signaled to Faninal, who sang his line again. I pointed to the Marschallin, staring into her eyes from two feet away, trying to mesmerize her. Apparently, I succeeded. "*Ja, ja*" came out just right, sadly and quietly.

I kissed her hand. "That was wonderful. Do it just like that tonight." She responded with a bewildered nod. We were minutes away from closing the rehearsal. We could all rest and prepare ourselves for the big evening.

That was the moment the house manager chose to stomp in, breaking the news of Richard Strauss's appearance. Just like that! Now it was I who almost went to pieces. The orchestra members sprang to their feet, all shouting at the same time, the chorus crowded onstage, joined by supernumeraries, stagehands, and workmen, mixed up together, jostling each other and yammering without listening to each other.

"Ruhe! Stille!" I shouted. Their faces shone with pleasure at the prospect of the composer's visit. "What an honor!" they were saying to each other. *What an honor, indeed!* But I had everything to lose if found deficient. Whatever reputation people believed I had suddenly seemed fragile.

"Let's have a short break," I said, "but I need you all back at a quarter to three. Ladies, I regret keeping you longer. We still have to polish up some odds and ends. I will not hold you for more than fifteen or twenty minutes, I promise you."

They packed into my office: all our department heads, also Herr L'Orénoque, Herr Kalandrelli, and the von Krefeld fellow—eyes dancing, all babbling. I felt endangered and reacted foolishly. Despite the gravity of the situation, I couldn't keep from chuckling. It had something to do with my panic. When the others looked surprised or frowned, my chuckles developed into open laughter. I was unable to stop.

"One would think," I sputtered, tears rolling down my cheeks, "that a visit by Richard Strauss to our opera house is the best news that we could hear."

"Well, it certainly merits discussion." The concertmaster tried to be helpful.

I responded with a loud peal of laughter. People looked at each other and rolled their eyes. Although he tried to control himself, the burly Herr L'Orénoque was the next to laugh. He poured fuel on my flames, so to speak, and now both of us were helpless. Everyone else looked frightened.

On the surface, Herr von Krefeld was an oily and deferential Schweinhund when he addressed me, but I wasn't fooled. "I think the Elector's Box will be free this evening," he said. "Shall I give instructions to have it prepared for Herr Strauss and his party? I think he should be welcomed with a champagne supper—"

I waved my finger at him. "No, no, Herr von Krefeld. That would be completely out of the question," I managed before being overcome by laughter again.

"But, Herr Kapellmeister, why ever not? Don't you understand? Richard Strauss will be here, Germany's greatest living composer—he exists on a level with Wagner—" He went on, typically underlining the obvious.

"The Elector's Box is not free," I said. The room quieted.

Herr von Krefeld stood. "What are you talking about?"

"Are you questioning me, Herr von Krefeld?" I stood as well. "I repeat, I have other plans for the Elector's Box—many weeks ago, in fact. Herr Strauss will be perfectly happy with other accommodations." I tried to look severe but failed. I could not keep a straight face.

Herr Kopsch, the house manager—the man who had launched this crisis—broke in. "With respect, Herr Kapellmeister, no other boxes are free. This is, after all, a gala occasion. Would it not be possible—"

I ignored him and struggled not to laugh again. "Herr von Krefeld," I said, "I request that you speak to our chairwoman, Frau Augustina, about this. Herr Kopsch, I suggest you be prepared to dislodge people from another box to make room for Herr Strauss. You are the house manager. Kindly perform your office."

I stared at each man in turn. Neither met my eye. In one stroke, I had solved the dilemma and also begun to master Herr Strauss at the same time. That was important. I adored his music. But I had suddenly and unpleasantly become aware of the hazards of performing works by a living composer. Simply put, I feared his judgments. I never recalled similar problems with Mozart, Beethoven, or Wagner.

"So," said Herr L'Orénoque, "why don't you reveal the great mystery! For which secret guest is the Elector's Box reserved? Is it destined for a beautiful lady?"

I could not stare down Herr L'Orénoque. A guilty smirk crept over my face. Herr L'Orénoque uttered a great, knowing "Ah-hah!" After a moment, the company repeated it, accompanied by their own knowing smiles. Herr von Krefeld remained angry. But the mood in the room was comradely.

"As a matter of fact, dear colleagues," I began—each man beamed at that—"I had wanted to save for another occasion a somewhat delicate announcement." I was interrupted by another great "Ah-hah!" from the group, everyone winking and grinning. "But I am obliged by the unexpected arrival this night of all nights of Herr Richard Strauss to divulge that a certain lady has graciously consented—"

I was unable to finish. Herr L'Orénoque stepped up and crushed me to him in one of his suffocating embraces. "Heartiest congratulations!" he boomed.

I fought to free myself. "Please, gentlemen, please!" But I had lost control. The others crowded around us, attempting to slap me on the back or find a hand to shake. At last, I was able to make myself heard.

They fixed me with silly grins, grateful, I suppose, to have been permitted some intimacy.

"Please, meine Herren. I must request the greatest discretion. But for the arrival of Herr Strauss this evening, my intentions would not now be in danger of premature disclosure. I must exact an oath and a pledge from each man in this room—on his honor—that he will not reveal these intentions."

"But what exactly are your intentions?" Herr L'Orénoque boomed.

"And which fortunate lady is the object of them?" Herr von Krefeld's voice was unpleasantly thin. It cut through the hubbub like a knife.

I broke the silence. "Bitte, Herr von Krefeld," I said, "would you mind waiting here a few moments?" He shrugged and sat. I addressed the others. "Gentlemen, you are all dismissed until this evening. Please inform the company that they are dismissed as well. My apologies for making you all wait. I will see you at the performance. And"—I emphasized—"I will rely upon each man here to preserve my secret until I make an official announcement." Every face bore a grin of complicity. That was all right. I held the door open for them, nodding to each in turn.

Herr von Krefeld watched me, openly sneering, as they left. I walked over to offer a cigarette. He shook his head. My heart was beating. The moment had come.

I said, "Mein Herr, let us not waste each other's time. We have no fondness for one another—"

The other laughed. "You may be a guttersnipe—"

"—But I'm able to see what's in front of me?"

"I have no idea whether you can or not," he said, looking down his nose. "But from the first moment we crossed paths, you have intruded on me, on my family, and on my plans. You have done all this by becoming the most accomplished arse-licker I have ever seen. You spring out of nowhere, recommended mainly by Jews, I notice. Before one can turn around—*Punkt!*—you have become Kapellmeister of the Westfälische Staatsoper. Astonishing! A complete unknown, obviously without breeding, without class, without manners." He took out his own cigarette case and lit a foul-smelling Turkish specimen. "Arse-licker," he repeated.

Incredible. I was actually enjoying the moment.

"And now," he continued, "what is this pathetic nonsense about a marriage? I happen to know that you are the greatest whoremaster in Düsseldorf. You are known to treat women in the most shameless fashion, as your personal harem, ruining countless reputations. You are disgusting!" I found his indignation exhilarating.

I drew in a mouthful of smoke. "The young ladies of the opera are fortunate to have you to protect them. What are you planning to do with this ridiculous slander?"

"It's time to put a stop to you," he said evenly. "I have tried to inform my grandmother for some time, gently and by suggestion, but she doesn't want to listen. It's too late for delicacy. We have to get rid of you before you disgrace us all—my grandmother, the Staatsoper, and all our family. You have crawled your way into us like a parasite. You're not a Jew yourself, by any chance? That's the kind of thing they're known for."

"I repeat, it is all a slander," I said.

"You deny it? How shabby. How typical. It won't do you any good. I have friends in official circles. People who take note of what you do."

This was absurd. He was as vulnerable to scandal as I. "You have actually informed on me?" I was incredulous. "Isn't it possible you could be accused of similar misdeeds?"

"What are you talking about?"

"What I'm talking about, Herr von Krefeld, is your own questionable conduct in the area of morals." I fixed him with a severe frown, aware that I was making perilously large guesses. I had no friends in "official circles" to threaten him with. All I wanted was to make him less cocky and leave me alone. I began with a given. As far as I knew, all men needed sex. That was article one. I was well aware that there was more than one kind of sex. The telling thing was that I never saw von Krefeld in the company of women, young or old, except for his grandmother. But I constantly saw him together with those strapping, strutting young toughs who had SA Storm Trooper written all over them, even in plain clothes.

"Look, Herr von Krefeld," I said kindly, "I don't wish to cause difficulties or make problems. I hold no bitterness toward you— even though you call me such ugly names. *I* don't care in the slightest what you do in private, or with whom. Why should my own activities concern you?"

"What, if anything, do you know of my activities?" he asked.

"All I'm saying, Herr von Krefeld, is that when I make bumsen"—
I used the vulgar expression for sexual intercourse—"I do it with girls,
with women. You catch my drift? With any tasty piece of meat, as long
as she's a female." I leaned into him jauntily. "The fact is, *Herr von
Krefeld*"—I took pleasure in drawling out his name as insolently as
possible—"I don't care what the lady looks like or what age she may be
as long as she is young and irresistible." I roared at my own wit.

He drew back in revulsion. "That's final then. You have gone too
far. You are truly disgusting. I shall report these vile comments to my
grandmother and the board. Your papers of dismissal will be delivered
to you by morning."

Another fit of laughter welled up. "What is the matter with you?"
he snapped.

"You didn't permit me to finish," I chuckled. "Herr von Krefeld, I
said that I didn't care what the lady looked like as long as she was a *she*."
I grabbed him by the shoulders and brought my face close to his. "Can
you say the same of yourself, Herr von Krefeld?" I was enjoying myself.
It was as good as being in front of the orchestra. "When you make
bumsen with your *Amor*," I said, "do you know if it is a he or a she? Or
don't you care? When you are ready to plunge in, is your passage unim-
peded? Or does something get in the way, so to speak? And if it does,
do I take it there would be other avenues to explore? *So to speak?*"

He turned white. "You are insane to speak like this. Do you understand what you're involved with? This would be trouble even you
wouldn't know how to stop."

I blocked his exit. "Before you go, Herr von Krefeld, I beg to
remind you of something significant. Last summer, you know that one
of the Führer's top lieutenants, Captain Ernst Röhm, chief of the
Brownshirts—perhaps his dearest comrade—plotted against him and
his vision for the Fatherland."

He paused. "What has that to do with me?"

"I know that you are proud to be a member of the SA."

"What of it?" he snapped. "Yes, I am proud to be a member of the
SA. We did the dirty work for the movement. We shed our blood in
countless streets and alleys. Ever since the Führer commenced his crusade, the SA has been at his side—"

"But your Captain Röhm wasn't content to be at the Führer's side,
was he?"

"Why do you keep bringing up Captain Röhm? I'm talking about the SA."

"Yes, indeed. But if I remember correctly, Captain Röhm was looking for more than the Führer was willing to give. When the Führer was named Reich Chancellor, it wasn't enough. Captain Röhm demanded a second revolution. He agitated for the Führer to destroy the capitalists, the aristocrats, the army—all the Führer's allies."

Herr von Krefeld vehemently shook his head.

"*Ach*, it pains me to contradict you, but Dr. Goebbels himself has verified it. Captain Röhm not only opposed the Führer," I went on, "in itself a treasonous act, he actually meant to replace him. He wanted command of the army, he wanted to turn the Führer's movement into another Bolshevik Revolution. Everybody knows about it. What are you trying to deny?"

"That's a lie," the other shouted.

"And worst of all—" I continued.

"You have more filth?" he asked bitterly. "Believe me, when you insult the memory of Captain Röhm, you slander an exceptional man, a true comrade, and a loyal soldier." I raised an eyebrow. "Sneer as much as you please, Herr Kapp. There are traitors who crawl like rats about the Führer. If only he knew what was said and done in his name! But he is immersed in the mission of rebuilding the Fatherland, breaking the stranglehold of the Jews." He lowered his voice. "Lies, black lies have been spread about Captain Röhm by opportunists who scurry about the Führer like rats."

He must have been the most stupid man in Germany. The source for my information was Dr. Goebbels, who had broadcast the news to a horrified nation. Captain Röhm had plotted in league with Gregor Strasser, another false comrade. Just in time, all was discovered. The Führer himself—aided by Dr. Goebbels, General Göring, and the SS—had arrested Röhm, Strasser, and countless numbers of top SA people. They had all been shot, swiftly and ruthlessly. It was *Die Nacht der langen Messer*. Those men had risen up against the leader they had sworn to follow. But ruthlessness is the only way to deal with revolts. I faced similar situations every day with my orchestra and crushed them.

"I've heard enough from you, Herr Kapp," he said. "I advise you to be most careful. The SA is still the bulwark of the new Germany.

You would be wise to take it seriously. My friends are powerful. I have the ability to make you disappear, to have you shot. I can do that."

A kind of terror grasped at me, but I laughed. "Do you agree," I giggled, "that Röhm was not merely the leader of a plot against the Führer but also the center of an organized, subversive attack by the queers against normal, healthy life? I'm referring to the moral health of the Reich."

"You don't give a fart for the moral health of the Reich!" he sneered. "You're signing your own death warrant." He may well have had a pistol on him at that moment. I didn't care. I felt immortal.

"If anything happens to me," I declared, "friends of mine have instructions to deliver envelopes personally to Dr. Goebbels, in his capacity as minister for Public Enlightenment, to General Göring, in his capacity as minister of the Interior, and to Heinrich Himmler, head of the SS." It was pure fabrication, inspired by countless Hollywood gangster films.

"What kind of letters?"

"What kind do you think? Disgusting I may be, as you choose to say, but certainly not stupid. The letters anticipate the threats you are uttering. You are not the only person in the Reich with open eyes. I have been observing much about you."

"And what have you observed?"

"Merely this," I said piously. "Even though the Röhm traitors have been eliminated, I suspect that an enthusiastic community of queers remains as a danger to a clean-living nation. Why the Führer would tolerate the SA—"

His face twitched. "The Führer remains loyal to his Old Fighters," he broke in.

I shook my head. "I don't understand what an artistic sort of fellow, a musician—even a dreadful one like you—was doing, breaking heads at street brawls. Are people with *von* in their names known for that sort of thing? Don't you realize that the entire nation was embarrassed by the rioting, by Captain Röhm's love for street toughs and bullyboys? Or were you yourself drawn to their sturdy masculinity? Nowadays, Brownshirts with any brains are abandoning the SA in droves. They're switching to the SS. The uniform is much better, for one thing. Smart black jackets instead of creased and rumpled brown shirts." He said nothing.

"The fact remains," I lectured, "that the SA is politically treacherous and morally corrupt. Everybody knows that." I poked him in the chest. "Don't worry, Herr von Krefeld, I included a full description of your associates and the times and locations of your meetings." I was lying through my teeth. "For instance, would it surprise you to learn that the Gestapo and the Kripo are in competition to clean up the city of Düsseldorf, which has achieved fame as a vibrant center of the queers in this part of Germany?" That last statement at least was true.

"I don't believe you could have been so busy," he said with narrowed eyes.

"You could always test me," I replied. "You could always carry out your preposterous threat and find out for yourself. Just one idiotic move on your part and you'd be hauled off to Berlin, to Plötzensee Prison, and thrown in front of a firing squad in ten minutes. Think of your poor grandmother!"

I seized his head between my hands and kissed him hard on the mouth. His eyes widened with shock and horror. He broke away, glared, and plunged out of my office. I collapsed on a leather armchair, laughing like a madman. *Why in God's name had I done that?* Were matters not difficult enough? I was too exhausted to think. I released a huge gust of air. My god! I had the premiere of *Rosenkavalier* in three hours. I was so tired that I immediately fell asleep, just as I was.

* * *

Herr Kopsch discovered me about two hours later and, with great difficulty, roused me. He informed me that Frau Augustina had made reservations for a late supper with Herr Strauss, his family, and the entire cast. I resolved to include among the guests Fräulein Margarethe (for whom I was demonstrating my utter suitability as a marriage partner) and her "dear Mutti." After many cups of black coffee, a quick tub in my private bathroom, and a change into a set of spare evening clothes, I was ready.

For once, I wished to enjoy a great musical occasion without hurry or pressure. Apparently, not possible. Just as when I conducted my triumphant *Walküre*, I have no clear recollection of the *Rosenkavalier*. It all passed as a blur. At the end of the first act, people said it was working well—vivid, vital, full of life and gaiety—yet with appropriate undertones of sadness. Oktavian's second act entrance and his presentation of the silver rose to Sophie were sheer splendor and magnificence for both eye and ear, but touching as well. The third act's noisy burlesque and tomfoolery go on for too long, if you ask me. But with the composer present, I put off to a later date my idea of making cuts. The scene finally quieted. The music transformed into the heartbreaking beauty of that final trio and duet. I had little fault to find. Truly, I made music wonderfully, leading my singers and players with both deliberation and pleasure—even though I wasn't sure what Herr von Krefeld intended for me. I was half-expecting a bullet in my back during the entire performance. Or to be taken into custody by his SA cronies at the end. Mercifully, neither occurred.

Finally, it was over. The great dark red velvet curtains parted, and the perspiring singers gathered onstage—Sophie, Oktavian, the Marschallin, Baron Ochs, Faninal, even the Little Black Boy. The last, of course, was a German white child appropriately slathered with greasepaint. The French army's black colonial occupation of the Ruhr had ended some years before, but one occasionally saw the unfortunate fruits of that presence. What on earth had possessed those young German women? In any case, everyone agreed that it would be imprudent these days to present a real black child on our stage. Hands joined, they advanced to the footlights, bowing, smiling, sweating. As I made my way to the stage, I was joined in the wings by the composer himself—I had forgotten all about him. Tall, distinguished-looking, getting on in years, but ruddy and vigorous, he grasped my hand, delighted to walk out and share the applause.

It was wonderful not to have been shot. Of Herr von Krefeld I saw no sign. But his grandmother, Frau Augustina, reminded us of our supper reservations. She had commandeered a private dining room in the Schlossturm, a thoroughly exclusive and expensive restaurant housed within the turreted museum of the same name. Like a mother hen, she shooed Herr Strauss, Frau Strauss, their son, and his wife toward a regal black Mercedes. I followed in another car with my guests, Fräulein Margarethe—my Gretl—and her mother, Frau von Hassel, a severe, angular woman, who stared out of the window during the whole drive. Margarethe, on the other hand, seemed happy to be close to me after watching the back of my head from the Elector's Box all evening, and would not stop chattering. The cast took taxis. When we got past the forbidding stone walls of the Schlossturm, the restaurant's interior presented a kind of savage elegance. As soon as we appeared, bowing hosts showed us to a magnificent medieval wood-paneled room, at one end of which was a roaring fire. The walls were covered with ancient weapons, horned helmets, hammered iron, boars' heads, sets of antlers. Awaiting us were bottles of Sekt, which were opened with loud pops, the wine poured by deferential waiters.

"I would have preferred champagne," grumbled Herr L'Orénoque, "but the German patriots here would hardly approve."

Frau Augustina made her way over to my guests. "In the name of the Staatsoper, I welcome you." She beamed at Frau von Hassel and took the hand of Fräulein Margarethe. "And it gives me pleasure finally to greet the intended bride of our esteemed Kapellmeister."

The remark produced immediate consternation. I groaned. Fräulein Margarethe turned pale. "What?" she stammered. Frau von Hassel leaned forward. "Excuse me, Frau von Krefeld, what did I hear you say?" Frau Augustina playfully wagged her finger. "Was I premature? I will hold my tongue. No one shall know too early."

The mother frowned. "No one shall know what, Frau von Krefeld?"

Frau Augustina behaved like a doting aunt. She regarded me and Margarethe with a conspiratorial smile. "*Ach*, nothing is the same since the war. Didn't we just hear this in the opera tonight?" She repeated Faninal's line: "*That's how young people behave. In this modern world,* Frau von Hassel, one must be grateful that at least some of the proprieties are observed."

"Apparently, not enough of them," said the other. She wheeled around to her daughter. "Child," she said, "do I understand that you have actually conducted some kind of liaison behind my back? And you have taken it upon yourself to arrange a marriage? And I am obliged to learn of it in this fashion? What would your father have said?"

All around us, people paid no attention, munching on *Vorspeisen*—mainly small dishes of maultaschen, pickles, and slices of *Weisswurst* on mushrooms—all the while talking, laughing, downing glasses of Sekt. It was a lunatic scene. Frau von Hassel, Frau Augustina, and Fräulein

Margarethe—all three stared at me. A waiter broke the tension by thrusting a tray of raw radishes at us. We ignored him.

Frau von Hassel turned to me. "Young man," she said severely, "times have changed indeed. When I was a girl, nothing resembling this could have happened. Courtships, proposals, acceptances, refusals—taking place either in secret or at a public gala? Unbelievable! I don't know what would be more embarrassing, to take our leave at once and have these people talk about us, or stay and pretend to enjoy ourselves."

Bewildered, Margarethe attempted to protest her innocence. I felt for her but suddenly realized that an unbelievable opportunity had presented itself. I would strike at once. I seized her hand. She was too startled to object.

Frau von Hassel frowned. "My child," she said, "have you actually formed an attachment to this young man—of considerable talents, I understand—but whom I have never before met, therefore of whose means and social standing I know nothing?"

Margarethe turned pale, gazed at her mother and then at me. At last, she said, "If he will have me, I shall be his." I almost dropped. Frau von Hassel looked appalled.

Someone nearby must have told a funny story, for there was a sudden outburst of merriment.

Margarethe started and seemed to recover. Now, all at once, she sounded decisive, in command of herself, altogether her mother's daughter. "Frau von Krefeld," she said clearly, "we should all appreciate it so much if you would say nothing at this time." I was astonished. *Where had the simpering gone?* "My dear Mutti should be the one to make any announcement, which would be by way of the society pages, as is family custom." Her mother did not look appeased.

Obviously, I was fated to become involved with unconventional young women. I had believed Margarethe blushing and docile—those were among the qualities for which I had selected her. But, in addition, she was turning out to be resourceful. I shouldn't have been surprised. She ran her young girls in the GuS with efficiency. Thinking back to Vienna, I recognized Lotte and Klara as other examples of womanly self-possession, only they had frightened the life out of me. Krisztina had also amazed me. Now, I could only admire Margarethe's handling of things. All these young women—so exciting and desirable! But you couldn't take your eyes off them a moment.

Frau Augustina broke away from us and clapped her hands. "Let us be seated, meine Damen und Herren," she commanded. I watched to see whether Frau von Hassel might leave. After a few seconds, she grimly led Margarethe to the table. I sighed with relief. Margarethe's eyes were bright. She threw me a wave.

We seated ourselves at long tables gleaming with white damask and elegant crystal. At the head table was Frau Augustina. To her right was Herr Strauss; I sat on *his* right. Frau Strauss, the Strausses' son and daughter-in-law were on her left. Of Herr von Krefeld, there was no sign. Frau Augustina got to her feet and rang a tiny glass bell, clearly the chairwoman of the board. "Meine Damen und Herren," she began. "First, let me invite you to rise for a toast to our beloved Führer, Adolf Hitler." We pushed back our heavy chairs, raised our glasses, and together uttered the words, "Der Führer." The gentlemen clicked their heels.

"Next, it is my honor and privilege," she resumed, "to welcome in the name of the Westfälische Staatsoper the greatest living German composer, who has graced us with his presence tonight." People noisily stamped their feet. She beamed at Herr Strauss, who half-rose and bowed in acknowledgment. "Herr Strauss paid me the great honor of sharing my box. He was gracious enough to say that he had been hearing good things about our opera for many years and regretted not being able to visit before now. You all know that he was recognized by the government of our nation, having been appointed by Dr. Goebbels to the post of president of the State Music Bureau, and has rendered great service to German music. Unhappily, for reasons of health, he has since been obliged to resign. On a happier note, he was good enough to remark how moved he was by tonight's performance, led by our brilliant young Kapellmeister, Herr Kapp-Dortmunder"—there was a second interruption as the company applauded me. I too beamed and rose. "Herr Strauss said that Herr Kapp-Dortmunder's interpretation was the best he had ever heard—except for his own, of course." We all chuckled. "Meine Damen und Herren," she concluded, "would you all rise and drink a toast to the health of a great gentleman of German art. Herr Richard Strauss!" We stood again, lifted our glasses, turned to Herr Strauss, and roared out a hearty "*Prosit!*"

Next, Frau Augustina summoned the Oberkellner, who briskly announced what he was serving at this late supper. "We begin with some fresh oysters, then a *Sauerbraten mit Apfelmus* and *Kartoffelklösse.*

To accompany that, I will fill your glasses with a wonderful red *Spätburgunder*. Finally, *Schwarzwälder Kirschtorte*. Nothing heavy. And of course, to conclude, liqueurs and Kaffee." Frau Augustina leaned to ask if I had seen her grandson. I could only shrug. The company settled down to dine and talk.

Glad as she was to be seated next to our distinguished guest, Frau Augustina seemed typically more interested in the domestic side of things. She sensed that Frau von Hassel should be left in peace for the moment, so she struck up animated conversations with Herr Strauss's wife, Pauline; his son, Franz; and his daughter-in-law, Alice. I had learned that Alice was a Jew and that, therefore, Herr Strauss would have a *Mischling* for a grandson. *My god, what an embarrassment for Germany's greatest living composer!* I couldn't help staring at the daughter-in-law. I had certainly seen Jews before, but they had acquired an evil mystique these days. I'm not sure why. Probably because we were bombarded with such dreadful stories night and day. But stare at her all I might, I failed to see anything unusual. No swarthy complexion, no shifty eyes, no large nose. She looked like any well-born, cultivated German woman, no different from the society ladies who occupied boxes at the opera.

While relishing my oysters, I continued to study her. What then was the difference between Alice Strauss and Aryan women? I honestly didn't know how to answer that. As far back as I could remember, people had nothing good to say about Jews. I had my own sour memories, I don't need to tell you. Remember that theory I shared with you about Carmen, gypsies, and Jews? I don't believe I am so excitable about it these days. But Jews indeed had a foul reputation, from the murder of Jesus, using the blood of young children to bake their Passover bread, their usury, their worldwide control of business, their inventing Bolshevism—all the way to their corrupting our souls by dominating German music and art. Yes, Jews were wrapped in an evil mystique. *Did I still share those beliefs?* Frankly, it depended on what day of the week you were to ask me. And it would depend on how I felt that day.

Just then, Alice Strauss exchanged a whispered remark with her husband, Franz. They shared a fond smile, looking into each other's eyes. *Now, was she a typical Jew?* What *was* a typical Jew? I had known Herr Schneidermann, Frau Malteser, and the decent Herr Fridolin Karl in Eisenstadt. There had been the shady Herr Zuckerweiss and

Fräulein Klara. Mama had claimed that Madame Polkovska and her cousin, Mellnicz *úr*, were also Jews. If this were so, it was not a simple question. Jews seemed to come in all shapes and sizes, not so different from us. But, you see, the Führer had made it plain, that was how they wormed their way into our lives. The German people were going through a terrible crisis, a battle for identity and existence. The stakes were enormous. In such a circumstance, with a known enemy, one had to be ruthless.

But I confess to a subversion of my own. Despite the Führer, the whole matter was of minor importance to me. The Nazis might be voted out; people's attention would turn from the Jews and fix on something else. But I thought it wise to travel with the tide. I had a career to build. That absorbed me. *Isn't this true for everybody?*

People were in awe of Herr Strauss and didn't dare disturb him at dinner. That left me and him to ourselves. He was warm and put me completely at ease. He said he had heard about me here and there, but nothing in detail. He immediately detected traces of Hungarian and Viennese in the way I spoke and inquired with friendly interest where I had come from, where I had been trained, how I had found myself in Düsseldorf. We only sampled the food—we were not really hungry—but we drank the wine, lit cigars, and talked and talked as though we were alone. He could not have been more charming to me as his face grew ruddy.

"You know," he said, "your performance tonight was truly fine." He impatiently waved aside my protests. "Both you and most of your singers are unknown to me. But the direction, the staging, your feel for the music—in fact, the entire production—not only fine, but superb! What productions of the opera had you seen before this?"

"None whatsoever, Herr Strauss."

"Is that a fact? I could have used you back in Dresden in 1910. We had all kinds of struggles over the premiere. Max Reinhardt rescued us with a new staging. Otherwise, the first night of *Rosenkavalier* would have been a disaster."

Again, he brushed aside my demurrers. "No, Herr Kapp-Dortmunder, both of us are much too busy to share empty compliments. I must tell you again, I have not heard many in your cast before. But your feel for the music, your ear, and the way you trained your singers—I wouldn't hesitate to place them close to those goddesses, Lotte Lehmann and Elisabeth Schumann. Perhaps not quite yet at the level of the divine Maria Jeritza—she is in a class of her own. But in many respects, close, close." He kissed his fingers. "And the way you handled the waltzes. Correctly gorgeous. *And sarcastic!* Well done, mein junge, well done."

I vibrated with excitement. "Let me ask you," he went on, "have you been out of Düsseldorf? Have you traveled to Dresden or Berlin? Have you met Furtwängler or"—he chuckled—"Clemens Krauss, who should now look over his shoulder when it comes to conducting my operas? Or have you made acquaintance with Herbert von Karajan, a young man who gets himself talked about these days? I think you and he are about the same age." I shook my head. "Well," he said, "you ought to be showing yourself around Germany and abroad; in your own country, Hungary; and in Austria too." I frowned at that: I had no wish to run the risk of seeing Dr. Böhm or Krisztina's father again. "The world deserves to know you."

His words made me glow. It was late, and we were too exhausted to eat much. But that great man wanted to continue talking to me. He got up, ignoring everybody else, and beckoned me to follow him to a small table over by the fireplace. A waiter poured brandy in huge snifters. We stared into the flames for a while, undisturbed by loud bursts of merriment arising from the others.

When he spoke again, his voice had become thick and indistinct, probably the brandy. "Yes, mein junge, I might have been helpful to you a year ago. Now, I don't think so anymore. I seem to have lost influence." He motioned me closer. "That business with the State Music Bureau. I can tell you that I didn't resign because of ill health." He wagged his finger. "When Dr. Goebbels appointed me president, I thought, *Ja*, I have a chance to do something for German music. The copyright rules were in a mess. I wanted to see composers paid for their work, players for their performances. My committee drafted rules to punish lawbreakers. I was successful too. The Reich government actually signed the appropriate international agreements last year."

"Yes, I heard. Congratulations." I raised my glass.

"But that wasn't everything. There was a bad side." He stared mournfully into the blazing logs. "I suppose I am incredibly naïve," he said at last. "Dr. Goebbels appointed Furtwängler as my deputy—he was hungry for official recognition, although like me, he had no need of it. I believed I could be left to my music and that Furtwängler would handle administrative details. But they expected me actually to become a civil servant. When I thought I could avoid Dr. Goebbels, I fell into the path of Dr. Rust."

I raised my brow.

"Dr. Rust is Reich Minister for science, education, and national training," he intoned, so solemnly that I knew he meant me to smile. "Dr. Rust is a remarkable man—he told me so himself. I was expected to keep office hours, to be on call, involve myself in all kinds of idiotic things. Keep records of programs played all over Germany, from the great orchestras of Berlin, Munich, and Dresden, down to dance bands and anonymous trios that perform at teatime in hotels. I was to ensure that no Jewish music, domestic or foreign, was heard. I was to be responsible for that. I cannot tell you what a stupid enterprise that turned out to be. When it comes to the popular music that people really love, everything—and I mean everything—comes from America, and it's not only all Jewish, but also all Negro. Just try explaining that to Dr. Goebbels and Dr. Rust." He struck his armrest with a fist.

"You know," he continued more quietly, "I began a long time ago. I composed and conducted for the great ducal courts. I made music for the royal houses—Hohenzollerns, Hapsburgs, and Wittelsbachs. I have conducted all over the world. I tried, through music, to console the nation after 1918. I rejoiced at our survival under Weimar. And now, under the Nazis, I believed in the recovery of our spirit—and still do. I still do." He shook his head. "But I must be incredibly naïve. I wished only to compose, conduct, and play. How was I supposed to do that and at the same time be a pen-pushing flunky? I had no interest in politics or administration. Do you believe that?" I nodded. "A crowd of self-important, ignorant men demanded that I join them." He looked about him and lowered his voice. "You cannot believe how ignorant and provincial they are. They sought to make a watchdog of me."

I knew what he would say. Those watchdogs had condemned Jewish music as morally corrupting: composers like Mendelssohn, Mahler, Offenbach, Meyerbeer. "I was supposed to supervise what others might and might not play." Herr Strauss's voice became louder. "Worse, they attempted to dictate what *I* could and couldn't play at my own concerts. Certain, shall we say, proscriptions were applied to me!"

I feared that he would become excited, but I believed him when he said he was naïve. However, he was making a fuss over something that might not last.

"The pen-pushers learned that I meant to perform the *Nocturnes* and *La Mer* of Debussy. I was obliged to withdraw them. *Debussy?* Is Debussy Jewish? I never knew. But what made me ill and unhappy is the whole stupid, tragic business over Zweig."

"Zweig, Herr Strauss?"

"Have you not heard about Stefan Zweig? My new librettist."

Of course I had. It was a great scandal. I couldn't predict what Strauss might say next, but based on the indiscretions he had already uttered, I thought it wise to continue pretending simplemindedness. "Your former librettist, von Hofmannsthal, of course was a genius. I know that well enough from *Rosenkavalier*. It must have been a terrible loss when he died."

"Did people think I should have died as well?" he asked bitterly.

"No, maestro, by no means."

"Yes, it was a great personal and professional sorrow to lose Hugo," he said. "It must be four years now. But I was determined to carry on. There was the premiere of *Arabella* in '33, which we had worked on. Then, by great good fortune, I came across Zweig, also an Austrian, like Hugo. I'm surprised you hadn't heard of this. And I'm surprised you hadn't heard of the ghastly struggle over my new opera, *Die schweigsame Frau*—meant to be a pleasant comedy." He sighed and signaled to a waiter for more brandy.

"Von Hofmannsthal was a Jew," he resumed. "I don't know if you knew that, or if you care. People have been making a huge noise about such things these days, but he and I are responsible for some marvelous work over the last thirty years—I don't care if you think I'm boasting or not. But it's true!" He drank from his glass. "So I begin meeting with Zweig. We take a liking to each other; it seems that we might work together, and we agree on an idea by that English Elizabethan playwright, Ben Jonson. Something worthwhile and wonderful was emerging. Then the authorities got wind of it and became unpleasant. Turned out Zweig also was a Jew. It became impossible for us to work together. Soon after the new government was installed, Zweig fled to Switzerland. We were obliged to do our work by post and telephone. Complete and utter madness!"

"But you managed to finish it."

"We managed to finish it," he sighed. "But then, more madness. The opening took place earlier this year in Dresden." He peered at me. "Are you quite sure you've heard nothing about this?" I shook my head. "When I entered the opera house there, I happened to catch sight of the programs. Zweig's name as librettist did not appear. I made a tremendous fuss and threatened to leave. They quickly printed new programs. A victory for the cause of art," he chuckled. "The Führer and Dr. Goebbels were expected at the opening—expressly in my honor. But they did not appear." He rubbed the side of his head. "Could they really take so seriously all this stupid Jewish nonsense? To thus interfere with the integrity of music and art?"

I was stunned. *Could he be serious?* Herr Strauss had described himself all too well. Naïve!

"There were only three more performances. Then they banned *Schweigsame Frau* altogether. They obliged me to resign from the State Music Bureau." He fell silent and stared into the fire. The dining room had become quieter, the hubbub died down. People had run out of things to say and were draining their demitasses and liqueurs.

Herr Strauss laid his hand on my arm. It shook slightly. "It had all begun so well." His blue eyes were wide and pleading. "Two years ago, when the Nazis first got in, they descended on prominent Jews like Klemperer and Bruno Walter—I'm sure purely for symbolic reasons. I never got along with Walter, but that's neither here nor there. In March of '33, he was supposed to conduct the Berlin Philharmonic at an orchestral benefit. The authorities warned him, if he did so, there would be a riot in the hall and the Brownshirts would see that the place was destroyed. Walter was horrified to hear that and naturally withdrew. The Philharmonic's impresario—also a Jew, by the way— begged me to take Walter's place. No fee was involved. As I say, a benefit. Some people condemn me now for filling in for Walter. But it was for the orchestra, you see."

His eyes still held that pleading look. "And there's more. That same summer, Toscanini was supposed to conduct *Parsifal* at Bayreuth. You know how Toscanini loathes the Fascists at home. He immediately broke his commitment for Bayreuth because he didn't approve of the Führer. The Wagner family made a personal appeal to the Führer. Their season would be ruined, they said. Dr. Goebbels was concerned that the new regime might—again—be tarnished by the violence of the Brownshirts. So I volunteered to go to Bayreuth to conduct *Parsifal*. I wanted to assure the world that *nothing* had changed in Germany, that we were not in the hands of barbarians. Am I not to receive credit for that?"

He heaved a deep sigh. "Really, I find it impossible to keep up with such a contradictory way of handling life. We are proud Germans. Why must we display how beastly we can be? We seem to take pride in it. We take pride in displaying infinite varieties of it." He chuckled. "What about a new tone poem, *Variations on the Beast*!"

He was not naïve. He was mad. Terror in my heart, I realized that Frau Strauss and Frau Augustina were approaching us. I rose, my legs shaking. A long line of guests wanted to say good night. Herr Strauss and I had completely ignored them. He had his eyes still fixed on me, as though I could tell him something of comfort.

"*Liebchen*," said his wife indulgently, "you have been selfish to have stolen away the Kapellmeister and kept him all to yourself. Was it not possible for one evening to get away from business talk? I looked forward to getting to know this talented young man myself."

With an effort, Herr Strauss broke his gaze away from mine. He blinked. "It must be late," he said. "It has been a long day, and I am tired." He reached out to me. "Please help me, young man. I must get up"—he smiled—"only to go to bed." Herr Strauss was a large man. It took me, his son, and his daughter-in-law, all together, to help him rise. The brandy might have had something to do with it. He focused on the long line of well-wishers with dismay.

"My friends," he began, "I am sorry to have neglected you this evening—" He was interrupted by cheers and applause. Flushed faces and reddened eyes indicated that the company had also imbibed. "I would have liked to thank each of you personally for coming." He looked around at Frau Augustina. "This has been a memorable night for many reasons—your magnificent hospitality and"—turning to me—"a performance of my work that equals the best I have heard. I thank you all deeply for this." Clasping my hand, he added, "And you have a Kapellmeister here who ranks with the best. Germany and the world will come to treasure him. And now, forgive me, it is time for me to rest. I take my leave with the promise never to forget the Westfälische Staatsoper. This will not be the last time we see each other." He gave a modest wave and made slowly for the door, his family around him. The crowd broke into more cheers and applause as he slowly left.

Frau Augustina was having her hand kissed several times as guests passed her. When the last disappeared through the oaken doors, she sat down heavily beside me. "*Mein Gott*," she sighed, "I am exhausted." I nodded. I too had expended enormous energy this long day. "Have you seen anything of Manfred?" she asked. I had not given her odious grandson a single thought and, again, shrugged. I helped *her* to her feet.

"Good night, dear Kapellmeister. We are all indebted to you. We shall speak in the morning. I was so pleased to meet your young lady. Good night, good night." I bowed and kissed her hand. After taking two steps, she turned back toward me and opened her jeweled bag. "Which reminds me!" She pressed a folded note in my hand. Except for the waiters discreetly clearing dishes, no guests remained.

"A thousand thanks, Frau von Krefeld," I said, bowing again. "I thank you for making this night truly memorable." She turned to leave, her driver waiting, but turned back once more to embrace me before walking out.

I opened the note:

My mother requests the pleasure of your company for tea tomorrow afternoon at four o'clock. I trust that you find the day and hour convenient. Fondly, Margarethe von Hassel.

No shrinking violet she. The address was to the south of the opera, on the Klosterstrasse. I would have to look for it. I began to chuckle. This whole day had been full of triumph and success. By the time I put on my hat and coat, I was laughing out loud once again, this time with genuine pleasure. Everything had gone well. Moreover, I was spared from having to drive home at that hour. Courtesy of Frau Augustina, a car awaited.

When I stepped into the dark outside the Schlossturm, I was startled by two male figures, one huddled against the chill, the other stamping his feet to keep warm.

"Klein? Lehrmann?" Two Jewish members of the opera orchestra. "What are you doing here at this hour?" Lehrmann's teeth were chattering. The taller of the two, he played principal second violin. "Forgive us for disturbing you, Herr Dirigent," he said, "but we had bad news today affecting the Jewish members of the orchestra."

Oh God, I moaned to myself, *the Jews again*. "Gentlemen, can't it wait until morning? I doubt if I have the clarity of mind to hear you after such a day."

The pair exchanged glances. "Forgive us again, Herr Dirigent," said the other, Klein, a cellist, "we have been standing out here quite a while. Your gala went on for hours, and we are quite frozen!" *Whose fault was that?*

"Gentlemen," I said heartily, "why don't we go back into the restaurant, sit down, warm up with a *Schnaps*, and you'll tell me all about this emergency of yours. You have to be short and sweet. I don't think I can keep my eyes open." I laughed again.

"We cannot do that," said Lehrmann. "No Jew is permitted to enter the Schlossturm. The staff knows us, and in accordance with the Nuremberg Laws, refuses to let us in. Not for Jews."

"We could at least get out of the cold and talk in your car, Herr Dirigent," said Klein, the less polite one. I bowed and ushered them to the limousine Frau Augustina had ordered. I requested the driver to roll up the partition so that we could be private.

"Gentlemen, what is your pleasure?"

"Being barred from the Schlossturm is the least of it," said Klein heatedly. "Why would anyone waste money in that pretentious establishment!" Lehrmann put a hand on his knee. "We have more important things to say, Herr Dirigent. Have you heard? The government has finally dismissed all Jewish personnel of the opera."

I had heard something like that was afoot. They had been getting rid of Jews in orchestras and theaters all over Germany. Evidently, our time had come. It would be a distinct hardship. I would have to set about scrambling for replacements in midseason. Where would I find the time? "Lehrmann, what are you talking about?"

He drew a letter from his breast pocket. "I received this today from SS Sturmbannführer Hans Hinkel. He used to be a high *Macher* in the Berlin theater bureaucracy. Now he's responsible for running the Jewish Cultural Association. He's setting up ghetto orchestras strictly for Jews!" He smiled sadly. "Instead of the three *B*s—Bach, Beethoven, and Brahms—it will be strictly the three *M*s—Mendelssohn, Mahler, and Moskovski. Jewish music for Jews."

I should have paid more attention to this. I had been swamped with administrative work of taxing detail. In addition, arranging my affairs to come up with a wife of whom Frau Augustina might approve.

I meant to become Generalmusikdirektor. I recalled the numerous pieces of correspondence that Herr Kopsch, our house manager, had piled on my desk. I had promptly swept them, unread, into a drawer. "And what, precisely, has the Reich government to do with our opera?" I asked.

"The Nuremberg Laws," said Lehrmann, "officially state that Jews are forbidden to be employees of the Reich. Another decree confirms that all members of opera companies, orchestras, and theaters must officially be listed as civil servants—"

"Which means we are automatically thrown out of work," Klein interrupted. "What are you going to do about it, Herr Dirigent?" The fellow was damned disrespectful. "I have given twenty-two years' faithful service—good times and bad," he went on. "I was here before you, before Franz Liebermann, and before Spangemacher, the Kapellmeister before him. I am a young man still, only forty-eight. Where am I supposed to work now? Must I move? My family has lived here in Düsseldorf for two hundred years. Why didn't I get out of Germany two years ago, like Franz Liebermann?"

Yes, you hopeless fool, why didn't you? But I held my tongue. I had no need to speak. The SS, the SA, the Gestapo, Dr. Goebbels, and this Hinkel fellow—all seemed to be doing their jobs. The date of the Jewish ban must be buried among my unread letters. I had better think of an answer for the authorities when they questioned why I had retained my Jews this long. What might save me was that the Düsseldorf Gauleiter was a pig, without cultivation or brains.

Klein was still seething. I turned to his companion. "Tell me, Lehrmann, how many Jews are in our orchestra?"

"I can tell you exactly, Herr Dirigent," he said impassively. "Out of our normal complement of seventy-seven, fully twenty-three are Jewish and have to go."

Aghast, I sank back into the leather cushions. I hadn't realized there were so many of them. The Nazis were correct to complain of Jewish domination.

"How will I ever find decent substitutes?" I groaned. "And when will I have time to do it?" Resentment burned in me. The damned Jews were complicating my life.

Lehrmann stirred. "Herr Dirigent," he said. "If you permit me, I have an idea that may help." I wearily inclined my head. "Please."

"It has not escaped our notice, Herr Dirigent, that, in contrast with the fate of our co-religionists throughout Germany, our employment at the Westfälische Staatsoper had been maintained so far." I stared stonily to my front. "And we all know who is responsible for that. You have said nothing about your part in this—and that was perhaps the prudent thing to do. But Klein here and I know—indeed all the Jewish members of the Staatsoper know—that it is to you, Herr Dirigent, that we owe so much for preserving our livelihoods." His eyes shone with gratitude.

I turned to him in astonishment.

"Whatever you have done, Herr Dirigent, and however you have managed it, we both are tremendously thankful—even though at the moment Klein is upset and frightened. We thank you from the bottom of our hearts." Impulsively, he leaned over and, despite our cramped positions, kissed me, first on one cheek and then the other, all the while gazing into my eyes. "It was a good deed," he said.

I was stunned. It was grotesque that I be thanked. "Now, Herr Dirigent, my idea is this," he continued. "See what you think. By your own talents and strength of will, you have become a major force in Düsseldorf. We may be in the provinces, but you have enormous influence in this part of the world—ask anybody. That which you demand will never be denied. Those whom you protect will never be harmed." He leaned forward eagerly. "Do you see what I'm saying, Herr Dirigent? If you take a stand and resist, you will be heeded. I am certain of it."

How could anyone be so incredibly naïve? He was Richard Strauss and Eduard van Vleiman rolled into one. Could he not see what was happening around him? Did these Jews, all of a sudden, have butter in their skulls instead of brains? Take me. I never could afford to live in such a cloud-cuckoo world. I refused to.

I sighed. "Lehrmann, Klein," I began. They were gazing at me with tremulous hope. "I appreciate your expressions of thanks. What I have managed to do so far"—I shrugged—"I have done. Unhappily, I can do no more." They sat listening, waiting, tentative smiles still on their faces.

"You can do no more?" whispered Klein.

"I'm afraid that is correct. Let me be honest with you. Let me be frank. What possible good would it do if I took a stand on your behalf at this time? The authorities have spoken. This is not a good moment. We have to be patient and bide our time. You would put at risk the entire Staatsoper." I thought of my earlier confrontation with Manfred von Krefeld. "Don't fool yourselves, gentlemen. Our masters, these National Socialists, take matters like this very seriously." There was a silence.

"Herr Dirigent," said Lehrmann at last, "perhaps some of us could be spared this purge. Not all the Jewish players are necessarily recognized as Jewish. Myself, I try to be religious. I serve as the secretary of my synagogue." *Why was I listening to this futility?* "Now Klein here, he's different," he continued. "I'd be surprised if he'd ever stepped inside a synagogue. But you know he's a marvelous cellist—why should you lose him because of these crazy laws? Besides, he's only half-Jewish. He has a Christian mother. He's even married to a Christian woman. Actually"—he attempted a smile—"he hardly counts as a Jew."

"I said I could do no more," I said with a sigh.

They sat still for a while. I had passed beyond exhaustion, more dead than alive. Lehrmann looked at Klein. "We have to go. We can apply to the Jewish Cultural Association. At least, we will not abandon music. It is next to life itself."

Klein didn't move. Tears ran down his cheeks. "After twenty-two years of service, I must beg this snotnose, half my age, for my job?" He stared at me full of hatred, not three feet away. I wondered if I should call for the driver for help—he was in his front seat, smoking. "You have done all you can?" Klein sneered. He leaned in my direction and deliberately spat in my face.

Lehrmann was horrified. "*Mein Gott*, Klein. What have you done?" He dug in his pocket for his handkerchief, which I disdained.

"Surely," I said slowly, "I have received not one but two significant gestures from the Jewish community. One spits in my face, a mark of his true feelings toward the German people. The other kisses me on both cheeks, supposedly in gratitude and friendship." I used my own handkerchief to wipe my face. "I wonder which gesture is worse"—Lehrmann looked more horrified—"honest, open hatred or the lying kiss of Judas." If I had not been so exhausted, I might not have been as spiteful.

I leaned to open the car door. "Gentlemen, good night," I said politely. "I believe our business is concluded." Lehrmann started to say something, but Klein pushed him out. I tapped on the glass partition. "Please, back to Neuss," I told the driver.

I have no memory of the drive. I must have immediately slumped into deep sleep. The next thing I knew was that we had arrived and the driver was trying to shake me awake. The town lay dark and quiet. The old clock in the Stiftkirche was chiming the third hour of night. As I handed him his tip, I assured the driver that, despite my fatigue, I could manage on my own, had my house keys, and was able to let myself in.

When I entered my flat, my soft, tinted lights, my "seduction illuminations," were glowing. *Had I left them on?* Then, overtaken by a huge yawn, I slipped out of my overcoat, let it drop to the floor, and kicked off my shoes. When I stumbled into the bedroom, I was surprised by the presence of more such lights. Then someone in the bed stirred and moaned. I seized a poker from the fireplace to attack the intruder.

A woman arose from the silken quilts. "*Liebchen*," she said in a sleepy voice.

For one delirious moment, I thought Margarethe von Hassel had miraculously come to astonish and delight me. She had already revealed herself as daring and adventurous. I immediately abandoned that thought. Margarethe could be full of surprises, but I didn't think she would create scandal.

All at once, I gasped. Of course. Not Margarethe at all! It was Huberta. *Huberta Menzel*, a new member of the opera chorus, a beautiful young woman with a provocative mouth. Memory flooded back. Of course! Huberta and I had arranged this tryst three days ago! In the meantime, not only had my mind been completely overwhelmed by the premiere and by Manfred von Krefeld, I had also been taken up by Margarethe and invited her to *Rosenkavalier*. In addition, there was all the excitement over Richard Strauss—and this new unpleasantness over my Jews. For three days, I had been immersed in tumult. Huberta had not been in my thoughts. She had not been in the cast of *Rosenkavalier*, and I had completely forgotten about her. Evidently, there were limits to what even I could do. But here she was.

Now, Huberta was sitting up. She appeared not to be wearing

anything and looked pink and warm in the subdued light. She rubbed her eyes, trying to focus. Then she smiled and leaned to one side to pour wine from a bottle in an ice bucket. She held the glass out to me. "*Liebchen*," she licked her lips. "Drop your clothes and come to me. Let me take care of you."

I stared at her in dismay. My limbs felt like lead. The spirit may have been willing, but the body was barely there. The clever girl understood immediately that for the time being I was *kaputt*. She darted to my side, a ravishingly slender naked presence, and led me to bed, efficiently undressed me, swung my legs up onto the bed, and covered us both. She switched off the lights and wrapped herself completely around me from behind so that her softness clung to my back. She gently stroked my head. I felt warmed, loved, and comforted after the mighty struggles and strains of the day. I wanted to express my happiness but was too weary even to form words.

"Shush, *Liebchen*, shush," she murmured. "Everything is well. There is no need to say anything."

Please, God, I prayed, *always send me a woman like Huberta.*

* * *

My marriage to Margarethe took place three months later. Just before the ceremony, I stood in the vestry, chatting with Herr L'Orénoque, our large-boned designer, who had agreed to serve as best man. I never quite understood Herr L'Orénoque's support of me, which had been loyal and consistent ever since I had taken over the Staatsoper. And what I could not understand, I did not altogether trust. But that's for another time.

As we talked over a surreptitious cigarette, I happened to glance at the arched entrance to behold a halting, infirm woman, one hand holding a cane, the other clutching Frau Augustina's hand. My patroness's face was wreathed in smiles as she glanced back and forth between me and her companion.

"Just look at who is here," she said.

I had to peer at the stranger for several seconds as she neared. The woman broke out into sobs and spoke to me in my native tongue. "Ferenc, I thank God for letting me see you once again."

"Mama?" I exclaimed. I was dumbfounded. Until you actually hear these words from a mother, you cannot dream how soft and melodious they sound. I sobbed as well. When she reached me, she took my hand and kissed it as though I were a bishop. I was shocked. She looked so frail. Her head did not reach as high as my shoulder.

"How long is it since you've seen your dear Mutti?" inquired a beaming Frau Augustina, "I thought it might be such a wonderful thing if she could be here on this special day. I was naughty and made all the arrangements without telling you. Will you forgive me?" Mama's sobs grew louder.

I was immediately plunged into embarrassment and humiliation. I did rapid calculations. I had last seen Mama when I left Szombathely for Vienna in 1927. That had been—only eight years ago? How could she have changed so sharply in that time? She must have been ill. If so, it had obviously been serious, and she had never let me know. She appeared like an aged cripple! I had always intended to visit but somehow had never found the time. Always busy, always breathless, always immersed in one thing or another. Do I need to explain?

* * *

Ninth Variation

Berlin 1941

To be German in 1941 was to approach as near heaven itself without actually entering the next world. The Führer had proved himself without equal in the arts of diplomacy, outwitting those smug gentlemen in Whitehall and the Quai d'Orsay. Without effort, he had recovered those lands that had been criminally stolen: Memel, the Saarland, the Sudetenland. Czechoslovakia was ours. He had gathered Austria back into the sacred German soil, all without firing a shot. And if the degenerate English and French were thinking of protest, our Führer proved equally eloquent in war. At Guernica, the Luftwaffe had spoken sternly with bombs on behalf of General Franco.

Then we witnessed a thrilling game of chess. Finally, the English and French woke up to the Führer's profound dissatisfaction with the so-called Polish Corridor that split us from East Prussia. They signed a pact with Poland, threatening to fight us if we took what was ours. *Was it checkmate?* All Germany was sleepless. Some lost heart and began to grumble. "The Führer has gone too far," they said over their beers in the *Kneipen*. Such malcontents were watched and questioned—rightly so.

Then, like a thunderclap, the impossible occurred. We signed a pact of our own. And with whom? Even today, two years later, it fills me with wonder. The Führer pulled off the most audacious diplomatic coup of the century. He masterminded a nonaggression treaty with the Bolsheviks, with Stalin, his most loathed and hated enemy!

Such brilliance took the breath away. This was checkmate. Double, if not triple, checkmate. The English and French choked with rage.

They were finished. I joined teeming crowds outside the Wilhelmstrasse and screamed for the Führer to appear, which he did most graciously, extending his arm in salute. At his side were Field Marshal Göring, Reich Minister Goebbels, and Foreign Minister von Ribbentrop, who had conducted the negotiations in Moscow. We too raised our arms, all Germans, united in a demonstration of confidence and affection. We sang *Deutschland über Alles* over and over. One could not fail to be uplifted and deeply moved.

However, the stupid English and French chose war with us anyway. So pathetic! We smashed, crushed, and humiliated them within six weeks. The war was practically over. Poland was ours, also the Netherlands and Belgium. France was ours. The haughty British Empire was on the brink of collapse. Our Führer had only to give a tiny push to make the whole rotten structure collapse. Our Führer was a mighty man of battle.

Well, as people know, it is rare when things go precisely to plan. One must expect a hitch now and then: this one came from the English air force. Their Spitfires, now fighting over their own country, were stubborn, but in vain. Furthermore, they were foolish and spiteful enough actually to bomb Berlin itself! Their attempts were pitiful, mere pinpricks, which served only to ignite the wrath of all Germany. The Führer himself was never interested in humiliating the English. But when the sacred soil of the fatherland was attacked, we struck back with devastating nightly air attacks on London and other cities. Churchill needed a good lesson. We resurrected that useful phrase from the first war, *Gott strafe England!* We repeated it to ourselves in great happiness.

Besides military glories, these years had been wonderful for me personally. Marriage to Margarethe had spelled instant social acceptance. My elevation to Generalmusikdirektor at the opera made us natural fodder for *Ufa* newsreels and the glossy pages of the *Berliner illustrierte Zeitung*. All Germany could catch photos of Margarethe and me skiing at Garmisch-Partenkirchen, laughing as we sped off in our Mercedes sportster for a Bavarian holiday, or bursting through the North Sea spray in our yacht at Wilhelmshaven. We were the perfect couple: young, glamorous, successful. We personified the New Germany. One disappointment: I imagined my bride would be accompanied by money. Her aristocratic name had given promise of that. I was mistaken.

And then there was Huberta. You know I am a man of large

appetites, which no one woman could possibly satisfy. Huberta provided levels of satisfaction impossible to abandon. I secured for her a position at the Berlin Municipal Opera, mainly chorus work, once in a while small solo parts. Why Berlin? Düsseldorf was entirely too exposed: people knew each other's business. Berlin, I don't need to point out, is anonymous, a metropolis. I had plausible reason to visit there once a month, which was about all I could afford to devote to Huberta in time and energy. She was delighted with the move and relished the busy city, the crowds, and cabarets. I got her a charming flat in the Wilmersdorf district, just off Nollendorfplatz, full of artists, émigrés, quaint cafés, and Russian shop signs—memories of czarist refugees. There we would meet, dine, and make love. Like Margarethe, she presented problems, but Huberta's turned out to be potentially terrifying and highly dangerous. Those who accuse me of being motivated solely by ambition can judge my conduct for themselves.

It was Huberta who opened a most touchy subject. "Every time we are together, I feel that I place my life in your hands," she announced one evening.

"What are you talking about?" I could barely speak. We were in bed, bodies dripping with sweat after just having driven each other beyond madness making love. Instead of answering, she glued her soft mouth to mine in a long, never-ending kiss. At last, she drew back, relaxed on the pillows, and placed her hand companionably, as though she owned it, on what we both called my center of pleasure.

"And it seems that mine is in yours," I beamed.

She fixed me with her beautiful dark eyes. "I'm serious, Herr Generalmusikdirektor," and leaned up to kiss me again, at the same time giving me a friendly squeeze in the right place.

I tried to keep a clear mind. "Did I really hear what you said just before—when we were in the middle of…doing it—that you wished I weren't married?"

Her face transformed into irresistible beauty when she smiled. "Yes, I did," she breathed, "and what is wrong with that?" She kissed me again.

"There is nothing wrong with that. I often wish the same thing. But, *Liebchen*, you also said something else. Or did I imagine it?" I struggled with the words. "You also said—I *think* you said—that you were Jewish? Did I hear you right? Why would you say such a thing? You were joking, of course."

Her eyes widened until she looked a bit mad. She made me nervous. "Well, Dr. Freud must be correct," she said.

"What do you mean?"

"I must have a death wish," she said. "Why on earth would I come out with that? At that moment, I was on fire. My god, the things one blurts out at such a time! I suppose I wanted to be completely honest with you. And besides, aren't you the reason I remain here in Germany? Yes, indeed, my life is in your hands."

Was she serious? *What did she mean, the reason she remained in Germany?* I was flooded by memories of Klara, whose lovemaking back in Vienna had been every bit the equal of Huberta's. I wearily closed my eyes. The Gestapo was thorough at Jew-hunting, but still, "they" could be found everywhere.

"Why should it ever occur to me that you might be—" Conditioned by Nazi epithets, I found no neutral way to utter what had become a most derogatory expression.

"A Jew?"

I held her close so that she could not read my face. "Yes, thank you. A Jew."

"Actually only half-Jewish," she chuckled.

"Oh yes? Only half-Jewish?" It was far from amusing. I felt too unsettled to be sarcastic. "Only half-Jewish" would mean nothing to the Gestapo. I tried to think. What had become of that daughter-in-law of Richard Strauss I had met? She had been a Jew. As I lay next to Huberta, a dazzle of emotions swept over me: profound dismay at the revelation, coupled with more than a flicker of rage. *Why had she not told me before?* I had not suspected it. As with Strauss's daughter-in-law, Huberta's looks did not arouse suspicion. But I felt increasingly distraught and nauseated. Even lying down, I had the impression that the whole house was toppling. I feared I might succumb to one of the crazy fits that used to plague me, which some lunatic quack in Düsseldorf once had diagnosed a form of epilepsy. *Stupid fool!*

I steadied my nerves. "*Ach, Liebchen, Liebchen,*" I cried. "You need have no fears about me! I don't care what you are. We mean too much to each other. My marriage is nothing but a joke. My wife and I—we have never been soul mates like you and me. You and I know the real meaning of love."

She reached across me for a cigarette. "Darling, sometimes when you try to sound sincere, you end up positively tinny, like a bad libretto. I'm amazed, with all your gifts, you don't possess a more genuine language. I know you have one." Her smile rankled. I hated being patronized. I lit my own cigarette and drank wine. At a time like this, you'd think, if a woman believed her life was in your hands, she'd watch her tongue.

Of course, I didn't realize how stupid we both were, nor how relentless and single-minded were the Gestapo and all the machinery of the Reich, not only to make the lives of Jews extremely unpleasant, but also to kill them. I swear I knew nothing of this at the time. All that counted, once she stopped her nattering, was how joyful we could make each other, how, like a pair of children, we could revel in pleasure, uniting flesh, spirit, and the soul of music itself in varieties of love. I could never give her up, maddening as she was. I assure you, this whole Jew business really meant nothing to me. For the most part, we got along famously. She was both adoring and adorable and generally uncomplaining, except for her uncomfortable jibes. For instance, what do you make of the following episode?

I had only just calmed down after her astonishing revelation; my breathing had returned to normal. She propped herself up on one elbow and subjected me to an appraising look. "You know, Kappi"—by chance, both Margarethe and Huberta used to call me that—"you never speak about the days when you were a piano student in Vienna. I recently ran into an old acquaintance of yours, someone younger who knew you from the old days. He wonders if you remember him. His name is August Wiedner. He says he was expelled from the Vienna Conservatory for being the laziest student in living memory and that he got you a job playing the piano in a nightclub. Is that true? And that you had to leave that job under what he said were interesting circumstances. He said you were a far better musician than he. I'd have arranged a reunion, but he was only passing through Berlin."

My god, another Viennese memory. August Wiedner—Gustl! After all these years. I was not delighted. I preferred keeping the various parts of my life separate.

"Well, darling," she resumed, "he couldn't stop talking about you. '*Ach*, that Hermann Kapp'—he remembers you by that name—'he was absolutely astounding. The way he played Beethoven and Schubert. Unbelievable, brilliant. Not only brilliant but also profound and deep!' That's what he said, Kappi. 'Profound and deep.' And, if that's true, I want you to tell me why you no longer play as a soloist."

I did not want to be reminded of Gustl or Vienna. Huberta rolled across me and looked me in the eye. "Kappi, I've always admired the way you deal with music. You're not always easy to be with, but you truly thrill me when you make music. You are a thrilling lover. You are a thrilling Kapellmeister. You are a thrilling leader of men. But Gustl mentioned something different. He talked about art, profundity, depth. About poetry!" My discomfort increased.

"I grabbed my friend August by the ears and shook him," she went on. "I couldn't help laughing. 'What are you talking about?' I asked. 'What poetry, what profundity? The Herr Generalmusikdirektor—' I didn't breathe a word that I knew you other than professionally— 'is a shrewd manager,' I told him. 'I've seen him at work. He is a politician, he is masterful, a bully when he has to be. He doesn't care what he does to get what he wants. He serves music with the same passion as a soldier serves the fatherland. I have watched him. He plots and plans. He spares nothing and no one. A poet, you say? I would not think of a poet when I think of him. He is a presence, a force.'" She gave me another kiss, her eyes shining. "There, Kappi, did I say it right?"

I gazed at her sourly. *What on earth was she going on about?* Vienna. Gustl. Krisztina. Klara. Lotte. Dr. Böhm. Eduard van Vleiman. There were far too many bad ghosts. Had I truly been an artist, a poet? If so, I was glad those days were over. Poets and artists are hardly constructed for efficient use. Heaven help Kapellmeisters who get lost in their own performances. You've seen them, swaying on the podium, eyes closed in rapture, transported, exalted—oh, so moved. Don't fall asleep, I want to shout! You'd better keep your eyes open. Somebody has to be in charge. You're here to run things, not enjoy your own bloody concert!

Huberta wouldn't stop rattling on. "The idea of it! Kappi, you are a commander, a Herr General, a Herr Feldmarschall. Artists and poets are pure gold, but also terribly fragile—poor things—damaged, starving to death, coughing up their lungs, raving with opium." Grandly, she flung her arms around me. "But that's not you. You are durable. Not gold at all. Better than gold. Solid brass, that's what you are! When the delicate vessels get dented or smashed, you will go on forever." Another kiss.

Brass? What was that about? Correct or not, it sounded more than vaguely disparaging. But it seemed to be the price I had to pay. Don't think for a moment that my eyes were not open. I was Huberta's willing captive. For one thing, her body never failed to astonish. I was no stranger to naked women. I fully understood the fascination they held for painters. Believe me, I wish I had the talent to practice a profession that entailed their endless contemplation. Naked women waged war with a silent language all their own. They had no need to utter a sound. Yet their weapons rivaled the most deadly arms. That must be a contradiction, but I speak as one who knows what it is to be conquered by both bodies and music.

Huberta's breasts, their fullness unsuspected while she was clothed—luscious areolas and nipples—never failed to make me gasp when she dropped her robe. Silken belly, swell of hips, the giddy swoon down to her pungent loins—if I had the capacity to exclaim, I would. Those breathtaking attributes, and her perversely amusing mind, bore no resemblance to the graceless person Margarethe had now turned into, pretty though she remained. I regretted only that the times and demands of my position prevented public acceptance of our liaison, like many another such arrangement. The Führer had ordered Reich Minister Goebbels to break *his* "arrangement" with Lida Baarova, the Czech actress. And after the war, of course, we all learned about the Führer himself and his Eva. Incredible! Naturally, Huberta and I had our differences and strains. Sometimes, like now, we skirted perilous edges. I lay there, shaking my head. So Hermann Kapp-Dortmunder had his Jewish mistress! It was good that no one knew about us. We would see what might happen. As she herself put it: her life, my hands.

* * *

Suddenly, my fame spread. Everybody wanted me. I was offered guest conductorships in Leipzig, Munich, Hamburg, Stuttgart—entirely too many for me to undertake. But how flattering! Because of the Führer, Toscanini refused to conduct at Bayreuth. It was suggested, because of the success of my *Walküre*, that I should cultivate Winifred Wagner and get myself invited there. But schedules could not be worked out in time.

Grammophon Gesellschaft invited me to consider a recording contract. But I would have to abandon the Westfälische Staatsoper.

"Believe me, Herr Kapp-Dortmunder, the faster you rid yourself of those provincials, with their third-rate standards, the better." I was seated in the Berlin office of Herr Wolfgang Pietsch, managing director of *Grammophon Gesellschaft*. The walls were covered with signed photographs of conductors, singers, violinists, and pianists.

"Surely you are not serious, Herr Pietsch," I said.

He tapped cigar ash into a porcelain bowl. "Let us be frank with one another. Düsseldorf has no particular distinction as a center of music."

"Herr Pietsch, that's hardly fair. Düsseldorf is hardly a backwater. It boasts quite a few estimable organizations. If you are talking about standards of musicianship before I took over, I might agree. But I can assure you, without false modesty, I have completely transformed performance levels to the point where I have created a demand for my services throughout Germany—because of which, you and I are speaking today."

Herr Pietsch stared at me and rolled his cigar around in his mouth with a plump hand. He put me in mind of Herr Zuckerweiss in Vienna. I wondered how Herr Zuckerweiss was faring now, after the Anschluss. What a surprise it had been when those charming Viennese had proved more beastly to their Jews than many Germans would have been—at first—and had turned on them. The papers had been full of pictures of Jews on their hands and knees, scrubbing public pavements, helped along by hearty kicks in the arse. Would our respectable, dull-witted Germans have thought of that? Inevitably, thoughts of Herr Zuckerweiss brought Klara to mind. She in turn summoned unwelcome visions of Krisztina on her deathbed—awful phantoms. Nothing to do with epilepsy.

"What about your manager?" Herr Pietsch broke my ugly reverie.

"I haven't got a manager. Frau Augustina von Krefeld, who is—"

"Yes, yes, I know who she is," said Herr Pietsch. "A fine woman of the old school but entirely undeveloped musically, entirely provincial, woefully ignorant of modern business practices." He waved aside my protests. "Look," he said, "I cheerfully acknowledge the tremendous effort you have undertaken to whip up those Düsseldorf people.

Grammophon Gesellschaft would be happy to undertake recording contracts, but not in tandem with that organization, and certainly not with that orchestra—"

"But could I do such a thing, Herr Pietsch? Would it be fair to them? I feel a responsibility."

"And you should be proud of that feeling, Herr Kapp-Dortmunder. It does you credit. Now let me try to enlarge your perspective. Have you any idea of the whereabouts of certain luminaries who were, until recently, prominent on our musical scene?"

"Of whom do you speak?"

"Oh, Bruno Walter, for one. Erich Leinsdorf for another."

I shook my head. "I have no idea."

Herr Pietsch registered incredulity. "Of course," he chuckled. "You have not the faintest idea about the activities of Bruno Walter, a man who has put an indelible stamp on German music. You claim to know nothing about him."

Was the man mad? I peered at him, plump in his faultlessly tailored suit, tiny yellow rosebud in his buttonhole, wearing a smart blue silk tie. He had in his lapel an enamel red-and-white party badge, black swastika at its center. "Why are we concerned with the activities of a Jewish polluter?"

Herr Pietsch giggled. "Please, Herr Kapp-Dortmunder. There is no need to say that. You are not among the Gestapo here. We are artists and musicians, you and I, and we are alone. There is no crime if we express an honest opinion about Bruno Walter."

Oh, isn't there! I stared at him. "Yes, I know about Bruno Walter, or should I say"—I added with a knowing smile—"Herr *Schlesinger*, as he used to be called. What do you wish to know? An exceptionally fortunate career, based probably on his influential Jewish connections. Most recently, four or five years in Leipzig at the Gewandhaus. Then, when the Führer came to power, the storm troopers promised to wreck the Berlin Philharmonic if he dared to conduct there. Then Dr. Goebbels banned him from Bayreuth—imagine, a Jew presuming to conduct Wagner! Then he quit the Reich altogether for the Salzburg Festival. After the Anschluss, he fled to America." I glared at him. "Have I got it right?"

"Very good, Herr Kapp-Dortmunder," he purred. "Despite your protests, you do know about him. And properly so, for he could move the earth."

My unease grew stronger. This talk was sheer disloyalty, if not trea-
son. From a man wearing a party pin, no less. Leinsdorf had been at
the Conservatory a year or two before me, quite highly thought of.
Bruno Walter had taken him under his wing as his chief assistant at
Salzburg. Naturally, one Jew assists another. Like "Bruno Walter,"
Leinsdorf had also changed his name. "Leinsdorf" used to be
Landauer. *Can anyone explain to me why Jews persist in attempts to con-
ceal themselves?* I'm joking, of course. Everybody knows the answer.

Herr Pietsch was making me uncomfortable. "You need not go
on," I told him. "You know better than I that the State Music Bureau
has been thorough in rooting these Jewish influences out of our lives.
Did they all go to America?"

"A fair number did. Many went to England."

Ah, yes, England. I would like to have performed in London, but
the war got in the way. A high party official who hung around the
Staatsoper had informed me what was planned for Jews who had fled
to Winston Churchill's ridiculous island. Records had been kept, lists
compiled. After the defeat of England, those Jews would soon be back
in the hands of the Reich. All that coming and going for nothing.

Herr Pietsch produced a bottle of Cognac and two glasses, which
he carefully filled to the brim. "The trick is to bring the glass to your
lips without spilling a drop and then throw it back down the throat."

"What are we drinking to, Herr Pietsch?"

"To the launch of a brilliant recording career—yours, in fact. *Prosit!*"

The man did not waste a moment. I straightaway rose to my feet
and threw the contents of the glass down my throat. *Mein Gott*, it was
powerful. I tried not to choke.

"Herr Pietsch, how have you made your decision so quickly?"

He beamed at me and refilled the glasses. "It was not difficult. The
departure of our Hebrew friends has created marvelous opportunities
for German musicians. We have so many excellent ones, but at the
same time, it's interesting"—he threw me a broad wink—"how many
wretched ones there also are who, because of that same departure of
Jews, imagine that they are entitled to places in our best orchestras,
even solo careers."

I knew what he was talking about. I myself had had a nerve-
wracking time auditioning men who, because of my own diligent
purging of Jews, imagined they had automatic rights to the vacancies.

Aryan credentials did not substitute for dreadful music-making. How many times did I have to fend off visits from that pig, the Gauleiter of Düsseldorf, pleading on behalf of one inept, tone-deaf fool or another?

In contrast, Herr Pietsch was dynamic, a vigorous German, despite his pudginess. He was decisive. I could do no less than emulate him.

"I put myself in your hands," I declared. I paused. *Where had I just heard that phrase?* "Now, do I remain in Düsseldorf? If not, which city am I to call home? Would I take over an orchestra already in existence or organize one from nothing? Am I to sever connections with the Westfälische Staatsoper right away?"

Herr Pietsch was wreathed in smiles. "*Grammophon Gesellschaft* is prepared to underwrite the formation of an entirely new orchestra to be based in Berlin. You and the orchestra will perform, record, and broadcast solely and completely under the auspices of *GG*. You and the orchestra will belong exclusively to each other, which means no joint directorships, except by special arrangement. Guest appearances with other orchestras or abroad will, similarly, be by express permission of *GG*, although I would prefer foreign tours be undertaken by the entire orchestra. What a splendid advertisement for German culture! I realize that opera companies in other cities or other nations may prefer their resident orchestras. But these are details to be discussed when the time comes."

More drinks were poured. "Now are you prepared to begin sketching an initial season's programs, together with the orchestral and choral forces that you require? I would be fascinated by your ideas. How quickly could you get to work on that?"

It was unbelievably marvelous and splendid. Herr Pietsch was like God. He said, "Let a thing be done, and lo, it was done." And it was as though he could read my mind, understand my desires. Huberta was already in Berlin. Margarethe had refused to leave Düsseldorf as long as her mother remained alive. Herr Pietsch was devising an arrangement dazzling beyond imagination. Not only Huberta, but also this.

I coughed. "You say nothing about—"

"Money?" Herr Pietsch giggled again, a sound to which I would rapidly become accustomed. Not only a decisive man, he seemed naturally happy. "If we do this well, Herr Generalmusikdirektor—and I have a feeling I am not mistaken—you will not have to worry about money for the rest of your life. This will be a genuine partnership. The compensation structure will be based totally on royalties rather than salary or fees for performances. It will derive from your appearances and recordings. When you sign the contract, you will be our partner. *Grammophon Gesellschaft* and you will succeed together. This is a business venture. This is our recompense for funding you—that and the satisfaction we derive from bringing to the world a profoundly exciting new artist."

I badly needed to discuss these proposals with a friend; at the same time, I realized I had no one. Rather than appear naïve or display ignorance, I kept silent.

"Frankly," he went on, "*Grammophon Gesellschaft* is banking heavily on your good looks. Like Herr von Karajan, you have a magnetic look about you—except that you are much taller. You can't ignore these things. They are vital components of a total packet." I was not entirely ignorant of my appearance but startled to hear so blunt an expression of its salability. He brushed aside protests. "I've already discovered that ladies form the secret weapon for success in a concert season. And you are aware, are you not, that you possess a pleasingly deep speaking voice. That also usually proves irresistible to women. I can't wait to hear you on the radio."

He scrutinized me, the way a man looks over a line of young women before asking one to dance. Nothing to do with music. "Turning to another matter," he continued, "*Grammophon Gesellschaft* holds the long-term lease on a most desirable property, a magnificent old hotel, very exclusive, very smart, right here in the center of town. It's on Unter den Linden next to the Pariser Platz, just by the Brandenburger Tor. The Hotel Adlon is right opposite. You could not ask for a swankier location. What do you say to that?" Another broad grin. I was feeling the effect of the *Schnaps*.

"We intend to convert the building into a concert hall, and we're going to set about it right away. It will be the most up-to-date concert hall in Europe, traditional in a traditional sense but up-to-date. And it will be ready for your inaugural concert within seven months. I have the ear of people who matter. Dr. Goebbels is a patron of the arts. As soon as I tell him what I need, Dr. Todt and Herr Speer will supply men and materials."

"Surely, the Wehrmacht and other essential state services have priority on materials and manpower."

"Not a bit, not a bit," he protested, still wearing his grin. "I happen to know that Dr. Furtwängler has got himself into difficulties over a few indiscretions, like speaking up for his Jews in the Berlin Philharmonic too zealously, and his occasional preference for programming music that, shall we say, is not approved of."

"I would be surprised by something like that," I exclaimed.

Another incredulous look. "I don't know how well you're acquainted with Dr. Furtwängler. Like Bruno Walter, he is a giant. But outside of music, he is, frankly, a fool. Have you forgotten the open letter he wrote to Dr. Goebbels? An open letter! I mean, he is such a simpleton! He claimed back in '33 that Bruno Walter, unlike some notorious examples, was one of the 'blameless Jews' and should be permitted to remain in Germany. The rest of the world would appreciate that gesture by the Reich. What an idiot!"

I remembered Furtwängler's letter. It had been published in the *Vossische Zeitung* and had certainly created a stir overseas but hadn't made much difference here, except effecting a change in the paper's editorial staff. Reich attitudes toward the Jews weren't altered. Why should they have been?

"For his part," Herr Pietsch continued, "Dr. Goebbels must proceed cautiously against Dr. Furtwängler because he is so widely admired. It is not easy to discipline him. But by speeding up our project, by enabling us to construct another musical presence here in Berlin, Dr. Goebbels makes it possible to—shall we say—deflate a man who has embarrassed him." His grin vanished. "To be so willful only encourages our enemies."

"Is there a name for this new ensemble?"

His grin returned as abruptly as it had vanished. "Of course, Herr Kapp-Dortmunder. As you know, we already have the Berlin this and the Berlin that. I propose that our new musical organization be associated with this entire historic region and be known simply, but accurately, as the Staatskapelle Brandenburg."

I liked it. Herr Pietsch refilled my glass. Strangely, the Cognac jolted my mind into clarity. Among all the unbelievable events of the morning was the realization that I had been chosen to disturb the Olympian tranquillity of a giant like Dr. Furtwängler. In the service of

Reich policy, no less. *Could anything similar be done about von Karajan?* His name and mine were coming to be linked with irritating frequency as bright young newcomers. Back in Düsseldorf, Magarethe had urged more than once that, if I wished to prosper, I should make formal application to join the Party, as von Karajan had done. As she herself had done. "He knew what to do, Kappi," she had said. "Learn from him!" I began to giggle. I sounded like Herr Pietsch. We drank more Cognac. I didn't realize what a strain I had been under.

I wondered if I should stay in Berlin for the balance of the week. Herr Pietsch and I still had much to talk about. I was about to uproot my life once more—in effect, part from Margarethe. I was sure that she would turn up in Berlin for important occasions, but she was fixed in our home on the Rhine. The thought of discussing my plans with her didn't occur to me. As I've mentioned, we may have seemed an ideal pair, but she was turning out to be a small person in spirit—pretty and charming, I grant you; nice and dainty—but very small, if you understand me.

For my part, I was prepared to be philosophical. After the first intoxicating months of marriage, one expects passion to diminish. But I found I had married a woman whose loyalties were, first, to her mother, second to the Führer, third to the Fatherland, and fourth—possibly—to me. She insisted, moreover, on continuing her work with the young girls in the GuS movement. I didn't think it prudent to be seen in public with Huberta. So, even though, while in Berlin, I spent many nights with her, I made my official Berlin address a pleasant residential hotel, the Askanischer Hof on the Kurfürstendamm, not far from the Schlüterstrasse. It was Frau Augustina who had suggested that I would appreciate its unassuming but comfortable atmosphere and the fact that established artists and writers liked to stay there. And so it proved. The Askanischer Hof suited me well. It was a massive, solid building, and besides, I was permitted to install a grand piano in my suite. It was a refuge from a no-longer-enchanting wife, a temperamental mistress, and the chuckling, intense roly-poly recording executive who was to become, in effect, my manager.

"*Also!*" Herr Pietsch boomed. He suddenly stood, walked around the desk, and clasped me in his short, pudgy arms. He failed to enfold me completely, but I was startled nevertheless. "Have you made plans for lunch? If not, come home with me—it's a short drive—we can continue to talk. Afterward, my driver can take you back to your hotel."

Before I had a chance to speak, there came an insistent tapping at the door. It was the plain female secretary who had shown me in that morning. She showed no surprise at our embrace but addressed her employer in a sibilant whisper. "Bitte, Meine Herren, forgive me for disturbing you. But it is most upsetting."

She continued to whisper. Herr Pietsch whistled. "No. He's actually here? Now?"

"Yes, Mein Herr, at this moment, standing in your outer office." She twitched with annoyance while trying to smooth her hair. "He insists on seeing you without an appointment. Even for a man like that, this is not correct behavior."

Yet another giggle from Herr Pietsch. After a moment, for no particular reason, I joined in. We were both tight. He strode to the door and ushered in a strikingly handsome man about my own age, his head topped by carefully nurtured, luxuriant hair. His chief flaw was that he was almost a half meter shorter than I.

"Herr von Karajan," I exclaimed, clicked my heels, and bowed. "Esteemed colleague, such a pleasure to see you again."

The other grasped my hand. He gave me a toothy smile as he bowed. "The pleasure is altogether mine. What brings you to Berlin?" He turned to Herr Pietsch, eyes twinkling but narrowed. "Are you gentlemen up to something I should know about?"

In response, Herr Pietsch placed his arms about both our shoulders. "Now why should you think that, worthy Herr von Karajan? Herr Kapp-Dortmunder here was merely bringing me news of musical happenings in the Ruhr." He lowered his voice to a confidential whisper. "The only problem, dear Herr von Karajan, is that we had only just begun our conversation and I wanted to treat him to an elegant lunch in the Berlin style and press him for details. And then you appear out of nowhere, dear Herr von Karajan, and expose our arrangement." He laughed again. "Have you come to see me about anything special?" He wagged his finger. "Ought you to be here, alone, without your agents and attorneys? It is surely not safe, my dear Herr von Karajan. Are you not owned, body and soul, by your managers and recording executives, those exalted magnates who have great things in store? What could our modest organization have to offer in comparison to mighty *Telefunken*, or even *Electrola*? But, seriously, can I perform any service? Do you require my help in any way? You need only ask."

Von Karajan edged away. He smiled but only with his teeth. "I should have let you know. I intrude." He bowed toward the secretary. "The young lady informed me that you were busy. But while walking through the Tiergarten, I experienced a kind of—what should I call it?—a cold breath, a kind of premonition about something. All of a sudden, I was impelled to come to this office. Something told me I had to see you." He turned a blank gaze toward me. For my part, I was experiencing my own cold breath. It was uncanny how von Karajan had chosen that moment to break in on us.

Herr Pietsch raised his arms in an apologetic shrug. "Alas, alas, my dear von Karajan, what can I do? Kapp-Dortmunder here must leave by the evening train back to Düsseldorf." That was a surprise to hear. "As I said, I'm interested in his plans—in a general way. Like you, he is neatly wrapped up and remains faithful to his commitments. He belongs, body and soul, to his beloved Westfälische Staatsoper. I have promised him my undivided attention for today. But tomorrow, dear von Karajan, if you wish, I shall see you first thing in the morning, no matter the topic. I promise you, we shall not be disturbed."

Von Karajan gravely studied our faces for long minutes, then nodded and silently walked to the door. It was clear he did not believe a morsel of what he had heard.

The secretary made to open the door for him, but he ignored her and turned back. "Herr Kapp-Dortmunder," he said, "if I may, I have been curious about something. I never had a chance to inquire about it before, so why not now? I assure you, the matter is hardly confidential."

I raised my eyebrows in polite invitation. "Perhaps it's too slight to mention, Herr Kapp-Dortmunder, and too trivial to recall. I refer to the music festival and conference held in Düsseldorf back in 1938. Surely, you remember it. It was convened by Reich Minister Goebbels himself. The express purpose was, first, to reveal to the world the exciting new composers nurtured in the Reich; second, to investigate to what degree our native German music might be corrupted by Jewish influence. I'm talking about the works of formal composers like Meyerbeer, Mendelssohn, Offenbach, and Mahler—and the way, it is said, Jews can commandeer Nordic themes and then cleverly insert in them plaintive, unmanly, synagogue-like weeping and wailing." He gave me a look of bland innocence. "Would you happen to remember that conference, Kapp-Dortmunder?—in Düsseldorf, after all."

Of course, I remembered—an eight-day extravaganza heralded by bugles and flags. At the time, I was overwhelmed with work. There was a never-ending blur of activity: a new marriage, new productions, constant immersion in negotiations, dealing with musicians, minutiae surrounding every aspect of stagecraft and design, craftsmen, singers and dancers, dealings with Frau Augustina and the governing board of the Westfälische Staatsoper. I had enough to occupy me. I didn't need to worry about more Jews.

What kept me from the conference were the political quicksands of the Third Reich itself. I was able to control temperamental artists, but you could pay with your career or your life for political errors. It was worse than imperial Rome, worse than the terror of the guillotine, worse even than the Russian Revolution. Certainly, I supported racial inquiries into Jewish music but made sure not to be in Düsseldorf while the conference was in session. For the 1939 conference, I took a holiday in Venice. I *certainly* didn't need to worry about more Jews.

Von Karajan was saying, "I did not present a paper myself, but it was all enlightening. Friedrich Blume spoke about racial implications in the choice of tone and structure—fascinating and complex. But I was disappointed by some of the presentations: if you ask me, too much anti-Jewish rhetoric without the scholarship to back it up. I thought that party theorist Dr. Alfred Rosenberg had made all that material available."

I had nothing useful to add. "As I say," he continued, "I thought I might have had the opportunity to run into you at that time. I regret that I failed." He grasped my hand again. This time the smile was dazzling. "We must make it a point not to ignore each other, Herr Kapp-Dortmunder. I think we have much to learn." A bow for Herr Pietsch and me, and he left. I released in a gust the breath that I had been holding and was aware that sweat trickled down my body from the armpits. Herr Pietsch grandly gestured his secretary to follow our guest out, then turned to me, rubbing his hands in delight.

"Now, what did you think of that, Herr Kapp-Dortmunder? What did you think of that? It must be true what they say. The man must have occult powers! How could he have learned about our meeting? Isn't he satisfied with what he has? He's got the Berlin State Opera, and everybody knows he's first in line for the Philharmonic if ever Furtwängler is replaced."

What bothered me was von Karajan's noting my absence from the Düsseldorf conference. *Was it ammunition for later use?* I would have been rattled by his breaking in on us in any case. Just as mention of Erich Leinsdorf had disturbed me, von Karajan's visit reminded me that I didn't take well to explicit or implied comparisons.

"But mark my words," Herr Pietsch continued, "if you, my dear Kapp-Dortmunder, could only give the appearance of occult, mystical powers of your own—for instance, could conduct without a score, eyes closed, face lifted heavenward, make eloquent, but not too flamboyant, gestures—all that would create marvelous opportunities for publicity photographs. Women would write in for them by the thousand." His eyes gleamed. *Another madman*, I was thinking.

Abruptly, he seized my arm, took his hat down from a rack, and led me to the door. "Time for lunch," he said. "I want to show you my new house." For a plump man, he moved briskly. We clattered down three flights of broad marble steps to the brilliant sunshine of the Tiergartenstrasse, where a posh tan Mercedes waited at the curb. We got in, and the driver set off. It was a beautiful summer day. Berlin was thronged with strolling businessmen on their lunch breaks, fashionable ladies with their friends. The pavements were crowded with smartly dressed, confident people, chatting animatedly. Were it not for the many uniforms one saw—Wehrmacht, Luftwaffe, Kriegsmarine, SS, SA, Hitler Youth, and so on—one would never dream there might be a war on.

The car headed east on the Kaiserdamm, toward the great park of Grunewald Forest. Herr Pietsch was enjoying the ride. He hummed to himself at the sight of those untroubled Berliners. A policeman held up his hand and halted us at the Charlottenburg traffic circle. "Tell me, my dear Kapp-Dortmunder, have you had a chance to see this morning's papers?"

"Why? Something special about the war?"

"No, something about Russia."

I frowned a moment but had come to learn that Herr Pietsch's questions were far from innocent. "Oh yes, there were a couple of small items about Russia. One was on cultural exchange. There's to be a visit to Berlin by the Bolshoi Ballet sometime in 1942. And the other mentioned the regular monthly petroleum deliveries from the Caucasus. They were on time. No mishaps or delays. What's the problem with Russia?"

He brought his head close to mine and checked whether his driver could hear us. "I shouldn't speak," he whispered, "but you'll soon be reading interesting news."

"About Russia? What are you talking about?" I whispered back. I didn't see the need for further help from Russia beyond what we were getting. Ever since the non-aggression pact with Stalin, everything had been wonderful. The Soviets had been immobilized with no special effort on our part. In the West, the British Empire was on the point of collapse. General Rommel was wiping the floor with them over in North Africa. We had taken Greece and Yugoslavia. Now we had room to breathe. Our laughable Italian allies were worse than useless, good only to cook spaghetti. The oxlike Russians had barely worked their way out of the Middle Ages, revolution or not. Already, they served us as a vassal state, supplying grain and oil, and that would be sufficient. Heaven forbid that they should join the war with us as allies. We had no need of that!

I communicated as much to Herr Pietsch. To my surprise, he roared in amusement. "What allies are you talking about? What do you mean, *allies*?" he hissed. Dropping his grin, he gripped my arm. "The truth is, we're going to smash the hell out of them. The Russians, I mean. We're not going to trade with them. We're going to break them to pieces and take what we need. Wouldn't you like to visit the steppes? When we've finished, German *Lebensraum* will rival the Wild West in America."

"Are you talking about widening the war?"

"Yes, I'm talking about widening the war. The decisions have been taken. It's going to be a mighty struggle. But they will collapse like a house of cards, like rotten wormwood. Those we permit to live will serve as beasts of burden."

I recoiled. "Where have you heard all this?"

The grin returned, but he still looked mad. "Perhaps we drank too many glasses of *Schnaps* this morning. But"—he nodded at me—"just pay attention to your wireless set this Sunday morning. I know what I'm talking about. My information is reliable. I have friends high up in the Party."

The car had entered a majestic realm, the Grunewald itself: broad tree-shaded avenues, flanked on both sides by gracious homes separated from each other by enormous gardens, shielded from the road by tall trimmed hedges. We halted in front of a three-story stone villa that resembled a giant Swiss chalet, with broad balconies and large sloping eaves. We got out after the car had swung into a graveled driveway.

"Yours?" I asked.

"Mine," he responded, rocking up and down on his heels. I was impressed. "It looks"—I searched for words—"how shall I say, venerable, *distingué*, but at the same time fantasy-laden."

Herr Pietsch clapped his hands. "Correct. I couldn't have said it better."

"Has it been in your family long?"

He didn't reply but put his hand on my shoulder and steered me up the driveway. The door was opened by a butler in a formal winged collar and black tie. As one entered, an immense paneled room rose to the height of the building and formed a grand reception hall. At the rear, a large staircase curved its way to the upper floors. Wherever one turned, there were paintings and bowls of flowers. I caught sight of more pictures as Herr Pietsch bustled me through a formal art gallery on the way to lunch on a garden veranda.

"I'll give you an opportunity to look at some of these pictures after lunch," he said. "They appear to be good. I haven't had a chance really to examine them yet."

"I thought you owned this house."

"I do, I do," he boomed. "Don't be tiresome and make me explain everything."

Waiting outside was a buffet laden with excellent salads and an array of cold meats and fish, toward which my host guided me. I immediately forgot my worries about impending war with Russia—I concluded that what I had been told in the car was fanciful bravado. I could not believe that a man as indiscreet as Herr Pietsch would be entrusted with military secrets. On a bed of lettuce and cress, I assembled a dish of stuffed trout and crayfish with asparagus. When I sat, the butler offered a choice of either *Gewürztraminer* or *Vouvray*. I chose the Alsatian wine.

Herr Pietsch waited for his servant to withdraw. "Now," he said, chewing vigorously and draining his glass of *Vouvray*, "in answer to your question. I have inhabited this splendid house precisely four months. It used to belong to Hans Rothenberg—have you heard of him?" I shook my head. Herr Pietsch poured himself more wine.

"Rothenberg, a Jew naturally—only those people could afford places like this—was a big name in international finance. That is, before our people came in. For all his cleverness, Rothenberg was an idiot. He said Hitler would never last, that he had more right to be in Germany than Hitler: at least he had been born here. He even referred to the Führer as that 'Austrian nobody.'" He let slip a giggle. I just sipped my wine. "Rothenberg could have managed to leave a hundred times over, but he didn't."

I helped myself to more food. "By chance," Herr Pietsch resumed, "I was in Reich Minister Goebbels' office, at a meeting about cultural trends, a burning concern of his—there were a dozen of us there. All of a sudden, the Reich Minister had to take a telephone call at his desk, a report from one of his people. As he listened, his face grew dark with rage, and he cursed. 'Meine Herren,' he said, 'I am reminded that I have apparently neglected some important matters. After eight years of the Führer's leadership, after eight years since I became Gauleiter of Berlin and began addressing the problem, I learn that there are *still* too many Jews here, oppressing our lives. I'm not talking about groveling merchants or slimy intellectuals and scientists, I'm referring to major bloodsuckers still in our midst.' Well, people knew there were Jews still in Berlin. Perhaps the Reich Minister had not noticed them on the streets, wearing their yellow stars. My thoughts immediately turned to Rothenberg. He was still permitted to live in this house with his servants as a kind of caretaker—in a way, to maintain the place before he was finally ejected. He well knew the clock was ticking.

"The Reich Minister was developing a genuine rage over the matter. One of his aides later explained that he had simply taken on too much work and could not handle everything. 'This infection will soon be terminated,' the Reich Minister said, throwing his hands in the air. 'This is Berlin, after all. There will be an end to this.' He slapped his palms on the table."

"What happened finally?" I inquired.

"Finally? As soon as I left the Reich Minister's conference, I made my way over here. I had known of this house for years, and I had always admired it. Herr Rothenberg had been a silent partner of mine in some business ventures back in the old days, and I had dined here. 'Look,' I told Rothenberg quite bluntly, 'the game is up. It's all over. If you haven't realized that by now, there must be something wrong with you. I'm telling you confidentially but definitively that Reich Minister Goebbels is enraged to rediscover that there are still Jews in the capital. He says he cannot understand it. The only Jews he is willing to tolerate are working in munitions factories. Are you willing to do that?' He looked aghast. He was an elderly fellow, after all. I told him that the rest would be resettled in the East.

"You have to understand," Herr Pietsch continued, "Rothenberg was in his sixties by that time. He was a widower, and his two married sons had left for America back in 1934. So he lived here in this magnificent house, with his antiques and drawings and paintings—I understand there's at least one Rubens and a Caravaggio. Also some good Flemish engravings, all first quality. And Rothenberg? All alone in the house, except for the servants and his ninety-two-year-old mother. A waste, really."

He broke off as the butler entered, accompanied by a maid. Silently, they carried away plates, poured coffee into espresso cups, and set out dishes of almond gingerbreads and *Berliner*. I grabbed one of the tiny doughnuts and noticed the maid wore a party swastika pin on her lapel, just like her employer.

"Karl," Herr Pietsch addressed his butler, "whom did you prefer working for, your former master, Herr Rothenberg, or me? Be honest now, you have nothing to fear." He swung around in his seat to give me a broad wink.

The butler paused in his tidying. "Herr Pietsch," he said, "I speak for Liesl here when I say that, since the advent of the Führer, all Germany has prospered."

Herr Pietsch persisted. "I was asking about Herr Rothenberg. You worked for him in this house, caring for these same possessions, for more than twenty years."

I wondered if Herr Pietsch, despite his joviality, were not indeed a thoroughgoing sadist. Clearly, Karl was reluctant to speak. It was Liesl the maid, presumably Karl's wife—wearing her party badge—who rushed forward, seized Herr Pietsch's hand, and kissed it.

"*Ach*, Herr Wolfgang," she gasped, "we thank you for everything. When they came for those old Jews, God knows what would have become of us and this house. Thanks to you, we retain our posts. Karl and I are grateful to you for taking care of us." She kissed his hand again. Gratified, Herr Pietsch dismissed the servants.

He turned back to me. "Ah yes, must finish the story." He snipped the end off a cigar and carefully lit it. "I was directed to the office of a most distinguished and influential person, Professor Dr. Theodor Vahlen, none other than the president of the Prussian Academy of Sciences, and sought his advice. Dr. Vahlen agreed it would be a sin if this house were to fall into the hands of some Brownshirt ruffian. There was every danger that it might—people's tongues were hanging out at the thought of picking up plush Jewish houses on the cheap. He directed me to Herr Hans Hinkel, secretary-general of the State Cultural Affairs Bureau. You can count on the German Civil Service to be scrupulously honest. But Herr Hinkel revealed what wonderful levels of corruption and rectitude a man may achieve at the same time. Once bought, he remained bought. Upon Dr. Vahlen's prompting, he took care of all formalities and legalities and signed the necessary papers. His imprimatur and position ensured that I wouldn't be questioned. Oh, don't misunderstand. Other ambitious party members had their eyes on the place. I appreciated Hinkel's sense of propriety. I made him a generous gift—of course, nothing near the market value of the house—but sufficient to take care of him and his friends. And"—he emitted a mouthful of fragrant smoke—"that's how it happened."

"And what happened to Rothenberg?" I asked.

Herr Pietsch shrugged. "I wasn't here. When Liesl—you know, the maid—went upstairs to help the old Jewess with her coat and shoes, she found her lying on a sofa, quite dead. Rothenberg was in his room next door in the same condition. Apparently, he had given a draught of poison to the old lady and then taken a tumbler of it himself. Karl said that Liesl was terribly upset, had an attack of hysterics. But you can see for yourself, she is fine now and performs her duties in a most satisfactory fashion."

He puffed deeply on his cigar. "It's a terrible shame, and I personally regret it," he said. "I repeat, Rothenberg could have saved himself a thousand times over. Do I feel responsible? Definitely not. It's the fortunes of war and historical inevitability, my dear friend. The German people were destined to wreak justice on their Jewish oppressors. It had been building over time. Now Rothenberg is gone, but the house is safe; these splendid pictures are preserved, and I trust that Reich Minister Goebbels rests easier at night."

He gazed at me sleepily out of a cherubic face, looking like a man ready for a long nap. "You might ask, is this the only way things could have been accomplished? Perhaps not. But I repeat, I was not responsible. We are all in the grip of history. I am only a grateful beneficiary. Through our association, you will be another."

The chauffeur drove me back to the Askanischer Hof. I decided to return to Düsseldorf that evening. My train was to leave at four. A sense of disturbance had been building in me most of the day, beginning with von Karajan's appearance, heightened by what Herr Pietsch had told me: Rothenberg, his house and pictures in the Grunewald; his ninety-two-year-old mother; Herr Pietsch's design for my life; even his wild story about impending war with Soviet Russia that weekend—all that induced a general nausea. I thought of taking a taxi to Huberta's but immediately rejected the idea. I might get some cosseting but wasn't up to the battle of wits that would accompany it. I should have gone to my desk and started making concrete all that Herr Pietsch and I had discussed, but I was unable to concentrate. The lunch I had eaten stuck in my throat. Nothing would go down. The room began to spin, and I had to lie down. But it got worse.

Near tears, not knowing what else to do, I got up again and staggered to the piano I had installed. I managed to open the lid and began to play. Without intending to, my fingers found their way to a Bach piece I had not touched for at least twenty-five years, the B minor prelude from the "Great Forty-Eight." Incredibly, as I played, the room began to settle and my head to clear. I felt better. It has generally been thus with music and me. Whatever ailed, music was the healer; I knew the world would come to order. The prelude, with its grave downward strides in the left hand, produced in me an incredible calm. Once again, I was struck with wonder. *What sort of man had written this?* Had Bach's heart beat as mine did? And the fugue—also noble and grave, but assertive and proud—laid down widely spaced percussive intervals, like measured pronouncements from God himself. The universe was indeed coming to order. I was able to catch some sleep before I got my train.

* * *

As soon as I returned to Düsseldorf that night, I broke the news to Margarethe. I had to wait to break into the chatter over which she presided. She was having late coffee with a group of ladies. They must have just returned from the theater. She listened calmly to my news but seemed not to comprehend, for she asked me in a humorous tone to be sure to telephone her at least once a week while in Berlin. Then she resumed passing out tea cakes, accompanied by the titters of those silly women. No cry of regret or astonishment. No congratulations. Had she somehow learned of Huberta?

Next morning, I visited Frau Augustina. In contrast, she greeted me warmly, but I found myself unable to respond. I remained on my feet in that familiar tapestried living room and fixed my gaze on the opposite wall, ignoring invitations to sit or offers of refreshment. If I looked her in the eye, I would be unable to speak.

I drew a deep breath. "Frau Augustina, something urgent has arisen. I must break my association with the Westfälische Staatsoper as of this moment."

After a blank stare, she gasped and rose to her feet. "What in the world are you saying to me, Herr Generalmusikdirektor? Did I hear you correctly?"

"I said I must leave Düsseldorf as soon as I can. A new opportunity has presented itself that I may not ignore. I am not at liberty to say what or how this opportunity may manifest itself. It is sufficient that it requires my immediate presence elsewhere."

She sat down again, dazed. "Have you been called to military service or something like that? Doesn't your post at the Staatsoper qualify as essential work?"

She had understood nothing, another stupid woman like Margarethe. My first inclination was to laugh. But as I was about to respond, a terrible realization fell on me like a blow on the head. Herr Pietsch and I had signed nothing. Nothing, not even a memorandum of understanding! Yesterday, I had felt too ill, and he had given me the impression he was about to slump into deep sleep. *Why had I been such an idiot? I was truly a child.* I began to speak rudely to Frau Augustina. I hadn't intended to. Of all people, she did not deserve it. She had put complete trust in me, even supported me in preference to her own grandson, the unfortunate Manfred von Krefeld.

My panic caused me to raise my voice. I found myself shouting at Frau Augustina. Even though I had achieved prominence in Düsseldorf, why couldn't she see that my fame was spreading, that I was on the brink of great things? *Why should she wish to hold me back?*

As I carried on, I was, of course, committing many more stupidities. I should not have bellowed at my benefactor. It had nothing to do with her. I understand now, many years later, the culprit, again, was that deplorable German habit of bowing and scraping to superiors. All it taught was hatred of those superiors and trained one to be beastly oneself. Added to that was the knowledge that I was surely antagonizing Frau Augustina without being certain of whether Herr Pietsch would keep to what he had promised. I was terrified. I could present no proof that yesterday's conversation had even taken place. As the Bulgarians say, I had shit in my own bowl of soup.

I did the only thing possible in the circumstances: I succumbed to another of my hysterical fits, just like yesterday in Berlin. My breathing once again rapid and shallow, I became lightheaded, began to see double, and finally was unable to stand. Frau Augustina caught fright and summoned her manservant. I soon came to myself but refused to be taken to hospital. Instead, I demanded a car and had myself driven home, where I immediately ordered the maid to repack my bags. I needed to head for the station, there to board a train back to Berlin as soon as possible. While I was taking care to include my miniature busts of Bach, Beethoven, and Brahms, Frau Augustina appeared at my front door, together with her servant, and attempted to plead for a measure of balance. I was shocked that she had followed me.

She addressed Margarethe. "The Herr Generalmusikdirektor has not been well," she said. "Has he told you that he almost fainted in my house and refused medical attention?"

Margarethe didn't know how to deal with things if she was not the center of attention. But, after all, this was Frau Augustina. She produced a bright social smile.

"There is nothing wrong with my Kappi," she declared. "He is, as ever, deeply moved by his work. We are so grateful for your unfailing protection." *What a lickspittle!*

"Perhaps he has been overdoing things, and neither of us has noticed," Frau Augustina replied. "He has far too many responsibilities. And this war—the things we are called upon to perform for the Führer and our Fatherland. It is all a great strain."

"But we do it gladly, Frau von Krefeld," Margarethe gushed. "We do it gladly."

Frau Augustina ignored my unkempt appearance, my urgent wish not to miss the Berlin train. "The Herr Generalmusikdirektor should not undertake any tasks over this summer. Instead, the two of you should take a holiday together in the mountains, Switzerland or Italy. The air will do you good. And you will return to work with renewed energy. You will require your strength for the new *Tristan*. And besides," she added archly, "your contract requires it."

What was this about a contract? I fixed Frau Augustina with a furious stare, fighting an impulse to strike her. "Frau Augustina," I declared, "with respect, there *is* no contract between you and me. There never has been—"

"You are quite correct, Herr Generalmusikdirektor. I was speaking figuratively, about the deeper understandings that prevail between friends."

"On the contrary," I grated, eyes fixed on the ceiling, "it means that there are no legal impediments to my freedom. I repeat, Madame, I am mindful of all your considerations, but now, as I related to you this morning, my presence is required by other opportunities. I hope I may inform you about them at an appropriate time."

Margarethe finally comprehended what was going on. "Kappi," she broke in with a nervous titter, eyes flickering back and forth between Frau Augustina and me, "I thought you were joking yesterday. I really didn't pay attention." Speaking rapidly, she turned to Frau Augustina. "You know what a witty man the Herr Generalmusikdirektor can be. Lord, how he loves his jokes and pranks. I think it must relieve his mind when he becomes too pressured." She burst into high-pitched laughter.

Frau Augustina rose from her chair. Her servant handed her a walking stick, upon which she leaned. "Frau Kapp-Dortmunder," she said, "I grasp what the Herr Generalmusikdirektor is saying. I have an idea that you are an innocent in this sorry business." Turning to me: "For you, Herr Kapp-Dortmunder, I have no words."

She turned to go, leaning on the arm of her driver. Naturally, I went to assist her. She halted, averting her head as I approached, whereupon I too stopped moving. As soon as I did so, she bowed to Margarethe and left the room. The maid saw her out.

Margarethe burst into tears. "Kappi, what on earth have you done? What has possessed you? Do you realize the influence that woman commands in Düsseldorf? There will be nothing here for us. We will be excluded from everything!"

She enraged me all over again. "You stupid woman, is that all you think about? You're like my numbskull orchestra. Nobody pays attention unless I scream." I had never before let out blasts like that at home. It was a relief to do so. And although I regretted parting from Frau Augustina, I was within my rights. There was no contract, hence, no legal encumbrance. I had given her excellent service, and she had paid me. Why should there be wounded feelings? Frau Augustina had trusted me, but I was not, after all, part of the family. She had not, for example, adopted me, made me her heir.

I was back in Berlin late that afternoon. I hurried past Herr Pietsch's secretary, into his office as insistently as had von Karajan the day before. I half-thought to see him there! But Herr Pietsch was alone. "I did not expect you until later in the week, my dear Kapp-Dortmunder. Have you already been to Düsseldorf and returned? Surely, you cannot have settled your affairs with Frau Augustina von Krefeld and the Westfälische Staatsoper in this short space of time."

I must have looked ridiculous. I was disheveled and out of breath. I had come straight from the station without pausing at my hotel. Herr Pietsch shot me a keen glance and nodded at a sheaf of papers on the desk. "I have prepared a draft of our contract," he said. I could swear he was laughing at me. "Please have your lawyers examine the terms, and then let's meet to discuss any questions you might have. I want you to be completely satisfied, dear Kapp-Dortmunder. We are going to do great things together."

There were many pages. I riffled through them, but the great number of clauses and conditions made me dizzy. I had no experience with this sort of thing. I knew no attorneys nor had need of any until now. For all my new so-called freedom, I was not truly at large but had merely passed from one master to another.

"I assure you, my dear Kapp-Dortmunder," Herr Pietsch was saying, "I am not promiscuous in my preferences. But as of this week, I find myself strangely beset by all the kapellmeisters of Germany," he twinkled. "They smell blood, they cannot wait to visit me. First, you and I met yesterday. Then, von Karajan mysteriously turned up. Next, it was Clemens Krauss out of the blue late yesterday afternoon, feeling me out about possible representation. And, wonder of wonders, who should telephone this morning but Hans Knappertsbusch, 'just wondering' whether we could meet. I don't understand how, but I'll wager they got scent of you. You are bringing good fortune to *Grammophon Gesellschaft*. You are our talisman."

* * *

That Sunday, just as Herr Pietsch promised, I awakened to the triumphal broadcast sounds of Liszt's "Les Préludes." Dr. Goebbels himself took to the air to proclaim that, after repeated and intolerable provocations, the armed forces of the Reich had undertaken to rid the world of the Jewish-Bolshevik plague. From the Baltic to the Black Sea, no fewer than three-and-a-half million men had surged eastward in this righteous crusade, accompanied by three-and-a-half thousand tanks and almost three thousand planes. All along this vast front, the Soviet armies, ill-prepared and riddled with corruption, were collapsing. Newspapers displayed our soldiers greeted with smiles and flowers by populations grateful for liberation from Bolshevik tyranny. Herr Pietsch had been absolutely correct. I resolved never to doubt him again.

During the following months, I had no time for Huberta. I was furiously busy assembling my new orchestra. Within four months, I had one—not necessarily the one I would retain, but definitely of superior quality. Herr Pietsch made it possible for me to recruit members of existing organizations by letting it be known that he would pay higher salaries than customary. Despite the Führer's and Reich Minister Goebbels' support of the arts, the pay of first-class musicians was not huge. Back in 1941, the average player would draw down five hundred *Reichsmarks* a month. First-desk men could make more and, of course, soloists much more. This may be compared to Furtwängler's pay during the same period, which averaged between four thousand and five thousand *Reichsmarks* for a single performance. His was a special case, but the example provided inspiration for my own future negotiations. The wholesale departure of the Jews was certainly a godsend for the capable, but as always, one had to make an effort to find them. Herr Pietsch's confidence in me made the task easier. From time to time, I was taken to the site at Unter den Linden to observe the progress on my new concert hall—despite the new war in the East. And although I was not bringing in revenue at this time, I did not lack for money. Herr Pietsch paid me generous sums, duly noted down, advances on the future.

On the other hand, my task was made difficult by the battleground

Berlin had become in the arts, especially its orchestras. What you had were two of the most powerful figures in the Reich struggling for the right to be considered State Cultural Kommissar, Reich Marschall Göring and Reich Minister Goebbels. One, Göring, declared himself master of every institution labeled as "Prussian," because, among the titles he held was prime minister of Prussia. The other, Goebbels, claimed for himself most ensembles beginning with the designation "Berlin," because he was Gauleiter of Berlin. Thus the Berlin State Theater, the Berlin Philharmonic, and the Berlin Opera "belonged to" Goebbels. Göring was chief of the Prussian State Opera.

The rivalry between these powerful men created hazards. Woe betide anyone caught between them. I often marveled where they found the time, seeing that the Reich Marschall must have been stupendously busy as air minister, even running day-to-day operations of the Luftwaffe, and director of the Four-Year Economic Plan. Dr. Goebbels managed the propaganda ministry, the massive winter relief programs, and had responsibility for the overall domestic war effort. He was to be found everywhere, encouraging the nation. Surely, it shows the value those men placed on music and art. But, I repeat, it did not pay to be caught between them. And if that were not sufficient, Party Theorist Dr. Alfred Rosenberg's Fighting League for German Culture was in the thick of the battle; then the handsome Baldur von Schirach, leader of the Hitler Youth and a fine poet himself, had some favorite musicians and soloists of his own, whose careers he was promoting; third, Hans Frank, governor-general of Occupied Poland and a distinguished jurist, also a prominent music lover, would regularly intercede from his headquarters in distant Krakow on behalf of one promising musician or another. I thanked my lucky stars to be under the protection of Herr Pietsch, even though hardly as prominent as those other gentlemen. Moreover, I blessed him for the inspiration of naming the new ensemble the Staaskapelle Brandenburg, bypassing the perils of labeling it either "Berlin" or "Prussian." But our new orchestra belonged to Berlin without actually announcing it.

The construction of my new concert hall took longer than expected and apparently had something to do with what was happening in Russia. After a brilliant initial campaign, during which our armies along that entire front swept from victory to victory—inflicting grievous losses as they went—until within sight of Moscow, they ran out of fuel. Indeed, the Soviets managed to drive our brave men back some distance. I didn't dare say what had been on my mind ever since Herr Pietsch told me of the impending attack. I remembered thinking, *That place is too vast. I'm not a military thinker, but at school in Szombathely I had read of Napoleon's destruction in 1812.*

Even with our special priorities, it was not until the following spring that the hall was ready for inspection. It was certainly a handsome and gracious auditorium: bare of adornment, because of wartime shortages, yet impressive with its four levels, chandeliers, and agreeable quantities of red plush. The overall impression was of strength and refinement, without descent into effeminacy.

As I say, the orchestra was ready before the hall. We had held auditions and winnowed out our prospects in a cinema in the center of town. I judged them ready for performance, but Herr Pietsch was reluctant to display them before the hall was ready. Orchestra and auditorium would make a joint debut.

"This orchestra must be put into action and soon; otherwise, it will become rusty," he said. Then he told me he had a brilliant idea. The time was right, he said, for a tour outside Germany: Paris, Brussels, Amsterdam, and Rotterdam. It would be good if I prepared programs to flatter those nations. Reich Minister Goebbels was absolutely enthusiastic when he heard about it. Music was the international language. The project would not fail to make friends for the Reich. But I never joined that particular enterprise, even though many colleagues did. One of the assistant conductors from Düsseldorf, with whom I had remained in touch, informed me that he had accompanied a German orchestra to Paris earlier in the year and had prepared just such a program designed to flatter the French—Berlioz, Bizet, and Gounod. He told me, when he stepped out to the podium at the Théâtre des Champs Élysées, nothing could be seen in the audience but row upon row of Wehrmacht, Luftwaffe, Kriegsmarine, and SS uniforms. Not a French civilian in the place, apart from Vichyites and known supporters of ours. I heard of others who toured similarly in Denmark, the Netherlands, and Bohemia. I saw no point in a similar exercise.

As the date for our opening concert drew near, Herr Pietsch and Reich Minister Goebbels arranged a press conference in the ornate, gold-trimmed main salon of the Propaganda Ministry on the Wilhelmstrasse, right next to the State Cultural Affairs Bureau. It was exciting. However, Margarethe chose not to attend, and Huberta naturally could not. After warm opening remarks before a hundred or so German and international correspondents, Reich Minister Goebbels turned the meeting over to Herr Pietsch and me.

"This is a signal event in the cultural life of Berlin, and indeed for Germany as a whole," Herr Pietsch began. "At a time when the Reich and its allies are fighting for civilization itself against the forces of Jewish-inspired Bolshevik and capitalist domination, we are declaring that there is more to life than brutality. Meine Herren, with the construction of this magnificent concert hall, with the formation of this magnificent new orchestra, we reaffirm the high principles of German art. In the immortal words of Hans Sachs, found in the glorious closing pages of *Die Meistersinger*:

Honor your German masters and preserve the powers of good.

"We call upon the world to witness that, even while engaged in this life-and-death struggle, we do not forget the spirit. For without the spirit, what are we but mere beasts."

Correspondents from the German press applauded while furiously taking down everything he said, particularly reporters from Reich Minister Goebbels' own newspaper, *Der Angriff,* as well as those from the *Berliner Tageblatt, Frankfurter Zeitung,* and *Völkische Beobachter.* Others, perhaps journalists from neutral countries, listened more than they wrote.

Now it was my turn. I took care not to outshine the oratory of either the Reich Minister or Herr Pietsch. I was confident that the eloquence of my music-making would serve. I spoke in general terms about the thinking that had gone into my choices of programs and repertoire. My performances would draw largely on the established giants of German music. I had shared all this with the Reich Minister and Herr Pietsch, and they had indicated their approval. At the end of my remarks, Herr Pietsch called for comments and questions.

The reporter from *Der Angriff* remarked that he was inspired by all that he had heard that morning. He had been impressed by the scope and range of the outlined programs. He wanted to add that he was humbled but proud to be a member of the German race, to know that he was of that same stock that had given birth to the likes of Beethoven, Bach, Wagner, and Brahms. He sat, accompanied by applause.

After a moment, a tall man in the third row got to his feet. "*Die Zeit*, Zurich," he announced. "A question for Herr Kapp-Dortmunder.

Herr Generalmusikdirektor, I am somewhat puzzled as I look over these projected programs for the coming year. I cannot help noticing that you include few contemporary or experimental works—not even new German music. For instance, while I notice a generous representation of Richard Strauss, the programs are largely made up of Beethoven, Wagner, Bruckner, and Brahms. I am surprised by the near absence of composers that Minister Goebbels himself has publicly praised as representative of new, dynamic German art."

I hadn't expected this. Dismayed, I looked about me. To my left, Herr Pietsch seemed amused by the question. To my right, Reich Minister Goebbels had thrown himself back in his chair and positively roared with laughter. I later reflected that he would hardly exhibit public annoyance with a journalist from a neutral country. For my part, I managed a weak smile. I knew what the Swiss gentleman meant. Where were the stalwarts of Third Reich modern composers? Where were Carl Orff, Gottfried von Einem, Werner Egk, or one of a dozen more? To tell the truth, I could neither stand them nor comprehend them. Either unbearably dull or outlandish in their futile attempts to be Stravinsky or Bartók. Praise God, I didn't have to deal with either of them, or with the likes of Arnold Schoenberg and his fellow uglies.

Reich Minister Goebbels rose to his feet. "Meine Herren, I cannot imagine what you think we do here in the Reich. That question seems to assume that we conduct life here under some kind of thought control. Obviously, you are thinking of the Kremlin. The Reich is locked in mortal battle with its enemies. Therefore, we do require military security. But to imagine that we would impinge on, or seek to influence, the free choices exercised by our artists is abhorrent." Everybody chuckled.

"No, Meine Herren," Dr. Goebbels concluded, "Herr Kapp-Dortmunder is revered for his interpretations of the works of established German masters. The public will flock to his concerts to hear them. Other musicians will perform what they wish. That is the way things are done in this Germany of ours." The German press rose to their feet, applauded, and raised their arms in salute. The neutrals politely got to their feet.

In due course, we had our gala inaugural concert. It was, as they always say, "a glittering affair." Distinguished foreign visitors, glamorous ladies, generals, admirals, high party officials circulated up and down the marble staircases, lined by SS guardsmen in dress uniform standing at attention. Then the dignitaries made their appearance: Reich Minister Goebbels, Reich Marschall Göring, SS Reich Führer Himmler, Herr von Ribbentrop, von Schirach, and many, many others, all accompanied by their wives. My colleagues in the music world were there, except—conspicuously—von Karajan. Of course, Margarethe was with me. At the stroke of eight, the Führer made his appearance. An SS band in the spacious vestibule struck up our national anthem. We snapped up our right arms and sang with tears in our eyes. The Führer walked slowly down our reception line, shaking hands and exchanging greetings in his own inimitable way, giving his penetrating look that seemed to search and comprehend one's soul. It was the first time that he had met Margarethe, and he paid us the compliment of holding on to her hand and lingering in conversation. We felt honored, particularly when we learned he had just returned from the Eastern Front.

It was all terribly exciting. We began with the third *Leonore* overture. The players were motivated to be especially responsive, the performance was thrilling, and the audience, already pleased with the interior of the new house, responded with cheers.

Herr Pietsch and I had kept the rest of the program a surprise until that moment. We had engaged three of the most distinguished pianists in Germany, each of whom would play a Beethoven concerto. When the names were announced, applause was heard at first, then unrestrained cheers. First, Edwin Fischer came onstage to play the Third Concerto in C Minor with a superb juxtaposition of defiance and lyricism. Next came Walter Gieseking, who played the Fourth Concerto in G with all the melting tenderness he is known for. After the interval, Wilhelm Kempff gave us the Fifth Concerto in E flat, the "Emperor." How can I describe it? He was pure poetry and fire.

The three soloists gathered with me onstage to receive the love and adulation that poured from every quarter, every tier of the house. Herr Kempff and I, soaked in perspiration, the other two soloists having had opportunity to change, stood in a row with clasped hands, bowing, placing hands over our hearts. The Führer advanced from his front-row seat, the other luminaries behind him, to applaud us. He summoned me down from the stage to join him. As I did so, like magic, the whole house fell silent. The Führer turned to an aide, who handed him a small flat leather case.

"I take pleasure," the Führer said in his still Austrian-sounding but compelling voice, "in bestowing on a great artist a mark of personal appreciation. Like me, he comes to Germany from Ostmark, our sister community to the south. And though, unlike me, he is not a soldier in the true sense of the word, he performs a highly valuable national service for which the Reich is grateful. It gives me pleasure to bestow upon him the Military Order of Merit." I was overwhelmed. I extended my right arm in salute again, my eyes shining. Again, the entire audience rose to sing *Deutschland über Alles.*

* * *

Tenth Variation

Berlin 1945

I awoke to terrible pain but at least alive. My head felt as though it had been beaten repeatedly with iron bars. I was unable to see. My eyes were open, I knew: I felt the lids scrape across them. I had been struck blind. Splayed out on my back, I wanted to touch my head but was unable to move. Paralyzed too? After a while, I realized I could not budge because of the crushing weights that held me there. Limbs, torso, muscles—I was unable to stir, lost in a stupor without the strength to feel frightened.

After I couldn't tell how long, a faint light struggled in from behind me. *Hurrah, I was not blind.* I was immersed in a deep silence, broken only by the sound of dripping water. How had I got here? Memory returned in painful splinters. Margarethe had been with me. We had been eating and drinking and talking. *What had happened to her?* Soon, fresh waves of agony enveloped me. I passed in and out of consciousness, able to draw breath only in shallow spurts because of the weight on me. I couldn't cry out, could make out only vague shapes. Perhaps I was indeed blind. The light I saw was the kind that flashes on the retina when sleep is disturbed.

One pain overwhelmed the rest. My bladder was stretched to the fullest. But my upbringing, my importance in the world, required me to hold fast. Whatever happened, a man in my position does not soak his trousers. Soon, it was impossible not to. I would burst. I relaxed the sphincter and, at first, pissed in a trickle, then more and even more. It was an incredible pleasure, better than making love. It created wonderful warmth around me—which rapidly turned cold. Now I was freezing. I wished I had held it in. But it was such a relief! The whole thing

319

was absurd, I wanted to laugh; but the weight crushing me didn't permit me to breathe.

I *had* been talking to Margarethe. *But what was this place?* Thought was painful. Through the profound silence, I thought I heard tapping. Then nothing. After a while, I could swear a dog was barking. I must have imagined it. *What had Margarethe and I talked about?* More time passed. Despite the pain and crushing weight, I felt hungry, my throat was parched. Above all, I was cold. I drifted again into darkness.

A heavy bang jolted me awake, not far from me. Another loud bang. Voices, barking dogs. And I was not blind! There was light on all sides. A new agony—thick dust invaded my tomb, choking me, stinging my eyes.

Outside, somebody shouted. "Silence! Is anybody there?"

I wanted to shout back but could not draw breath. I heard bricks scraping, debris dragged aside. Another shout. Then a fusillade of barking. "The dogs have found something!" The voices and barking were close. Suddenly, a hole tore open right by my head. Light poured in. Now I was truly blinded. A dog poked in its snout and licked my face. I still could not breathe.

A man's gruff voice. "All together. Now!" A cry of many men, accompanied by the groan of straining wood and the screech of metal. The weight on my body suddenly disappeared. I was starved for air, but my attempt to gulp breath came with fresh pain. I looked up. I saw a dozen burly, sweating Civil Defense workers in Wehrmacht helmets. They had raised massive beams and were holding them up while four of their fellows seized me and placed me on a stretcher. At a signal, the dozen released their hold; the wreckage fell back with a dust-laden roar. I must have fainted again.

When next I opened my eyes, I was in a dimly lighted corridor. No pain now, no feeling, everything numb. I caught sight of women in white, cloths around their heads. Nurses? Nuns? Men walked by in long white gowns, stethoscopes around their necks. But this was a grimy passageway, not a ward. *When had I last been in a hospital?*

"He's awake." A nurse, young but plain, sensible-looking rather than attractive. "How do you feel, Herr Kapellmeister?"

"What's happened to me? What is this place? How do you know who I am?" The words came in a whisper.

"You're not supposed to talk," the nurse chided.

"Then how can I tell you how I feel?" I gasped.

She straightened up, out of my vision. "Herr Doktor," she called.

A new face replaced hers. An elderly man, white-coated, carefully sat down next to my cot. Elderly. Younger men would be facing the Russians. He studied a chart. "Herr Kapp-Dortmunder?" I was able to nod. "I am Dr. La Rivière," he said in a tired voice. "They found you this morning in the ruins of the Hôtel Park Sanssouci near here in Potsdam. Do you have a memory of that?"

I tried to think. I could make no sense of the hotel name. As you know, when in Berlin, I stay at the Askanischer Hof.

"There was a bad raid last night," the Herr Doktor continued, "our British friends. A lot of damage, they tell me. The hotel suffered a direct hit, the entire building collapsed. The rescuers couldn't begin to work until the All Clear blew at four in the morning. Then work was interrupted when the Americans struck this morning." He had mournful eyes. "Anything you can tell us? Was anyone with you?"

Margarethe. Yes, definitely. We had been talking and eating. But why hadn't it been the dining room of my usual hotel? Why the Sanssouci? *What had Margarethe and I been saying?* I screwed up my face, trying to think. But that hurt too much. I could not turn my head. I managed to see that my cot was lined up with others ahead of mine, single file, on one side of the dismal corridor. Doctors, nurses, and too young or overaged orderlies hurried back and forth. At one side of my cot, fluid dripped from a bottle leading to my arm.

Dr. La Rivière was speaking. "While you were unconscious, we had opportunity to do a set of X-rays. You suffered heavy blows about the head. We saw no skull fracture, but there was severe concussion. As for the rest of you, your chest was crushed. You have four fractured ribs on the right, severe trauma to three more on the left, a fractured right tibia, and a fractured right clavicle. Your left leg, your two arms, and your fingers are bruised but otherwise unharmed." He permitted himself a faint smile. "I recognize you and have attended some of your concerts, Herr Kapellmeister. You will play the piano again. And, after rest and treatment, your collarbone will be as good as new. You will swing the baton once more." He rose and hung the chart at my feet. "They will move you when a bed becomes available," he said. "I regret that accommodations are tight these days. I'll be back when you are settled." When he left, I struggled to raise my head. My chest was encased in Plaster of Paris. Also my shoulder and right leg.

The nurse appeared. "We shall be moving you within an hour at most. You must be hungry. I'm afraid the kitchens are closed, but I can get you some soup. Would the Herr Kapellmeister like that?"

My bladder was once again stretched beyond the limit. "What the Herr Kapellmeister would like," I managed, "is *pissen*." I had not startled her. "Very urgent!"

"I'll bring you a bottle."

"Will you put up a screen?" I asked.

"No screens, no time, and no help. But I'll assist you."

She produced a long-necked flask, folded back the covers, exposed my member to the world, expertly fitted me in the thing, and waited, peering intently. I was beyond shock. There was much noise around me, nurses and orderlies hurrying back and forth. I was unable to deliver. The pain in my groin was intense.

Suddenly, she made a rapid *whish-whish* sound with her mouth. My mama used to do that in the night when she awakened me for a midnight pee. I couldn't help laughing at the memory. But it relaxed me, and I was able to perform.

"Sehr schön, Herr Kapellmeister," she praised as she rearranged the blanket and handed a full bottle to a passing orderly.

"What happens when I have to …" I could not think of the polite expression. "Scheissen?

"We'll help with that. Do you need to now?" I shook my head as far as I was able. She reminded me of Krisztina, guileless and direct.

"Would the Herr Kapellmeister like some soup?"

"Would the Fräulein Nurse kindly cease this horrible formality and address me like a human being. She has already seen the best of him." I was glad when she laughed.

Talking and movement continued painful. "There's something you can do for me." She waited with a tilt of her head. "Can you bring me a looking glass?"

"Oh, I don't think that's a good idea," she said.

I liked her, so direct. So different from—I was just thinking of her but couldn't remember her name—so different from…oh yes, Margarethe. I frowned, trying again to remember. *What had happened to her?* We had been together in the Hôtel Park Sanssouci, if Dr. La Rivière could be believed. She had been shouting at the top of her lungs. Then another louder scream from outside had overpowered hers. Loud enough to fill the universe, to wake the dead. That's when memory stopped.

The nurse brought a small mirror. "Please, don't tell the doctor I did this." She held up the glass. I couldn't believe what I saw. Except for my face, my head was wrapped in bandages. I had expected that. But my face was one giant purple bruise—eyes blackened, cheeks swollen, jaw in a brace. Not a hint of natural color. All black and blue. The nose looked twice its size. Dr. La Rivière had said it was not broken. My arms and fingers? Horribly bruised also. And I was encased in plaster.

It was ridiculous to plan one's life, but the end of the war was clearly in sight. I had already given more than one thought to how I might carry on if the unthinkable were to occur. If the Reich went under, my sense of duty to the cause of music would compel me to survive. All the same, I couldn't help grinning at my reflection. *Only thirty-five years old, and see what I look like!* The air was foul with odors of rot, disinfectant, and unwashed bodies. Nurses hurried back and forth, their cheeks shiny with sweat, once-white uniforms grimy and stained. Orderlies, carrying stretchers, tunics dirty and creased, faces unshaven, struggled around them, though there was no room to get by. I had an urgent need to piss again. Already? I was unable to call out, unable to recognize any of the people that darted rapidly past my cot.

My angel of mercy reappeared. "Do you need help again?" Once again, she expertly stuffed my limpness into a long-necked bottle—I could feel nothing—and watched me with a critical eye as I performed.

"How did you know?" I gasped in relief.

"Why wouldn't I know?" She gestured to the container attached to my arm. "You are receiving intravenous fluids, and it's good that your kidneys are working." Again, she handed the bottle to a passing orderly and squinted at the hanging container to check what remained.

Two orderlies appeared and pulled my cot out. "We've got a place for him."

Instead of a regular ward, I was wheeled down the corridor into a large underground room on the same floor, crowded, with the same dank lighting, the same foul smells, the same bustle. The only difference was that this new space was vast, almost a low-ceilinged arena. Beds lined all four walls and were arranged in at least eight or ten long rows in the center. The figures in the beds, many of them heavily bandaged, lay silent;

but I heard groaning from some. My cot was maneuvered into a narrow space by a wall. I preferred that to being lost in the center.

I asked the orderlies where I was. "We're in the sub-subcellar—whatever they call it—of the Emergency General Hospital near Wannsee," one said. "They brought you here from Potsdam. That's badly banged up now, all services broken down. No picnic here either. Bombing all the time, so it's too dangerous to return upstairs to the wards." They straightened my bedclothes with gray weary faces.

My informant bent closer. "Those bastards, the American and British fliers, are above us day and night," he hissed. "When they get shot down, we don't bother taking them prisoner anymore. We shoot them on the spot. Or the crowds beat them to death. My brother told me. He's in the auxiliary police."

"What about the rules?" I stammered.

He laughed bitterly. "There are no fucking rules."

All at once there was a bustle in the underground ward. Someone had entered, I couldn't see who. Doctors, nurses, orderlies—all sprang to attention. Someone big had come. I was unable to raise my head to see. My two helpers hurried away. I heard a spatter of Heil Hitlers and at last made out a group of uniformed visitors making their way down one row of beds and up another. Every so often, the group paused at a silent bandaged form. Those at attention stared rigidly into space.

Now the group arrived at the foot of my bed. A small, thin man, well known to me—to us all—wearing a gold-braided peaked cap and long tan leather coat, limped to my side. He wore his usual bony smile, intense and penetrating. "Herr Reich Minister," I gasped, "you do me great honor." Dr. Goebbels leaned over and smiled down at me. He raised a hand. A chair magically appeared.

"Hello, old friend," he said. "It is awful to see you under such circumstances. The Führer and I were distressed to learn that you were among the injured. What utter barbarians our enemies are! But these ordeals make us stronger. Thank God you were spared. The Führer wishes you a speedy recovery and promises that those devils will be repaid a thousandfold." He made to grasp my hand. Just in time, my nurse intervened. "Herr Reich Minister, please, this patient cannot use his hands."

A displeased aide, wearing an adjutant's golden *aigullette*, drew close. Dr. Goebbels was not accustomed to reproofs from staff nurses.

But even though this one was not particularly attractive, the Reich Minister was known to be attentive to all women. He gave one of his half-menacing, half-appealing wolfish grins, so familiar from the news-reels, and waved the young man away. "Herr Kapellmeister, the Führer and I express our profound regrets at the injuries you have suffered, and"—he lowered his voice—"our profound sorrow at news of your beloved wife's death." I recoiled in shock. "What did you say, Herr Reich Minister?" I whispered.

Dr. Goebbels was surprised. "Does the Herr Kapellmeister hear this for the first time?" He glared about his group. "Who is responsible for this lapse? It's downright inhumane to withhold such information. Especially from such a distinguished servant of the Reich." He summoned Dr. La Rivière, standing nearby.

"I heard what the Herr Reich Minister said, and I am as baffled as you to learn this," he observed. "We have no knowledge of her. As far as I know, when the Herr Kapellmeister was discovered under the rubble, he was alone."

The young uniformed aide bent over to whisper furiously in the Reich Minister's ear. "Unacceptable," Dr. Goebbels snapped. "Completely unacceptable! I order an immediate investigation—results instantly reported to me." He turned back to me. "My friend," he said, "it is terrible to learn of your loss in this heartless fashion. But don't be ashamed to weep." He gazed into my eyes. "We Germans are stern when we have to be. But we are known for our capacity for profound feeling. Our music is evidence of that—the music *you* have brought to us. Just read our poets, wrestle with the concepts of our great thinkers, penetrate the mysteries of our Aryan past."

As I listened, my mind cleared and I began to remember. I had indeed been speaking with Margarethe. We had met at a hotel. Not where I had first thought, but where Margarethe, pretentious as ever, insisted on: nearby Potsdam, at a place her mother always spoke of and that Dr. La Rivière had accurately identified, the Sanssouci. Other than that, nothing made sense.

You must be aware that I had long wearied of Margarethe and of her talent for filling life with meaningless ritual, with simpering niceness. She had always been so *nice*. My impatience soon converted into irritation and frequently into fury. She was so maddeningly ladylike. The damned dainty teacups, the tiny finger crooked just *so* as she sipped, the ostentatiously refined way she spoke! Sometimes, I deliberately belched loudly in her company. *How had I ended up with such an impossible woman?* No matter what intimacy we achieved, I seemed always to end up—in my own home—like an uninvited guest at a formal tea party. My frequent absences—wartime travels, concert tours on behalf of German culture—were all that prevented me from having murdered her before this. Besides, I think I mentioned that no estates or fortune were attached to that *von* in her name. For all her fastidiousness, for all her Mutti's snobbery, the family was as poor as church mice. The late colonel's wealth had vanished in the Great Inflation.

I was remembering more. When bombs had struck the Sanssouci, the entire ceiling must have collapsed. Now it was coming back to me. Margarethe and I had indeed met for dinner. I didn't expect it to be pleasant, and I was correct. The location was at her request. The dining room was sparsely filled. Frankly, I was surprised that the place was open at all. Reich Minister Goebbels had tried to close down restaurants like this—and also cheerful, naughty cabarets—in the interest of equally shared burdens. On the other hand, Reich Marschall Göring tried to keep them open. He was particularly fond of the girls at Frasquita's. People needed diversion these days, he said.

To one side, an aged string quartet was doing its work. When the obsequious Oberkellner showed me to Margarethe's table, the silly cow actually offered me her hand to kiss. I ignored it. The fatuous social smile faded, but only for a moment. Appearances had to be maintained.

"This place is still so elegant, don't you think, Kappi?"

I studied the menu in silence and ordered a triple Calvados. France had been back in the hands of the Allies for almost a year, but I was confident that the Sanssouci would still stock that wonderful import, bombing or no.

"Will you not ask what I would like?" she asked with a saccharine smile. I sighed. She had not changed. The Oberkellner, eyebrows raised, pencil poised, made to participate in this sad charade. "Please tell him yourself, my dear. I have not thought about what you do or do not like for a long time."

She was actually taken aback. I had long despaired of witnessing genuine emotion in her. *Was she perhaps capable of vengeance or malice?* She had chosen to meet in this Potsdam hotel for a reason. She must long have seethed at the way I slighted her. Perhaps she had finally grasped the point. She must long have wished to get rid of *me* but was reluctant to invite gossip. Two new factors might have changed her mind. One was the recent death of her mother, who had terrified her—except for the defiance she had exercised in marrying me. The other was simply how the war was going—loosened standards, despair, hedonism, end-of-the-world madness. Margarethe, who had never had an original thought, may have wished to settle accounts.

"Kappi," she said coyly, "have you any idea why I wished to see you tonight?"

"Not the slightest," I replied.

The woman was infuriating. I debated whether to walk out right then or eat first. The klaxons warned of an impending air raid. The Oberkellner shooed guests downstairs into the cellar. "Not as comfortable as our dining room, Gnädige Frau und Mein Herr, but we are prepared to serve you here. You will be safe." The sad group of players reassembled and began scraping show tunes once more in this dank place, where waiters had to stumble to and fro with stooped backs so as not to bump heads on the ceiling.

I ordered another Calvados. Margarethe fiddled about in her usual irritating way and finally settled on some local trout from the River Havel—amazing that people actually continued to catch fish with all that was going on.

She took a sip of wine. "For some time now, Kappi, I have not been *contente*, not as a wife should be." Her use of the French word shocked me and immediately transported me back to Vienna, to Krisztina, to the sweet innocence of our first love. "*Je suis contente*," she had whispered to me.

I gazed at Margarethe with loathing. "I have been experiencing profound neglect from you," she was saying but looking not a bit sad or put out. "I have tried to be a good wife, I have tried to be a good German, and I have tried to be a loyal and faithful servant of our Führer. I understand that you are a great artist. I completely understand the need for your absences and travels. I myself come from a family devoted to service. The von Hassels are accustomed to give their strength, their blood, their lives. But, my dear Kappi, even when you are present, you are never there. I hold your body in my arms, speak to you, try to learn what pleases you, but you are never there."

She stared at me with downturned mouth. "I believed the example of my family could inspire you to decency. But I see now there is a quality, a tradition, a breeding that makes me completely different from you. My poor Mutti tried to reason with me, but I refused to listen. I was dazzled by you and believed that I had the same feelings for you that I had for my poor father and now have for our beloved Führer." *Why did I waste my time with this pathetic mouse?*

"I am descended from an old family," she declared. "Behind me are ghosts of an aristocratic, soldierly past you could never understand. Here in Potsdam, my poor father trained as a cadet at the Military Staff College. He was schooled in the shadow of the old Garrison Church, where Frederick the Great lies buried. It was here in Potsdam that he met and courted my dear Mutti. At this hotel my parents held their wedding reception. I do not expect you, Kappi, to understand this. I now realize that you are not capable. You come from dirt, and your conduct reveals it."

She peered to see how I might react. When I made no response, her eyes filled with rage. "I do not stand alone, you realize." Her usually syrupy voice grew louder, despite looks from others. "I am filled with the courage of those who came before me. You have imposed a scandalous separation on me. I have finally decided to make it formal. I have commissioned our family lawyers; they will serve the necessary papers." She blinked away what I considered a crocodile tear. "I do this with great reluctance, Kappi," she said loftily. "I do not know which would have been more horrible—to learn of your death while away from me or to endure your absence of spirit and contempt while at my side." Huberta would have properly labeled this speech operatic. "Our difficulties lie in your utter lack of breeding."

There, she had broken away. Now she could expose me, the grubby parvenu she believed me to be. She would disparage my talents, my accomplishments—my profound services to music, to the Reich, to the world. But I was free!

I smiled. "I cannot tell you how relieved your words make me, my dear. I thank you for your honesty. All this time, I thought you a fragile flower, too delicate for real life, behaving like a dainty geisha. And all this time, you were eating, pissing, and shitting like a real woman. Once in a while actually fucking!" I raised my voice too. She turned pale, then red.

"Thank God, I never depended on you for affection," I continued. "I can tell you, now that we are slamming the doors on this miserable charade, that I have always looked to others for warmth, for love, for passion, for joy, right from the beginning—"

"And don't think I haven't known about every one of them," she screeched.

The quartet stopped playing. The Oberkellner, distraught, hurried to our table and stood, eyes popping.

"And I cannot wait to see the end of you," I roared.

As soon as I uttered those words, Margarethe amazed me. She became openly enraged, hurling insults and obscenities. She hurtled around the table and flung herself on me, spitting, scratching, clawing. A wild animal. *My god, this encounter was ugly, but at least genuine.* Where had this Margarethe been hiding? Had this Margarethe been in evidence throughout our marriage, perhaps I would not have needed to seek earthier women—at least, not as much.

At that moment, as we stared wild-eyed at each other, came the unmistakable howling rush of a falling bomb, clearly heard from the outside, even down here, followed by an explosion. Everybody turned white. The musicians' bows were suspended in midair. Another howl and a second explosion, much closer. There must have been a third—I didn't hear it because the building collapsed on us. I hadn't seen Margarethe since.

All this while, Dr. Goebbels stared down at me, speaking rapidly, but hadn't observed that I wasn't paying attention. We were both unseeing. His eyes were glazed. He addressed not me, but untold thousands, perhaps at some unseen giant rally. It was eerie. *And how had he learned of Margarethe's death?*

Finally, he fell silent and grinned down at me, surprisingly cheerful. "By the way, Herr Kapellmeister, I bring astonishing news from America." I started. *What had he said?* "From America?" I murmured.

"Yes, wonderful news from America. Would you like to know?" He laughed at my disbelief. Then he bawled at the top of his voice so that the entire underground ward could hear. "It's Roosevelt. The greatest criminal in the world! That Saujude has just croaked!" Everything came to a halt. People craned their heads. "He has had a stroke. And, *pfft,* he is no more. It's official. All over the American radio."

"Roosevelt was a Jew?" I asked.

He shared a conspirator's smile. "We're not entirely certain but reasonably sure. We certainly place no credence in that fable about supposedly Dutch ancestors. The family name is Rosenfeldt. Certainly the name is Jewish. Reich Führer Himmler has commissioned the SS State Racial Bureau to carry out studies."

Talking about it excited him. He hobbled rapidly up and down beside my bed. "It makes perfect sense," he cried. "Why do you think Roosevelt led the world Jewish conspiracy to bring down the Nordic peoples? Now he is dead. We still struggle against harsh and brutal enemies, but we shall prevail." His bright eyes peered into mine.

He glanced about and lowered his voice. "Of course, the Führer has set his mind on total victory, a crushing defeat for our enemies—both the Jewish plutocrats of the West and the Jew-trained Bolshevik hordes from the East. Roosevelt's death at this critical hour is truly a sign from heaven. The burdens the Führer carries on his shoulders are not to be imagined. I went to him directly, bearing the news. I said to him, 'Mein Führer, heaven has sent us a divine signal. You are to be congratulated. The archcriminal Roosevelt is dead.' He looked long and deep into my eyes. He actually wept. I said, 'Mein Führer, all the auguries have predicted that Germany's fortunes would dramatically change in April.'

"Not for a long time had I seen our Führer so filled with joy. 'Goebbels,' he said to me, 'I can guess exactly what you are about to say. It's about Frederick the Great, isn't it?' 'Mein Führer,' I replied, 'you never fail to astonish me. You never have to be told anything.' He fixed me with his most frank and generous smile. 'Even today,' he said, 'people still doubt my intuition—to their grave cost.' He gripped and wrung my hand, thanking me for bringing him this wonderful news."

The Reich Minister looked down at me, his face creased in smiles. "I speak of the events of 1763. Frederick the Great was hard-pressed by his enemies in the Seven Years' War. All seemed lost. All at once, the Czarina Elisabeth of Russia inexplicably and miraculously dropped dead. It happened in April, just as with the death of Roosevelt. She had led Frederick's enemies. Her sudden death caused the collapse of the alliance against der Alte Fritz. The Führer believes that such a miraculous day for Germany has dawned again. I believe it too."

In my injured condition, in spite of my being thus favored, it was overpowering to be so close to him, subjected to his enthusiasm. "It is no accident that fate has brought us together in Potsdam, Frederick's city," he chuckled. "The miracle is about to happen again. Have no pity for our enemies. Do not forget who is responsible for all our troubles. The Jews imagined that they could break us, but we are

330

going to dance on their bones. All auguries point to it." His eyes bored into mine.

Then he limped away from my cot and addressed the entire underground room. "Even though Berlin itself is now beset," he cried, "the Führer has given his word: all will be well. Berlin is now a mighty fortress. Fortress Berlin will save us. The genius of German science brings new weapons every day—weapons of unspeakable horror for our enemies. Even at this late hour. Fresh armies under General Wenck are massing, the joy of battle shining in their eyes. They cannot wait to come to grips with our enemies. The Führer has pronounced it; he believes it with all his heart. And I am privileged to bring the message of his unshakable faith to every one of you."

He flung his right arm in the air. "Sieg Heil!" he shouted at the room. And twice more: "Sieg Heil! Sieg Heil!" His aides stood at attention but were silent.

But for a few moans from here and there about the vast cellar, most of the bandaged forms on their cots were silent, might already have been dead, for all I knew. One final triumphant stare, and the Reich Minister hobbled briskly to the door, followed by his entourage. Strange coincidence. I had just been pulled from the ruins of Potsdam, and the spirit of Frederick the Great was supposed to save us at this perilous hour.

Dr. La Rivière approached. "It's a shame to learn of your wife's death in this way. Even one month ago, this kind of inefficiency would never have occurred."

I could barely speak. "But I still don't know what has happened. I remember being dug out of the ruins of the hotel. I remember Margarethe—that's my wife. We were…discussing things. But where has she gone? Why hasn't she been found? And how did Dr. Goebbels know about it?"

"If it's any consolation," said Dr. La Rivière, "I could attribute the confusion to the priorities accorded certain activities and not others. For example, we are excellent at putting each other under watch. Reich Führer Himmler has kindly brought us the benefits of the People's Reporting Service, by which neighbor informs upon neighbor and everything is known, whether true or not. Our leaders need constant reassurance. What are people saying about them? Food, medicines, relief of all kinds can't get into Berlin. Bombing night and day has practically brought the city to a stop. Our armies face the Russians and the Western allies. We don't receive reinforcements or ammunition. Our soldiers die of trivial wounds. But information—informing and reporting—is what's valued." I gasped. He was speaking pure treason. *Had anybody overheard?*

"Two contributions to the war effort operate at peak efficiency," he continued. "One is the SS Death Squads, who roam the city and arrest deserters. Of course, there are many to be found these days. My own son was accused of desertion. He was a medical officer attached to the Fifteenth Corps. He managed to get back after the collapse of the Vistula Front. His unit was in shambles. He was on his way here to make himself useful, trying to find an officer to report to. He was picked up by one of those squads."

"What happened to him?" I whispered.

"They shouted one or two questions at him and hanged him from a lamppost with a sign around his neck. I didn't even get the chance to see him. Let Dr. Goebbels be damned together with his auguries of total war and total victory!" I squeezed my eyes shut, unwilling to hear more. But he would not stop.

"The second efficient element," he went on, "is that relentless gathering of information. The police, the SA, the SS, the Hitler Youth, the Gestapo—there is no lack of busy informers. I'm sure that one of them discovered that your wife had been killed. Why had you not been informed? I have no idea. How did they discover that? Had her body been found? Had it been removed? I could not tell you. Perhaps it was, and perhaps the body was looted before it was identified. But, somehow, it is known. Perhaps somebody who might have let you know feels guilty, terrified, and ashamed. This is a nation of paranoia and guilt." The nurse gave me a sedative. I slept.

* * *

I drifted through morphine into ongoing pain. My head, my chest, and all my bones united in a great throbbing ache. Merely opening my eyes caused me to groan. As my vision cleared, I saw a new visitor. A middle-aged man wearing a hat and a shabby long raincoat, even though we were indoors, sat by my bed, clutching a notebook and pencil. When he saw me stir, he began to talk without any introduction. "I must take down some particulars," he said. Right away, I saw he had a dreadful twitch. Not so much a twitch as a frightening grimace. He would abruptly open his mouth, bare his teeth, as though he were about to bite at me, then snap it shut again—about once every minute or so. It was both horrible and fascinating to see.

"You are Herr Kapp-Dortmunder, eminent conductor of the Staatskapelle Brandenburg?" he managed before another display of jaws and teeth. "Can you tell me the circumstances of your being at the Hôtel Park Sanssouci, the name of your companion, and where she is now?"

"Excuse me, please," I whispered, "I was hoping that you could tell *me* what happened. Besides, you seem to know all about it. I feel weak. I want to rest, need to sleep." Another huge, silent grimace. I should have displayed better manners, but he looked so ludicrous that, in spite of my discomfort, I couldn't help grinning.

"You find an interview with the authorities amusing, Herr Kapp-Dortmunder? I am Obersturmführer Funk of the Gestapo. Heil Hitler!"

What could the Gestapo want with me? And why did it employ as a plainclothesman someone with so grossly identifiable a mannerism as the spasmodic Funk?

"Are you well enough to speak?" he asked. "If not, I will come back later. The only thing is that the longer you wait, the more you will forget." Another violent facial shudder. "We need your account to be as fresh as possible." I felt profoundly exhausted. I had no energy—to talk, even to keep my eyes open. Reich Minister Goebbels' visit had sapped me. I fell asleep even while Funk was speaking.

When I awoke again—after how much time?—feeling was certainly returning. Pain was alive and throbbing throughout my body. I was aware of my bladder too, about to burst again. It was enraging to be dependent in this way. And, on top of all this, also hunger. I had not eaten for days.

Obersturmführer Funk was at my bedside. "Heil Hitler," he said. "You're awake. I thought you might be in a coma, and we were about to lose you." His mocking stare was swallowed by one of his spasms.

"Obersturmführer." I still had to whisper. "Would you kindly call the nurse and tell her to bring my piss-bottle. And the Herr Doktor. Everything hurts." He flushed with anger but found my nurse, who performed her rituals deftly.

Dr. La Rivière appeared. "He must be getting better," the nurse said. "He feels pain." He gently palpated me. "There is still much swelling and tenderness," he murmured. "To be expected, but that should subside." More palpation. I winced. "One good thing, no sign of infection," he added.

"Could you give me something for the pain, Herr Doktor? It's bad." He shook his head. "Sorry. Medications are hard to find, especially anesthetics and analgesics. Reserved for soldiers at the Front, poor devils. If you find it impossible to bear, we could find some more morphine." I didn't know much about morphine, but I feared it.

"Nurse," he said, "you have much to do, but try to keep an eye on the Herr Kapellmeister. He is one of Germany's treasures." I detected an ironic edge. But he actually smiled. He resumed his neutral air when he caught the Obersturmführer watching. "I'll be back from time to time," he concluded.

"Heil Hitler," said Funk. Dr. La Rivière nodded and left.

"I don't want to disturb the Herr Kapellmeister unduly," Funk said, "but I still need his account of what happened three nights ago during the raid." *It had been three nights?* The nurse shook her head and left. Funk took out a notebook and a pencil. "Now, Herr Kapellmeister." There were stabbing sensations all over my body. Fiends were driving knives into me. Sweat trickled down my face. I was feeling worse but managed to nod. After all, I was a German icon.

"Can you tell me what you were doing in the Sanssouci in Potsdam?" How was it the Gestapo's business what I was doing? It was a private matter; he had no right to ask. After the war, I told people about this "act of resistance." People thought I was crazy. "Only your position saved you," they said. "One did not defy the Gestapo." *Well, perhaps.* As I stared into his face, the image of Margarethe flashed before me again. Yes, we had been shouting at each other in public. But, believe me, I really had no wish to share these matters.

"I'm sure, Herr Obersturmführer, you ask questions to which you already know the answers. I was dining with my wife. She disappeared during an air raid. She—or her body—has not been found. Do you know what happened to her?" He remained silent. I became angry and glared back at him. I can only attribute this lack of caution to my injuries and pain.

"Anyway, why is the Gestapo so interested in my whereabouts?"

The Obersturmführer suffered another facial convulsion. "Herr Kapellmeister," he said, "we are in possession of requests for train reservations and travel permits for two. One is in your name and the other is in Frau Kapp-Dortmunder's. But it is known that you and Frau Kapp-Dortmunder had maintained separate residences for at least four years. It is curious that you and she had suddenly found each other again. When did you effect this reconciliation?"

"Again I ask, what business is it of yours, Obersturmführer?"

"Please answer my questions. You paid in advance for those reservations with a check drawn on a Berlin branch of the Kommerzbank." He drew a slip of paper from his briefcase. "Do you recognize your signature? The reservations are for your use—yours and for that of a lady, obviously not Frau Kapp-Dortmunder. We are also interested in that woman's identity." I closed my eyes.

"There is no evidence of a request for return tickets. By the way, had you received those tickets?" I had to think a moment. "No, I had not," I replied.

"Would you happen to know why not?" he asked. I shook my head. "Really, Herr Kapellmeister! You surprise me. A brilliant and informed gentleman like yourself thinking he could leave Berlin at a time like this! Do you really have no idea of our situation?" He stared down at me with contempt.

This is absolutely lunatic: one day, Dr. Goebbels favors me with confidences gleaned from the Führer himself. On the next, the Obersturmführer treats me like an enemy of the Reich. When his face twisted again in one of his violent convulsions, I wanted to jump out of the bed and run away. *Please, someone save me before anything terrible happens.*

"You must be aware that it is impossible to leave Berlin now," he said as though to a child. "The fellow at the booking office didn't inform you of that fact, but he did inform *us* of your intentions. What particularly caught our notice was the destination you requested. You were planning to travel to Lindau, in the far south of the Reich. What commitments might you have in Lindau, might I inquire?"

"I am not accustomed to my movements being questioned, Obersturmführer."

"Of course," he said. "The problem is that you intend to leave just as Berlin must fight for its life. Moreover, my information tells me that you are still fully engaged for the spring season with the Staatskapelle Brandenburg, which has four weeks to run. How could you be in Berlin and Lindau at the same time?"

Hadn't he heard? There were no concerts anymore. How to convey the obvious to this lunatic?

"Obersturmführer, it must be plain that the bombing in recent weeks has become terrible. The British by night and the Amis by day. I have complete faith in the Führer's assurances of final and crushing victory, but I cannot help feeling—"

"Nervous?" he put in solicitously. I was sweating, partly because of the pain, partly because of him. "Obersturmführer, let us be frank with each other." Perhaps I shouldn't have said that. One thing you should not do when speaking with the Gestapo is be frank. It must have been the pain. He waited.

"There must have been a hundred air raids on Berlin since January. People are picking their way through ruins. The Russians are on our doorstep. Of course, I share the Führer's—and Minister Goebbels'— unshakable faith in total victory. But with no buses or taxis, unreliable elevated and underground trains, without gas or electricity, food and water uncertain, how can people make their way to concerts at the Schloss Charlottenburg?"

He frowned and consulted his notes. "What are you doing over there? Does the Staatskapelle Brandenburg no longer use that theater next to the Pariser Platz?"

What was this? Something he didn't know? "Surely you remember, Obersturmführer. That auditorium was hit at least two years ago, has been in ruins ever since." For once, he looked perplexed, which cheered me up. Speaking of Dr. Goebbels reminded me. "Are you aware that the Reich Minister himself has authorized Dr. Furtwängler and the entire Berlin Philharmonic to suspend performances until further notice? And—and—Wilhelm Kempff has canceled *his* recitals. Robert Heger has left the city, as has Ellie Ney. She is of course known for her fierce devotion to the Führer and for her wonderful performances of the Beethoven sonatas—almost as good as mine. I was merely seeking to act in the same wise way."

A strained smile to cover his confusion. Once again, it is the German way—either grovel or terrorize. "I know, Herr Kapellmeister," he said, "what a legend of courage and devotion to the Führer you are as well," he said. "I was present just last summer when you conducted that open-air concert here at the Olympic Stadium. We looked down at the thousand singers and musicians, all Germans, and all communing as one. It was an experience never to be forgotten." He startled me and other patients nearby when he suddenly broke into a raspy baritone. *"Alle Menschen werden Brüder!"* he croaked and beamed down at me. "Never before had I experienced Schiller's words and the music of the divine Beethoven so directly." He actually had tears in his eyes. "German art is the best in the world."

He was truly sickening, perhaps insane. And presumptuous besides. Over the years, high party officials, accompanied by their ladies, had come backstage to tell me how deeply my performances had affected them. *But someone of this stripe?* You could tell just by looking at him that he was a soulless functionary, a brute—necessary for clearing out undesirables and maintaining order, but not to know socially.

I licked my dry lips. "You were at that open-air concert?"

His eyes widened in reproach. "Not as a policeman, Herr Kapellmeister, but as a lover of music and a son of the Fatherland. I am a musician myself, you know. I play the oboe." All at once, he was confiding. "You are too fearful, Herr Kapellmeister. Life goes on in Berlin. I have a ten-year-old son. This evening, after my duties— and before air raids begin—I shall take him to the Odeon to see *Kolberg*, the new film about Gneisenau's epic fight against Napoleon. Such miracles are likely to be repeated." I didn't know whether to laugh or weep.

"It was your destination that seized our attention. As you know, such a destination could be interpreted as defeatist. Perhaps punishable by death," he smiled.

"Now, as for Reich Minister Goebbels," he said, "in addition to the heavy burdens of being minister of propaganda and Gauleiter of Berlin, he has just been named Reich Kommisar of Defense for the city. He will watch to see who follows his leadership. What's more," he went on, "he would immediately perceive that Lindau is right up against the Bodensee—Lake Constance—next door to Switzerland." He raised his brow. "Were you actually planning to make winter sport in April? In any case, it wouldn't matter. There are no trains, no buses, no roads out of Berlin."

"We are cut off?" I asked.

"That's right," he replied heartily. "Now the world will discover what we are made of. We're going to stand and fight until relieved by General Wenck."

I'd never heard of General Wenck. My guardian nurse arrived to rescue me. "The Herr Kapellmeister must rest now."

My visitor rose and bowed stiffly. "Our business is not yet concluded. While we speak of Switzerland, I wish to introduce a fresh matter that we are investigating."

I couldn't repress a groan. "What now, Obersturmführer?"

Another twisted smile. "I'll just mention this for a start. Have you, by any chance, had anything to do with transferring sums of money to Swiss banks?" I went into silent shock. "For some reason," he continued, "the name of Herr L'Orénoque, principal scenic designer at your former Düsseldorf opera, appears to have a connection with these suspected transfers. I'm sure you know that such would be absolutely illegal."

For the first time, I felt afraid. I tried not to reveal it. "If there is anything you want to say to this," he said, "you might consider preparing an appropriate response. You will thank me for helping rediscover your courage." One more Heil Hitler, one more massive spasm, and he left.

The nurse leaned over me. "Are you all right, Herr Kapellmeister?" I was unable to speak. I had never expected the Obersturmführer to stumble on my financial dealings, matters known only to myself and one other person. I had kept mention of these matters as close to myself as possible. I mean, if one cannot trust the Swiss, then whom?

I looked up at this kind and solicitous nurse. But she looked tired, not as young as I had thought. In her middle or late thirties? A plain woman. "It's difficult to understand," she was saying. "One moment, you have Reich Minister Goebbels as a visitor, and the next, you are interrogated by the Gestapo. What on earth is happening?" I was as baffled as she. How indeed had the Obersturmführer unearthed information about my secret banking transactions, the participation of Herr L'Orénoque? That alone would be enough for a people's court. If they also learned about the existence of Huberta, my half-Jewish lover, it might well mean a firing squad.

How to balance Dr. La Rivière with Funk? Herr Richard Strauss's words came back to me, that night I had presented *Rosenkavalier*. He remarked that if our Nazi masters were proud that we could behave like animals, he could compose a musical score for that particular horror, *Variations on the Beast.*

338

Nurse Paulina's hand felt cool on my forehead. "That's good, Herr Kapellmeister. Temperature seems normal, the discoloration is improving, and the swellings are going down." She placed a thermometer under my tongue, withdrew it, and frowned over it in the poor light. Finally, she brightened. That honest, sturdy smile far outshone the mincing sneers of society women. I suddenly craved honesty. The wealthy sluts who had fawned over me in countless gilded reception halls disgusted me. They couldn't hold a candle to this good, hard-working woman.

During that night, sleep eluded me. Obersturmführer Funk was nothing but a menace. He had his claws in me. Berlin was destined to perish, and I together with it. We would be bombed to pieces by the British and the Americans. Then we would be overrun by the Russians, who would grind us to fine powder. One could see what lay ahead. At least, the Americans, British, and French were like us, inhabitants of the West. The Russians were different. The days of Tchaikovsky and Pushkin were done with. These present-day Soviets had no understanding of artists. We were to be overrun by hordes of Mongols and savages. Our salvation depended on accommodation with the West, people who knew about paved streets and running water and who wore shoes.

Was I a defeatist? Call me what you like, but my Third Reich phase was ending. I had left Hungary without regret—the same with Austria. Now it was time to say goodbye to the Reich. The Führer's utterances had become too operatic, like Margarethe's. I didn't understand strategy, but I certainly knew opera. I had produced enough *Götterdämmerungs* not to recognize reality. Nazi grand pageants—Nuremberg rallies, torchlight processions, Olympic Games—had made the heart proud and beat faster. But sometimes productions fail. When that happens, one analyzes what went wrong and abandons or restages the production. One does not stubbornly repeat a poor plan so that the scenery collapses at precisely the same point every night.

Another restless night. I groaned when I opened my eyes. True to his word, Obersturmführer Funk was there again. But instead of his customary smirk, he wore a broad grin, actually seemed happy. The constant pain that had been mine for the past few days seemed lighter but still there as well. However, Funk's demeanor was puzzling.

He glared at me in triumph and launched right in, à propos of

339

nothing in particular. "Good morning, Herr Kapellmeister. You know, I was once privileged to hear Reich Führer Himmler when he spoke about our war of survival against the Jews."

Oh, God in heaven, I muttered. *Not now*. But he carried on.

"I heard the Reich Führer complain that the Germans themselves were the chief obstruction to carrying out this war. Those good, solid Germans may have been all for putting Jews out of business or for setting fire to a few synagogues. But each one of them had a so-called decent Jew they didn't want touched. I myself had to break some stupid German bones in the basement of the Prinz Albrechtstrasse because of this treasonous sentimentality. 'Don't people remember how the Jews stabbed us in the back in 1918?' Himmler shouted at us. 'Don't they remember Weimar? All that degenerate immorality? It's all because of the Jews.' I remember clearly how the Reich Führer looked us in the eye. 'We have the moral right,' he said, 'to exterminate this race that wants to exterminate us.'"

What was all this leading up to? The state had nothing to reproach me for. With regard to the Nuremberg Laws and the anti-Jewish policies of the Reich, I had always publicly done my duty. Everyone would vouch for that.

I began to perspire. The Obersturmführer had been correct. I too knew "a couple of Jews I didn't want bothered"—one in particular. What with the switch in the fortunes of war, it might now be prudent to strengthen pro-Jewish perceptions in the right circles. People like the Obersturmführer would struggle to the end. That was his sworn duty. He was a soldier. But what about tomorrow? Thoughts about tomorrow were behind my attempt to journey to Lindau, which, as the Obersturmführer had correctly noted, was next door to Switzerland. I admit to not having thought out the escape stratagem sufficiently well. And, honestly, no word had reached me, as recently as a week ago, of Berlin's having been cut off. To tell the truth, Reich Minister Goebbels didn't always trust the people with the facts. My information had been unreliable. But wasn't I a sufficiently meritorious person to deserve escape if I chose?

Germany's struggle had been heroic, feats of arms without parallel. We had indeed made the world sit up and take notice. But the game was over for now. On the other hand, our matchless contributions to mankind—to music, art, literature, science, and thought—could never pass into extinction. People like me, transmitters of culture, would be essential for Germany's tomorrow. I was startled when I heard the Obersturmführer say, "The struggle will continue to the last man, woman, and child."

"What are you talking about?" I whispered.

"Reich Minister Goebbels, in his capacity as Berlin's defense chief, has sent a direct communiqué to all army, Gestapo, and police commands. It calls for the utmost exertion at this inspiring hour and proclaims the Führer's faith in final and total victory."

"For my part," I declared, "I want to assure you of my own inextinguishable faith in the victory of our arms. You have inspired me with renewed courage."

He gazed down at me with naked derision, until overtaken by another of his facial spasms. "So far, I have kept my suspicions to myself, Herr Kapellmeister," he said pleasantly. "I remind you that my inquiries are still not at an end. But in your situation, you are not likely to escape. You are where I can find you."

I contained my despair until he had gone. I was helpless and in danger. I had to communicate with someone. *But with whom?* The Obersturmführer had been absolutely correct. I had indeed made plans to leave Berlin, and I would have been gone had I not received that hysterical message from Margarethe begging me to meet her. Because of sentimentality—and, yes, guilt—I had indulged her. Now, the Hôtel Park Sanssouci had collapsed on top of me, all but crushing me to death. Margarethe was dead, they told me, but I was stuck in Berlin, suspected of treason and defeatism. And yes, the Gestapo had it right: I had intended to go to Lindau, and from there hire a boat to take me to Switzerland. Three or four days ago, I still might have succeeded.

I had to get out of the hospital. It was only a matter of time before the Obersturmführer, obtuse as he was, would discover the identity of the woman who was to accompany me. Once that was revealed, all would be lost in the last, spiteful, vindictive throes of the Reich. Hearing what had happened to Dr. La Rivière's son convinced me of that. It truly would be *Götterdämmerung*, the end of everything.

This is what I planned. I had intended to leave Berlin and go to the south in the company of Huberta—of course, you remember, my sweet consolation. No longer in Wilmersdorf—bombed out twice—she was now living in Moabit, a working-class district. We had been seeing each other as often as we could. However, since '42, she had been obliged to exist as what people called a "U-boat," in virtual hiding, because, whether she wore a Jewish star or not—and she refused—it was equally perilous. But I had two trump cards to play in my own fight for survival: my status as an artist and Huberta herself.

First, sooner or later, one of the invading armies would arrive. If it were the Russians, things would be terrible. Those Jew-Bolsheviks wouldn't wait to tear the heart out of us, wreaking pillage, rape, and mass murder. But if one of the Western allies reached us, they surely would respect the reputation of a great musician.

Second was Huberta. I had to find her in all this chaos. You remember that she had magically appeared just after I became engaged to Margarethe. We had been together ever since for ten full-blooded years, not only a difficult and independent lover, but also a devoted and provocative companion. And then—stroke of luck—I had discovered, among her many talents, that she was also half-Jewish! You could say that I had protected her these ten years. Now, she would be my passport to safety.

My guardian-angel nurse, whose name I still did not know, came on duty at 6 a.m., but she was being run off her feet. There had been much coming and going of dead and wounded during the night. Air raids, night and day, were increasing in ferocity. People tried to live—they queued up amid the ruins to buy food or even went to the *Kino*—but things were truly dreadful. Citizens were brought in with crushed bodies and ripped or missing limbs. They mingled with the muddy, bloodstained soldiers—if they had survived—dragged back from Küstrin and the River Oder. The Russians were getting closer. The floors filled with the wounded, sitting along the walls or lying down, waiting for grimy dressings to be changed. Finally, I caught the nurse's attention.

"You need something, Herr Kapellmeister? You see how it is," she said, attempting to pin straggling locks under her cap. "I need to walk," I replied, "go on crutches if I have to." She wearily shook her head. "You know that your ribs and shinbone are fractured. It's much too soon—"

"Nevertheless, I insist that I try. It's important." She hurried off. A few minutes later, Dr. La Rivière appeared, dark blotches of fatigue on his face.

"What is it that you want, Herr Kapellmeister? As you see, we have been driving hard all night. We have not slept." With a sigh, he sat down by my bed.

"I need to get on my feet, one way or another."

"Didn't Nurse Paulina inform you that it was too soon?" So that was her name. "I didn't say I wanted to walk on the leg, but get used to crutches."

The doctor sighed again. "There is no one to help you." Even though it hurt, I reached up to grasp his arm. "For God's sake, Herr Doktor! I am in great danger here. I must leave the hospital and get out of Berlin."

"But this is absurd," he said. "You are in no condition to walk, let alone leave the hospital—or Berlin, for that matter. Do you understand the nature of your injuries?"

"The devil with my injuries," I snapped. "Haven't you noticed? I'm being hounded by the Gestapo."

"Yes, I have noticed. A man of such distinction!" Irony again.

I spoke in a low voice. People bustled back and forth. "The story given out is that my beloved wife was killed at my side in the wreckage of the hotel in Potsdam." Dr. La Rivière raised his brow. "But that is only partly true, Herr Doktor. Yes, that woman was my wife, but hardly beloved. The fact is, for the past ten years, I have loved someone else, a beautiful good woman, and she has loved me." The doctor waited. I swallowed painfully. This was the terrifying moment. "The reason that I hadn't divorced my wife and married the woman I love is that she"—I lowered my voice further, I was trembling—"is Jewish." His expression did not change. "We both feared the worst, but I refused to give her up."

Why didn't the man say something? At last, he stirred. "What a dilemma," he said wryly. "I can tell you something about that. My own wife is Jewish." My mouth sagged. "Her family was 'resettled in the East'—that's what they called it. We haven't heard from them for two years. We are afraid to imagine what has happened to them. On at least two occasions, the Gestapo ordered my wife to the railway station together with other Jews married to Germans. By that time, they must have been the last Jews *not* in hiding. I went together with her. Most of the other spouses were wives of Jewish husbands—I think I was only one among the few husbands there with a Jewish wife. We refused to stand for this attempted deportation. We all gathered outside the building on the Rosenstrasse where they were holding them. We screamed and howled in protest for two days. Yes, Herr Kapellmeister, I actually did that."

I stared at him. *That contained, dignified man?* He had actually screamed at the SS? In the streets? I couldn't comprehend it.

"The SS men screamed back at us," he went on. "They ordered us to disperse. They set up machine guns. We thought we were going to die. Germans killing Germans! Finally, our husbands and wives were released and told to go home. It was a sort of miracle. But we were prepared to die with them. My question is, Herr Kapellmeister, would you have done the same?" His voice was without passion, as though pursuing some philosophical inquiry. "You say your devotion is of long standing. It is perhaps too much to ask that the story be published in Dr. Goebbels' newspaper, but would you have made such a gesture? I never thought *I* could. But just see!" I didn't know what to say.

That afternoon, by stupendous effort by the entire ward personnel, some degree of order was achieved in our "bunker." The dead were carried out, doctors and nurses were able to separate severe wounds from the light, dressings were changed. Orderlies actually managed to scrub bloodstained and grime-encrusted walls and floors. It was a massive undertaking. A miracle of German efficiency!

Nurse Paulina stopped by. "You're a privileged man, Herr Kapellmeister. It's a spring day outside. The Herr Doktor has approved your sitting in the sunshine awhile."

"How do you suggest we accomplish this? I thought I couldn't be moved. And what about air raids?"

"Funny thing," she said, "we had terrible bombing by the Tommies last night, but the Amis didn't come over this morning as usual. It's been quiet all day. You said you wanted some air. I can have you taken upstairs for a while. Don't worry," she added, "you'll be near the doorway. We'll bring you inside if anything happens."

With the help of two orderlies, and a lot of wincing from me, she managed me into a wooden wheelchair. I discovered that, although my chest and right leg were encased in Plaster of Paris, I could bend at the waist. I could sit up. I was trundled up a series of ramps to the sunlight—my first view of it for almost a week, even though it had to struggle through a pall of grit and ashes, heavy with the stench of burning. I was grateful to feel the warmth. Across the park toward the

Havel, I could make out ruins of apartment blocks and churches. I closed my eyes and tried to bask.

I awoke as my chair was wheeled back indoors by two nurses. At the bottom of the ramp, one of the orderlies startled us by rushing out of an inner office, blocking our way. He was gray in the face and shaking. "What's the matter?" I asked.

He gulped. "I'm just sitting down here, having a smoke in the switchboard room. I'm all alone. It's quiet for once. No air raids. All of a sudden, the phone rings. I pick up. A voice with a funny accent comes on the line. 'Hello, Fritz, hello, Fritz,' he says. 'Hello yourself,' I say. 'Who's this?' The voice says to me, 'What do you mean, who's this? This is Ivan,' he says. For a moment, I don't understand. 'Ivan, Ivan!' he shouts at me. Then the voice laughs and speaks in Russian, I guess, to other people. Then he says, 'I bring you greetings from Comrade Marshal Zhukov and the First Byelorussian Front.' I nearly had a heart attack. Then the voice asks if I'm enjoying the afternoon. I ask him what he's talking about. He says, 'A whole day without an air raid. Did you enjoy it? But don't get too comfortable, Fritz. From now on, you're within range of our heavy guns. We're coming to collect the bill for Stalingrad!' That's what he said. Then I hear a lot of laughing, and that's it. The line goes dead." He looked at us, stunned.

Almost immediately, from upstairs at street level we heard two huge explosions. There was immediate pandemonium. Policemen, women ambulance drivers, civil defense workers—faces ashen, weeping, eyes wide in shock, many covered in fresh blood—streamed down into our underground ward, where the staff had just heroically restored some order. One of the women drivers was sobbing. "We heard explosions to the east, from Kreuzberg or the Tiergarten. We looked up at the sky but couldn't see any planes. Then there was a terrible whooshing sound. Two enormous yellow flashes right in front of us in the parking area! Then these two deafening bursts—we were knocked off our feet. I think my eardrums are broken." Others staggered down, more ambulance drivers, messengers, and medical auxiliaries—boys and young women among them—who had congregated during a break to smoke, flirt, and have a chat.

"It's the Russians. They're shelling us now." The orderly who had received the call from "Ivan" solved the mystery. His sergeant, hearing this for the first time, was terrified that the failure to report the intelligence might be laid at his door. Both left at the double to report to an officer.

Everybody was busy with the new casualties. Because of them, I had not been put back on my bed. I was tucked away, still in my wheelchair, in a small storage cubby next to the telephones. Once in a while, a nurse or orderly would check on me. I had no visit all day from the Obersturmführer. I assumed he had been absorbed by new urgencies. By six o'clock, the ward was quiet again, the batch of newly injured attended to. I was pleased to see Dr. La Rivière. "Are we really shelled by Russian guns?"

"That's correct, Herr Kapellmeister," he replied. "An official communiqué from Eisenhower. Everybody heard it in spite of attempts to jam the broadcasts. We'll have no further bombing. The Russians are taking over the attacks. By the way, are the works of Shostakovich and Prokofiev in your repertoire?"

His levity was dangerous, but I had no time to remonstrate. "Herr Doktor, for the love of God, I implore you to use your influence to get me out of Berlin. I already told you, I am in grave danger here. And it's all a ghastly mistake, absolutely without cause, a gross injustice. I must leave."

He pulled over a chair and spoke in an uncharacteristically fierce whisper. "Mein Herr," he said, "how ironic to hear you speak of gross injustice. For twelve years we have lived under maniacs and gangsters. Gross injustice is a way of life with us. I know you are not a naïve man, Herr Kapellmeister. But like many of us, you are possessed of a selective gaze. You choose to see and not see. You choose to know and not know. May God forgive us for the crimes that our beloved Führer committed in our name. And to celebrate which we all cheered and shouted in joy."

"Crimes?" I stammered, glancing nervously at the door of our cubby. He gazed at me with pity. "Please don't insult my intelligence. We are supposed to be the clever ones, yes? The cultivated and the knowledgeable?" He leaned in. "We gave our souls willingly to the devil, you know," he said. "But is this really news to you?"

Was he not going to help me? I had no need of this hand-wringing, but I couldn't move. I was obliged to listen.

"Now, something has occurred that our Führer promised would never happen. The Russians are here. For them, Berlin is the place to crush. I told you what happened to my son. Since '42, he served as a doctor on the Eastern Front. When he was home on leave, he described such horrors—murders, slaughters, burnings, monstrous cruelties beyond description. We were stunned but said not a word. And what about the Jews—his own mother's people? Yes, besides, he was a Mischling, a half-Jew, and always in danger because of it!" He glared as though I were responsible. "I had many colleagues and teachers among the Jews. I said nothing when they were expelled from their posts or driven to their deaths. I woke up only when my own wife was threatened. My son brought nightmare stories from the East. Jews, not famous people but humble men, women, and children without number, shoveled into death. But we huddled in fear."

"Herr Doktor, please. Later perhaps."

He ignored me. "Now, we have reaped the whirlwind, Herr Kapellmeister. It is not swarms of contemptible, helpless Jews that we face. That would have been simple. Now we have an enemy who exceeds even us in savagery. I always said that we made a terrible mistake in Russia. We provoked a devil more terrible than ourselves. Who knows why we had to go there. Did nobody remember Napoleon?" I had thought the same thing. "Now the Russians are here, and they will tear the hearts out of our breasts. But first, we civilized Germans will tear ourselves to pieces. Like mad dogs. Today, everyone is suspect, a traitor, liable to be shot."

I tried to tell him that I realized that.

"Whenever I attended conferences at great centers of medicine or at our ancient universities," he said, "I tried with all my heart to rediscover those decent German colleagues with whom I had done research, or my teachers, the men who had inspired me. After the general meetings, I sought to be in touch with those good men again. With few exceptions, they were difficult to find."

I awaited his next words with fear. "Do you want to know what had happened to them? Like you and me"—he paused and closed his eyes—"and I do not absolve myself, they had all cultivated that selective gaze. They chose not to see. Did they know? Of course, they knew. But being brilliant, thoughtful, subtle men, they concocted the most ingenious reasons for not knowing. They knew. Not only knew, but contributed. Some few were deeply ashamed, but most were not disturbed or even made uncomfortable. They could look me in the eye and enjoy life. I still find it hard to believe. The best and the worst—you cannot tell them apart."

Nurses and other members of the night staff began to filter

through the ward, checking patients and charts. A nurse poked her head into our room and, seeing us in conversation, quickly retreated.

"But, Herr Doktor," I said, "you cannot condemn an entire nation—least of all yourself. I see what you do. You pursue the noblest profession, selflessly, tirelessly, to the detriment of your own health—"

He held up his hand. "I'm sorry," he said, "I cannot listen to such words. They sound hollow and bombastic, something that would emanate from Dr. Goebbels. I can't listen to them anymore." He wiped his eyes and blew his nose. "And you, Herr Kapellmeister? I'm sure you played your own dutiful role in the elimination of Jews from your orchestras, yes? In the elimination of *Entartetemusik*, degenerate music. No Jews, no moderns, except for the approved, boring ones."

What could I say? The times were what they were.

"Herr Kapellmeister, I've been well aware, as has Nurse Paulina, of the incongruity of your visits from both Reich Minister Goebbels and Obersturmführer Funk—two ends of the Nazi social spectrum but equally despicable—being both lauded and hounded by the Reich on the same day. Is that sufficiently insane for you? But no matter. I think I can help you." He lowered his voice further to a barely audible murmur. "I propose to sign a document attesting that you suffered a hitherto unsuspected fatal cardiac arrest, no doubt brought on by your grave injuries. A great loss to Germany."

Now that was extremely creative of the elderly fellow. I brightened. "What would have happened to my body? You don't know the Gestapo."

"But I do know the Gestapo," he said. "They may be relentless, but they don't believe in wasting effort, especially now. They will have too much to worry about. You will have been buried behind the hospital in one of the mass graves that we Germans have made so popular. I imagine that Dr. Goebbels would have mounted a state funeral."

"And what happens next?"

"Some roads to the south are still open. We would have time to send a few more medical convoys out of Berlin, the hopeless cases. You will travel with one of them. I know where you want to go. If you're lucky, you may succeed. The Allies and the Russians are closing in rapidly. But if you go due south from Potsdam, from Babelsberg through Torgau, you may be able to reach Dresden before the Russians arrive. If you meet any Americans, your ambulance markings will probably help you through.

Once in Dresden—or what's left of it—keep heading south." Another glance left and right. "The BBC said an American army, General Patton's, has reached close to the Czech border. It's worth trying."

"Will you come with us?"

He shook his head. "I must stay and do my duty. It may sound ridiculous and far too late. But I should be among the Germans who accept responsibility."

He sounded not merely ridiculous but preposterous. In his own way, he shared the grandiose pretensions of the Germans. Operatic! I was beginning to understand how German lack of reality and over-weening ambition could lead the people into disaster. So surprising in a nation steeped in philosophy and science. After all, I can speak about the Germans objectively as an outsider, coming from Hungary as I do, and having lived in Vienna. The Germans would be inclined to blame everybody but themselves for their own troubles. As the Austrians liked to say, when asked who was responsible for some misfortune: "The rabbit did it!"

"Who will be in charge of this ambulance?"

"We have a number of French forced laborers who have worked for me as medical orderlies. They've done their best, poor devils. They were forbidden to fraternize with the German population, but I'm sure they did their part to father French babies on German women whose husbands were in Russia."

"French forced laborers? Will I be safe with them? I'm still helpless, you know."

"You will be safe," he smiled. "France is still a civilized place. In fact, Herr Kapellmeister, they will be traveling with safe-conduct permits from me. You will have papers attesting that you are one of them, gravely injured in an air raid. All Berlin will celebrate your departure. Fewer useless mouths to feed."

"And why, Herr Doktor, are you doing this for me?"

He gazed up at the low, grimy ceiling. "Let us say that I was touched by what you said about the woman you really loved—you know, your special friend, with the special circumstance. She sounded close to my own special circumstance."

Huberta was already proving useful. But I hadn't seen her for at least three weeks, long before my Margarethe-inspired disaster. *Whom could I dare trust to send a message?* The only person I might think of was Nurse Paulina. And with her, certain interesting possibilities might develop that would preclude Huberta. I could tell that Paulina liked me. But which one would prove more useful? At this stage, having a Jew speak on my behalf—even a half-Jew—could be more valuable than gold. On the other hand, whom might I need more urgently than a skilled, intelligent nurse? And if I decided on the one, how would I persuade her to make room for the other?

"When does your convoy leave Berlin?" I asked Dr. La Rivière.

"As soon as possible," he replied. "There's not much time." From ground level outside, there sounded a deep, muffled roar. Dust drifted down from the ceiling.

I came to a decision. "Herr Doktor, I would like to take advantage of your generosity. And would you be willing to provide an additional safe pass?"

"For whose benefit?"

I swallowed. "For the woman I have loved all these years."

"You mean your special woman? She's here in Berlin?"

I tried to raise myself. "Herr Doktor, can you have her brought here? I can give you her address. It's in the Moabit district. Perhaps try her telephone number?"

"It's better I don't know. It will be difficult enough to get you out. Everybody is nervous. The street patrols are liable to shoot anybody."

Suddenly, I didn't want to abandon Huberta. She was my passport. Also, when I had last seen her, she had managed to remain utterly captivating despite the strains of her own difficult life.

"Hazardous," the Herr Doktor said. "It would be too much to expect of the Frenchmen—having two fugitives, and one of them a Jew." He looked around him warily. "On second thought, if you can trust me with her address, I'll see what can happen. Only it would have to be done later, after you have gone."

I dictated the street number of a quiet courtyard off the Emdenerstrasse. Huberta had moved there after the Wilmersdorf flat had been bombed. I still used to visit there one or two times a month—of course, after taking elaborate precautions. Dr. La Rivière was right. First priority was my safe departure from Berlin. I was not returned to my bed but kept out of sight in my snug cubby room.

No sleep. The rumble of the Russian guns, though muffled, was constant. More restless hours. The doctor returned together with four short, stocky men, who silently and carefully dressed me, inching my legs and arms into trousers, shirt, and sleeves. They finished by making sure that my leg splints and arm slings were prominent.

"Merci beaucoup, messieurs," I grinned. No reply.

At precisely 4 a.m., I was wheeled up the ramps. A convoy of three ambulances waited, utility vehicles with only canvas flaps at the rear. Although April had arrived, there was still a chill in the air. To the east, white and red flashes peppered the black sky all the way from north to south, accompanied by ceaseless rumbling. Once in a while, there were sharper explosions; and we heard shells screaming closer to us, bursting some streets away, but thankfully not in front of the hospital as before.

One of the Frenchmen nudged me and smiled coldly. "Les Russes," he muttered. "Les bolschéviques." I said nothing. "Maintenanent, votre Führer sera kaputt, je crois." They skillfully lifted me into the back of the first ambulance and secured my wheelchair. When Dr. La Rivière approached to say goodbye, their manner became respectful, their affection for him obvious.

"They understand you're in a fragile state," he said. "I don't know the precise condition of the roads, but please be prepared to get bumped or even thrown about. Another thing, I have information that the street patrols are active. And jumpy besides, itching to shoot. I pray that your papers provide sufficient protection." He placed a light hand on my shoulder. "Good luck, Herr Kapellmeister. I don't think we shall see each other again." He turned abruptly and disappeared down the ramp.

The driver of my ambulance started his motor. Through the rear flaps I could see another injured man carried toward my vehicle on a stretcher. He was lifted up and placed on the opposite wall. This new passenger was so heavily bandaged, head and body, that he looked like a mummy or a corpse ready for burial, not moving or speaking. Dr. La Rivière had said there would be no extra riders.

"Who is this one?" I muttered as one of the Frenchmen sat between us.

The man sniggered. "You, monsieur, are a national treasure, according to the good Dr. La Rivière. Me, I am a simple man and have no understanding of things like that. But if Dr. La Rivière says it is so, I believe him. He may be a damned boche, but he is a decent man, and I believe him. Besides"—he paused to strike a match and light up a filthy-smelling cigarette made of ersatz tobacco—"he was once French:

look at his name. Him"—jerking his thumb at the silent passenger—
"he's a different story, monsieur. He's here because of a private transaction that he himself made with us."

That was baffling. I looked over at the other rider. He never stirred.

"Oui, monsieur, this gentleman has made a private arrangement with us that Dr. La Rivière knows nothing about—and that you will never discuss. Compris?"

"He himself made an arrangement with you, to have himself drugged?"

A shrug. "Bien sûr. That's what he wanted. Maybe it's your Führer under all those bandages. He certainly paid us well to smuggle him. He will not move or speak a word for hours." I couldn't understand something like that, a man actually paying money to have himself rendered unconscious.

Our ambulance started off with a heavy jerk. Almost immediately, the poor condition of the roads became apparent. The driver stayed in low gear in order to negotiate bumps and torn surfaces. He was constantly swerving and lurching. After only a few minutes into our journey, he called back to us through his window.

"Attention! Les patrouilles!"

We ground to a staggering halt. The engine panted like an aged bulldog. I heard my countrymen outside barking orders, banging on the side panels.

"Your papers!" they shouted.

Our driver scrambled out to present documents—the same as other members of our convoy. After a minute of silence, I heard the leader of the patrol. "They're all French? We'll see about that." A moment later, he thrust his head through the flaps, holding up a shielded lantern with which to peer at us. He was an SS Oberscharführer (staff sergeant), wearing tank destroyer badges on his sleeve, a hard-faced man. "And what's going on back here?" He fidgeted with his automatic pistol. "You bastards, why aren't you doing your duty to defend Berlin? We need everyone. Are all you Frogs deserters? I'll have you lined up and shot."

The Frenchman took off his cap. "We're all sick men, mon sergent," he pleaded, "not good at fighting anymore. These others have been hurt in the bombing. "Ils sont blessés. Sérieusement, badly injured. Mutilés," he added. He pretended to struggle with German, which I knew he understood. "C'est à dire…sehr verwundet, mon sergent. We have special passes, special permits personally signed by our chief."

The German spat on the floor. "And what's wrong with you?"

The Frenchman responded with a long, wrenching cough right in his face. "Die Tuberkulose, mon sergent. Sehr schlecht." The Oberscharführer jerked his head back. He turned his attention to me and to the silent bandaged body. "Their papers too." The Frenchman fished into a breast pocket for realistically tattered documents.

The German addressed me. "Who are you?" I hadn't expected to be questioned. My French wasn't good. I gestured at my throat helplessly.

"He doesn't speak? No voice?" the German demanded. "And what about him?" He pointed at the "mummy." The Frenchman shook his head. "Très grave," he said.

"Damned stupid Frogs!" the SS man sneered. "No wonder you people can't do anything right, much less fight. The whole lot of you wouldn't be worth shit if you met the Russians. And you actually wangled a petrol ration to drive around Germany with a bunch of corpses! I feel like shooting the lot of you for that alone. Perhaps I should. Last night my boys shot eleven Dutch Waffen SS they caught trying to sneak away from their post. It's no problem for us. You're all the same, you shitty foreigners. What are you doing here, anyway? Can't trust none of you."

Terror clutched at my stomach. *Was our journey to end before it had begun?*

Just then, an unearthly screech that never in my life had I heard before overwhelmed my ears. It swelled in an instant to an unbearable level and ended in a series of six deafening explosions about two hundred yards away. *"Katyushas!"* the Germans shouted as the rockets burst, flinging themselves down on the torn-up roadway. Shards of shrapnel whizzed through the air. Luckily, nothing near us. This broke the tension. They got up, brushing mud off their tunics.

"Let them run if they want," said the Oberscharführer. "They're worthless pieces of shit. I wouldn't waste a bullet on them. Their papers seem all right. It's their funeral. Now get out of here before I change my mind. Heil Hitler!"

The Frenchmen lost no time in returning to the ambulances. We set off once again at the same slow grinding pace, which picked up as we passed Wannsee.

My guardian was mopping his brow. "That's just what I needed, mon ami, to survive four and a half years of this filthy war and be killed just when it's ending." He offered me one his dreadful cigarettes. I accepted it gratefully. My hands were shaking.

"By the way, monsieur," he said with the first smile he accorded me that night, "I want to tell you my name in case anything happens to me and I lose my companions. It's André. André Chevin, from Briey."

"Never heard of it," I said.

"Small village near Metz."

"Enchanté, André. And what should I do with this information?"

His smile vanished. "Idiot," he snapped. "Don't you listen? I said, if anything happens to me, you should do the decent thing, even if you are un sale boche, and get word to my family." He had lost his momentary lightness, this dour Frog. I nodded. After all, I was in his hands.

We bumped along for about an hour. I must have dozed. I started awake when the ambulance stopped. André threw away a cigarette stub, stuck his head through the rear flaps, and whistled. The sun was up. We were in the country, no longer alone in the world. The road behind us was filled—women, children, old men—trudging along, all in our same direction. People were walking by themselves or leading children by the hand. Many carried suitcases or sacks over their shoulders, some struggled to push wagons laden with furniture, family pictures, pots and pans, belongings of every description. Some carts were pulled by horses. There were farm animals, small clusters of cows and sheep. One grizzled old man rode an emaciated horse, holding a young girl and boy in front of him. Strangely, no sound was to be heard, not even crying from the children. All was dumb fatigue and misery. Who were they? They didn't look like Berliners.

André was grinning again. "Sales boches," he chuckled. "I think they're farmers from Silesia—maybe far away as Königsberg—running from the Russians. This time, it's the Germans running. You don't know how much joy this sight gives me."

I could not bear to look at him.

"Mon ami, this reminds me of 1940. Only then it was our children, nuns with schoolgirls, soldiers without their officers. And now, just look at what some time can do. That and a couple of million bolschéviques." He chuckled again.

"But there are women and children here too," I protested.

He became furious, far different from the obsequious orderly he had been with Dr. La Rivière. "Are you completely stupid? You already know that you're un idiot. Yes, I can see that there are women and children here. But the same thing happened to our women and children. The very same thing. And what about the other forced workers from l'Union Sovietique and la Pologne? *Mon Dieu*, what terrible things they had to see done to their wives and children!"

"But what did I say?" I protested. "This is elementary humanity—"

"*Tais-toi*," he hissed. "Or I'll kill you myself, even if you are a so-called national treasure." He took a deep breath. "Monsieur, I used to be what they call a civilized man; but after years among your people, I think I need to drink some blood before the pain goes away. That's right. A taste of German blood would make everything much better."

I began to shake again. Why did everyone need to lecture me? First, Dr. La Rivière. Second, that menacing Oberscharführer. And now, this unspeakably arrogant Frenchman. Just like Dr. Böhm in Vienna. He had humiliated me after the terrible business with Krisztina. Honestly, what had I done? I was guilty of nothing but of being an artist, a man sensitive to cruelty. Nothing more.

I stared gloomily back along the road and was astonished to see not only civilians but also an occasional tank and army lorry in our funereal procession, some actually towing artillery. *Why were they not trying to stop the Russians?*

"The only difference between 1940 and now," said André, "is that the Russians are not flying over our heads machine-gunning and bombing everything in sight just like your Luftwaffe did to our women and children—at least, not yet. But if they catch sight of all this military equipment"—he gestured outside. "We've got to get away from this rabble. It's dangerous."

He signaled to the ambulances behind. All three vehicles inched their way to the side of the road. André jumped down and held a consultation over a map. None among the passing refugees and soldiers exhibited curiosity or sought to ask questions. On the other side of the van, my bandaged, unconscious companion remained silent and unmoving. I was coming to believe that he might be dead. That Oberscharführer had been correct. What was the point of transporting corpses across Germany?

One of the Frenchmen broke away from the group and approached my ambulance. He was not short and stocky like the others. Under his cap, his features looked strangely youthful. I could have fainted from shock when "he" arrived at the tailgate. It was my angel of mercy, Nurse Paulina, dressed in men's rough clothing.

"Good morning, Herr Kapellmeister," she said. "Are you all right thus far?"

"Fräulein, what are you doing here? Are you abandoning Berlin too?"

"You are too intelligent to ask a question like that. If I am to be sacrificed, I'd like to choose the time and place of my death." So much for Dr. Goebbels' call for unity and total war. "I came to see if you needed help," she added.

I was astonished to see her. And I could not believe that a true German woman would leave her post. But first things first. "Fräulein," I begged, "are you by any chance equipped with a piss-bottle. I am dying."

She roared with laughter. The refugees eyed us with curiosity as they stumbled by. Miraculously, she discovered one in the ambulance and deftly eased my discomfort.

"I don't know how I could manage without you, Fräulein," I gasped.

"If I didn't know you better, Herr Kapellmeister," she replied, "that might sound suspiciously like a proposal of marriage."

How refreshing she was. How different from the suffocating Margarethe. "But you don't know me at all, Fräulein," I said. "Perhaps I mean it."

The smile vanished from her face. "This is not the time or place. We are trying to save our lives, Herr Kapellmeister. Germany is finished. I'm not a fool. Everybody hates us, and we are to blame. Look at all these people marching by—hungry, thirsty, and suffering. They are inches from being savages. If they had the remotest idea we were carrying food or medical supplies, they would forget their self-control and tear each other to pieces to grab them."

I sighed and closed my eyes. Another lecture. People were taking everything the wrong way. "Fräulein," I said, "I merely wanted to thank you for helping me."

André returned. "We've decided to head for Stuttgart. A French armored division might be striking in that direction. But we have to get off this road. If the Red Air Force doesn't strafe us, this mob will surely kill us for our supplies. It's too dangerous here."

We crawled along, but at the first opportunity turned to the left down a narrow, unpaved cart track. It was muddy and bumpy, but we were able to make speed because we were alone. André shared his bench with Paulina, who elected to ride with us.

Then came another shock. Because of the unevenness of the road, which caused the ambulance to pitch and sway, the heavily bandaged "mummy" on the other side of the van actually rolled off his stretcher and dropped to the floor with a heavy thump. From under the bandages came loud, deep moans. It was a man, and he was alive. Paulina and André instantly kneeled and loosened the wrappings around the head.

From my wheelchair, I had an excellent view as the face was revealed. At first, it was muddy gray, a corpse coming to life. The eyes flickered open and rolled about without comprehension. They stared up at us angrily, trying to focus. The face suddenly contorted. I thought he was about to sneeze. Instead, a tremendous, silent convulsion seized his features. There came another and then another. I began to laugh. Paulina looked at me as though I were mad, but I couldn't stop. It was one of my typical fits, half hilarity, half hysterics. I wanted to shout and wave my arms, but of course it was impossible in my condition.

"It's Funk," I sputtered, almost helpless with glee. "Of course you remember Obersturmführer Funk, Fräulein? The bravest of the brave, the strongest of the strong, ready to shed his blood for Führer, Volk, und Vaterland." I leaned over him. "Guten morgen, Herr Obersturmführer," I said, "where is your darling ten-year-old son? Who will take him to see the next performance of *Kolberg* if you are not there? Is he good at languages? How long would it take him to learn Russian, do you think?"

Furiously, Funk stared up at me, mouth open, gulping for air, face twitching wildly. More I was unable to say. I was laughing too hard.

Sufficiently hard to make my shattered ribs ache badly.

The next moment, the laughter strangled in my throat. I sudden-ly remembered. Somehow, Funk had learned about my Swiss bank accounts. Who else knew?

* * *

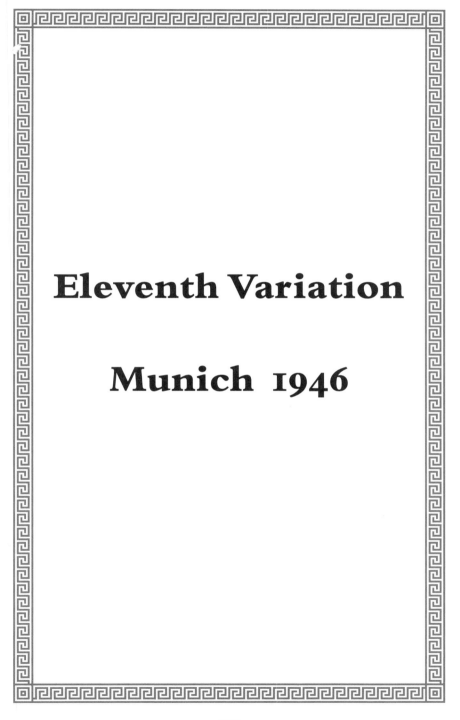

Eleventh Variation

Munich 1946

Palace of Justice. Allied Military Government, Germany. U.S. Army Provisional Headquarters, Judge Advocate General's Corps. March 18, 9:45 a.m.

PRESENT: The Accused, Hermann Kapp-Dortmunder, musician; Maj. Hugo H. Turner, U.S. Army, interrogator; Lt. Harvey M. Greenspan, U.S. Army, interpreter; Sgt. Lucy-Anne Sullivan, U.S. Women's Army Corps, court reporter; M/Sgt. William Jones, Corps of Military Police. Lieutenant Greenspan and Sergeant Sullivan each swore that they would render true and faithful translations and transcriptions of the proceedings.

ACCUSED (*rising*): I want to begin, gentlemen, by protesting in the strongest and most vehement terms to this ordeal. I am not well. As you may observe, I am obliged to use a cane. I have not recovered from injuries I suffered as a result of the Allied bombing of Berlin—

MAJOR TURNER: The accused will resume his seat and remain silent until asked to respond to questions. These hearings have been instituted to investigate the conduct of certain citizens of the former Third Reich, not necessarily leading members of the Nazi Party or of the Armed Forces High Command, before and during the late conflict. The purpose is to determine whether or not those citizens committed, participated in, or benefited from crimes against humanity, military or civilian, by members of the party and Reich government. If evidence of such crimes is discovered, appropriate charges will be leveled, and the accused will stand trial. As for the medical condition of the accused, I have been assured that he is physically and mentally competent.

ACCUSED: I wish to say at the start that I had no knowledge whatsoever—

MAJOR TURNER: Again, I direct the accused to resume his seat and to remain silent until invited to make a statement or asked a specific question. I hope it will not be necessary to station the military policeman at his side in order to restrain him.

ACCUSED (*still on his feet*): I have no wish to violate the rules, Herr Richter (Judge). Perhaps you are not aware that I have been unable to practice my profession for a whole year. Not only am I recovering from crippling war injuries, but I suffer personal and professional hardships that are inhumane and monstrously humiliating—

MAJOR TURNER (*rapping his gavel*): Once again, I direct the accused to be seated and to be silent. Sergeant Jones, I instruct you to stand at the side of the accused and be ready to remove him from the hearing room should he once again ignore my instructions. I have no compunction about deferring this case in order to deal with other matters. It is the accused who requires a certificate of denazification in order to resume his profession, not I. (*The accused sat*) Now then, for the record, the accused will state his name, age, address, and profession.

ACCUSED: I am Hermann Kapp-Dortmunder, thirty-six years old. I reside at the Hotel Askanischer Hof in Berlin—but this is utterly absurd, Herr Richter. Everybody knows who I am and that—

MAJOR TURNER: Just a moment, just a moment, please. Has the accused always been known by that name?

ACCUSED: I was born under the name Ferenc Kapp.

MAJOR TURNER: Well, what is your origin? What kind of name is that? It doesn't sound German to me.

ACCUSED: My first name is Hungarian.

MAJOR TURNER (*addressing Lieutenant Greenspan*): What did he just say? He was mumbling. Did you catch it?

LIEUTENANT GREENSPAN: Sir, he said it is a Hungarian name.

MAJOR TURNER: Is the accused a Hungarian national?

ACCUSED: I was born a citizen of the former Austro-Hungarian Empire. I decided some years ago to identify myself with the dynamism of the Greater German Reich. This is something that you, coming from a powerful nation, Herr Richter, might understand.

MAJOR TURNER (*addressing Lieutenant Greenspan*): Lieutenant, are you accurately rendering the remarks of the accused into English?

LIEUTENANT GREENSPAN: Yes, sir, to the best of my ability.

MAJOR TURNER: Is the man actually attempting to talk his way to the gallows?

ACCUSED: Would I be permitted to ask a question of this tribunal?

MAJOR TURNER: In spite of repeated admonitions? Perhaps I was remiss not to have requested a psychiatric evaluation.

ACCUSED: Just as an aside, I was admiring the superb German-speaking ability of your interpreter, Herr Richter, and I wonder how he acquired it—idiomatically correct and with a cultivated accent.

MAJOR TURNER: The man is impossible. Lieutenant, do you feel like responding? You are not obliged to.

LIEUTENANT GREENSPAN: No objection, sir. I was born in Magdeburg and went to school there. In 1938, my parents sent my sister and me on a *Kindertransport* to seek refuge in England. The next year, we were sent to America. Leaving Germany when we did saved our lives, but we haven't heard anything of our parents since we left.

MAJOR TURNER: Does that satisfy the accused? Will he now respond to our questions, not the other way around? He is aware, is he not, that the Reich and its so-called dynamism are thankfully things of the past. They are what have earned Germany the opprobrium of the civilized world.

ACCUSED: I just wanted to observe that it hardly seems fair that the interpreter in these proceedings is a former German citizen of the Jewish faith and who, therefore, might not be objective—

MAJOR TURNER (*rapping his gavel*): Does the accused not understand? My patience is at an end. At the next provocation, this case will be held over indefinitely. He has not worked for a year? Would he be willing to try for two years or three? If he determines that Allied military justice is lacking, perhaps he would be interested in learning about other versions. This case might be transferred to the Soviet Zone for adjudication.

ACCUSED: I apologize, Herr Richter.

MAJOR TURNER: Now then, let's return. It is documented that the accused enjoyed a special, protected relationship with the former propaganda minister, Joseph Goebbels—and by implication, with Hitler himself—by means of which he secured prominence, reputation, and wealth.

ACCUSED: I don't know what the Herr Richter means. I feel secure that I owe any advancement I enjoyed to my own gifts and hard work—

MAJOR TURNER: Please answer the question. Were you acquainted with Goebbels?

ACCUSED: Yes, of course I was. The late Reich Minister was a patron of the arts. It was inevitable that he would take an interest in me.

MAJOR TURNER: Did you consider yourself his friend?

ACCUSED: It didn't matter whether or not I considered myself his friend. The point was that the Reich Minister had noticed *me*. I had nothing to say. In any case, I saw no point in contravening the wishes of one of the most powerful men in Germany.

MAJOR TURNER: And because of his wishes, your career flourished?

ACCUSED: Is that fair to say, Herr Richter? As I have just observed, I had been building my career for many years. I have always loved music with utter devotion—

MAJOR TURNER: Weren't you instrumental, if I may use the word here, in the expulsion of Jewish musicians from that opera house in Düsseldorf? Are you saying that it's admirable to love music and at the same time behave despicably to musicians?

ACCUSED: Herr Richter, this is a complicated issue. I hardly know where to begin. You must realize, while the party was in power, we Germans were not masters of our own house. We were completely in the hands of our leaders. Reich Minister Goebbels dictated artistic policy; he and the entire regime, of course led by the Führer, were in charge of the nation. Those leaders, for reasons I fail to understand, were obsessed, utterly obsessed, with the idea that the Jews were responsible for all the bad things that happened to the German nation in 1918—and for hundreds of years before that.

MAJOR TURNER: You deny subscribing to those opinions?

ACCUSED: Not only do I deny them, I am horrified that the leaders of the country would carry out policies that may have harmed the Jews.

MAJOR TURNER: May have?

ACCUSED: As the Herr Richter is aware, the newspapers have been filled with terrible accusations and rumors—

MAJOR TURNER: Rumors?

ACCUSED: They are hardly to be believed. These wild estimates of hundreds of thousands, millions of deaths! I refuse to believe them! They do not make sense. They are directed against the most highly educated and cultivated nation in the world.

MAJOR TURNER: Why are they are hard to believe?

ACCUSED: It stands to reason. I personally know of no one who might have committed such acts.

MAJOR TURNER: Indeed? Does the accused recognize the name of Wolfgang Pietsch?

ACCUSED: Of course I recognize the name. Wolfgang Pietsch did nothing wrong in his entire life. He was not politically prominent. He was a hardworking businessman, a concert manager, and a record company producer. I owe him much, much more than I can ever express. Excuse me, please, may I have some water? I am overcome by emotion when I think about him and the horrible way he died.

MAJOR TURNER: The records indicate that Wolfgang Pietsch was indeed a person highly important in the career of the accused. He was also responsible for the looting of property and art works owned by Jews, and for whose deaths he may have been responsible. It is an irony that his own death was caused by a Russian prisoner of war whom he employed in his household as a slave-labor gardener, part of the spoils of war.

ACCUSED: Herr Richter, the man was beaten to death with a shovel. I feel quite overcome. He was like a father to me.

MAJOR TURNER: Were you aware of how he acquired his property?

ACCUSED: Of course not. How should I have known?

MAJOR TURNER: Would a father not have told his son things of this nature?

ACCUSED: The Herr Richter is mocking me. I meant that, like a father, Herr Pietsch guided my career, advised me on what, and what not, to say or do.

MAJOR TURNER: Would that include what I referred to earlier, namely the expulsion of Jewish musicians from your opera house in Düsseldorf?

ACCUSED: No, no. That unfortunate episode occurred before I knew Herr Pietsch.

MAJOR TURNER: Yes, the accused is quite correct. My records tell me that you ousted the Jewish musicians in Düsseldorf several years before you met Pietsch—

ACCUSED: I beg the Herr Richter's pardon. I did not, as you say, *oust* anyone. The Reich government laid down those decrees, known as the Nuremberg Laws, the results of which, when carried out, were horrifying. They included—

MAJOR TURNER: The accused need not enumerate the terms of the Nuremberg Laws. They are well known. Essentially, it is the position of the accused that he was carrying out orders. Is that not so?

ACCUSED: Herr Richter, I had no choice in the matter.

MAJOR TURNER: What does the accused mean, no choice?

ACCUSED: I don't understand the question.

MAJOR TURNER: What is there difficult to understand? Was the accused obliged to obey orders? Was he a member of a military organization? Was Germany in a state of war in 1935?

ACCUSED: You could say that, in a certain sense, the Reich considered itself at war. And in a war, drastic measures sometimes have to be taken to save the nation—

MAJOR TURNER: By eradicating Jews from German life?

ACCUSED: Please, Herr Richter you were not here. You didn't know what it was like. The Reich had lost its way. It was the Führer who restored the nation's balance and direction, pulled it together, gave us promise of a brighter future…and…

MAJOR TURNER: Go on. Why has the accused so abruptly fallen silent? What brighter future? I invite him to continue. This is fascinating.

ACCUSED: Forgive me. I had not intended to speak in this vein. I believe the question concerned why I felt I had to carry out the terms of the Nuremberg Laws.

MAJOR TURNER: That is correct.

ACCUSED: What was a loyal German citizen supposed to do? I *had* to carry out state policy.

MAJOR TURNER: Had to do it?

ACCUSED: Yes, had to do it. What were the alternatives? Should I have thrown away my career, gone abroad, lived like a vagabond, without identity or a mother tongue to sustain me? What are you suggesting, Herr Richter?

MAJOR TURNER: What about men like Bruno Walter, Otto Klemperer, Kreisler, Leinsdorf, and all the other musicians who were forced to leave? Did not they and countless others do the same? They managed to remain alive. And, amazingly, they thrived. Would you not have experienced such a fortunate outcome, given your gifts, had you followed them into exile?

ACCUSED: But what have such men to do with the case? First of all, they are not actually Germans. The Herr Richter has just demonstrated the Reich government's point, that these men—these Jews—were able to live and prosper anywhere. Historically, these people have always been wanderers. Just take your own interpreter: the gentleman says he was born in Magdeburg but has settled down and managed to prosper without harm or effort in his new country. I happen not to share that tradition. That's all.

MAJOR TURNER: Sergeant Jones, I instruct you to take the accused to a holding area and watch him carefully. We will resume in fifteen minutes. I require some air.

ACCUSED: Herr Richter, I am eager to proceed with all dispatch—

MAJOR TURNER (*raps his gavel*): These hearings are recessed for fifteen minutes.

* * *

MAJOR TURNER: Let the record indicate the resumption of these hearings at 11:15 a.m. I remind the accused that he is still under oath. I want to return to the issue of the Jewish musicians you expelled from the Düsseldorf opera. By any chance, did you keep in touch with those men? Were you at all concerned about their welfare, fellow artists, with whom you had performed for years? To hear you describe it, you had created art together. Can one be indifferent to the fate of such creatures?

ACCUSED: Again, Herr Richter, these are not simple questions. I say once more, you had to have been here in Germany to understand. And I say again, it would have meant the end of all I had worked for if I had defied the government. And for what?

MAJOR TURNER: So the answer is no. You were not concerned about the men you discarded like so much rubbish—or their careers, families, and children.

ACCUSED: (*inaudible response*)

MAJOR TURNER: Please speak up. We were unable to hear you.

ACCUSED: I said, perhaps I might have done things differently.

MAJOR TURNER: Oh? And how would you have handled your government?

ACCUSED: The Reich government would not have been easy to handle, as you put it. Perhaps I could have gone abroad.

MAJOR TURNER: Even though not a Jew? Interesting. In connection with those expulsions, what was the role of the chairwoman of the board at your opera company, Frau Augustina von Krefeld?

ACCUSED: You mean about the enforced departures of the Jewish musicians?

367

MAJOR TURNER: Precisely.

ACCUSED: It is no secret that Frau Augustina—unlike myself, I should point out—was indeed a member of the party. It was she who was responsible for creating a virulently anti-Jewish atmosphere at the opera. In light of both the Nuremberg Laws and that virulent atmosphere, there was nothing I could do.

MAJOR TURNER: Are you suggesting that you and she were in conflict?

ACCUSED: Not in conflict exactly. But our differences grew to such a dimension that it was impossible for me to remain in Düsseldorf.

MAJOR TURNER: Frau von Krefeld has already been questioned at her home in Düsseldorf in connection with these proceedings. Her account of your separation and yours do not agree. Even though she is of advanced years, she has indicated her readiness to appear at these hearings to testify. Would it serve any purpose were she to do that? She could be here in Munich by tomorrow afternoon.

ACCUSED: I feel that nothing useful would be served by her appearance. As you say, Herr Richter, the lady is afflicted by advancing age, and I would doubt the reliability of her memory. There were other issues, certainly, at play—

MAJOR TURNER: Evidence indicates that in 1941 you received an offer from the late Herr Pietsch, an offer so compelling that, without notice of your intentions, you abruptly withdrew from your obligations at Düsseldorf, abandoning ongoing projects—

ACCUSED: I knew that she would accuse me of something like this. The fact was, legally, I was not bound to the lady.

MAJOR TURNER: I have not the slightest interest in that dispute. What concerns me is that there were no apparent differences between you and Frau von Krefeld over the expulsion of the Jewish musicians. You performed the act, and she assented.

ACCUSED: That was not what I meant to say—

MAJOR TURNER: It is of no importance, other than to indicate the accused's lack of veracity or decency. If it comes to that, all these expelled Jewish musicians did possess valid contracts, which did nothing to help them. The testimony of Frau von Krefeld emphasizes the undeserved brutality of the accused toward his benefactor. Unhappily, the accused cannot be prosecuted for his abuse of Frau von Krefeld. In any case, both she and the accused behaved despicably toward their

Jewish musicians in that they carried out, or did not protest, application of the Nuremberg decrees. The accused may have treated his benefactor callously, but she, on her part, accepted what happened to her musicians. In my opinion, they deserved each other. Has the accused any comment to offer?

ACCUSED: Nothing at this time.

MAJOR TURNER: Let us turn to another matter. Not only did the accused enjoy a privileged relationship with former Propaganda Minister Joseph Goebbels, he also maintained a spirited correspondence with Hans Frank, one of the major defendants currently on trial in Nuremberg. As you well know, Frank was governor-general of part of Occupied Poland, known in Reich parlance as the *Generalgouvernement.*

ACCUSED: Minister Frank is a most cultivated gentleman. I have never met him and know him only as a devoted lover of music and the fine arts—

MAJOR TURNER: You are surely aware that Hans Frank is on trial, together with codefendants Göring, Hess, Ribbentrop, Keitel, and others, and faces the death penalty for mass murders committed in the territories he administered. I would be happy immediately to transfer this case to Nuremberg if the accused thinks he has something to contribute to that tribunal—or, again, to the Soviet Zone.

ACCUSED: May I respectfully state that that will not be necessary.

MAJOR TURNER: I'm glad to hear that. May we proceed. What in the world would the director of such organizations as the—help me with the pronunciation, Lieutenant, if you, please—

LIEUTENANT GREENSPAN: Sir, the Staatskapelle Brandenburg, the Westphälische Staatsoper—

MAJOR TURNER: Thank you, Lieutenant. Why in the world would the accused have been in regular communication with a man whose own countrymen, now the war has been lost, have labeled a sordid butcher?

ACCUSED: As I have already stated, Herr Richter, I was acquainted with the governor-general purely as a fellow lover of music, poetry, and painting.

MAJOR TURNER: What an amazing people you are! The Nuremberg Tribunal has already heard that Frank expanded the orders issued by SS Security Chief Reinhardt Heydrich, which brought about the slaughter of millions of Jews and Poles. At the same time, like Herr Pietsch, he loved art so much that he engaged

369

in the wholesale looting of it for his personal enrichment. The accused declares that he is an artist and therefore above suspicion. Hans Frank loves music, we are told, which somehow mitigates his crimes. Is the accused aware that the murderous Heydrich, before his assassination by Czech partisans, is described as having been a sensitive and exquisite violinist—could have been on the concert stage?

ACCUSED: Herr Richter, I never met either of the men you are discussing, and I swear I know nothing of these sad events.

MAJOR TURNER: No, of course not. None of you knows anything—except when you are cornered! Has the accused been informed that the defendant Frank has admitted his guilt before the Nuremberg Tribunal? Actually expressed his profound contrition. He has converted to the Catholic faith and asks God to forgive him. It wasn't his fault, he swears. He was misled by your Führer! Now I ask you again, what was the nature and content of your frequent correspondence? How did you have so much to say to each other?

ACCUSED: The governor-general, for some reason, was in the habit of communicating with me on the subject of certain individuals—musicians—who had caught his attention and thought that I would be interested in hearing about them.

MAJOR TURNER: What sort of individuals?

ACCUSED: Promising young musicians, usually, with whom he came in contact, who he believed displayed unusual talent and deserved a chance for wider recognition.

MAJOR TURNER: The accused makes the defendant Frank sound as though he was engaged in concert management rather than the wholesale extermination of a civilian population. Were these individuals usually women?

ACCUSED: Many were women, yes. But not all.

MAJOR TURNER: Of what nationality were they?

ACCUSED: German, of course. Members of the Wehrmacht, the Waffen SS, and so on. I recall that he was enthusiastic about one member of a women's Luftwaffe medical unit, Magdalena Mertens, who he said possessed an extraordinary soprano voice. The governor-general is said to have often held musical soirées at his residence in Krakow. You must understand, Herr Richter, that musical training and appreciation are important fundamentals of a German education—

MAJOR TURNER: Every time I'm made aware of this, I experience shock and disbelief. In fact, it makes me feel unwell.

ACCUSED: I'm not sure what the Herr Richter means. It's absolutely true.

MAJOR TURNER: Never mind. Go on.

ACCUSED: The governor-general was eager that someone influential in music be told about Fräulein Mertens and, if possible, see that she met the right people.

MAJOR TURNER: Which you managed to do, despite your heavy commitments.

ACCUSED: Which I managed to do—which I was happy to do. The young woman in question turned out to be extraordinarily talented. The governor-general had been absolutely right. It would have been criminal if she had not been noticed. Magdalena was released back to Berlin by special dispensation of the governor-general and, with my help, gained entrance into a superior music school. It turned out that she was a natural artist. Within a year, she was on the recital stage. People were uttering her name in the same breath as that of another of Germany's great singers, Elisabeth Schwarzkopf.

MAJOR TURNER: I remind the accused that we are not participating in a polite discussion over tea. How does the accused respond to the charge that he aided these special friends of Hans Frank, not only out of admiration for their musical abilities, but rather because Frank provided the accused with opportunities to enrich himself with quantities of foodstuffs, works of art, textiles, gold, and silverware looted from Jewish and Polish citizens within the jurisdiction of the *Generalgouvernement*. Further, that—following the example of his own mentor, Wolfgang Pietsch—he accumulated considerable treasure from proceeds of the sale of these properties. How does he respond to this?

ACCUSED: With the most indignant and heartfelt denial.

MAJOR TURNER: I see. Would it interest the accused to learn that this tribunal is in possession of sworn affidavits from one Gunther-Pierre L'Orénoque, former chief designer at that opera company in Düsseldorf—

LIEUTENANT GREENSPAN: Sir, the major means the Westfälische Staatsoper?

MAJOR TURNER: Much obliged to you, Lieutenant. This L'Orénoque testified that, over a three-year period, you shipped to him, as I say, large quantities of foodstuffs by military transport, including cured hams and other preserved meats, beet-sugar, and sacks of grain.

Hams and sacks of grain, for God's sake! In the middle of a war where your people were dying like flies! L'Orénoque declared under oath that you had instigated his complicity in this enterprise, that Hans Frank was the source not only of these foodstuffs but also of paintings, tapestries, Jewish religious artifacts, and other valuables. These were regularly smuggled across the border to Switzerland and sold, the bulk of proceeds going to Frank, a smaller portion to you, and yet a smaller, but still significant share, for L'Orénoque. Would the accused like to reconsider his denial?

ACCUSED: I am shocked to hear such an accusation by Herr L'Orénoque. I have not seen him since I left the Westfälische Staatsoper in 1941. He cannot be serious. I have known him only as a man of earnest devotion to his craft, a man of good spirit. Why would he say such things? I would like the opportunity to confront the gentleman.

MAJOR TURNER: I fear that is not possible. L'Orénoque was seriously wounded after having been called up to join an auxiliary militia—

LIEUTENANT GREENSPAN: Sir, the Volkssturm—

MAJOR TURNER: Precisely, Lieutenant, to be a member of such a unit. He was severely wounded and taken prisoner while fighting in the vicinity of Düsseldorf by elements of General McLain's Nineteenth Corps. He subsequently died. His sworn statement was in the nature of a deathbed confession and is therefore taken seriously. If the accused's description of him is correct, it makes his statement all the more plausible.

ACCUSED: How can I respond to such an accusation, Herr Richter? I have never studied the law, but the absence of your chief witness against me—would not that be a weakness in your allegations? I'm surprised that the Herr Richter has not attempted more with what would be equally laughable allegations of my anti-Semitism.

MAJOR TURNER: Why does the accused raise that particular issue? I wish to further examine his participation in wholesale plundering, looting, and spoliation. Claims by the accused that he was merely furthering musical careers and thereby enhancing German culture are ludicrous. Our investigators are attempting to scrutinize the Swiss records. Incidentally, the Swiss authorities must have guilty consciences themselves, the way they block access to information about Nazi use of their banking system. Indeed, we have information from another source regarding this matter. It appears that the accused himself was the object of an investigation by the Gestapo in this matter. It's remarkable that he was being scrutinized by his own government for illegal transfers of wealth abroad. That investigation, according to our notes, was in process of being conducted by a man named Funk. It provides stronger incriminating links between the accused and Hans Frank. Does the accused recall having been questioned by the Gestapo officer, Funk?

ACCUSED: I have no knowledge of him. But, Herr Richter, I must emphasize that I can present evidence that I protected Jews.

MAJOR TURNER: I would be glad to hear it. But haven't we just heard information that strongly suggests that the accused directly committed and colluded in anti-Jewish acts in Düsseldorf and Berlin? As well as by sworn allegations of the proceeds of his arrangement with the defendant Frank. But I'm curious. Is the accused eager that we turn our gaze away from the *Generalgouvernement* and direct it elsewhere?

ACCUSED: Not in the slightest, Herr Richter. But I have nothing further that may be of use.

MAJOR TURNER: Well, perhaps I can assist your memory. In statements of your activities during the war years, which we requested of you—and which you swore were complete and comprehensive—you say nothing about a one-week visit that you paid to Theresienstadt in the early summer of 1943.

ACCUSED: Yes, the Herr Richter is absolutely correct. I ask his pardon for omitting this. Much has happened during these years, and as he says, it was only a brief visit.

MAJOR TURNER: What were the circumstances? What connection did the accused have with a Bohemian transit camp for Jews on their way to extermination?

ACCUSED: Please, Herr Richter. Again I swear that I had no knowledge of this.

MAJOR TURNER: The accused was not aware that Jews were rounded up and deported? He was not aware of that?

ACCUSED: Of course I was aware of resettlements. But Theresienstadt was special.

MAJOR TURNER: Yes? Special in what way?

ACCUSED: Reich Minister Goebbels had emphasized that this was but a first step in the Führer's vision for a solution to the age-old Jewish question. The Reich Minister was extremely sensitive to accusations from abroad about alleged mistreatment of the Jews. After the party came to power, not everybody appreciated our new political system. It presented problems for some. The simple fact is that, as soon as we Germans had defined our mission, the Jews no longer felt comfortable in Germany. You could say it was by mutual consent. The party had a plan, which was to move Jews outside the German sphere of influence. Theresienstadt was a step in that direction. The party also wanted to dispel the slander of inhumane treatment and show the world with what humanity and consideration the Jews were treated—even at the expense of the war effort.

MAJOR TURNER: And what precisely was the role of the accused in this?

ACCUSED: In my capacity as a musician, as a Kapellmeister, I made a thorough inspection of the place. Wherever I went, I observed that the Jews were busy, absorbed in meaningful activity. Shoemaking, carpentry, furniture building—of course, tailoring, at which many were already adept. All the useful crafts. And, most important, the arts. Many were happily engaged in design, painting, and sculpture. And what about music, you may ask? Theresienstadt possessed an orchestra, an opera company, and several chamber ensembles—all of creditable quality. That's why I was sent there, Herr Richter. That's what I observed. That's what I reported to the Reich Minister.

MAJOR TURNER: Did the accused come across people he knew in this musical paradise for the Jews?

ACCUSED: Strangely, Herr Richter, I did. Someone I had not seen for years.

MAJOR TURNER: Who was he? I'll bet you and he fell into each other's arms.

ACCUSED: The Herr Richter is pleased to make light of it. The man's name was Klein. He used to be principal cellist in the Westfälische Staatsoper. Excellent musician!

MAJOR TURNER: So you and he were on good terms.

ACCUSED: The very best! In fact, I was desolated to lose him. Were it not for the actions of Frau von Krefeld—

MAJOR TURNER: Once again, the accused seeks to lay responsibility elsewhere. We have an affidavit from one Sigmund Lehrmann, a Jewish former violinist in the opera orchestra, who swears that, during a nighttime conversation held in a hired limousine in 1935, you refused to intervene when he and Klein, the cellist, informed you that the Jewish members of the orchestra had been expelled from their posts. Lehrmann testifies that Klein responded to the refusal by spitting in your face. Do you recall the incident? I consider it a persuasive detail.

ACCUSED: I would certainly remember such a thing, had it occurred.

MAJOR TURNER: So Sigmund Lehrmann was lying. Would it sadden the accused to learn that the cellist, Walter Klein, whom he admired so much, was later taken to Auschwitz, with most of the other Theresienstadt musicians and their families, and there gassed and their bodies incinerated. As is the German custom, state functionaries kept excellent records, and many of these records have survived, despite attempts to destroy them. We know when Klein was transported. We know the date of his death.

ACCUSED: I am horrified to hear that, but I cannot believe it. As for Auschwitz, I have no coherent idea of it. I would say that many Germans are in a similar position.

MAJOR TURNER: Indeed! I am astonished to hear the accused make that statement. Would he care to reconsider it?

ACCUSED: I don't mean that literally, Herr Richter. Of course, many Germans have heard of the place, but most would be ignorant of alleged crimes—

MAJOR TURNER: Let's say the accused is correct. Let's say many Germans are ignorant of the crimes. But that would hardly be true for the accused, would it?

ACCUSED: I don't know what the Herr Richter means by that.

MAJOR TURNER: I ask again, would it be true for you?

ACCUSED: Would the Herr Richter object if we might have a break in these proceedings? I see by my watch that it is 12:15 p.m. I would much appreciate a pause in order to visit the rest room. In addition, a friend of mine, I know, is waiting outside with sandwiches and a flask of coffee.

MAJOR TURNER: No objection at all. Good suggestion. Of course, the accused will be under supervision. We shall reconvene at 1:30 p.m. sharp. Sergeant?

SERGEANT JONES: All rise. These hearings are recessed until 1:30 p.m.

* * *

MAJOR TURNER (*raps his gavel*): We are once again in session. Did the accused enjoy his sandwiches and coffee?

ACCUSED: I thank the Herr Richter for his consideration. Before we continue, may I once again beg the Herr Richter's indulgence. The friend whom I mentioned, the friend who brought me my lunchtime refreshments, is a lady with whom I have enjoyed a special and intimate relationship for the past eleven or twelve years. By the gift of great good fortune, we have rediscovered one another after the horrors of war and destruction. She is a lady of impeccable reputation who knows me well. She stands ready to give evidence on my behalf.

MAJOR TURNER: Who is this lady?

ACCUSED: I hesitate to reveal her name should she not be called at this time.

MAJOR TURNER: Lieutenant Greenspan will secure that information for use if needed. In any case, this is an investigation, not a formal trial.

ACCUSED: I should mention that she is Jewish, a Jewish woman, willing to speak on my behalf.

MAJOR TURNER: I take the request under advisement. In due course, the accused will be notified whether or not we hear this woman's testimony.

ACCUSED: I am grateful, Herr Richter.

MAJOR TURNER: Now, would the court reporter refresh my memory? What was the last substantive question before lunch, please?

SERGEANT SULLIVAN: Sir, you asked, "Let's say many Germans are ignorant of the crimes. But that would hardly be true for the accused, would it?"

MAJOR TURNER: Thank you, Sergeant. As you know, I was referring to crimes against humanity committed at Auschwitz. Has the accused considered a reply?

ACCUSED: I don't know how to answer such a question.

MAJOR TURNER: Doesn't the accused mean, once more he doesn't know how to answer the question?

ACCUSED: Herr Richter, I have been advised that there exists in the United States Constitution a prohibition against self-incrimination.

MAJOR TURNER: Such constitutional protections are not available to the accused, and it is futile for him to pursue them. I remind him once again that these hearings are held by authority of the Interallied War Crimes Tribunal to investigate whether there are sufficient grounds for prosecution and trial. The question stands. Does the accused claim ignorance of the purposes and functions of the Auschwitz camp complex, yes or no?

ACCUSED: I state categorically, Herr Richter, I did not know.

MAJOR TURNER: Well, now, such a position poses an awkward contradiction for the accused. On one hand, he says he knows nothing about Auschwitz. On the other, we have testimony and affidavits that physically place him there.

ACCUSED (*stands*): Herr Richter, that is a downright untruth! When? Where?

MAJOR TURNER: Sergeant Jones, please see that the accused resumes his seat. Thank you. When the accused completed his inspection of Theresienstadt, did he return to his duties with his orchestra in Berlin?

ACCUSED: Of course I did, Herr Richter.

MAJOR TURNER: Right away, I mean?

ACCUSED: As God is my witness.

MAJOR TURNER: Now, here we have a prime example of a downright untruth.

ACCUSED: I swear it, on my mother's memory.

MAJOR TURNER: Here is the problem. After his visit to Theresienstadt, witnesses observed that the accused boarded a train, which took him from Bohemia, by way of Breslau, to Krakow, where, despite denials, he was indeed the personal guest of Nuremberg defendant Hans Frank, governor-general of occupied Poland. We have in our hands travel documents and papers attesting to this. We are also prepared to offer witnesses who were present when the accused played a piano recital in Frank's mansion, attended by Frank and a group of guests. We even know that the program included works by Mozart, Haydn, and Schumann. The next day, an SS chauffeur drove the accused and two companions the fifty kilometers to the Auschwitz complex. There, after a tour of that complex, as though it were some kind of resort, the accused was joined that evening by a junior officer—a guard who supervised prisoners' labor gangs—and a physician, a member of the so-called medical research staff. These two men, who now are the object of intense worldwide search for crimes against humanity, participated with the accused in the performance of chamber music works in the Auschwitz residential quarters. My sources indicate that the highlight of the evening was a performance of Beethoven's "Archduke" Trio. After spending the night at Auschwitz, the accused returned to Krakow for two more days as the guest of Hans Frank. It seems to me that this visit, amply witnessed and recorded, afforded the accused sufficient scope and opportunity not only to discover what went on at Auschwitz but also to set up his arrangements in the spoliation and plunder with which he himself is charged. Any comments?

ACCUSED: I deny all of it. And I will say no more.

MAJOR TURNER: I must inform the accused that, in my judgment, things are out of our hands at this point. We have presented evidence and charges. The accused resorts only to denial, without mentioning the existence of documented counterevidence—except for one witness who, as far as I understand, cannot attest to anything substantive. I am now prepared to make a ruling. It is that the record of these hearings be passed up to the executive council of the Interallied War Crimes Tribunal, with the recommendation that the accused be held for trial as a war criminal within the meaning of guidelines laid down at Nuremberg. As of this time, the accused will be held in custody without bail until a trial date has been set. There is, in my judgment, a risk of flight. We are adjourned.

SERGEANT JONES: All rise.

* * *

I spent a wretched night. It was too humiliating. I was marched down to a cell in the basement of the Palace of Justice, cold. I couldn't think of changing into pajamas. I remained fully dressed and wrapped myself in the two threadbare blankets that were given me. They didn't do any good. The heating system didn't work. At six the next morning, I was awakened and handed a mug of dreadful coffee—far worse than ersatz—a piece of black bread, and a small slice of ham. There was humiliation and shame, but also a certain pride. It was no accident that the Allies had selected me as their target, just as they had chosen other artists and musicians. If they could break the spirit of German art, they would break the spirit of the entire Volk. At the same time, I was frightened. What would happen to me? Ruthless sentences were being imposed daily on both men and women who had only done their duty, who had only obeyed the orders of their superiors: death or long prison sentences. And I had done nothing! I was innocent of any crime. I had not been a soldier, had not even been a member of the

Party. But that interrogator and his Jew accomplice had sought to brand me the blackest villain known to man.

At ten o'clock, two jailers came to unlock my cell with much clanking of keys and motioned me into the corridor. "Exercise time," one of them barked. *Lackey! One day serving the Reich, next day the Americans.* They took me through dark passageways into a yard surrounded by high walls. It was freezing. I was glad I had brought my coat. "March around the circle. You've got twenty minutes. No talking." The yard contained just one other prisoner, a short fat man, perhaps in his sixties. I didn't recognize him and didn't attempt to speak. We trudged around in silence, at equal distance from each other, flailing our arms, trying to stay warm.

Back in my cell, I was left to myself, aware only of a silence occasionally interrupted by the distant slamming of doors. There was no midday meal. My watch had been removed; I had no idea of the passage of time, except by a barely visible patch of darkening sky. I had nothing to do, nothing to read, no pen or paper with which to write. *This is inhuman.* I lay down on my cot and dozed. A clash of metal, right by my head. The jailers had entered and dropped a tray: a bowl of thin broth with a few bits of carrot, a piece of sausage, more black bread, and an apple. In addition, a Bible, a blank notepad and two pencils.

"Lights out at eight o'clock," one of them barked.

"When will that be?" I demanded. "I haven't got my watch." I was ignored.

The next day was a mirror of the first—no visitors, no one spoke to me. At exercise time in the courtyard, I saw my mysterious companion again. If he was someone like me, deserving of solitary treatment, I should have recognized him. But no. I was tempted to signal him in some way. He seemed in no way interested in me, simply stared at the ground as he marched round and round. He might have been some Gauleiter I had never heard of. When I returned to my cell, I began to make marks on my notepad. At first, they were only idle scribbles to fill time. Soon I discovered that I had been writing Krisztina's name over and over—just like that—quite unconsciously. A whole page was covered with her name. I buried my face in my hands and wept.

Soon another woman came to mind: Nurse Paulina at the hospital in Berlin and that insane ambulance journey together with

Obersturmführer Funk. The French hospital orderlies with whom we drove—God, it seemed ages ago, but it was only just last year—had intended to meet up with a Free French army unit. But everyone, I was relieved to note, was equally intent on not being swept up by Russians coming from behind us out of the east. Our drivers, therefore, drove straight westward. We got to somewhere around Halle before we were halted by advance patrols of the American First Army. The Frenchmen were ecstatic—couldn't stop laughing and crying at the same time. The Obersturmführer was divested of his shroud wrappings, denounced—I could not say by whom—and immediately placed under arrest. Nurse Paulina, that sturdy, sensible young woman, for whom I had entertained certain fantasies, immediately volunteered to work in an orphanage in Erfurt. She promised to keep in touch with me but failed to do so.

I was taken to a hospital in Ulm and well cared for. Once I got well, I looked forward to the resumption of my career. Promises were made but somehow never carried out. I heard that Furtwängler and von Karajan—and all manner of distinguished German artists—were running into similar obstacles. They wouldn't let us perform. It was senseless, cruel, and disgraceful. Since when were Mozart and Beethoven political?

By the third day in my cell, following the same routines, I was becoming crazed. After exercise hour, the guards told me I had a visitor. I received the news almost with indifference. *What did it matter? My fate had been sealed.*

I was taken to a small room with barred windows and ordered to seat myself at a wooden table. After a few minutes, a key rattled in the lock. Huberta was led in by a guard, who remained in the room. She was told to sit opposite me. We were forbidden to approach or touch each other. I studied her face. Even though she had been my lover for many years, I thought it ironic that Krisztina's name should now be splayed all over my notebook. I had been thinking, during those final terrible months of the war, how the strains of life had affected Huberta. I grant it was not easy to be a Jew in Germany, but she could have taken greater pains with her appearance. She had attained her thirties. Her skin did not glow with the same freshness. It bore a pinched, sallow aspect. Despite makeup and her good spirits, she could not hide the circles about her eyes. Her waist had thickened. Her breasts, though still wonderful, had begun to droop. I was no longer trapped in enchantment. I could see clearly again, if you know what I mean.

"How are you, Kappi?" she asked.

I glanced at the guard, unwilling that he overhear the endearment. "What are you doing here, Huberta? What is the point of coming to see me? Don't you realize I'm finished? I'm in the hands of wolves and hyenas. You know what happens with all these so-called war crimes trials. Them, you know whom I mean, they're in power now—"

She broke in. "Kappi, shush, don't get excited. You will be permitted a lawyer, a German who will be on your side. They didn't tell you that before—"

Her stupidity was enraging. "Yes, I know I'm permitted an attorney. But not until a trial. We haven't had a trial yet. What's happened so far was not a trial but an interrogation. An interrogation, understand? Besides, it won't make any difference."

"I hope you're not trying to upset me, Kappi. One of us should keep a clear head."

That was Huberta, undeniably captivating but also sarcastic and disrespectful. For years, I had wanted to ask her whom she thought she was dealing with. As she herself had said, her life had been in my hands.

"I'm trying to tell you, Kappi, that I think you ought to engage a lawyer, even though a trial date has not yet been set. Wouldn't it be better to be prepared?"

I was increasingly irritated. The guard, clearly an illiterate oaf, had to witness the spectacle of Hermann Kapp-Dortmunder being reprimanded by his Jewish mistress. But I was more deeply outraged by the absence of any German supporters. Where were my colleagues, the orchestras, the music societies? Where was public opinion? Were my supposed transgressions greater than theirs?

"I don't feel well," I told her. "I must lie down."

Huberta stood in alarm. The guard shrugged but immediately took me back to my cell. I did not look at her or say goodbye.

On the next day of this dreary charade, I was taken back to the visitors' room. This time, the guard ushered in four men. I rose to my feet, recognizing only two of my visitors, my sadistic interrogator and his Yid interpreter. The third man was a high-ranking American officer, bespangled with stars like a whore—two sets on his collar, two sets on his shoulders. The fourth visitor was a severe-looking elderly German civilian.

My heart sank. They had come to present formal charges. The Herr Richter regarded me with an unpleasant scowl. Surprisingly, the senior American officer was smiling as he extended his hand. Without thinking, I took it.

"Orville Shannon," he announced in a deep, hearty voice. "Major-General, United States Army. I represent the Judge Advocate General's Office and the Interallied War Crimes Tribunal in Europe. I have waited a long time for this moment and the opportunity to make the acquaintance of such a distinguished man." I was dumbfounded. He pumped my limp arm up and down. My interrogator did not relax his hostile stare. General Shannon indicated that I should resume my seat.

The elderly civilian gave a precise bow. "Dr. Heinz Cornelius," he said. "Permit me to inform you that I had been retained to be your defense attorney—"

"*Had been retained?* My defense attorney? By whom?" I really had no need to ask. Dr. Cornelius allowed himself a thin smile. "I see that the Herr Kapellmeister is a perceptive and educated man. I deliberately employed the pluperfect tense, and he emulated me by employing it in return."

This was rapidly turning into a species of madness. On top of everything, now a grammar lesson! Dr. Cornelius became severe. "I said had been retained as your defense lawyer, employing the pluperfect tense. You asked, by whom I had been retained. I replied that I *had been retained* as your lawyer because, as your interrogator lately informs me, my services will not be required after all. And that, Herr Kapellmeister, is a triumph for you personally and for the German people as a whole."

I wheeled around to stare at the Herr Richter, the man who had subjected me to such a humiliating ordeal. I felt dizzy. I slumped back in my chair. The strain of the past days was more than I had been willing to acknowledge.

"Why, Herr Richter, do I no longer require a lawyer to defend me?"

The Herr Richter addressed me in a voice uncharacteristically loud and harsh. "Doesn't the accused understand? I'm here to inform him that there will be no trial. His statements have been reviewed by a supervisory body of the Interallied War Crimes Tribunal. In the opinion of that superior authority, no sufficient or reliable evidence has been amassed. Therefore, the War Crimes Tribunal will have no further interest in this case. Papers of exoneration will be delivered in due course."

The Herr Richter stared at me with burning eyes. He had not shouted, but one might tell that he was angrier than anyone I had ever seen. Abruptly, he stiffened to attention as he turned to address General Shannon. "Sir, do I have the general's permission to withdraw and attend to other business? Lieutenant Greenspan and I have a full schedule pending." The general nodded and exchanged salutes but did not remove his admiring eyes from mine. I was used to the sight of such admiring gazes. We did not glance away as the two junior officers strode out.

But now, I had to contend with the grammarian! In the presence of the general, whom I dared hope might be a friend, Dr. Cornelius addressed me:

"Last evening, as I was sitting down to dinner," he began, "Fräulein Menzel came to my house on your behalf." *God, Huberta was unstoppable.* "As soon as she mentioned your name, Herr Kapellmeister, I set everything aside. The dreadful news of your detention and possible trial was in all the papers. Herr Kapellmeister, we Germans took it hard. People ask, where will it end? What more do they want of us?" He exchanged glances with General Shannon. Both men looked rueful. "Yes, our leaders led us astray," he went on, "some of them. But why hound people like von Karajan, Furtwängler, or Gieseking? Or people like you, Herr Kapellmeister? These are our musicians! These are our teachers, exemplars of our Kultur! It makes no sense. I'm sure our conquerors have no wish to grind our faces in the dirt." General Shannon nodded.

Dr. Cornelius droned on in this vein for several minutes. It gave me opportunity to absorb the incredible, unbelievable, astounding news. I was to be released without a trial. *How had that happened?* I needed to recover my balance. I had to make a rapid decision about Huberta. If I were now to be cleared of charges, matters between us would require radical alteration. She and I had been close for many years. She had become especially devoted during the years of the bombing and before the Russians were at our throats. What was most insane was my addiction—the only word for it—to the body and love-making arts of my Jewish mistress. Yes, that was utterly insane! I remember, back in '41, when she had first told me that she was Jewish.

She said she must have been responding to some kind of death wish to reveal it. *Well, how would one label my own conduct?* I would often work with Reich Minister Goebbels by day, fulfilling tasks he assigned me, but at night I would steal back to Huberta.

I have a suspicion that both Huberta and I were motivated in our mutual passion by a hunger for the bizarre. As a Jew, her consorting with me during the war was indeed foolhardy. She courted danger every day of her life. She once brought home one of those Jewish stars that every member of the tribe had been ordered to wear in public. She actually put some glue on the back of it and surprised me by sticking it onto my naked body while she danced around me, laughing. Whatever substance she had smeared on it, I had a painful devil of a time detaching it from my chest hairs, which only provoked her to laugh harder. Why had she been so perversely careless about a matter important to the safety of us both? It defies rational explanation. Only now, released from her spell, do I recognize the danger in which she had placed both of us. I shudder when I think how often I may have approached death because of her.

And now, Dr. Cornelius was telling me, Huberta awaited me upstairs in the vestibule. What more was expected of me? While I was in hospital recovering from my injuries—the war coming to an end— I had kept in mind the possibility that it would be helpful if Huberta were to speak on my behalf. As I say, what better witness than a Jewish lover? But as I sat, bored stiff by Dr. Cornelius and his droning, it came to me that I needed no one, not Cornelius—and certainly not the assistance of Huberta. The benign countenance of General Shannon was testimony to that. Like the blinding moment when I realized that I was no longer bound to Frau Augustina, it came to me that I was truly free of Huberta. Once again, I could see clearly.

I stood and bowed to Dr. Cornelius. "Thank you for taking the trouble to come to me in prison. Most grateful! I'm glad that your services indeed were not required. Good morning to you. I can find my own way out of this place, thank you."

Taken aback, he automatically took my hand. "Delighted to have been of service. However, there is the matter of the fee. It is not considerable, but I *was* summoned on your behalf outside my usual consulting hours, given to understand an emergency—"

"Dr. Cornelius, forgive me for interrupting. I don't wish to appear ungracious, but as you accurately observed, it was not I who summoned you. Again, good morning." I stood up to be taken back to my cell.

General Shannon insisted on walking with me and my guard. I was flattered and welcomed his company. I still felt unsteady. Another American officer, who had been waiting in the corridor, fell into step beside us.

"Colonel Gilbreth, my assistant," the general said. The two Americans conducted me to my cell. Once there, I could not help collapsing on my cot.

"Please forgive me, Herr General, but for some reason, I am exhausted. The strain, it's all been too much. You and I have only just become acquainted, Herr General, but I sense in you someone I might trust. Could I ask you, please, be kind enough to explain what has just happened. As of this moment, I have no comprehension of it. None whatever." Colonel Gilbreth offered me brandy from a flask.

Between the general's German and my English, we managed to communicate. The story was unbelievable. He took me right into his confidence, I thought to an alarming degree. I could hardly imagine a German officer of his rank, indeed of any rank, sharing information of this kind with a stranger, particularly a recent enemy. How on earth do these people—I mean, the Americans—guard their national secrets? I can only conclude that my face appearing on countless record albums throughout the world had something to do with it. I am known—widely recognized—and that must have done the trick. My fame was partially responsible for the miraculous reversal of fortune—from reviled criminal back to my proper place.

A new political climate was emerging, the general said. While we Germans had been scrabbling for crusts of bread and lumps of coal, the Russians were behaving like certifiable paranoids, and the Americans were responding in kind. Both sides seemed actually to be preparing for a new conflict, unbelievable as that sounds. German scientists, like the rocketeer Wernher von Braun—just lately working to destroy London—were now working for the Americans on long-range missiles.

None of this would have happened, General Shannon said, had not the Russians unaccountably turned hostile and transformed the recent mutual comradeship into a thing of suspicion. *My god, the Führer had been absolutely correct. Wasn't this what he always predicted? The capitalists and the Bolsheviks tearing each other to pieces?* Why the devil couldn't it have happened a couple of years earlier, when it might have done us poor Germans some good! The Führer, say what you like, had been one of the most farsighted human beings this earth had ever seen.

Now General Shannon was inviting me to the officers' club. "There are rules against American soldiers fraternizing with German women, and your people are barred from certain social events; but such restrictions would hardly apply to a distinguished guest like you. I'd like to see you back at the head of your orchestra as soon as possible. Given what's going on with the Russkies, it makes no sense to further antagonize you Germans by hounding your artists. We're taking care of the top Nazis—and some others. We want criminals punished, but we don't want to decapitate the entire nation. What kind of justice would that be? And I can tell you that our British cousins agree with us."

Had the Herr General read the transcript of my interrogation?

"Did I read it? Hell, I did better than that. Gilbreth and I were in the next room, listening to the whole thing, hooked up by radio wire."

Had the Herr General formed any opinion?

"You bet. I formed the opinion that it's time to end this. We've made our point. We need to find our friends."

"Perhaps the Herr Richter will not share your opinion."

"Major Turner, you mean? He's one of my best men, but he doesn't always get the big picture."

With much regret, I declined the Herr General's invitation to dine that evening. I needed to return to Berlin as quickly as possible. I bowed and shook his hand with warmth. I could get to like this man. He had a businesslike mind and could clearly discern priorities. We said goodbye outside my cell, exchanged warm wishes, and hoped we would meet again soon. Colonel Gilbreth was particularly solicitous, asking more than once if he could help carry my belongings. I politely declined.

One or two formalities remained. One floor up, the head warder personally saw to it that my wallet, money, watch, and other valuables were returned to me and directed me to the exits with much deference, bowing several times, addressing me most respectfully—markedly different from the treatment accorded me earlier.

I climbed some stairs and turned a corner. By a stroke of good fortune, I caught sight of Huberta sitting at the far end of the vestibule. She didn't see me. I was able to slip out through a side door, hail a taxi, and be on the noontime train to Berlin with scant minutes to spare. Life beckoned again.

∗ ∗ ∗

Finale

Vienna 1960

Margot and I arrived back at the lodge at about a quarter to two in the morning. It had been a long and exhausting night. However, during the past fifteen minutes, I began to feel rejuvenated—not the least bit sleepy. I jumped out of the Daimler; Josef swung open the door for Margot. She immediately started up the front steps. I ran around the car and, to her surprise, seized her in my arms under the porch lamps, kissing her face and neck. Josef discreetly looked away.

"Darling," she protested, laughing. "What on earth are you doing? It's late. Don't you realize what time it is?" She attempted, without success, to avoid my mouth. "My hair," she grimaced. "What are you doing to my hair?" *What the devil was she worrying about? It was bedtime. Why carry on about her hair?*

"Josef, before you go to bed, I want you to bring iced vodka and caviar to the library. Your mistress and I wish to bring this wonderful day to a fitting close."

As soon as Josef was out of sight, Margot broke free and, with a touch, sought assurance that I had not disturbed the perfection of her blond upsweep. "Darling," she said. "Were you actually leering at me in front of Josef? How indiscreet. And did I hear you ask for vodka? Haven't you had enough tonight?"

Her amusement was glacial. She was smiling, but how remotely. Even after seven years of marriage, I could not claim that she was mine, that I had ever possessed her. Come to think of it, there was always something palpably absent in all the women who had charmed me—but for one. You could describe me as an incorrigible romantic. The pursuit was always more satisfying than the conquest.

I resumed firm hold of Margot, but she avoided being kissed. "Darling. *Darling!* Are you listening to me?" She continued to wriggle in my grasp, battling like a large muscular fish. "I don't want to go to the library to drink vodka at this hour. I don't want you to make love to me tonight. Be a good Kapellmeister for now, my darling. I'm tired"—she slapped down my wandering hands—"I said I am tired."

Josef reappeared. "I have placed vodka and caviar in the library as you ordered, sir. Will there be anything else before I go to bed?"

I leapt back from Margot, panting with frustration. "No, thank you, Josef. You may go." Josef bowed and said good night. Margot took the opportunity to dart out of reach. She paused at the top of the front steps and swept into a deep curtsy.

"Sorry, but I am *so* tired," she laughed. "I will say good night, Herr Kapellmeister. Perhaps I will see you in the morning before you leave." She slipped into the house. I felt exhausted again, but I refused to go to bed. *I would go inside, damn it, and drink and eat caviar by myself.* I slammed the heavy library doors behind me with a crash that shook the house.

I kicked off my shoes, poured an iced tumbler of the excellent Swedish vodka I preferred, downed it in a gulp, and immediately poured another. Before collapsing into my leather armchair, I clipped and lighted one of my especially imported Havanas and reached over to switch on the high-fidelity system, always tuned to a twenty-four-hour music station in Salzburg. I broke into a smile as sound welled up through the massive speakers. It was one of my own recordings— the wonderful second act of *Meistersinger* taken from a live perform- ance I had directed at the Cologne Opera four years before. I was glad Margot was not in the room to savor my pleasure. Why should she? She didn't deserve it. However, my poor dear Mama's eyes would have glistened with pleasure. I scooped up a generous portion of beluga and carefully arranged it on my toast. Lying back, I listened while savoring the delectable saline crunch of the caviar between my teeth, punctuat- ed by icy swallows of the Swedish vodka—far better than the Russian swill, all the propaganda notwithstanding.

My tightness dropped; I felt easier and had a chance to reflect. I had really not done so badly with my life. One way or another, the promise had been fulfilled. Of course, I was most grateful for the benefits of my secret Swiss bank account. I said daily prayers for the repose of Hans Frank's soul—wherever it was. Thanks to him and his farsighted vision, I was able to support myself comfortably on the proceeds of our enterprise. The biggest disappointment had been those arch-hypocrites, the rest of the Germans. I received absolutely no support from my fellow musicians after the war—none whatsoever. The Western allies, steeped in blood and guilt themselves, did their best to make life difficult, even though I had done nothing wrong.

Then the Adenauer government, every member an arsekisser, actually had the gall to declare me unwelcome in the new German Federal Republic. I was profoundly shocked because I had made so deep a moral commitment to the Reich. But I was consoled when the Austrians let me know, because of past citizenship, that I could find a home with them.

I settled down here in Vienna again, a more forgiving city. Even so, those Austrians turned out to be arsekissers themselves. They actually claimed, astonishingly, to have been victims of the Reich—its first conquest—rather than its joyous colleague, savoring with the Reich each and every glorious victory, freely contributing both honored service and its own citizens. I am not as indignant about it as I used to be. One has to do what one must to survive. At least, I was able to work again. Engagements were few at first, but the orchestras and choruses were willing, even though still fearful and shell-shocked. I was surprised to find that people had not forgotten me and were demanding my return. In 1948, I was profoundly moved when the call was taken up by survivors and remnants of what had been my old orchestra, the Staatskapelle Brandenburg, who miraculously filtered their way into Austria, determined to find me. They labored to secure hard-to-find work permits in order to make music and record once more under my direction. Many Austrian musicians joined them, and together, we formed a brilliant new organization known as the Stadtkapelle Wien, with its flattering allusion to my old group. I was astonished because, as may not be widely known, I am not the most congenial of conductors. I have standards and am not easy to please.

I'll never forget that initial concert of the Stadtkapelle Wien. I determined to keep everything optimistic, despite our circumstances, despite a miserably cold winter. The audience had to sit bundled up in greatcoats, scarves, and gloves. We started with the Brahms First Serenade in D, which immediately encouraged the right mood, with its bright melodies and cheerful horn calls.

Then came a revolutionary surprise, the sort of thing I like to spring on people. Nobody expected it. My manager, Gessler, had brought a young woman to me, a pianist. Three things astonished me about her. One, she was black. Really black. Of course, one comes across many Negroes these days, particularly among American soldiers. But I never saw any as profoundly black as she. Her eyes were large and lovely. To look into them was unsettling, gazing into depths. The second thing was that she was young, twenty-three or so. The third thing was that she was bewitchingly beautiful. Despite her race, I confess to falling instantly in love with her. But, alas, it was not to be. This bewitching young woman came from French West Equatorial Africa, had been educated in Paris, and spoke only French, affecting not to understand German or English. But she was a pianist—and what a pianist! She wished to perform under my direction. And only that. After hearing her play, I made an immediate decision. She would be my soloist in the Beethoven "Emperor" Concerto. When I led her to the stage, the audience really woke up. Black people were rare those days on European concert stages. But her performance was dazzling. Even more dazzling was the shimmering white off-the-shoulder gown she wore, and the way it contrasted with the glowing, glossy blackness of her incomparable skin. It took enormous bravery to wear such a garment that freezing night. Her first name was Monique, her second unpronounceably African. After the performance, she left the country. I never saw her again. In the second part, after the interval, I gave them more Brahms, the Fourth Symphony. Everything went well, except for the lamentable disappearance of the exotic Monique.

I became reacquainted with my old haunts: the Conservatory; Rosalie's Kaffeehaus, or where it used to be, now a bomb site; the street where the ugly Frau Malteser's house once stood, few Jews left; the Café Gonzaga in the Old Town, a boarded-up ruin, no sign of Herr Zuckerweiss; my flat near the General Hospital, still there. I could not help shedding many a private tear for dear Krisztina. *Why, despite all the accolades, did happiness always elude me?*

Leaning back, puffing my cigar, I found the broadcast recording, *my* recording, captivating. The Eva in the cast, the pure and innocent

Eva, was performed by the same Magdalena Mertens that Hans Frank had sent to me from the *Generalgouvernement*. Had I mentioned what a vibrantly beautiful young woman she was? When we first met in 1942, like Monique the African, she must have been twenty-two or twenty-three years old and already possessed of a glorious voice. That voice and that beauty inevitably exerted hypnotic power over me; but since I knew her to be the special friend of the governor-general, I was nothing if not respectful. Some years after the war, I happened to attend a recital she gave in Vienna. The voice and beauty had grown, if possible, even more glorious. By that time, I was rapidly becoming an international figure and once more permitted to work in Germany. As such, my manager secured a half season for me with the Cologne Opera and its excellent orchestra. I immediately set about securing Fräulein Mertens for performances and a recording of *Meistersinger*. It turned out to be one of the best things I had ever produced, as you can hear from the recording. But that was not the end of it.

By that time, the glamorous Margot and I had been married for three or four years, and she had quickly laid down her vision of the union. She required constant travel to ensure the smooth functioning of her international design interests. What could I say? My own commitments were worldwide. I was constantly on the move. We were lucky to be reunited for Christmas and the summer holidays. And I was always happy to see her. She was exquisitely beautiful and elegant, always so magnificently coutured. Whenever we stepped out of our limousine for an opening or a reception, she carried herself in her gowns, necklaces, and tiaras like some grand duchess, only infinitely more lovely. My heart burst with pride.

But, of course, that was not the whole story. What had just occurred on the front steps of the lodge was typical. Margot was sleek and exquisite, but untouchable, more like a porcelain Dresden shepherdess than a woman. So it should have surprised no one that, in Cologne, while working on *Meistersinger*, Magdalena and I launched into a deeply sensual and satisfying affair. The woman was incredible! We remained in the city for about three months, doing our contracted seven performances and working on the recording.

I must say that Magdalena had so enchanted me that, once again, I entertained illusions that I had truly found love. I seriously contemplated leaving Margot. But I confess to having been deluded once again. Magdalena principally desired the cachet of having made a recording with the renowned Herr Kapp-Dortmunder, and while highly diverted by the man himself, did not entertain thoughts of a life together. In that sense, she was not unlike Margot or me—perpetual seekers and wanderers. But I was grateful that, if we happened to find ourselves in the same city, Magdalena and I would invariably arrange to meet. We still do in fact.

The second act was drawing to a close. Eva—my Magdalena—melting in anticipation of marriage to the handsome and gallant Walther, does not know that the villainous town clerk, Beckmesser, is scheming to subvert the free choice of the lovers. The honest shoemaker, Hans Sachs, is faced with a quandary. For true love to triumph, he will have to "influence" things. This Hans Sachs, the embodiment of upright German artisans, will prevent Beckmesser from winning the *Meistersinger* contest, if necessary with chicanery. The composer Richard Wagner teaches Germans a valuable lesson. It is sometimes necessary to break one law in order to uphold a greater one. This Beckmesser—one doesn't have to strain the imagination to deduce whom he might represent—is typical of those who achieve wealth through haggling and usury. He stands in sharp contrast to the honest artisans—shoemakers, tailors, coppersmiths, pewterers, goldsmiths, and furriers—all of whom elect to place art above everything else. In the words of Eva's father: "In the entire German Reich, we craftsmen alone cherish art. In contrast, the burghers don't care about it. But art builds honor. We treasure all that is beautiful and all that is good. I intend to reveal the value of art to the entire world."

This, in my humble way, was what I always strove for. Nothing less than that.

It was late. I had to be at the Vienna airport by one tomorrow afternoon—no, this afternoon, to catch the flight to Buenos Aires. There was simply no respite. I was to present a season consisting of *Fidelio* and three Mozart operas. At the same time, I was scheduled for performances of the German orchestral repertoire in New York, Cleveland, Chicago, and Los Angeles. There would be considerable flying back and forth between the northern and southern hemispheres.

I switched off my audio system, carried the remains of my solitary collation to the kitchen for the maids to deal with, and crept upstairs. I wanted merely to spend the rest of the night in tranquillity with

Margot, perhaps wrapped around her. She liked that sometimes. But the bedroom door was locked again. I tried again to turn the handle, tapped softly, and with increasing loudness. Still no response. I couldn't very well break down the door. I had attempted that some years ago and failed. I sighed and went across the hall, where I had a private study with a comfortable daybed. But as soon as I lay down, all my ease vanished, to be replaced by mystification. At least, I would be flattered had Margot taken offense at something I had said or done. But she gave me the impression that she did not care one way or the other. I switched on a desk lamp and poured myself some brandy from a stock I kept there.

My journey to Buenos Aires the next day reminded me. I unlocked a bureau drawer and extracted a letter I had been handed some six months earlier. The writer's identity was soon revealed.

> Dear Kapellmeister,
>
> I am certainly the last person you expected to hear from. But since your name is brought to my attention in the newspapers and magazines almost every day, you may say that somehow it is you who have provoked me to write.
>
> You see from the return address that I now go by the name of Miguel Otto Negrón, but I am sure you remember me as Obersturmführer Otto Funk of the Gestapo. We came to know each other in less happy circumstances than I assume we both enjoy today.
>
> First, let me say that I was happy to read that you are doing so well and that you have acquired such a beautiful and charming wife. If I may say so, from her pictures, you look as though you suit each other.
>
> We have both enjoyed miraculous recoveries. Let me tell you about mine. We last saw each other, I believe, near Halle, having been driven in an ambulance by those Frenchmen. One of them, quite sadistically, gave me away to the Americans as a Gestapo officer. As a result, I was not put into a POW compound but taken across country to a special prison near Heiligenstadt with other members of the SS. You cannot imagine what I went through there—endless interrogations,

deprivation of sleep, and beatings. There were about fifty of us. Finally, we resolved somehow to do away with ourselves. Whereupon—and this is the first miracle—I and two others were awakened in the middle of the night, given women's clothing to wear, and smuggled out of the camp.

Well, as you know, I have disguised myself in the past in order to escape danger. Only this time, the enterprise was run by my Kameraden. And the enterprise functioned well! Within eight days, traveling only by night, we had made our way through southern Germany and Austria, ending up in North Italy by way of Innsbruck and the Brenner. We arrived at the small mountaintop abbey of San Vigilio, where, to our astonishment, the brothers in charge turned out to be part of the enterprise. They told us, naturally on the sly, that this rescue had the support of certain high papal ministers deeply committed to assisting anti-Bolsheviks.

The first thing that happened after we were fed and rested was that our underarm SS tattoos were surgically removed. I can tell you that our arms were so sore we couldn't raise them for a week! Then we were photographed and given new travel documents. It was superbly organized. The rest was simple. We took a train south to Brindisi, boarded a freighter, and enjoyed a leisurely sunny cruise to Buenos Aires. To our further surprise, Kameraden were awaiting us, working with the warm and friendly cooperation of the Argentine government. They helped us with jobs, accommodations—even with social introductions. You cannot imagine what a boon that was to friendless outcasts, grateful for crumbs, after we had been forced to leave the fatherland.

Herr Kapellmeister, should you find yourself in Buenos Aires, permit me to extend an open invitation. These days, I work as a tourist guide, and a quite comfortable living it is. I know the city and the surrounding countryside extremely well, and I can reveal all the sights and attractions. Furthermore, I take great pleasure in informing you that I have remarried and am proud to boast of five wonderful children: Evita, Miranda, Uwe, Maria, and Otto. It would delight me if you could come to visit someday. You would love the children. And, saving the best for last, you would have the opportunity to become reacquainted with many fine Genossen living here, whose hearts beat fiercely and proudly, always cherishing the knowledge of who they are and for what cause they shed their blood.

Heil Hitler.

Yours faithfully, Miguel Otto Negrón
(formerly Otto Uwe Funk, Obersturmführer, SS)

I tore up Funk's letter, drained my brandy, and gathered a rug to cover myself. *What wretched impudence! What outrageous presumption!* No, I did not wish to see that dreadful man again. News of my presence in Buenos Aires, I'm sure, would not be a secret, but I had ways of fending off unwanted visitors and phone calls.

I must have dropped off to sleep soon after. The next thing I knew was Josef shaking me awake—he had found me in the study before this—announcing that it was nine o'clock in the morning, my bags had been packed, and there was just time for me to breakfast and shower before he drove me to the airport. I stumbled out across the passage and tried Margot's door again. It opened easily. Two housemaids were changing sheets; the floor was strewn with bed-clothes and pillows.

I charged into the inner dressing room. "Where is your mistress?"

One of the maids curtsied nervously. "Frau Margot is out riding, Mein Herr."

"When will she return?" I had no time.

Another curtsy. "She said she might not be back for several hours. She intended to visit the Herr Graf von Grozny and have lunch with him."

I exploded. "Was she not aware I was flying to Argentina this morning?" The two maids clutched each other in terror. I calmed myself immediately. It was not the fault of these stupid young women. It was always Margot and her instinctive knowledge of my sensitive spots. Particularly with regard to young von Grozny. That slimy gentleman had made no secret of his being attracted to her, and she had made no secret of her response. Simpering, batted eyelashes, the lot.

During the drive to the airport, I pieced together Funk's letter, hastily retrieved from the wastebasket. I might pay a call on him after all. The shoemaker Hans Sachs in *Meistersinger* behaves not at all criminally when he deceives the slimy Beckmesser. Rather, he permits Beckmesser's own greed to do the work for him. He is wise enough to know, in order to produce a good result, it is sometimes necessary to break rules, even to break heads. The trouble with me has always been my restraint and good breeding.

Funk might suggest a solution to my difficulties. I was not clear what it might be. But I understood the rigors of his orderly mind and, given his background, he would surely not miss one trick in contemplating variations on the beast.

* * *